SCOTTISH SEDUCTION

Ramsay settled down beside Cassie. He peered into her face for a long silent moment and then he took her hand and kissed it, an endearing spontaneous gesture that startled Cassie. Their eyes met over her hand while it was still pressed against his mouth. Desire burned in his green eyes.

"I'm glad you agreed to come," he murmured.

Though it was her hand that he kissed, a surge of heat rustled through Cassie. Did it show—that his touch affected her body? Certain that he could see how he thrilled her, a blush burned in her cheeks.

Swiftly, he dropped her hand. His eyes searching hers, he seized her shoulders, drew her close and kissed her hotly, hungrily. Cassie surrendered to the kiss, offering him every sort of response her mouth could give. Almost guiltily she slipped her arms around his neck and acknowledged to herself that this was what she'd wanted and hoped for from the moment she'd agreed to go away with him. This kiss, this intimacy that he'd introduced her to on the river barge. This piece of himself that she knew he kept hidden and protected.

He wanted her and she wanted him. No man's touch had ever made her feel so feminine, so desirable—so hungry—as his did.

She gave herself over to it . . .

Books by Linda Madl

BAYOU ROSE
A WHISPER OF VIOLETS
THE SCOTSMAN'S LADY
THE SCOTSMAN'S BRIDE

Published by Zebra Books

THE
SCOTSMAN'S
BRIDE
LINDA MADL

Zebra Books
Kensington Publishing Corp.

http://www.zebrabooks.com

ZEBRA BOOKS are published by

Kensington Publishing Corp.
850 Third Avenue
New York, NY 10022

First Printing: March, 1999
10 9 8 7 6 5 4 3 2 1

Printed in the United States of America

To my editor, John Scognamiglio,
for believing in my work.

ACKNOWLEDGMENTS

Though a book comes from the author's head and heart, there are always those who contribute in many and varied ways.

Thank you all and especially thank you
to Kayla Westra for loaning me Sir Calum, Heather Heath-Frank,
Margaret Ohmes, Leann Shoaf, Kristine Hughes, and to my agent, Evan Marshall.

from "The Princess"
Now sleeps the crimson petal, now the white . . .
The fire-fly wakens: waken thou with me . . .
Now lies the Earth all Danae to the stars
And all thy heart lies open unto me . . .
Now slides the silent meteor on, and leaves
A shining furrow, as thy thoughts in me.
Now folds the lily all her sweetness up,
And slips into the bosom of the lake:
So fold thyself, my dearest, thou, and slip
Into my bosom and be lost in me.

—Alfred, Lord Tennyson

CHAPTER ONE

London, 1828

Victory over the McKensies was so near Ramsay Forbes could taste the sweetness of it. This plot would not fail as his last one had, he vowed silently. He'd been careless before. From here on, he'd make certain nothing went amiss.

"Does this seating suit your lordship better?" asked the wide-eyed waitress of Bunter's Bakery and Tea Shop. Her voice quavered.

Pleased with the amount of fear his glowering demeanor had instilled in the serving girl, Ramsay, Marquis of Linirk, eyed the table's position, then peered beyond the column toward the empty table on the main floor below. The view of the seating arrangement he'd orchestrated for Cassandra St. John and Dudley Moncreff was excellent. While he could see all he needed to see of the couple, he would be sufficiently hidden by the column to remain unobserved. He gave a curt nod. "This will do nicely."

Relief washed across the waitress's face and she bobbed a curtsy. "Shall I bring tea and cake for one, then?"

"Port and apricot tarts for two. A gentleman will be joining me." Ramsay stripped off his black leather gloves, aware of the waitress's curious gaze on him. He decided to give her a soothing smile. "That's what this shop is known for, isn't it? Apricot tarts?"

"We have the best apricot tarts in London, if you please, your lordship," the waitress bragged, bobbing another curtsy. "Port, then, and apricot tarts for two."

"Excellent," Ramsay said.

She scurried away.

The tea shop was nearly empty at this early hour. It was an unusually large, elegant shop decorated with fine woodwork and shiny mirrors. The tables were covered in white damask and brightened with fresh flowers. Sun streamed in the large front window. Ramsay had chosen to arrive at this early hour to avoid curious glances. He knew how out of place he and Graham would appear: he in his austere black garb and Graham in his tartan trousers. But once he and Graham were seated and the tea shop crowded with refined ladies and gents, they would never be noticed.

Just as Ramsay seated himself, his foster brother, Graham, appeared at the top of the stairs. Ramsay waved to his kinsman. Graham spied him immediately.

"It's all arranged," Graham said, seating himself awkwardly in the dainty chair opposite. He was not quite as tall as Ramsay, but was more solidly built.

"They will be seated there?" Ramsay nodded toward the table below. "We shall be able to see it all?"

"Aye, my lord, at that very table," Graham said, his hands planted on his thighs as if he feared touching the smooth white tablecloth before him. "We'll not miss a minute of it."

Ramsay said no more. He knew that Graham did not agree with what he was doing. He seldom ignored his foster brother's counsel, but Ramsay was certain this plan would work. He was not about to allow the McKensie clan to win back Glen Gray through a simple marriage contract with Charlotte St. John.

The feud that the Forbes and McKensie clans had waged against each other for three centuries would never come to an end that easily. In about an hour all Ramsay had to do was make the acquaintance of the soon-to-be-free Cassandra, Charlotte's twin sister. Then Ramsay would win Glen Gray back from Davis St. John. Then Graham would appreciate the brilliance of the plan.

The port and apricot tarts arrived. Soon the shop began to fill with groups of ladies and couples. The clink of silver on china tinkled throughout the room and the murmur of voices grew to a din. Steam rose from teapots. But still the designated table remained empty. At first Ramsay wasn't too concerned.

"Perhaps Moncreff got cold feet," Graham said, awkwardly reaching for a tiny tart covered in sticky icing.

"Moncreff won't let us down." Ramsay had great faith in the power of intimidation and extortion. The last thing Dudley Moncreff wanted was for his father to learn about his gambling debts or for his fiancée to find out about the little affair with the upstairs maid. Cassandra St. John was too young to turn a blind eye to that sort of indiscretion in her future husband. No, the Viscount of Monksleigh was caught between a rock and a hard place. The lad would do as he was told. Ramsay was sure of it.

But another half hour passed before the couple appeared.

"Ah, here they are at last," Ramsay murmured, sitting back in his chair to better admire Cassandra's feminine figure.

As the waitress showed the stylish couple to the table Ramsay had secretly arranged for them, he studied Cassandra St. John with new interest. She wore a fashionably demure Clarence blue gown and bonnet. He'd only glimpsed her at the opera weeks ago and he'd forgotten how pretty she was—her red hair so vibrant, rich, and coppery, and her kittenlike blue eyes dark and lively. Unlike many freckled redheads, she had smooth white skin that begged to be touched. He wondered if Monksleigh had ever given in to the urge to stroke her flawless cheek.

To Ramsay's satisfaction, Tophet, the Nairn hound he'd

hand-raised, walked on a leash at Cassandra's side. He was certain the dog, his engagement gift to the couple, had done exactly what he'd intended—planted thoughts of himself in Cassandra's head and driven a wedge between her and Monksleigh.

"She is quite spoiled, you know," Graham was saying as he also watched the young couple. Disapproval gleamed in his keen gray eyes and furrowed his heavy brow. "She's not going to be some docile English maid who will stare at you agog and be glad to do your bidding."

"Aye, I'm aware of that," Ramsay said, already conscious of the truth in his foster brother's words.

"I don't see how turning the lass's life upside down is going to be of benefit to us," Graham continued. "It's not going to keep Connor McKensie from wedding her sister."

"No, it won't, but that's not the point." Ramsay found himself strangely intrigued by the challenge Cassandra St. John presented. She was known to love a good prank. He'd only recently heard the rumor that she and Monksleigh had once masqueraded as highwaymen. Graham was right: a few sweet words and expensive gifts were unlikely to win over the lady. "Be patient, Graham. The important thing to remember is that Cassandra St. John is the key in reclaiming Glen Gray for the clan."

"Aye, and I wish it wasn't so," Graham said, his frown still in place.

When Cassandra and Monksleigh were seated across from each other, Ramsay could see them as well as he'd expected. The back of Monksleigh's head was toward him, but he had an unhindered view of Cassandra's face. He suspected that her expression would tell him all he needed to know about what was being said.

She appeared to be carrying on a lively but somewhat one-sided conversation. Monksleigh appeared to be saying little. Soon their tea and apricot tarts arrived and Cassandra tackled the pastries as if she had an appetite. Words continued to flow from her and her face glowed with happiness. Monksleigh sat stiff and silent. Ramsay smiled to himself in dark satisfaction.

"My lord? I believe we need more port," Graham said, bringing Ramsay's attention back to the table.

Ramsay glanced down to see that his port glass was still full and his apricot tarts were untouched. But the plate in the middle of the table was bare and Graham's port glass was empty. He'd downed everything.

"Suit yourself," Ramsay said, unconcerned about food at the moment. When he turned back to spy on Monksleigh and Cassandra, he saw that shock had stolen the happy glow from her face. She sat frozen for a long moment with her teacup in midair, her face pale and her expression blank. Ramsay cursed silently. He'd missed it. The crucial moment he'd been waiting for.

But from the shock written on Cassandra's face, he was certain it had happened. The young viscount had not let Ramsay down. Monksleigh had just broken his engagement to Cassandra St. John.

Bunter's Bakery and Tea Shop, Cassandra's favorite place for tea and pastries, was crowded as usual and she was pleased that she and Dudley had been able to get such a good table near the window. She loved watching passersby. The day was gorgeous and their carriage ride in the park had been fine and invigorating although Dudley had been quiet. She usually did not have to drag conversation out of him like she did today. But that was all right, because she was in a fine enough mood for both of them.

With Tophet, her Nairn hound, sitting at her feet, she surveyed the large, high-ceilinged room over the rim of her teacup.

"I'm surprised there is no one here we know today."

"No, there isn't," Dudley agreed, glancing around only briefly. "Not a soul. Frankly, I'm glad."

"Glad, but why is that?" Cassandra asked. "I thought you

liked hobnobbing with the ladies we meet here. I was hoping the Duchess of Hollerton would be here or maybe Aunt Dorian.''

When Dudley said nothing more, Cassandra flirtatiously nudged his calf with her kid boot in the hopes of bringing a smile to his lips. ''Don't look so downcast, darling. It's a beautiful day and the bakery is not yet out of the apricot pastries. Sometimes they are by this time of day.''

''Yes, we are fortunate in that, aren't we,'' Dudley agreed without an ounce of enthusiasm.

''Did I mention to you that Mr. Bunter does the most exquisite layered wedding cakes here?'' Cassie asked.

Dudley shook his head.

''Why, only yesterday Mama and I were talking about it,'' Cassie went on, thinking surely talk of their wedding would lighten his mood. ''Bunter's wedding cakes are absolutely works of art, with sugared flowers for decoration.'' Then, to emphasize her point, she leaned across the table. ''And what's even better, the cake tastes good.''

Dudley stared at his teacup.

''Dudley?'' Cassandra was beginning to worry about him. He was hardly ever this downcast for this long. She touched his hand. ''What is it?''

''Actually, I brought you here for a very special reason.'' Dudley pulled away, tucking his hands beneath the table.

''You mean for some reason other than the apricot tarts?'' Surprised by Dudley's withdrawal, Cassie turned to Tophet, broke off a piece of tart, and fed it to the dog. She brushed pastry crumbs from her hands, then glanced at Dudley once again. When she did, she was shocked by his paleness. Why hadn't she noticed his unhealthy color before now? ''Are you feeling unwell, Dudley?''

''No, nothing like that,'' he said with a dismal shake of his head. ''I'm quite well.''

''That's good to hear,'' Cassie said, relieved but still mystified. She picked up her cup again. ''Did you skip your breakfast this morning?''

"No, it's just that I have to deliver some bad news." Dudley's eyes flickered across Cassandra's face, then he seized his teacup as if it held some kind of salvation.

Teacup hovering in midair, Cassie noted with growing dismay that Dudley's hands were trembling so the amber liquid sloshed into the saucer.

"Deliver bad news to whom? To me?" Hurriedly she set down her cup. "Out with it. You know I believe in being direct about things."

"But you're not going to like this news." Dudley sat stiffly in his chair with a frown on his face.

"I understand that," Cassandra said, a bit alarmed now, but how bad could it be? "However, I dislike dithering even more."

"Then I shall get right to it," Dudley said, meeting her gaze at last, but glancing away just as he spoke the next words. "I am crying off our engagement."

Her breath caught in her throat. She stared unblinking at Dudley, thinking that she had not heard him correctly. The tea shop had grown crowded. She leaned forward and whispered across the table, "It's noisy in here, Dudley. What did you say?"

Dudley glanced across at her from the corner of his eye. He looked absolutely sick this time. "Don't make me repeat it, Cassie. You heard me. For pity's sake, don't make a scene. Not here in front of all these people. Think of the gossip."

Cassandra sat up straight in her chair and stifled a small cry of dismay.

Tophet stirred at her feet.

Cassie bit her tongue. Distractedly she touched the dog's head to reassure him before he snarled at Dudley as he was wont to do. She forced herself to take a small breath. "Surely you jest, darling. This is some kind of prank, is it not? Are you trying to find a way to keep from going to the opera with me? I've been able to change many things about you, but I know I've failed where the opera is concerned. For many it is an acquired taste."

"It has nothing to do with the opera," Dudley mumbled, his gaze straying everywhere in the room but to her face. "I do not jest. I meant every word I said. I'm crying off."

"Yes, I heard you," she said this time, slightly short of breath. Crying off? Crying off! The humiliating words echoed in her mind. She could not believe what she'd heard him say. She and Dudley had been betrothed for nearly a year and were planning to wed in another year. It had all been arranged carefully with the full approval of both their families. The contracts had been negotiated and signed. Papa had been especially pleased. The Viscount of Monksleigh was heir to an earldom and Cassie would one day be a countess and her children, the St. John grandchildren, would be little aristocrats. It was all planned, written, and ordained.

"But, Dudley, have you thought this through?" Cassie asked, still unable to believe that he truly meant what he'd said. They were destined to be husband and wife, and he owed her so much. She'd made him the sensation of the London Season only a year ago. He couldn't possibly be serious. This was betrayal. This was humiliation.

Cassie struggled to control her panic. "Remember how you came to Town dressed like a country squire hardly able to get an invitation to a decent soirée or ball? Remember the afternoons at the tailors and the day we selected the best hat for you?"

"I remember all of that," Dudley said, misery in his voice. "I am truly grateful to you, Cassandra, but we simply aren't meant for one another."

Cassandra wondered who had put such a stupid idea into Dudley's head. His aristocratic family and their ancient house, joined with her good taste and her money, made for a perfect match. All of Society thought them the impeccable couple. Frantically she searched her mind for all the differences they'd had in the last few weeks. "Is this about Tophet? I know you're offended that he does not like you."

"I could do without that bloody mutt," Dudley admitted, pointing an accusing finger at the dog. Tophet glared back. "I almost think Lord Forbes knew the hound would hate me. And sometimes I think you enjoy it, too.''

Tophet sniffed disdainfully.

"That's nonsense," Cassandra cried, although she had indeed taken petty pleasure in the dog's preference for her. "If Tophet is the problem, we shall find a trainer who can—"

"A dog trainer is not what we need." Dudley shook his head. "Please don't make this difficult, Cassie. You've always been such a good sport. We've had a good time, but it's over. I'm going to the Continent to do the grand tour. I don't know how long I'll be gone."

"But that's wonderful," Cassie said, perching on the edge of her chair, eager to rescue herself from humiliation. "Don't you see? No need to postpone the wedding. We'll honeymoon in Geneva. Right on the lake. How romantic."

"No, Cassie, you will not be going with me," Dudley said, his mouth pressed in a thin line. "No honeymoon in Switzerland. No marriage."

"I could wait for you," Cassandra volunteered, suddenly aware that she was beginning to sound as if she were begging. Wait? What was she saying? "Or maybe I won't."

"No, Cassie, I don't want you to wait for me," Dudley said.

Silence settled over the table. The gravity of what Dudley was saying took on reality in Cassie's head. Still she could not shake her disbelief. "You are serious? But, I thought we were in love. You told me just last week that you loved me. Now you cry off because you are going on a grand tour of the Continent?"

Dudley shook his head. "Our engagement is at an end. I hope you'll try to understand. I hope you won't embarrass both of us by making a big issue of it."

"Make an issue of it?" Cassandra exclaimed loud enough to make Dudley start and glance around to see if anyone else had heard her. "So that's why you brought me here. To cry off in a public place so I wouldn't make a scene?"

"Please lower your voice, Cassandra." Dudley ducked his head.

No one seemed to take notice of them. Indignant and betrayed, Cassandra continued, her voice only slightly lowered. "I can't believe you are doing this to me."

"You've been generous," Dudley said. "Please don't think that this reflects on you. We'll simply tell people that we decided to call it off together. We will say that I wanted to go to the Continent and that you wanted to stay in London. We agreed that we'd cry off together. Is that fair enough?"

Her chest growing tight and her breath coming in shallow gasps, Cassie considered the story he offered. It made a certain amount of sense. Everyone knew how she loved Town life: the shops, the theaters, the parks, and gardens.

"That's it, then. We both agree to this end of our engagement." Numbly she tugged off her left glove and pulled at her betrothal ring. Her finger suddenly seemed reluctant to release it.

Seeing what she was doing, Dudley glanced uncomfortably about the tea shop once more. "For God's sake, Cassandra, not here. Send the ring to me. People will start to stare."

"No, I want this finished now," Cassie said, finally managing to slip the ring from her finger. "There. Done. Over. Finale."

Vengefully she held the ring up for Dudley to see. The diamond flashed in the sunlight.

"Cassie?" Dudley glanced around the room self-consciously. "Just put the ring on the table. I'll get it."

She knew she was being spiteful, but if felt so good under the circumstances. With a smile of mean pleasure she stretched across the table and dropped the diamond ring into Dudley's teacup.

Cold tea splashed onto the tablecloth. The diamond and gold clinked against white porcelain.

"Blast it, Cassie," Dudley muttered between thin lips as he peered into his teacup. She could see at last that he was losing his patience. "Was that really necessary?"

"Dreadfully necessary," Cassie declared, her heart feeling a bit lighter.

Just as she'd expected, Dudley glanced furtively around the tea room once more. When he was satisfied that they were unobserved, he grabbed his spoon. Desperately he plunged the utensil into the cup, clattering silver against the porcelain. Suddenly he stopped, glancing about again to be certain he was not being watched, then he scooped the ring out from the tea leaves. *Drat,* Cassie thought as he dropped the ring into his napkin. No one in the tea room seemed any the wiser—no scene.

"Cassie, I knew this would be difficult for you to accept," he said, as he dried the ring then dropped it into his waistcoat pocket. The sincerity in his voice was enough to convince her that he regretted calling off the engagement. His contrition soothed her raw feelings—a fraction. "I'm truly sorry. But I must ask that you promise me one last thing."

"What?"

"You won't incite your father to press a breach-of-contract suit or anything like that, will you?"

"Certainly not, though I know Papa thought highly of you and will be most disappointed in your behavior," Cassandra snapped. She had no more interest in being part of an embarrassing public lawsuit than Dudley.

"Perhaps you should consider spending a few weeks in the country," Dudley offered.

"Pooh, a few weeks in the country will only allow the rumors to be batted back and forth like shuttlecocks in lawn tennis." Cassie could already hear the ugly rumors in her head. She sat staring with unseeing eyes at the unfinished tea and pastries on the table. She was an unencumbered young lady once more. The humiliation of it was mortifying, almost enough to bring her to tears. The girls who had gaped at her in admiration and envy last Season would now whisper behind her back, their voices full of pity. *There goes poor Cassandra St. John. Her fiancé cried off, you know.* What embarrassment, to be cast off like so many used goods.

"Come, I will see you home." Dudley reached for her hand. Tophet growled.

Cassandra snatched her hand off the table. "I'll see myself home, thank you."

"Be sensible, Cassie," Dudley said, appearing relieved and confused all at once. "I can send you home in my carriage if you desire privacy."

"Privacy? For what?"

"If you might—might wish to weep."

"Weep, indeed," Cassandra said, closer to tears than she cared to admit. "I shall see myself home and you can be assured I won't make a fuss of this. I have no need to force anyone into marriage. Before I took you under my wing, I had scores of men calling at my door and filling my dance card."

Cassandra rose from the table.

Dudley scrambled respectfully to his feet.

With her head held high so he and everyone in the room could see that there were no tears on her cheeks, Cassandra took up her reticule and Tophet's leash. "Good-bye Dudley."

"Are you sure you don't want me to see you home?"

"I can hire myself a hackney, thank you. Good-bye," Cassie repeated, eager to walk out of the shop with dignity. She'd never hired a carriage in her life, but that was unimportant at the moment. Without another word, Cassandra armed herself with composure and strolled toward the shop door.

She was almost there, already savoring the comfort of fresh air in her lungs when Mr. Bunter hurried from behind the counter and stepped into her path.

"Miss St. John, it is so good to see you here again," the master baker greeted, wreathed in smiles and ducking his head in rapid bows of respect. Cassie was a frequent patron and he knew her well. "I hope you found everything to your liking today."

She sucked in a breath, wondering what to say, how to

extricate herself gracefully and get out of the suffocating tea room as quickly as possible.

Then inspiration struck.

"Mr. Bunter, your pastry was as light and fine as always," Cassie said, shaking the man's pudgy, flour-covered hand. "So sorry I must be off in a hurry today. I'm going to meet my mother for a gown fitting." Then she leaned closer to confide, "See the gentleman there, yes, my fiancé, the viscount. He thought your food so fine he would like to make everyone in the shop his guest today as a compliment to you."

"He doesn't look very happy to me," Mr. Bunter said doubtfully, gazing in Dudley's direction.

"But he is," Cassie assured the master baker, patting his arm. "He is just unhappy that I had to leave so soon. Please announce his kindness to your patrons, and of course, you must make a great show of thanking him for his generosity. Good day, Mr. Bunter."

"Yes, of course, good day," the baker said, moving off toward Dudley's table. "Lord Monksleigh, how kind of you to treat my patrons . . ."

Smiling with vengeful pleasure, Cassie whisked out the tea-shop door.

Outside on the pavement, her dignity seeped away in the face of her embarrassment. Cassie began to stroll down the street with Tophet at her side. Several carriages bearing crests waited at the curb, including Dudley's. She walked past it, looking for a hackney to hire, but none appeared.

Actually, she might be able to walk home, she thought. It wasn't so terribly far—or was it? And the weather was fine. On the other hand, in some places the street was filthy and the costermongers could be troublesome. Sometimes there were pickpockets in the form of street urchins, but her sister Charlotte had learned how to deal with them. Surely she could too. With a toss of her head Cassandra decided she would brave whatever the streets sent her way. Why did she need a man to escort her home? She struck out down the street in the direction she was certain her home lay.

She strode along with her head held high, ignoring inquiring glances, and braving rude leers. The sunlight warmed her face and the brisk air invigorated her. Perhaps she had no footman following along in her wake, but she had Tophet. Woe be to anyone who bothered her. A snarl from her great hound would clear the path.

CHAPTER TWO

Ramsay never took his gaze off Cassandra St. John. Her oval face was so expressive he liked reading the expressions that passed over her features, over her delicate brow, fine, straight nose, and tantalizingly pink, bow-shaped mouth. There would be no second-guessing her. Her face would tell all. Ramsay was vaguely aware that the young gentleman sitting across from her ducked his head as he spoke. As Ramsay watched, Cassandra's sunny smile faded. Bewilderment clouded her eyes. Confusion furrowed her clear brow.

"I told you Monksleigh would not let us down," he murmured as he continued to watch. The imbecile had cried off. For a moment Cassandra looked so shocked and vulnerable that Ramsay almost took pity on her.

"Aye, the lass looks bloody unhappy," Graham agreed, reaching for the last pastry on the second plate that had been brought to the table. "She might take this harder than you think. Remember that spurned lass who drowned herself in the loch back home?"

"Nay, Cassandra St. John will not drown herself over the likes of Monksleigh," Ramsay said, but he studied Cassandra closer. In her confusion she had abandoned her food and she scratched nervously at the tablecloth. When she spoke, her eyes searched Monksleigh's face, but Monksleigh avoided meeting her gaze. She appeared indignant and argued with the young viscount as if she could change his mind. When that didn't seem to work, she pleaded, all to no avail.

Once Ramsay thought she was about to weep. At the prospect of tears welling in her eyes an odd pain struck him in the gut. He shifted in his chair, feeling a bit ashamed of himself. The end of her betrothal was in her best interest, too—he reminded himself—not just for his own purposes. If she knew the truth about her viscount, which Ramsay never intended to reveal, she would be throwing her betrothal ring in the young man's face. Monksleigh might be an amusing companion during a prank, but he was unworthy of Cassandra St. John. It hadn't taken much digging for Ramsay to discover that fact. If her father, Davis St. John, and Cassandra knew the facts about Dudley, they would thank Ramsay for bringing an end to an unsuitable match.

He felt better when he saw her drop her engagement ring into Monksleigh's tea. She did it so quickly he almost missed the action, but he caught the gleam of vengeance in her blue eyes.

"Miss St. John is leaving the shop alone, it appears." Graham wiped his hands on his napkin. "Was that in the plan? Be the lass more unpredictable than you thought?"

"No, it was not part of the plan," Ramsay muttered, annoyed with the unexpected turn.

Suddenly she was out the door and the baker was announcing that the viscount was treating everyone as his guest today.

Dudley's mouth dropped open. Ramsay laughed quietly.

"It seems the lady has her own way of taking revenge," Graham said.

"Indeed it does." Ramsay had expected Cassandra St. John to take exception to the breakup of her engagement, but he had not expected her to do anything rash—not right away, at least.

Hastily he rose from his chair and reached for his black cloak. "Stay here. I'm going after her."

On the street Ramsay caught a glimpse of Cassandra's back as she marched down the stone pavement, a proud, feminine sway to her skirts. Tophet trotted contentedly at her side. No one would guess she'd just suffered the most dreadful thing that could happen to a young woman of society. She'd been jilted.

She was walking toward home. As Ramsay watched, a beggar ventured forth, holding out his hat to Cassandra and begging for pennies. Tophet lunged to the end of his leash, his long white fangs gleaming in the afternoon sunlight. The ragged man jumped back.

Cassandra quickly brought the hound to heel and dutifully dug in her small bag for coins. From her pretty profile Ramsay saw no evidence of tears on her cheeks or morbid gloom in her expression. Her heart had not been broken—not that he would be troubled if it were. She was strong enough to weather this, he thought. He watched her drop several pennies into the beggar's hat and wondered if she had enough coins to get herself home. Nearly an army of beggars thronged the streets, all brave enough to approach an attractive, unescorted lady.

Ramsay signaled Grady, his henchman who loitered across the street, to follow the lady.

This was not how he'd planned to make her acquaintance. But he'd make do. He pulled his hat low over his face so he was difficult to recognize, and strolled after Cassandra.

The afternoon was fine, perfect for a turn in the park for a girl with a light heart. But in her present mood Cassandra longed for clouds and fog. No, a thunderstorm with a dark brooding sky and jagged bolts of lightning would reflect her mood best, she decided. Dudley had just cried off on their engagement. No matter how many times she repeated the fact to herself, in time to her footsteps, she still found it impossible to believe.

Cassandra's cheeks grew warm and she knew it was not because of the heat of the day. She had been discarded. Cassandra St. John had been cast aside.

Tears of humiliation threatened. Cassandra bit her lip and kept marching, head up and footsteps firm. She managed to cross another street and turn the corner before she encountered another beggar, much younger than the first. A child actually. Tophet growled, but heeded Cassie's command and sat at her feet. Thinking of Charlotte and her orphans, Cassie dug into her reticule once more and dropped several pence into the child's hand. "And share it with your sisters and brothers," she admonished.

The child bobbed his head and dashed off, apparently thrilled with his newfound fortune.

But the encounter made Cassie hesitate. She'd seldom encountered so many beggars on her outings. Perhaps that was because she generally went forth in the company of a maid and a footman, if not a gentleman as well. Turning around to take in her surroundings more closely for the first time since leaving the tea shop, she realized the row of houses behind her appeared to be slightly shabbier than she was accustomed to seeing in Mayfair. She didn't recognize the street, but that wasn't any great surprise. She seldom walked in this part of Town. Yet passersby appeared respectable enough. The equipages on the street looked genteel, but none bore a noble crest. Still, not a single hackney was in sight.

Cassandra set out once more, this time at a faster pace. She did not feel threatened, but it would be best to get herself home before deciding how she wished to proceed. She wasn't certain what she was going to do about her freedom. Perhaps Dudley was right; a few weeks in the country would be good for her. But now was not the time to wool-gather about it.

She'd gone about another block, past an ill-kept square when she heard halting footsteps behind her.

"Yer ladyship," a high-pitched woman's voice called. "Ye dropped something."

In the voice Cassandra heard an accent she did not recognize. Holding Tophet to a short leash, she stopped, and turned to see what it was that the woman wanted. The black hound growled. The woman addressing Cassie stumbled back a step.

"That be a big dog," she said, her milky eyes growing wide.

"Yes, what is it?" Cassie demanded, glad to have Tophet at her feet, but feeling suddenly uneasier than she'd ever felt on the street in her life. The old beggarwoman who approached her was dirty and smudged with soot and reeked of gin. At least Cassie thought it was gin.

The creature waved a soiled lace handkerchief under Cassie's nose. "Ye dropped this, yer ladyship."

"I don't think so," Cassie said, certain the item was not hers. Tophet continued to growl and she did not reprove him.

"Are ye sure?" the old woman persisted, stepping closer and shoving the handkerchief at Cassie once more.

Involuntarily Cassandra winced and put her hand out to ward off the soiled article.

Tophet snarled and leaped around her feet in another direction. He lunged at someone behind her and set up a fierce barking. His leash wound around her skirts, pulling her backward. At the same moment the old woman grabbed the reticule hanging from Cassie's wrist. Crying out in dismay and indignation, Cassie resisted. But the old woman kept tugging on the reticule with surprising strength. The silken cord bit into Cassie's wrist. At the sound of her cry, Tophet turned back to the woman. His leash snapped across Cassie's knees, in another direction. From behind someone grabbed Cassie's arm, grasping at the reticule. She smelled gin for certain this time, sour sweat, and cheap tobacco.

"Give that to me," a man demanded. He seized her elbow and jerked on the reticule again. Flustered but angry, Cassie fought him. Then he yanked her bonnet down over her eyes and pulled on her reticule once more.

The old woman had retreated in the face of Tophet's attack. The dog whirled, this time attacking the man behind Cassie.

The leash snapped across the front of Cassie's skirt again, yanking her off balance this time. Blinded by her bonnet, she tottered, struggling to regain a firm stance.

"Here, what's going on?" a new, deep male voice called from behind.

"Help!" Cassandra shrieked. She struggled with the brim of her bonnet as Tophet continued to tug on his leash. She could not see the man who'd called out the question, but she would engage his help if she could. "Help me, please. Footpads!"

Cassie heard the old woman turn and sprint down the street, little sign of age in her swift stride.

"That's enough of that," commanded the new but unseen man on the scene.

Tophet ceased barking.

Cassie's arm was released. She heard a smack, the violent sound of flesh striking flesh. Fearful for the first time, she struggled to unwind herself from Tophet's leash. A groan of pain reached her ears. But by the time she had turned, she caught sight of a short, shabby man, her attacker, staggering away. A tall man wearing black was about to pursue him. When she looked toward the corner, she saw other disreputable men waiting there.

"No, don't go after him," she cried, reaching out to her rescuer to waylay him with a touch on his sleeve. "No more trouble. I'm all right, really, I am."

Her rescuer turned back to her. "Are you certain? Do you not wish to report this to the authorities?"

"No. No," she gasped. Pressing her hand against her racing heart, she watched her attacker join his friends up the street. Together they hastily disappeared around the corner. When she glanced in the other direction, the old woman had vanished also. The last thing Cassandra needed was to report this to the magistrate and let all of Society know that she'd been strolling the streets alone after Dudley had cried off. "Really, I'm quite all right. And nothing was taken, thanks to you."

"I'm just glad I could be of service," her rescuer said, bending to pick up his tall black hat which had fallen to the walk in the attack. From the quality of his coat Cassie judged him a gentleman.

When he regained his full height, Cassandra was surprised to see that he was an older man—older than Dudley, at least—but younger than Papa. He was tall, nearly as tall as Uncle Nicholas. Her first impression of litheness made her think him slight. But on reassessment she saw that his shoulders filled out his black frock coat nicely and the skirt clung close to narrow hips.

Cassie's insides fluttered oddly as she stared at him, struck by the contrast and contradiction of him—the dark blondness of his close-cropped hair, and the dark green of his eyes. Everything about his dress was dark—black cravat, shirt, coat, gloves, fitted trousers, boots. Only the satiny texture of his black damask waistcoat relieved the severity of his ebony dress and his fair hair.

"You surely were not out walking without an escort," he said, his words softly accented with a northern burr. "Your maid or a footman?"

"What? An escort?" Cassie stammered, unable to take her eyes off his finely drawn face, the long, straight nose, the thin, stern mouth, and the stubborn, masculine jaw. "I have my dog."

She glanced down at Tophet. The dog was wagging his tail and eagerly gazing up at the man in black.

He reached down to pat the hound on the head. Tophet accepted the attention with a lolling tongue, as if greeting a long-lost friend.

"He doesn't look very threatening."

"But he is," Cassie cried, feeling betrayed by Tophet's cordial reception. The black hound had been invariably suspicious of all the men in her life. "He hates my fiancé—uh, my former fiancé—and he only tolerates my father. He absolutely despises my future brother-in-law. The only respect he shows to any man is to my cousin, Tony, and my uncle, Nicholas.''

"Uncle Nicholas?" the man repeated, respectfully continuing to hold his hat tucked beneath his arm.

"Lord Nicholas Derrington, Earl of Seacombe," Cassie clarified for him.

"Ah, yes, Seacombe," he said, as if he understood something not evident before. "A hero of the high seas deserves respect from dog or man."

"Do you know my uncle?" Cassie asked hopefully.

"Only by reputation," he replied. "And what, may I ask, is the niece of the Earl of Seacombe doing walking alone on the street?"

"I'm on my way home from the tea shop," Cassandra said, reluctant to reveal her true circumstances. She put her hands to her bonnet to resettle it—and her dignity—in proper place. " 'Tis only a few blocks."

"Then I shall escort you to assure your safe passage," he said, raising his hand to signal someone down the street. A second thought seemed to occur to him. He turned toward her once more. "If you will permit me the service. My name is Ravencliff, Lord Ravencliff."

Cassie inclined her head in acknowledgment, secretly relieved that her rescuer was indeed a gentleman. "Pleased to make your acquaintance, Lord Ravencliff. I'm Cassandra St. John."

"The pleasure is all mine, Miss St. John," Ravencliff said, offering her a courteous bow, but making no move to take her hand. His manner was distant, but charming. Cassie smiled at him. What would she have done if he'd not come to her rescue?

But when Cassie heard the rattling of a hackney coming down the street, she couldn't help but stare in disbelief. There hadn't been such a conveyance anywhere to be seen only a moment ago.

"What good fortune," Ravencliff said, gesturing toward the

hired carriage which promptly stopped at the curb for them.
"We'll have you safely home in no time."

Still shaking slightly from being set upon by footpads, Cassandra could think of no reason to refuse Lord Ravencliff's favor. She and Tophet were soon seated in the carriage with their rescuer at their side.

But when Ravencliff asked for the direction, after a moment's thought Cassandra gave him Aunt Dorian's house number.

He glanced at her askance and repeated the direction slowly. "Are you certain?"

"Yes," she said, repeating Aunt Dorian's street and house number once more. Her head was still spinning from Dudley's betrayal and her unfortunate attack on the street. She was not ready to face Papa, Mama, and Charlotte just yet.

He turned toward her ever so slightly, making polite conversation on subjects acceptable among social acquaintances. Tophet sat at their feet, quiet and complacent. Cassandra's pounding heart quieted in Lord Ravencliff's company. She learned that his small barony lay on the northern border and that he'd come to London on business.

"This is your home?" he asked, a hint of disbelief in his voice when the carriage pulled up in front of the Seacombe House in Mayfair.

"Near enough," Cassandra said, unwilling to explain herself to Lord Ravencliff. A lady didn't confess all to a gentleman, at least not to one she hardly knew. "I can't thank you enough, Lord Ravencliff, for coming to my rescue like a knight in shining armor. I hope my plight in the street was of no inconvenience to you."

"Not at all, Miss St. John," Lord Ravencliff said, apparently accepting Seacombe House as her destination. He climbed out of the carriage and reached back to help her out. "I'm only too glad to come to your aid, though I seem to have left my armor and charger behind somewhere."

"The hackney served well enough as a white horse," Cassie quipped, smiling up at him, feeling strangely better about the unsettling events of the day. Her rescuer wasn't a handsome man in the fashionable way—too austere, too intense. But still there was a confidence in him, a self-assurance and strength that made Cassandra breathe a little faster when she looked up into his emerald-green eyes. He radiated a power that made her want to let her gaze linger on his features.

"At the risk of sounding as though I'm lecturing, may I suggest that you not venture out without a proper escort again," he said, meeting her look. "Tophet is a good companion and an ally, but he can't fend off everyone."

"Yes, of course, you're correct," Cassandra said, curious about Tophet's acceptance of Ravencliff. "But usually he is an excellent chaperone."

"I'm glad to hear that," he said, taking her arm and leading her up the steps to the door. Cassie liked the strength she felt in his hand. He rang the bell. "Having delivered you to your destination, I bid you good day."

"Lord Ravencliff." Cassandra curtsied.

Ravencliff bowed politely, loped down the stairs, swung into the hackney and was gone. As his hired carriage disappeared down the street, Cassandra realized with dismay that she'd neglected to ask for his card. Not that she expected to see him again; that was quite unlikely. But she owed him a note or some token of thanks. She frowned a bit at the thought. And if she phrased her appreciation correctly, she might be able to ask him just how it happened that he knew Tophet's name.

"Well, I never thought you and Monksleigh were well suited," confided Aunt Dorian, the Countess of Seacombe, over her glass of sherry. She and Cassandra were seated in the family salon of Seacombe House. The doors to the garden were open and a sense of peace wafted into the room with the soft summer breeze.

When Cassandra arrived on her aunt's doorstep with the bad news about Dudley, Dorian had immediately taken her in and poured two glasses of sherry. As Cassie settled into the comfort of a cushioned chair with Tophet at her feet, she was very glad she'd decided to stop at her aunt's house before going home. She needed to gather her wits before she confessed to Papa the unhappy news about her broken engagement.

"But you never said anything," Cassandra said, mildly surprised to hear of her aunt's doubts. "Not even when our betrothal was announced."

"You seemed content, and unlike Charlotte, you've always seemed to know your mind." Aunt Dorian waved a hand airily. "And your father was ecstatic. Under the circumstances it was not my place to question the decision. I wonder what made Monksleigh cry off now? Well, 'tis done. But do not despair, Cassie. I know you do not think so now, but in time you will come to see that Monksleigh is no great loss."

With a broad smile, Aunt Dorian lifted her glass in toast. "To the future."

"I trust you are right. To the future." Cassandra drank, uncertain whether her aunt offered the toast in consolation or celebration. But she was glad Dudley's offense did not shock Aunt Dorian. Unlike Papa, Dorian was seldom fazed by the greatest of disasters. She always saw the bright side of a calamity. Best of all, she was never at a loss for what to do next. "Dudley suggested I go stay in the country for a few weeks until the rumors quiet down."

"Go to the country? What nonsense!" Aunt Dorian waved her hand once more, dismissing the thought. "That would be the worst possible thing for you to do. Burying yourself in the shires would only confirm that you've been jilted."

She paused and shook a finger at Cassie. "And don't let your father talk you into being packed off, either. No matter how downcast you feel, now is when you want to be out. You want to be seen with a smile on your face and a bounce in your step. The Little Season is but a fortnight away. Wear your prettiest gowns and buy yourself a few new bonnets. That's always good for a girl's soul."

"But wouldn't that be unseemly?" Cassandra asked, concerned that if she seemed to enjoy herself too much, people might think her heartless. "I'd been looking forward to the Hollertons' ball the day after tomorrow. I even had a special ballgown made and now—"

"And you must go." Aunt Dorian tipped her head toward Cassie. "You know what I think about 'unseemly.' You've done nothing wrong or dishonest. There is no reason to be concerned about other people's opinions."

"But who will be my escort?" Cassandra began, concerned that her aunt had forgotten an essential in these festivities, Dudley.

"Tony will adore squiring you about. Everyone knows he's your cousin. To be seen in his company will not put off any truly interested, eligible man."

Why hadn't she thought of Tony? Cassie wondered. Tony was always great company and a smashing partner in the waltz or in a prank. Then she wondered if Lord Ravencliff would be at any of the places she might go with Tony. Would he approach her again? Had he a wife? She remember noting that he wore no ring, but that did not signify one way or the other.

"Of course, I'd love to have Tony as an escort," Cassie said, still unable to dismiss other problems that troubled her. "But, Aunt Dorian, it's so embarrassing with Charlotte betrothed to the Earl of Kinleith and her wedding being planned and now—I have no one."

"Ah, is that what truly troubles you?" Aunt Dorian asked, casting a sly sideways glance of understanding at Cassie. "You suffer from wounded sisterly pride. You want to keep up with Charlotte. How I remember Davis and I competing with each other! Yes, that can be difficult."

"I know it sounds childish, competing with my sister, but I've always done everything first," Cassie added. Having the first broken engagement was something she was not proud of. The cheerfulness that Aunt Dorian had inspired began to fade.

"I'm so glad I was here when you came," Dorian said. "I

know just what you need, a new bonnet. I saw the very hat. Let's go have a look at it now. Yes, bring the dog."

Cassandra allowed her aunt to guide her out the door without protest. The carriage was ordered and they were soon on the way to the milliner's shop. Dorian talked ceaselessly, planning Cassandra's social life over the next few weeks.

"You must be seen at whatever it is that you like to do," Dorian explained. "The races or even the boxing matches if you like. Balls, soirées, theater, whatever invitations you've accepted. If Dudley is off to the Continent, then you needn't be concerned about the embarrassment of running into him."

"Yes, that is true," Cassie said, thankful for small blessings.

"Here we are," Aunt Dorian said as the carriage pulled to a stop.

When they alighted from the carriage Cassie saw the hat in the window that her aunt had been talking about. It was stunning— wide-brimmed with rucked mauve silk, and trimmed in pale pink feathers. Very unusual, but beautiful.

Inside the shop the milliner and Aunt Dorian quickly seated Cassie in a chair before a mirror. The hat was fetched from the window and fitted on Cassie.

"Magnificent. I knew it," Aunt Dorian said, standing back to admire her selection in triumph. "It was made for you, Cassie. Let that be your answer to Dudley's bad behavior. Wear it like a crown of courage."

Cassie stared into the mirror at the red-haired girl with rounded, slightly slanted blue eyes, who would never be a countess. She was unsure how disappointed she was about that. The hat was lovely, and did flatter her in just the style she'd adopted for herself. She had a sound sense of what looked good on her and Aunt Dorian's eye was right on target. However a new hat didn't solve her problem.

"But what about Papa?" Cassie asked, still uneasy about how her father would take the news. He had put great store in her betrothal to Dudley. She'd be lucky if he didn't send her off to the country forever. "What shall I tell Papa?"

The shop was empty, and the milliner far too polite and knowing to let on that she was witnessing a private conversation. Cassie knew that her father was bound to be disappointed. He would never accept the end of her engagement as easily as Aunt Dorian. Cassie could already see him storming about the house demanding she admit what she did to offend the Viscount of Monksleigh.

Aunt Dorian sobered. "Your papa will not take this news well. Leave him to me. I was planning to call on your mother this evening anyway. I will talk to your father. The important thing to remember is that Dudley has released you so that you are available for the Little Season."

"Oh, thank you, Aunt Dorian," Cassie said, relief washing over her.

Aunt Dorian took Cassie's hand in hers and sat down beside her on the bench before the shop mirror. "Your father is an ambitious man. In his favor I will say that he resists the tentacles of this yearning, but the pull is there. He's always wanted to be a member of the aristocracy, and he is so certain that it is the most prized thing on earth that he wants his daughters to have it, too."

"But you married into aristocracy," Cassie said. "Are you sorry?"

"Heavens, no," Aunt Dorian said. "But I married Nicholas because I love him, not because he was the twelfth Earl of Seacombe. That's the difference. Much as your father might preach the benefits of marrying nobility, remember, he married for his heart, too. He loves your mother very much—much more than any title. You know, he had a chance to marry into a noble family and he passed it up."

"Truly?" Cassie stared at her aunt. She'd never heard her mother or her father speak of such a thing. And she was certain that Charlotte didn't know about it either. "Papa had a chance to marry into aristocracy?"

"Yes indeed," Aunt Dorian said with a knowing nod. "Of course, it's not as simple for a man to marry into a noble line.

He doesn't just walk into a title in the same fashion a woman does.''

"The way you became countess, or I would have become a viscountess if Dudley hadn't . . .'' Cassie allowed her words to trail off.

"Yes, but the family of the aristocratic heiress with whom he'd formed an affection and who seemed to have some interest in him, was in need of funds,'' Aunt Dorian explained. "If they had wed, your papa, thanks to his fortune, would have been a member of a noble family and probably would have been knighted, though he could not have expected to receive an entailed or hereditary title. But he could not bring himself to do it. He married your mother. Though he remains ambitious, I don't believe he has regretted it for a minute. But what I'm trying to tell you, my dear, is that you should wed for the sake of your heart and not for the sake of ambition or position.''

A slow smile spread across the face of the girl Cassie stared at in the mirror. She understood better how Papa might be handled.

"Let me speak to your father,'' Aunt Dorian said, patting Cassie's hand. "But, about the hat. You must have it, my dear. A gift from me, an early birthday gift.''

"Then I accept, thank you,'' Cassie said, smiling at her beloved aunt, who had just given her insight and confidence—and a new, beribboned crown of courage.

CHAPTER THREE

The day after the Hollerton ball—and four days after Ramsay had first encountered Cassandra St. John on the street—he sat astride his new black stallion at the Newmarket horse races with an ear half turned toward his kinsman and his gaze searching the crowd for her.

The day was fair and warm. A blue sky stretched above the dusty race grounds. Bookies, food vendors, acrobats, flower girls, and gypsies thronged among the coaches, open carriages, and riders gathered to watch the races. Laughter and chatter carried across the grounds. Colorful clothing fluttered in the breeze. With the start of each race, telescope and opera-glass lenses flashed in the sun.

"Any hardy Highland lad can hike faster than these English steeds, racehorses or palfreys," Graham complained, a painful grimace on his face. He sat tense and stiff atop a gentle bay gelding as if he expected the animal to lurch from underneath him at any moment.

Ramsay had purchased their mounts at Tattersalls. In fact he'd spent the last several days getting himself and Graham set up to move in London Society as a Scottish marquis and his foster brother should. He'd rented a townhouse, purchased a carriage and horses, had servants hired, and visited a tailor. At first the St. James Street tradesman had balked at making everything in black, but had been won over with the prospect of extra pay. The only regret Ramsay had about establishing himself in London was that he hadn't done it sooner. Trying to orchestrate the acquisition of Glen Gray out from under Connor McKensie from Edinburgh had been a grave mistake. Pure folly, now that he thought on it.

"I can see that ye might believe ye need four-legged transportation to keep up with these Londoners, but for meself, you could have forgone the expense," Graham was saying.

"You'll get used to riding," Ramsay said, still scanning the crowd for the Derrington carriage. They'd been meandering through the crowd for the last half hour looking for the Earl of Seacombe's equipage without success. Yet he had it on reliable authority that Tony Derrington and Cassandra were here.

Someone waving a hat in the air across the course caught Ramsay's attention. He saw Grady there, pointing toward an elegant black carriage, its rooftop crowded with racing fans.

"There they are," Ramsay said, recognizing Cassie sitting on the roof. She wore a fashionable hat he'd never seen before. She was laughing at some jest her cousin Anthony Derrington had made. Despite all his dispassionate calculations about her lively temperament, when Ramsay saw her laughing in the sunlight, he could not take his gaze from her.

The late summer breeze tugged at her gray-and-white gown, molding the merino against long, shapely legs and fluttering the feathers of the most remarkable bonnet Ramsay had ever seen on a lady. The bold mauve creation of ribbons and feathers softened with a hint of lace suited Cassie. She looked up at her cousin and laughed as if she didn't have a care in the world. Then they both leaned over the far side of the coach roof as if they were helping someone climb up to join them.

"Does that look like a lass about to drown herself over a

broken betrothal?" asked Ramsay, mystified by the strange current of pride that coursed through him.

"She's not missed a ride in the park since that day in the tea shop," Graham admitted, with a frown.

"No talk of solicitors or breach-of-contract suits either," Ramsay said, repeating for his own satisfaction the information he'd compiled from his sources in Davis St. John's gentlemen's club.

"She hardly gave Monksleigh a second look when he cried off," Graham said, shifting uncomfortably in the new saddle. "Next thing you know she decks herself out in her best feathers and frippery and turns up at the Lord Hollerton's ball and now she is at the races."

"What else should a spirited lass do?" Ramsay couldn't resist an evil laugh. "I knew she wouldn't run off to hide in the country. Not Cassandra St. John."

" 'Twould have been simpler if she had," said Graham. "I know ye don't like to go about in Society, but I still don't understand why you didn't get yourself invited to Lord Hollerton's ball and secure an introduction to her there."

"And have her barely notice me among all the young bucks eager to present themselves to one of the richest heiresses in the kingdom? Oh, no," Ramsay said, finding himself anticipating the next few weeks with pleasure. " I'm taking no chances this time. I'm not leaving to others or to lady luck what I should have taken care of myself. When Cassandra St. John and I are together, I shall have her complete and undivided attention."

As Ramsay watched, a young gypsy fortune-teller scrambled on top of the Derrington carriage with the help of Tony and Cassandra. The young woman's dark curls fluttered in the breeze and her gold hoop earring glinted in the sunlight. The gypsy glanced from Tony to Cassandra with uncharacteristic wariness for a fortune-teller.

Ramsy wondered what kind of jesting was going on between the cousins. Tony was probably teasing Cassie about her future. Ramsay watched the fortuneteller and Cassie with growing unease. The gypsy was not part of his plan, but he immediately wished she had been. Prophecy—what a powerful way to gain influence over a young woman.

"Tony, you know I don't believe in fortune-telling," Cassie protested with a laugh. She was having a dashed good time, better than she'd had in the last year as Dudley's fiancée. Aunt Dorian's advice had been right on target. Society had hardly begun to gasp over Dudley crying off before Cassie distracted them with her frenetic social life.

The family was rallying around her. Society was taking her to their hearts. Dudley, who had scuttled off to the Continent, was dubbed the villain and a fool by the more gallant gentlemen. Hostesses were only too glad to welcome her to their social events with handsome Tony Derrington as her escort.

Papa, tight-lipped and clearly unhappy about the breakup, cast few recriminations on Cassandra. Aunt Dorian deserved thanks for that, Cassie knew. He also made no effort to aggravate matters with a lawsuit. While the whole affair had been over for Cassie when she'd dropped the Moncreff ring into Dudley's teacup, she was sadly aware of Papa closeted behind study doors with solicitors bent on nullifying marriage contracts and agreements.

But she'd become a free woman and she loved it. And maybe Tony was right about this being the time to learn of her future. She smiled at the young gypsy girl. "I mean no disrespect, dear lady—what is your name?"

"Jasmine, yer ladyship," the gypsy said, pulling her red-and-yellow flowered shawl closer about her shoulders, though the sun was warm. She seemed a relatively young woman to Cassandra. Her brows had a lovely arch and her skin was smooth and golden, like honey. Her eyes were that kind of dark, liquid brown that could melt a heart if the lady chose to do so.

"What say you, Cassie? This is when you need to know

what comes next," Tony continued. "We might be able to find out which one of those gents who came sniffing around you at the Hollerton ball is going to be your next husband. Isn't that right, Jasmine?"

"Perhaps," the gypsy allowed.

"I'm not about to become betrothed to any of those gentlemen," Cassie said, eager to spur Tony on. He could be such fun. Not one of those gents at the ball had interested her. She'd spent the entire evening hoping Lord Ravencliff would appear. "In fact, I've sworn off betrothals. I believe I'll swear off men as well, except for you, of course, dear Cousin."

"Thanks—I think," Tony said, an expression of mock injury crossing his handsome face. "But we've dragged poor Jasmine up here to learn what the future holds. Why not allow her to look at your palm?"

"Please, if ye will, yer ladyship," Jasmine pleaded, holding out her hands to take Cassie's. "I can tell ye what is to come. If a gentleman is in the lines of yer hand, I can tell you who you may wed. If I don't tell you true, your lordship don't need to pay me."

"There." Tony looked at Cassie and shrugged. "You can't complain about that kind of guarantee."

"No, I suppose not," Cassie agreed, still laughing. She pulled off her dainty net glove and proffered her hand to the fortune-teller. "Does this satisfy you, Tony? I'm submitting to your silliness. Here, Jasmine, tell me what lies in my future."

The gypsy immediately bent over Cassandra's hand, her thumbs tracing the lines of her palm. The fortune-teller's touch was firm, but exploratory.

"Yer ladyship has a long, strong heart line of a deep red color," Jasmine murmured, her head bending even lower over Cassie's palm, so all she could see of the gypsy was her glossy black hair and her golden hoop earrings glittering in the soft sunlight of the partly cloudy day.

"What does that mean?" Cassie asked obligingly, a silly thrill of excitement prickling down her back. She glanced over

Jasmine's head at Tony who was clearly suppressing a chuckle. What nonsense this was, but what fun.

"A long, strong red heart line indicates ye are deeply passionate, my lady," Jasmine said without raising her head. "Possessors of such a heart line are usually devoted to their chosen ones and bestow great happiness on their mates."

Disappointed and annoyed, Cassie bridled slightly. The humor of the situation was beginning to escape her. She tried to pull her hand from the gypsy's grasp. "If you have nothing more than generalities to tell me—"

Jasmine's grip on Cassie's hand remained firm. "I see, yer ladyship, that ye have a sister, a twin sister."

Cassie ceased pulling away. How could something like that be revealed in her palm? "Yes, I have a twin, Charlotte," she admitted. "What say you of her happiness?"

"She is recently betrothed to a handsome gentleman," Jasmine said, her voice hesitant as if she was finding her way through a dense forest. "They are very happy together."

"Yes, that is very nice," Cassie said. The fun of the palm-reading was wearing thin. Glad as she was for Charlotte and Connor's betrothal, her sister's happiness only made Cassie feel left out and alone. Besides, the gypsy could have gleaned information about Charlotte from any of the household staff.

"They are lovers," Jasmine added blandly, without looking up.

"Lovers?" Tony's dark, violet-colored eyes widened in shock.

Cassandra blinked. Sometimes Tony seemed so terribly youthful. But she was certain that bit of information was unknown to anyone but herself and Charlotte. "How do you know these things about my sister?"

"It is here, in your hand," Jasmine said, continuing to stroke Cassie's palm. "Your sister is destined for great happiness. But for you it is not so clear. In the last few days, something very upsetting has happened to you, yer ladyship. You lost something that was of great importance to you. Or it was withdrawn, I cannot see which, exactly.''

Cassie and Tony exchanged glances over the gypsy's head. They both knew the gypsy could only be referring to Dudley's crying-off.

"Right again," Cassie said, looking away. Tony knew all about her and Dudley, but they had silently agreed not to discuss it. She tried to pull her hand from the gypsy's grasp. "This is all ancient history. Enough for now.''

"You are not to trouble yourself over this loss," the gypsy continued without looking up. "You did nothing to make it happen. There was an impediment placed there by another.''

"Impediment?" Cassie and Tony repeated in unison.

"A dark figure directed the loss," Jasmine explained.

Cassandra frowned and tried to peer into the palm that Jasmine seemed to find so enlightening. Who would have arranged for a crying-off? She couldn't imagine Dudley's family encouraging it. The Moncreffs had been as pleased as Papa with their betrothal. When she cast a questioning glance in Tony's direction, he shrugged, clearly as mystified as she was.

"But what does the future hold for my cousin, Jasmine?" Tony asked.

"The dark one is part of the future," Jasmine said, still intent on Cassie's palm. With soothing strokes of her thumb she traced the map of Cassie's future.

"Who is the dark one?" Cassie asked.

"He will come again," the gypsy said, looking up into Cassie's face for the first time during the reading. Her liquid brown eyes had grown wide and fearful. "Beware of him. For he will bring much grief and sorrow into your life.''

"Of course, she means Tophet," Tony said, the solution to the puzzle bringing a smile to his lips. "Dudley never liked him and, you must admit, Cassie, the mutt is almost more trouble than he is worth.''

"That is not so," Cassie said, offended that Tony might

think the hound had caused Dudley to cry off. "Tophet is a wonderful companion."

"No, the dark one is a man, a heartless man," Jasmine said, stroking Cassie's palm once more. "I can not tell you more. This particular line is not clearly formed. It fades into several directions."

"But I thought our future was already written there in our hands," Tony protested as if he thought the gypsy had violated some rule.

"Our destinies are not always so clearly ordained," Jasmine explained. She appeared troubled. "What is to happen is not always recorded in the hand, but I see that the dark one exists and he is a powerful man who has brought dissention into your life once, yer ladyship. He will do so again. And there is something more I should tell you, yer ladyship."

"Yes? And what might that be?" Cassie asked politely though she was bored with the game now. "Am I about to go on a trip? What is it?"

Without meeting Cassie's gaze, Jasmine took a deep breath, as if she was about to dive into a river. "There is murder in your future."

"Murder? Surely you jest," Tony said.

Cassie scoffed. Her first inclination was to laugh, but when Jasmine suddenly looked up at her, the intensity of the gypsy's gaze robbed Cassie of mirth. "You need not concoct some drama to amuse me, Jasmine," Cassie warned.

The gypsy shook her head emphatically. "I make no jest. Nor mistake. If what I saw was of less importance, I would not reveal this sadness to you. But it is in the lines. Untimely death will come to someone you know. Beware of the dark one. That is important. More than that, I cannot tell you. But beware. Beware."

The gypsy scrambled to the edge of the carriage rooftop.

"Here is your fee, Jasmine," Tony said, pulling the coins from his coat pocket and holding the money out to her.

The gypsy paused in her climb, her eyes focused longingly

on the coins. She shook her head and made some gesture, warding off an evil eye or some such. "I cannot deliver such news and accept a fee for it. Thank you, you have been very kind, but I cannot take it. I thank yer ladyship and wish you well."

Jasmine was gone, disappearing down the side of the coach with the help of the coachman. Cassie watched as the gypsy melted into the crowd.

"That was strange," Tony said.

"Yes, indeed," Cassie agreed, a sudden chill coming over her. What nonsense! Still, the chill made her rub her arms as if the summer breeze was a cool one. "Don't you have a wager to make in the betting circle?"

"Yes, glad you thought of that," Tony said, climbing down from the coach. "Too good a tip to pass up. I'll be back soon, Cassie."

Tony was off the carriage rooftop in a flash, making his way through the crowd in pursuit of his favorite oddsmaker.

Still a bit unnerved by the gypsy's warning, Cassie stared down into her palm again. She saw no dark man, no murder, only innocent lines on pink flesh.

She was still staring at the lines, trying to make sense of them, when she heard her name called.

"Miss St. John. Miss Cassandra St. John," called a masculine voice with a vaguely familiar burr. "What a pleasure to see you again."

Cassie gazed over the edge of the carriage roof to see Lord Ravencliff smiling up at her from atop an elegant black stallion.

"My lord," she said, the pleasure of seeing her rescuer again erasing the gloomy mood of the gypsy's ridiculous fortune. "How glad I am to see you once more. I'm so embarrassed that I did not have the good manners to find out where I might send my thanks for your kind assistance."

"But no thanks are necessary, Miss St. John," Ravencliff said, sweeping his tall hat off his head so that the sun gleamed off his dark-golden fairness. Cassandra gazed down into the familiar stern, sculpted face. He didn't exactly smile at her, but she detected a hint of pleasure in his eyes. It warmed her, and she smiled in return.

As before, he wore all black, each garment of the finest cut and fabric. Only the sheen of his black silk brocade waistcoat livened the somberness. "I was glad to be of service to you, though I would always welcome any correspondence."

"I only wanted to express on paper how very kind I thought it was of you to come to my rescue." Cassie felt a silly school-room-girl blush rise in her cheeks as she felt his gaze settle on her. She'd forgotten what a uniquely good-looking man he was. He was far from being the first man to focus his attention on her. She normally basked and preened in the glow of a man's admiration. But for some reason this particular man's undivided regard flustered her.

"I'm certain your parents were most concerned for you," Lord Ravencliff said.

"Well, no, actually." Cassie leaned a bit over the edge of the carriage roof. "I did not exactly confess the details of my—our misadventure."

"I see," Ravencliff said with a solemn nod of his head. "You don't think they would wish to know?"

"They have so many other things on their minds," Cassandra said. "My sister's engagement and coming nuptials. And the outcome of our unconventional meeting was so fortuitous, thanks to you, I saw no reason to trouble them. You understand, I'm sure."

"Yes, in light of those circumstances, perhaps it is best not to trouble your parents with something that is done and over with," Ravencliff agreed, quiet approval in his voice.

Cassandra smiled and savored the warmth of his sympathy.

"And sometimes adventures are so much more precious when they are not shared with everyone," he continued. "Don't you think the best memories are kept whole and stored as treasure in our own private recollections?"

"Precisely." Cassie gave a slight start. "Yes, how well

you put it, my lord. That's just how I feel sometimes about experiences. There is such a thing as sharing too much.''

Ravencliff nodded slowly, a nod revealing great wisdom. A wonderful, mysterious smile lighted his face. When he met Cassie's gaze once more, his greenest-of-green eyes held her transfixed. ''Indeed, too much like giving something precious away.''

''Yes, I quite agree.'' A sudden chill shivered through Cassie. She loved secrets.

''But you are not here unescorted, are you?'' he asked, obviously noting that she sat on the coach rooftop alone. ''Where is your dog?''

Cassie did not miss the disapproval in his voice now. ''No, no, I quite heeded your advice, my lord,'' Cassandra said, eager for him to think her sensible. ''Tophet is in the carriage and my cousin, Tony, has only gone off to the betting circle. Please join us and watch the conclusion of the races.''

''Why, thank you, Miss St. John,'' Ravencliff said, reaching into the carriage to pat the hound on the head. ''That is very kind of you, but regrettably, I must refuse. I have business to tend to. But perhaps we will see each other again. I ride daily in Regent's Park at two o'clock.''

''Is that so,'' Cassie said, making a mental note of that particular piece of information. ''I, too, occasionally take the fresh air in the Regent's Park, but I don't recall seeing you there.''

''I am not a man to draw much attention, Miss St. John,'' Ravencliff said, reminding Cassie of the austere privateness that seemed to surround him. ''However, if I had known you were in the park and that I was missing such delightful company, undoubtedly I would have made myself known to you before now.''

Cassandra laughed, delighted with the gentlemanly flattery. ''Undoubtedly, my lord, and I would have been most pleased if you had. But 'tis not too late. Now, perhaps, we will encounter one another in the park soon.''

"I shall look forward to it." Lord Ravencliff smiled, as if he kept a wonderful secret, and replaced his hat. "Until that fortuitous moment, then, good day, Miss St. John."

"Yes," Cassie said breathlessly, her mind already laying plans for a ride in the park and another meeting with the mysterious, heroic baron from the north. Of all the adventures she'd embarked on as a free woman in the last four days, a meeting with the handsome black-clad gentleman promised to be the most thrilling. "Until then, Lord Ravencliff."

When Tony returned, Cassandra said nothing of Ravencliff's visit. After all, why tell all her secrets?

CHAPTER FOUR

In the three days following the encounter with Lord Ravencliff at the Newmarket races, it was impossible for Cassandra to arrange a ride in the Regent's Park alone. She was obligated to so many gown-fittings and social calls with her mother, aunt, and sister, her head was fairly spinning.

However, she never forgot that she had an informal assignation with Lord Ravencliff. In fact she'd quickly dismissed the silly gypsy's warning at the Newmarket Races. *"Beware of the dark one."* What nonsense, she thought. The only dark gentleman she knew was Connor McKensie, and he was engaged to Charlotte. He posed no threat to her. Dudley was brown-haired and everyone knew he was in Italy. Ravencliff was a fascinating man with golden hair and a calm demeanor that she liked, so unlike the young bucks who had pestered her at every soirée, theater outing, and ball. But he wasn't like Papa, either. Not stuffy or boring. Ravencliff was coolly confident in himself—and all male. No other man's voice nor any other man's nearness had ever sent shivers through her. The gypsy's reading had nothing to do with any of the men in her life, Cassie concluded. Jasmine had been telling tales to amuse.

Cassandra told no one about her meeting with Ravencliff, not even Tony. It was her secret. A treasure she had no intention of portioning out to others, even her twin sister. It was her delight. Her adventure to savor and cherish apart from the flurry of her broken engagement. Somehow Ravencliff, with his mature assurance, offered a haven to Cassandra. She had no intention of ignoring the healing refuge his attentions bestowed.

At last an afternoon without obligations arrived. As casually as possible—because the excitement threatened to bubble to the surface and betray her secret—Cassandra ordered her horse saddled, and hurried upstairs to her room. Quickly she donned last season's riding habit, a deep Devonshire brown ensemble with a small military-style hat. She chose it because of its subdued design and because the hat featured a veil she'd never used. As she admired her figure in the mirror, she was satisfied that her dress would not call much attention to herself. She would not have Lord Ravencliff think she was ostentatious. If they were to keep their meetings unnoticed, she dare not flaunt herself with conspicuous finery. Carefully she tucked her hair up beneath the dark veil.

She liked the effect of having her hair concealed; she appeared quiet and mature—like a lady, like Aunt Dorian. She'd decided after her second meeting with Lord Ravencliff that he was not a man to be impressed with the flutter of a lady's fan. He expected substance and poise from a woman. The hat was right, she decided. Then Cassie dropped the veil over her face. The girl in the mirror changed. The black netting added instant mystery. She became an enigmatic woman, and she liked the effect.

Who would think that she, Cassandra St. John, former fiancée of Dudley Moncreff, was already seeing a gentleman aristocrat? She studied the hat and veil in the mirror again, arranging the drape of the netting. The look was perfect. She prayed Lord Ravencliff liked the effect, too.

She slipped out of her room unnoticed, having quite forgotten the warning of the gypsy fortune-teller.

                          *   *   *

Since the day of the meeting with Cassandra at the Newmarket races, Ramsay had ridden every day at two o'clock just as he'd told her. Though his spies had informed him of the St. Johns' crowded social schedule, he had great faith in the young woman's cleverness. He especially had confidence in Cassandra's willfulness. If the young lady possessed the ingenuity to masquerade as her twin sister or as a highwayman as she had done in the past, then she was canny enough to arrange an unobserved meeting with a gentleman in the park.

On the third day, his patience was rewarded, as it always was. He had learned patience early in his life, and it invariably paid off. Give people enough time and they will oblige you.

Cassandra rode into the park on a pretty gray mare, followed by a dutiful-looking groom. The escort did not surprise Ramsay or concern him; he could deal with a servant. She wore a subdued but fashionable habit with a matching hat and a veil. Ramsay couldn't help but admire the trimness of her waist and the firm fullness of her breasts. As she rode, she glanced around frequently, greeting those familiar individuals she passed, but then looking past them, obviously in search of someone. Ramsay smiled to himself with cold satisfaction. She was looking for him.

Time to buy the flower, he decided. He gave her a few minutes to search the bridle paths and to see and be seen by the members of Society who were taking the fresh air. During that time he purchased a rose from the flower girl at the entrance. Then, when Cassandra seemed about to turn her horse toward the exit, Ramsay rode out of the shadows.

"Miss St. John, what a pleasure to see you," he called softly.

"Lord Ravencliff, I'd about given up hope of meeting you again," Cassandra said with charming, youthful honesty. She pulled her horse to a halt.

"Would you have been disappointed if you hadn't found

me?'' he asked, doffing his tall hat and inclining his head in greeting.

"Indeed, I always look forward to seeing my knight rescuer," Cassandra said with a slight toss of her head. "Would it trouble you to disappoint me?"

Ramsay sat back in the saddle and smiled, unable to resist. The sweet boldness of her response surprised and enchanted him. He was accustomed to more fainthearted responses from young ladies. "I believe I would, indeed, Miss St. John, be sorry to find that I had disappointed such an intriguing lady."

She rewarded him with an unexpectedly shy smile.

"I see you have a groom with you," Ramsay said, eyeing the servant who tipped his hat respectfully when he found himself under scrutiny.

"I heeded your advice," Cassandra said. "Albert has been with the family for years and is quite discreet."

"Albert." Ramsay nodded acknowledgment toward the man, then fished into his pocket for a coin. "Treat yourself to a lemonade from the vendors over there. Your mistress is in safe company with me."

"Yes, I'm sure she is, my lord." A smile flickered across the groom's face as he accepted the money. "Thank you, my lord." He turned his horse and headed for refreshment.

"That was very kind of you, my lord," Cassandra said as she turned her horse to walk along beside Ramsay's black stallion.

Not kind, just practical, Ramsay thought.

He led the way into the quieter, darker sections of the well-traveled bridle path. They exchanged customary comments about the weather and the loveliness of the day.

"And was your day at the races a success?" Cassandra asked, turning her pretty, eager face toward him.

"Successful enough," Ramsay said truthfully. He never lied unless absolutely necessary. "I was not there to wager, but to consider purchasing a racehorse for investment."

"And did you decide on the investment?" Cassandra asked.

"Not this one," Ramsay said. "The horse didn't look fit enough. Were your wagers successful?"

"Tony did quite well," Cassandra said, laughing at some pleasant memory. Clearly she enjoyed the company of her cousin. The knowledge strangely irritated Ramsay.

"Tony is the luckiest person I know," she continued. Her smile faded as some new thought came to mind. "I do not have the courage to try my luck these days."

"How is that?" Ramsay asked, his voice purposely full of innocence. When she did not respond, he went on. "Of course, it is none of my affair, but did I hear the St. John name connected with a broken engagement?"

Cassandra turned on him, indignation shining in her eyes. "What have you heard? What are people saying?"

"Only that young Monksleigh is a fool," Ramsay said, reaching inside his coat. "That is the word going around my club."

She shook her head vehemently. "I was the fool, to have ever pledged myself to a dunce so uncertain of his heart."

Ramsay smiled to himself, unaccountably pleased with her spirit. He extended the rose to her. "Well, I cannot speak for Monksleigh. He is a very young man. And youth is sometimes prone to foolishness. Please accept my apology for the stupidity of my gender."

At the sight of the flower, the defiance in Cassandra's face softened.

"Why, thank you, my lord," she said, staring at the rose, then across the distance between them. Gratitude and vulnerability shone in her gentle smile.

Unaccustomed guilt made Ramsay shift uncomfortably in his saddle. " 'Tis but a small token."

"But so kind of you to think of me," Cassandra said, sniffing the bloom she'd accepted. "Pink is my color and the fragrance is wonderful."

She tucked the rose into the lapel of her riding habit and sobered for a moment. "I've put on a brave face, but in truth, the loss has been difficult. I've told almost no one that, but I feel I can tell you.''

Ramsay blanched at the thought of her sharing a serious confidence with him. She should really be more careful to whom she confessed.

Cassandra continued, staring at the bridle path ahead, "I'm not sure people understand how devastating it is when someone whom you believe cares for you suddenly announces that they no longer wish to have a future with you. It has shaken me.''

"Perhaps people understand better than you think,'' Ramsay said, still sitting stiffly in the saddle.

"Do you think so?'' she asked, turning to him, her eyes wide and trusting, obviously prepared to believe his every word.

He forced a smile of reassurance to his lips. Smiles seldom came easily to him. "I'm certain, Miss St. John, that your bravery is a source of admiration for many young ladies.''

"Please call me Cassandra,'' she offered, smiling now, the shadows gone from her eyes. "That is good to know. I like to think that because of my example, other young ladies will take heart and not be forever downcast because some heartless gentleman let them down.''

"Precisely the way to look at it,'' Ravencliff said, anxious to put the topic of Monksleigh behind them. "How have you been passing your days since we last met at the races?''

She launched into a list of soirées, musicales, and theatergoing. Even though the Season was over and only the Little Season lay ahead, there seemed to be plenty of social events for a lady to enjoy.

"But everywhere I go,'' Cassandra was saying, "no one mentions Lord Ravencliff. Do you not go about in Society at all, my lord?''

"I prefer a quiet life,'' Ramsay said, making an honest reply.

"But how bor—'' Cassandra began, then stopped, clearly having second thoughts about what she was about to say.

"How boring?'' Ramsay finished for her. "I do belong to

a club in St. James Street and I am here in Town to conduct business affairs.''

"But I didn't mean to say 'boring,' " Cassandra said quickly. "I meant to say *lonely*. It must be lonely for you. Have you no family here to visit? No wife to keep you company?"

"I am not married," Ramsay said, secretly amused at how she had gotten around to soliciting that important piece of information.

"Not married," she repeated thoughtfully. He could feel her looking him over, wondering how he could be a baron without a wife, without an heir. Then a smile flashed across her face. "But, my lord, how the London hostesses would love to have you in their drawing rooms! You have but to say the word and I could see to it that you receive invitations to all the best soirées. Between Mama and Aunt Dorian we can get you into any social affair of significance in Town."

"Thank you, Cassandra," Ramsay said. "Your offer is kind and generous, but I do not care to join the social whirl."

"I see," Cassandra said, clearly not seeing at all. "You are in mourning?"

"No, it simply is not in my nature to stand in a hot room full of overdressed gentlemen," Ramsay explained, "nor to say things that I don't care to say or listen to conversations I don't care to hear."

"Oh," she said once more, apparently still mystified. "This desire to remain out of the 'whirl' as you call it, is that why you always wear black?"

Ramsay had expected that question. Women always got to it if he remained in their company long enough. "I wear black for a practical reason. Because I do not like making decisions about clothing."

Her solemn gaze flicked over him, from the toe of his boots to the top of his tall hat. "Are you certain that is the only reason?"

Simple decision-making was not the only reason why he wore black, but he had no intention of sharing of his personal philosophy with her. "Just what do you mean?"

"I thought perhaps you affected black dress to go with your name," Cassandra said. "Ravencliff. Such affectation is not unheard-of among gentlemen."

Annoyed, Ramsay frowned. He did not like being classed with dandies. "I do not trouble myself with such egotistical pretensions, I assure you."

"I'm sorry, my lord, I did not mean to offend," Cassandra sputtered, bowing her head in an apologetic gesture. "You surely will allow the connection—ravens and black—it is only natural and a bit intimidating, don't you think?"

"Perhaps," Ramsay allowed, aware that he'd always used that association to strike fear in the hearts of the people from whom he wanted things. Why waste time and energy earning someone's goodwill when a quick, intimidating appearance accomplished the same goal? What startled him was that young Cassandra St. John's question struck so closely at understanding his secret. He felt oddly guilty, as if caught in a lie—though he'd actually told none.

"Tell me about your country seat. What is it called? Ravencliff Court?" Cassandra said, riding ahead of him a few paces, thankfully changing the subject. "What is it like? You must be very happy there to be so content to stay out of Society."

"Ravencliff Court is my favorite place in the world," Ramsay admitted, expressing deep feelings he'd never spoken in his life. He'd traveled the Continent more than once and he always returned to the ancient manor house on the rise in the Raven River Valley with pleasure. Aware that Cassandra was waiting for him to go on, he added, "It is a sixteenth-century stone house with many Tudor windows."

"So, it is very light, then?" Cassandra prompted with a smile.

"Yes, light and airy for an old stone house." Ramsay found himself waxing nostalgic. "The woodwork is dark and worn, and smells of lemon oil and beeswax. The hearths are many, twelve in all, and each is tall and always ready for a fire."

"Is there a garden?" Cassandra asked. If she wasn't truly interested, she certainly sounded as if she was.

"Yes, a formal French style on one side of the house and a less formal planting on the other against the stone wall next to the kitchen garden."

"It sounds lovely." Cassandra halted her horse and leaned close. "Please, forgive me, my lord, but I must ask."

Ramsay quirked a brow at her. He was already becoming wary of her questions. "Yes? Ask."

"Is there a gray lady at Ravencliff?"

Ramsay blinked. "Who?"

"A ghost?" Cassandra said in a whisper, as if she thought someone might be listening. "A gray lady?"

"No ghost." Ramsay shook his head. Though he could sometimes still hear the echoes of his dead mother's and father's voices raised in anger, he knew there were no ghosts in the house. "Does that disappoint you?"

"No, I'm glad for you," Cassandra said, relief in her voice. "Ravencliff Court must be a happy place."

"Content enough," Ramsay said, touched by her youthfulness but sorry that the conversation had gone so far afield. She was nearly thirteen years younger than he. Despite Cassandra's painful loss, the world was still bright and welcoming to her. He could not expect her to be as content with obscurity as he was. "How did we get to the topic of ghosts? Never mind. What I intended to tell you is that the sobriety of my dress does not mean that I don't enjoy certain amusements, such as the Newmarket races or perhaps even the animals in the zoological gardens."

"Have you not seen the new zoological gardens, my lord?" Cassandra asked, clearly astonished with the thought that he had not. "Charlotte and I were there the first week it opened."

"As I said, I only take the *fresh* air here in the park. So far I have avoided the animals."

"But on a beautiful day like this, with the breeze blowing, you can hardly smell a thing," Cassandra said, her eyes sparkling with the prospect of seeing the exotic creatures. "I have yet to see the new elephant and giraffes. The news sheets have been full of their arrival.''

"An excellent point about the breeze," Ramsay said, glad she'd forgotten about the house. Her excitement was irresistible. A wry smile formed on his lips. "Then let's go see what wonders the animal kingdom has to offer us."

The Regent's Park zoological gardens' clock tower rose over the grounds, marking the camel house.

At the garden entrance Cassie unfastened the skirt of her riding habit from the sidesaddle and allowed Ravencliff to help her down from her horse. His large gloved hands spread wide across her waist and ribs, a curious heat seeping through layers of fabric between his palm and her skin. Cassie's heart fluttered strangely as he set her down on her feet. For a moment they stood so close together, his hands still on her waist and her hands on his arms, that she caught the scent of him, a pleasing mixture of lemon and leather. A light wave of dizziness made her sway.

"Steady?" he asked, looking down into her face.

"Yes, actually, quite steady," Cassie said, pushing away from him despite her lack of balance.

"Do you need help with your habit?" he asked, his gaze following her habit train clutched in her hand.

"No, not at all," she said, embarrassed that she was standing there with the tail of her riding skirt in her hand like a schoolgirl ignorant of how to comport herself. Dudley had never unnerved her so. She was quickly learning that entertaining Ravencliff was not as simple as flirting with Dudley. The baron from the north expected proper behavior from her. She did not wish to disappoint him. She drew a deep breath. "I just loop it over my wrist so and off we go."

"Good." Ravencliff offered her his arm.

Leaving their horses with Albert, whom Ravencliff had invited to rejoin them, Cassie allowed the baron to pay their shilling each admission. Then he escorted her down the stone terrace steps into the zoological gardens.

The elephant was outside, restrained by one leg chained to the ground. The few visitors, ladies, gentlemen, and children alike, fed the huge animal peanuts and marveled over its flapping ears and snaking trunk.

"Do you keep exotic animals at Ravencliff?" Cassie asked as they strolled past the elephant. She was unable to get a clear picture of Ravencliff in her mind yet. She could see only the stone walls and the sparkling diamond-paned Tudor windows.

"No," Ravencliff said. "There is a large deer park, and of course, the usual game and wildlife. Nothing more exotic than a kelpie or a brownie or two."

"But, of course, why go abroad for magic when it dwells at home," Cassie said with a laugh. In her mind's eye she placed a forest around the house's broad expanse of lawn. "Let's go see the giraffes over by the camel house. Charlotte and I've heard that when they mate, they twine their long necks together. Isn't that fascinating?"

The moment she realized what she'd said, the heat of a blush burned in her cheeks. She resisted the childish urge to clap her hand over her mouth. What was she thinking?

"That is indeed a fascinating piece of information." Ravencliff looked down into her face without cracking a smile, but amusement glimmered in his green eyes. "I shall remember that should I decide to raise giraffes at Ravencliff."

"Yes, well, perhaps we should go see the camels," Cassie said, exasperated with her own lack of sophistication. Her face burned.

"No, I want to see the giraffes," Ravencliff insisted, leading her along toward the giraffe pavilion. "Twining their necks, you say?"

Her cheeks still warm with chagrin, Cassie prayed the exotic animals would not embarrass her. She was doing quite nicely without help.

CHAPTER FIVE

To Cassie's relief the giraffes were far too intent on their feed to demonstrate their mating practices.

She and Ravencliff wandered along the paths and through the pavilions, amused by the long-necked creatures, the braying zebras, and the stately camels. As they chatted, the formality of their new relationship slowly evaporated. Though the day was warm, the breeze blew away unpleasant odors. Cassie relaxed, enjoying Ravencliff's quiet company and forgetting all about Dudley. But she did remember to guard her tongue against any more silly remarks about mating habits.

"Now we must go see the monkeys," Cassie said, as they left the haughty camels chewing their cuds. "They are my favorite because they look and act like little old hairy-faced men."

Ravencliff regarded her from the corner of his eye. "Have respect, my dear, you could be speaking of half of Parliament."

The unexpectedness of the humor caught Cassie off guard. She blinked at him for a moment before she realized what he'd said. She laughed. "You made a joke, my lord."

"So I did," Ravencliff acknowledged, with a rueful expression. "But don't expect more. I'm not known for my wit."

"Ah, then, if it is so rare, it must be of great value," Cassie said with another laugh, pleased that he felt comfortable enough to share his humor. She was certain that behind that stern facade there was so much to be discovered—humor, generosity, even passion.

How different a man's passion must be from that of a youth like Dudley.

"Lead the way to the monkeys, my lady," Ravencliff said, gesturing toward the path before them. "I have no idea where they are, if not at Westminster."

"They are this way through the tunnel to the other part of the garden," Cassie said, tugging on his sleeve and leading him toward the clever underground passage that connected the two portions of the zoological gardens. "The tunnel offers something really unusual."

The underground passage led downward, then rose slightly on the other end so that daylight was always visible. No one was around but the two of them. At the mouth of the stone structure Cassie felt suddenly foolish and sorry that she had mentioned anything about the tunnel.

"Well, it's just a silly thing that my sister and I tried when we were here before," Cassie added, venturing a few steps into the darkness of the passage and feeling suddenly childish and awkward. What must this man think of her, carrying on like a common serving-girl fresh from the country! "We never did it when anyone was around."

"No one is around now." He stood just inside the entrance with his hands clasped before him and a look of expectation on his face. "Well, I'm listening."

"Yes, well then." Cassie tossed back her head and sang a few notes of a schoolroom song that she and Charlotte used to sing. She stopped, listening to the soft echoes bouncing around her.

"What an interesting phenomenon," Ravencliff said. "Rather more distinct and prolonged than one expects to hear."

"If you sing in round," Cassie said, encouraged by his interest, "the echo seems to add rounds."

"Then you need another voice to make it work," Ravencliff said, walking farther into the tunnel and pulling off his gloves as if he had serious work to do. He winced when his voice bounced back at him. "It is a unique experience, certainly. Let's try another song."

Cassie started another child's song, her voice weak at first as she sang a schoolroom ditty. Quickly Ravencliff joined her, his voice deep and smooth. With him singing counterpoint to her song, Cassie sang out louder, feeling less foolish than before. Their voices bounced off the stone walls floating around them until it seemed that an entire church choir sang in the deserted tunnel.

They finished, laughing as their song faded into echoes, then nothing.

"You're right, it is unusual," Ravencliff said, gazing up at the walls, then smiling down at her. "Let's see how it sounds if we stand in the very center of the tunnel."

He led her to the lowest portion, where they stood in darkness but could see sunlight at either end. Then he drew her closer until they stood shoulder to shoulder. Cassie felt his warmth again, the same melting heat that earlier had spread from the touch of his gloved hands on her. This time it radiated from his shoulder into hers and tingled throughout her body. She did not move away, nor did he.

"Now, let's try it again," Ravencliff said, apparently unaffected.

"You start this time," Cassie said, slightly breathless from his nearness.

He glanced down at her and began to sing, and she joined in at the proper place. This time they raised their voices to the top stones of the arched passage. Chaotic echoes bombarded them, filling the darkness with song. They glanced at each other, and as if by some mutual signal, they began to sing the round again, raising their volume until the echoes rang in their ears.

"I say, what in the name of the King is the caterwauling going on in here?" boomed a loud, deep voice.

Cassie choked on her lyrics and turned toward the tunnel entrance to see a heavyset, stony-faced gentleman with an elegant lady on his arm standing there. Ravencliff stopped singing, too, and with a bland face slowly turned to their inquisitor.

"I hardly think such noise is necessary," the heavyset man added.

Cassie held her breath as she searched for a sensible explanation.

"The lady and I are merely indulging in a bit of high spirits," Ravencliff said, his eyebrow quirked and his mouth thin, as if to say he did not appreciate the interruption in the least. "You may join us if you like."

"Humph," the man said, continuing to grimace. "We wish to pass through the tunnel in peace."

"Then pass," Ravencliff said, gesturing the way without moving one inch. "We will not block your path."

So the couple marched through the passage, skirting Cassie and Ravencliff as if they were mad and their madness contagious.

As soon as she and Ravencliff were alone once more, Cassie began to giggle. "I'm afraid we shall become the talk of their visit."

"That does not signify," Ravencliff said gruffly, gazing down into her face. "They interrupted our song."

Cassie gazed up at him, entranced by the rare smile that lightened his face. The expression made him look younger and less formidable. "Shall we find the monkeys?"

"There is time enough for the monkeys," he said, taking her by the shoulder and turning her so that she squarely faced him. Then he released her and reached for the veil of her hat. "Let's leave this netting turned back, shall we?"

"I don't normally wear veils," Cassie said, every inch of

her body aware of his closeness. Gently he rolled the gauzy fabric farther from her face.

"No reason why you should." He leaned closer.

Cassie's eyes fluttered closed. Breathlessly she awaited the kiss she was certain would come. She'd been kissed often enough to know when a man wanted to steal a favor. The baron wanted to kiss her. She waited, her body alert, her lips nearly aching for his.

Instead of kissing her, he touched her cheekbone with the back of his hand. The warmth of his knuckles flooded into her and tingled along her cheek. She opened her eyes slightly. She could see his hand—large, but the skin smooth and tough, sinewy muscles stretching down his wrist in the shadow of his black sleeve. She could see his pulse beating, strong and steady. His fingers smelled of fine leather. Without looking up into his face, she stood perfectly still, feeling as if a spell had been cast over her.

He drew his hand down her jaw and around to the point of her chin. Cassie let her eyes close again, savoring the strange thrill of his caress.

"Just as I thought," he whispered. "Smooth as satin."

Cassie's heart began to beat rapidly. Dudley had never touched her so, never admired her with such intimacy. She gazed into Ravencliff's dark green eyes again. Even in the darkness she could see him searching her face. He sought something. She longed to know what it was. She would gladly give him anything he desired to have him place his mouth on hers right now.

At last he did, brushing his lips against hers as though sampling her taste, her warmth, her willingness. Then he withdrew. Her entire body tingled with heat and longing. She feared she'd done something wrong, had not let him know how much she longed for his touch. She leaned into him, hoping desperately for more. He did not retreat. She tilted her face up to his even more, inviting him to kiss her once again.

A child's shriek shattered the spell. Cassie and Ravencliff

started. A pair of boys came charging into the passage, screaming at the top of their voices. The din was almost enough to make Cassie cover her ears with her hands.

Ravencliff stepped back, his face turned away so that she could no longer read his expression. He took her arm and led her toward the light. "I believe it's time to find those monkeys."

Cassie sighed as he drew her along the path. She glanced aside to glimpse his reaction, but Ravencliff appeared unaffected. Yet Cassie couldn't keep from touching her lips with her gloved fingers. His kiss had been nothing like the hasty, overeager, sloppy mouth-on-mouth that Dudley had engaged in. It had been delicate, exquisitely fragile, and full of promise. She was sure of it. She smiled to herself. Full of more to come.

In front of the monkey cage Ravencliff bought Cassie a bag of peanuts to feed to the howling little pirates. The monkeys screeched, scratched indelicately, and swung from the cage bars, begging to be fed peanuts by the visitors.

"No, these are not politicians," Ravencliff remarked dryly as a greedy creature snatched a nut from his hand. "With a cigar in their mouths they might look like them. But I can tell you politicians don't work for peanuts."

Cassie laughed, wondering what transactions Ravencliff had experienced with Parliament, but she decided not to ask.

They moved on to the cats prowling the perimeter of their cages. From between the bars the tiger peered at them, majestic and regal. The lynxes skulked close to the floor. The lion stretched out in the middle of his cage regarded them with a keen, unblinking gaze.

"Look at them," Cassie said, admiring the sleek, powerful movements of the huge cats. "Such power. My sister's fiancé killed a Scottish lion with his bare hands. Connor McKensie, Earl of Kinleith. Do you know him?"

At her side, Ravencliff stiffened. She cast a sideways glance up at him in time to see the line of his mouth grow harsh. The warmth in him that Cassie had been aware of only moments before vanished.

"We met long ago," Ravencliff said, releasing her arm.

"Then you've heard the story?" Cassie asked, forgetting the great black-maned lion in the cage. She studied the baron, curious about his withdrawal.

"I've heard the story," he said. "Scottish lions are rare these days."

"So I understand, and this animal was quite vicious," Cassandra said. "Yet Connor defeated him."

"That is not an impossible task, to kill a lion with bare hands," Ravencliff said, staring at the cats in the cage. "It all depends on how determined one is to survive. McKensie is a big man with a strong belief in himself. Is your sister's betrothal a happy one?"

"She and Connor are very happy," Cassie said, the sudden shift in conversation reminding her of her twin's happy glow. Morning, noon, and night, Charlotte beamed with happiness that truly was beginning to annoy Cassie.

"Did they receive many gifts on their engagement?" Ravencliff asked.

"A number of fine things including a pair of lovebirds that are almost as vexing to watch as Connor and Charlotte are," Cassie admitted, with a rueful laugh.

"Their engagement troubles you?" he asked.

"No, I'm truly happy for them, really I am," Cassie said honestly. Another thought occurred. "But I wonder. Dudley and I received Tophet from the same gentleman who gave Charlotte and Connor their lovebirds. Now that Dudley has cried off, I wonder if I should return Tophet to the earl."

Ravencliff turned to Cassie. "I should think not. I suspect Tophet has been in the city too long to be any good for hunting."

"So true," Cassie said, pleased with the Ravencliff insights. "I've become quite fond of Tophet. I fear he enjoys lying in front of the fire better than pointing on the damp moors."

"Then don't give another thought to returning him,"

Ravencliff said. "I'm certain your father must be very pleased that your sister is about to wed the Earl of Kinleith."

"Oh, indeed he is," Cassie said. "Papa has always encouraged us to marry well, for our own good as well as his own."

"There is a certain wisdom in his ambition," Ravencliff said. "How does your papa feel about losing a daughter to the Scottish Highlands?"

"How perceptive you are, my lord," Cassie said. "I don't think he's too pleased about it. Papa has given Charlotte and Connor a townhouse in Mayfair not far from Aunt Dorian in Seacombe House. So we should see Charlotte some part of every year."

"Generous and practical," Ravencliff said.

"Yes, we will miss Charlotte," Cassie said, the loss of her sister suddenly overwhelming her. "Who will I talk to when she is gone? Who will I go to the drapers with and share fittings?"

"You can sing in the tunnel with me," Ravencliff offered, smiling faintly.

Cassie glanced aside at him once more, surprised and touched by his offer. "Is that more levity, my lord?"

"No, you must consider that a serious invitation." He grinned at her, his reserve gone. "I've expended all the levity I have to offer today."

"Thank you, then," Cassie said, dazzled by the rare glimpse of himself he'd given her. She extended her hand. "I shall call on you, then, when I need you."

Ravencliff accepted her hand and bestowed a light, proper kiss on it. "I look forward to hearing from you soon."

Cassie took back her hand, noting with a shiver of pleasure the sincerity in his green eyes.

Ramsay stood back and allowed Albert the groom to give Cassandra a leg up onto her gray mare. Although he longed to put his hands on her again, he'd decided to maintain a proper distance. After that little episode in the tunnel he dared not trust himself. He'd not intended to kiss her this soon. But she'd drawn him into that ridiculous round of singing to hear echoes in the dark and the time had seemed so ripe. And she seemed so willing to be touched and tasted as she gazed up at him, a smile on her full lips. She'd tasted good, delicate and feminine. As he watched her settle herself on her horse, he sternly reminded himself that the point of all this was to frighten her father into reconsidering his hard line on Glen Gray. Cassandra was only a puppet in the plan. He'd learned long ago deviating from carefully laid plans was always a mistake.

The Cassandra St. John he was getting to know was not easily alarmed by a minor impropriety. She was clearly capable of inviting indiscretion herself. She was, in all, a curious mixture of vixen and lady. The question suddenly assaulted him: What lay beneath the warmth and passion of her quicksilver temperament? Would she be like the other women in his life? Would she open up to him only to reveal a heart of ice?

Ramsay frowned. He had no intentions of finding out. Who and what she was, beyond being the daughter of Davis St. John, had nothing to do with his plan.

"Thank you, my lord, for a lovely time in the zoological gardens," Cassandra said, gathering up her reins and riding crop in her small gloved hands.

" 'Twas my pleasure," Ramsay said, doffing his hat and adding a formal bow.

"I hope I will see you again soon," Cassandra said, obviously hoping he would offer an appointment. Ramsay suppressed the impulse to shout victory. She wanted to see him again. He covered his feelings by replacing his hat.

"I'm here every day at two o'clock," he said casually. "I shall always welcome your company."

"What if I were to be riding and found you with a companion?" she asked, rearranging the reins in her hand once more, her casualness just as studied as his.

He allowed a smile of understanding to reach his lips. "That will never happen. I may be a hard man to please, Cassandra. But I will be here, always for your company only.''

She smiled at him and ducked her head a bit—a shy, pleased smile. He knew he'd said the right thing.

"Next week perhaps," she said.

"I'll be here," Ramsay said, hiding his annoyance this time. He wanted to move things along faster than that.

"Then good day, my lord," she said and turned her horse toward the park entrance.

Ramsay mounted his stallion and watched Cassandra ride out of the park with her groom following close behind. He'd learned almost nothing about Glen Gray, but about Miss Cassandra St. John, he'd learned a great deal.

Out of the shadows of the trees rode Graham. Ramsay's foster brother was once again mounted on the horse that had been purchased for him. They had agreed that he should remain out of sight because Cassandra would probably recognize him as the messenger who had delivered the lovebirds to her sister and Connor and Tophet to her and Dudley.

"Is the gelding working out better for you?" Ramsay asked, distractedly admiring the straightness and the taper of Cassandra's back as she turned her horse down the street toward Mayfair.

"I don't think I'll ever get used to sitting on the back of an animal which seems poised between sudden sleep or violent madness," Graham complained, his elbows akimbo as he pulled on his mount's reins. " 'Tis a mystery what this cursed creature is going to do next."

"It should do what you want it to do," Ramsay said, still more interested in Cassandra than in Graham's trials and tribulations with the horse. "You are the master, remember."

"Aye, and does the St. John lass know who is master yet?" Graham asked, in that cheeky voice he used when he wanted to get back at Ramsay.

"Don't compare her to a horse," Ramsay snapped, surprised by his own reaction.

Graham stared back at him, his eyes growing wide. "Surely ye donna like the lass? Or did she tell ye everything ye wanted to know of Glen Gray?"

"Neither," Ramsay said, mildly frustrated by his inability to learn more than he had. "She said nothing to make me think that her father has decided to give the property to McKensie as a wedding gift. The glen's disposition may still be undecided."

"Then ye still have a chance at it," Graham said, a smile of hope spreading across his face. "Does she suspect ye are not who ye say ye are?"

"No, because I am who I say I am," Ramsay snapped once more. Accusations of dishonesty always irritated him. Regardless of the faults one might lay at his door, he did not lie—unless it was absolutely necessary. "I am the Baron of Ravencliff, among my many titles."

"That probably won't satisfy her much when she learns the truth," Graham said, tugging on the reins of his horse to keep it from eating the grass alongside the bridle path.

"Probably not," Ramsay agreed, wondering for the first time just how Cassandra would react when she learned the truth. And learn it she would. Revelation of his identity was part of the plan. Once he'd ingratiated himself with the daughter, his intention had been to reveal himself to Davis St. John. Yet, he'd never thought about revealing himself to Cassandra. He'd never considered how she'd feel or react. Davis St. John could be counted on to be intimidated as any father would be. But Cassandra? Now that he knew her—now that he knew how lyrical her laugh was, how strong her spirit, how smooth her skin beneath his fingers—he suspected uneasily that when she learned the truth, she would be angry.

Ramsay frowned. He wished he could go back to the beginning and reevaluate his scheme. He had learned things today no spy could have warned him of—that the lady was warm, that the lady was playful, that the lady was astute and clever in a way he had never anticipated. But it was too late to change anything. He was committed to his course. One way or another, he would win the feud.

Davis St. John sat at the desk in his study and gazed in surprise at his wife who'd just come in the room and closed the door. Susanna seldom troubled him when he sequestered himself in his study to work at home.

"What is it, darling?" he asked, rising from his chair, certain she would only come to him about something serious.

"We must talk about Cassandra," she said, moving to stand near the cold hearth.

"She's just off on another shopping trip," he said, recalling Cassie's words over her tea, toast, and eggs. It'd all sounded innocent to him. "That's what she said at breakfast."

"Yes, something about a new riding habit," Susanna said. "But you know she's never liked horseback riding. Remember how she and Charlotte would trade places if any great amount of riding was required?"

"But they haven't done anything like that for some time. Do you really think we need to be concerned?"

"I'm not certain," Susanna said, settling down in one of the chairs that flanked the fireplace. "So much has happened in such a short time: Charlotte's engagement to the Earl of Kinleith; Dudley crying off. I think she feels quite deserted."

"We're talking about our Cassandra?" Davis asked just to be certain that he'd not misunderstood the topic his wife had come to him about. "Nothing troubles Cassie. She has always faced the world as if it were a great adventure. What makes you think something is amiss? Tears?"

"Not a single one," Susanna said, in almost a moan. "Charlotte confided in me that Cassie seems to be taking this broken engagement well. She hasn't wept once, but there have been moments when she has seemed downcast. Call it a mother's instinct, if you will, Davis. I just know something is going on. Something secretive."

"Cassie? Secretive?" Davis sat down in the chair across from his wife. "That is not like Cassandra." They exchanged looks. "Yes, well, except when she is up to one of her adventures," Davis said, sinking deeper into the leather chair. "You don't think she has some scheme cooked up, do you? I actually thought that Dudley's crying off might make her take her behavior more seriously."

"I honestly don't know, Davis." Susanna sighed. "I just know that something is different. Cassandra and Charlotte rarely spend much time together now, and many daily routines that they once shared as sisters have changed. Charlotte's time is almost totally spent with Connor or at the Foundling Shelter or some social event connected with the coming wedding."

"You think Cassie feels left out?" Davis asked. "Does Charlotte not ask Cassie to join her? I would think they'd be all aflutter with the wedding and such. By the way, did you put the Duke and Duchess of Deander on the guest list?"

"Yes, of course, I would not forget the duke and duchess," Susanna said, her mind obviously still on her daughter.

"Good," Davis said. The surly old duke and his duchess had never been an iota of help in his bid for knighthood—before Linirk's ultimatum or after. Not that his ambition mattered any longer. Davis's response to Linirk had been to withdraw all petitions for a title. The decision had been a hard one for him to face. Linirk's threat—and Susanna's good sense—had brought Davis back to reality. He'd given up his attempt for a title and he had no regrets.

Life had given him everything he could possibly want: two beautiful daughters, a successful business, membership in the best clubs, a dear, loyal sister and an honorable brother-in-law. But best of all, he had a loving, passionate wife. He eyed Susanna's slender ankle as she swung her leg distractedly. At the end of the day, he hoped she'd be able to put aside her concern about Cassandra. Because he was looking forward to crawling into bed beside her tonight.

Now that he'd refused Linirk's offer of help in obtaining a

title in exchange for purchasing Glen Gray, he wondered exactly how the heartless marquis would unleash his revenge. Would Linirk come after him in some way through business or would he threaten Charlotte and Connor? Davis no longer feared for Kinleith or Charlotte. The young Scots prizefighter and his loyal cousin, Erik Drummond, had proved themselves able to protect Charlotte.

But who could foresee what diabolical retribution Linirk might wreak on him and Susanna? Davis knew of one man Linirk had ruined financially and socially two decades ago. There were vague rumors about others in the years since. What would the marquis do to the St. Johns? The sooner Charlotte and Connor's wedding happened, the less time Linirk had to mount his countermeasures, whatever they might be.

"Well, of course Charlotte has included Cassie in planning the wedding, and she has invited Cassie to join her in the work at the Foundling Shelter," Susanna was saying, "but I think Charlotte doesn't want Cassie to feel she is flaunting her happiness when Cassie is feeling rather low."

"Yes, it's all become dashed awkward, hasn't it, the rush of it all?" Davis said, more touched by his adventurous daughter's plight than he sounded. He'd thought Dudley Moncreff a blithering idiot to pass up this opportunity to refinance his old, but nearly bankrupt family. They'd managed to hold on to their lands and old houses—fine old structures badly in need of repair and refurbishing. First and foremost, though, Davis thought the young man an absolute cad to disappoint Cassie like this.

"Yes, awkward indeed," Susanna said. "Cassie has no interest in going along with Charlotte to the Foundling Shelter. And she has little patience with a pack of noisy children."

"No, you're right," Davis said. His daring daughter was like him in that way, too. He was reasonably satisfied with the match Charlotte was making. McKensie seemed to treat her well and she seemed enthralled with the Scots earl. But Davis wanted joy in Cassandra's life, too, happiness every bit as glowing and complete as Charlotte's. "Dashed awkward."

"So you see," Susanna said, looking steadily across at Davis, "that's why I felt we needed to talk about this. What do we do about Cassandra? And what on earth do we do about the Marquis of Linirk?"

Cassie strolled dreamily into the deserted hallway, pulling on her gloves in preparation for her shopping trip. Finding something wonderful to wear when she met the baron next was a must. She wasn't sure when she would see Ravencliff again, but when she did, last year's riding habit would not do. Since the day in the zoological gardens, she could think of little else except meeting him again. Since the kiss in the dark tunnel her mind refused to concentrate. She couldn't resist licking her lips—as if she could still taste him there—every time the memory crossed her mind.

On a leash at her side Tophet paced contentedly. She was waiting for Betsy to join her at any moment. As she was fastening the glove button at her wrist and daydreaming of Ravencliff, she caught the low, earnest sound of her parents' voices. She glanced up to see that she was standing outside Papa's study. The seriousness of Mama's and Papa's tones told her they were engaged in a significant conversation. Then she heard her name. Curious, she glanced around to be certain that Horton wasn't lurking about. When she confirmed that she was alone, she tilted her head toward the door.

"No, I've heard nothing from Linirk since the day of the wedding breakfast when his foster brother brought in the gifts," Papa was saying. "Kinleith tells me he thinks the marquis is in Town, but neither he nor I have had official word from him, nor has anyone else."

"Do we invite him to the wedding?" Mama asked. "We did not invite him to the engagement party but he sent gifts anyway. He hardly could have drawn less attention by appearing dressed in his black coat and challenging Kinleith to a duel. God forbid."

A duel! Cassie pressed her fingers against her lips to stifle the sound of her gasp. Charlotte would be distraught beyond words if Kinleith and Linirk faced each other off in a duel.

"I'll not be party to anything like that," Papa declared. "I don't think Linirk would do anything that direct. But if we send him an invitation, what if he accepts? What kind of scene do you think he'll make then?"

Cassie glanced down at the black hound at her side. She loved Tophet, and had Linirk to thank for the dog, but she had little sympathy for a man who threatened her family's happiness.

"Better to know where he is and what he's doing, than to be wondering what he will do next," Mama said.

"Wise once again, my dear," Papa agreed. "Invite him. As you say, 'tis better to know what the Marquis of Linirk is up to—good or bad—than to know nothing."

"There you are, Miss Cassie," Betsy said, bustling into the hallway, her shoe heels tapping solidly on the marble floor. "Sorry to keep you waiting."

Cassie jumped and stepped away from the door. She didn't want Betsy to hear any of Mama and Papa's discussion. "That's quite all right, Betsy. The carriage hasn't been brought around yet. Shall we wait outside for it?"

"Yes, miss." Betsy led the way out the house.

Cassie followed, her head full of Mama's and Papa's words. *" 'Tis better to know what the Marquis of Linirk is up to, than to know nothing."* She knew that she and Charlotte lived a protected life, one ordered and provided for by Mama and Papa. How easy it was to dismiss thoughts of Mama and Papa worrying over them. Though she and her sister didn't like to think about it, deep in their hearts they knew their parents spared nothing for their welfare. Cassie wished as she climbed into the carriage that she could do something to help. If only she had it in her power to aid Mama and Papa. If only she could do something to keep Ramsay Forbes from hurting Charlotte and Connor.

CHAPTER SIX

The day was a fine one for shopping, sunny with a summer-blue sky above. The streets were teeming with life. The prospect of an outing was too delicious for Cassie to be long troubled over the Marquis of Linirk. As the carriage carried her and Betsy toward Henrietta Street, Cassie turned her thoughts to the venture at hand.

Cassie had never selected clothes without the advice of her mother, her aunt Dorian, or her sister Charlotte. She'd always had the sense of style necessary to make good selections for herself. But frequently shopping had been like a party, light-hearted and fun, with someone at hand to advise her—someone to keep her from becoming too adventurous in her choices.

But she did not care to explain to anyone why she was looking for a riding habit in a sober garnet or maroon when she generally favored brighter hues. It was time to put away girlish things. She sought the perfect sophisticated color to flatter her complexion and to complement Ravencliff's black attire. A warm tint was needed, nothing glaring. When she closed her eyes, she pictured herself and Ravencliff riding side by side, a striking, debonair couple: she in sedate burgundy, and he in his dashing raven black. Yes, a warm tint was required.

Today Betsy would be her ally. She could trust her maid to be discreet about the outing. And she could judge from Betsy's expression whether or not a color or style suited her.

When they disembarked at Henrietta Street where all the best draper's shops were, she immediately began to examine the offerings in the shop windows. She had no intention of going to their usual shop. She wanted this habit to be something new and different. She wanted a habit that made her look as feminine and mature as the Baron of Ravencliff's company made her feel. She wanted to become her own person, just as Charlotte was doing. She wanted to find a riding habit that would make the Baron of Ravencliff kiss her—again.

She and Betsy strolled along the street, critically eyeing one fabric then the next in the storefront windows. They made occasional comments to one another about the quality of a color or the texture of a cloth. But Cassie saw nothing that caught her eye. She stood staring at an amaranthus satin, not what she was looking for at all.

"You know, Betsy, that would make a lovely, sophisticated ballgown," Cassie murmured. "But I see nothing here suitable for a riding habit."

"Then order the ballgown," a deep voice replied.

Cassie started and turned to find Ravencliff standing on the walk behind her.

"My lord, you did startle me so." Cassie pressed her hand over her heart to still its sudden rapid beating. "I was addressing Betsy, my maid."

Tophet wagged his tail.

"Your maid is over there having a visit with the street vendor." Ravencliff gestured toward Betsy, who was purchasing herself an orange. Then he bent to give the hound a pat on the head.

"You do know how to make the servants happy, Ravencliff,"

Cassie said, realizing with a vague discomfort that he had taken control of the situation once again.

"I thought we could talk more freely that way." He offered his arm. "Shall we walk?"

"My maid can be trusted," Cassie said, feeling a bit insulted on Betsy's behalf, but taking his arm anyway.

"I'm sure she can," Ravencliff said. "I'm sorry if I offend you. But this is so fortunate, our meeting. And what brings you to this part of London?"

"I am thinking of some new clothes," she said, reluctant to tell him the truth lest she seem too eager to please him. It was never advisable for a lady to reveal too readily her pleasure with a gentleman's company. Men could become overconfident so quickly. At least the younger ones did. "A lady must keep herself informed on the latest styles."

"Yes, of course," Ravencliff said. "I'm certain that is important. How pressing is this matter of clothes?"

Without thinking, Cassie allowed him to lead her back down Henrietta Street. "Well—"

"I was thinking it would be a perfect day for a boat ride on the river today," Ravencliff said before she could reply. "In fact, I have to take a barge downriver to transact some business. Perhaps you would like to come with me. On the water there is a light breeze. I'm certain we could find some refreshment along the way."

"What a lovely idea," Cassie said, truly impressed by his suggestion. Despite her annoyance with his high-handedness with Betsy, she was glad to see him again so soon. He looked just as good to her today as he had three days ago in the park. As usual he wore all black, the only relief being the texture of his waistcoat. Today it was a simple black twilled sarcenet with velvet-bound pockets. "But I'm expected at home for luncheon."

"We'll send Betsy with a message that you decided to have luncheon with a friend," Ravencliff suggested without pause. "It's as simple as that."

"I haven't been in the country for weeks," Cassie admitted, more to herself than to Ravencliff as he led her back past the windows she'd just examined so carefully.

She was also thinking that it had been weeks and weeks since she'd enjoyed a true secret adventure. The last one had been her trip—in disguise—to the brothel where she and Charlotte had gone in search of the kidnaped Connor McKensie before he and Charlotte were betrothed. "An outing would be so nice. Lots of lovely green trees and contented cows in the meadow. Time away from the city and the reminders of Dudley."

"Precisely," Ravencliff said, his lips thinning at her mention of Dudley. At the corner he turned, ushering her toward the river. "We can board the barge at the St. James stairs at the end of the street. I've already made arrangements for my business trip with a waterman of good repute. That's where I was going when I saw you. Let's send Betsy off with her message, shall we, and be on our way."

"What about Tophet?" Cassie asked, hesitant for the first time about going off with Ravencliff beyond London's precincts. Her reluctance surprised even her. As much as she liked him, there was something about Ravencliff's masterful way, the ease with which he always dispensed with the servants, that troubled her. Yet Ravencliff had been the man who'd rescued her from the footpads. She always felt so secure in the baron's company.

"Bring the dog along," Ravencliff said, smiling at her. They stopped on the curb of the street and he took off his hat. The sun gleamed on his dark blond hair. The sternness of his face softened. "Tophet is good company and he will enjoy the river trip as much as you will. There's a quiet inn there where we can have luncheon and sit in the shade."

Cassie could think of no reason why the hound—or she— wouldn't indeed enjoy the outing.

* * *

Ramsay could hardly believe his good fortune. He'd been planning this business trip anyway, but when the St. John household spy sent him word that Cassandra was off on her own to do some shopping, he knew he must take advantage of the opportunity. He'd immediately adapted his plans. For his scheme to be successful it was important to keep things moving. He wanted Cassandra to continue to be aware of him. Besides that, he found himself eager to see her again—more so than was necessary. The kiss in the tunnel had left him looking forward to pushing their relationship on to more intimate terms.

That realization made him uneasy. Yet there was no reason why he should not enjoy himself during the outings. There was no reason why he should have to suffer in carrying out his plan. Cassandra St. John was a delight to be with, and he wasn't going to complain about it.

He would see her again, sooner than he'd expected, and he was glad of it. But when he sent Graham off to make the necessary travel arrangements, his kinsman had objected. In fact, Graham's angry reaction had surprised Ramsay. He'd accepted Graham's disapproval of this plan, but no amount of success seemed to satisfy his kinsman. And he was growing impatient with his kinsman's lack of vision.

"She's spoiled and unpredictable," Graham had railed. "There's no telling what havoc she'll wreak if she finds out what ye are up to before you're ready. I don't see why ye canna do this like ye would do any other acquisition."

"St. John refused my first offer," Ramsay said, impatient with Graham for forgetting so quickly how hard they'd both been working to acquire Glen Gray. "I thought for sure he'd swallow the offer for knighthood, but he didn't. He's not a man who will be bought off easily."

"Aye, so we threaten the family," Graham growled. "I saw him, you know."

"Who?" Ramsay said, at a loss to understand his foster brother's truculence.

"Connor McKensie and Erik," Graham said. "They go strutting around the city like they own the place."

"Did they see you?" Ramsay asked, concerned that if Kinleith saw himself or Graham, he would demand a confrontation before Ramsay could win St. John to his side.

"Nay, I made sure that they didna see me," Graham said.

"The important thing is that they don't own Glen Gray," Ramsay reminded him.

"But who knows how long we have? Is there no faster way than dancing to this lady's tune to have our land back?"

"We're working as fast as we dare," Ramsay admitted, troubled by Graham's impatience, but understanding exactly how his foster brother felt. "If we move fast today, this may be just the opportunity we need to move things ahead."

Graham had agreed, grudgingly.

Ramsay had found Cassandra in the street without any difficulty. At first she'd been reluctant to go along with him. Her resistance had surprised him, but he'd been persuasive and soon he'd dispatched Betsy toward home with the appropriate message to deliver. Then, just as he'd hoped, they were on their way to board the luxurious barge awaiting them at the riverside stairs.

He encouraged Cassandra to cling to his arm as he made way for them through the crowd and descended the steps to the river. Tourists, merchants, and city dwellers bumped shoulders and elbowed their way toward the barges and punts that offered alternative transportation to the hackney carriages and sedan chairs.

"That's our barge over there," Ramsay said, drawing her along with him through the press of other river travelers.

"A sturdy-looking craft," she said, jostling along beside him and wrinkling her nose as the stink of the river water reached them.

"And comfortable, I hope," Ramsay said, eager to get her aboard and have the waterman set sail.

Suddenly Tophet barked and leaped to the end of his leash. He threw himself back into the crowd away from the river. The force of his hurdle snapped the leash tight and pulled Cassandra away from Ramsay. Her hand was ripped away from his arm. She staggered after the hound, unable to stop his pursuit of someone.

"Tophet, heel," Cassandra cried, vainly resisting the pull of the dog.

Ramsay started after her. He seized her wrist when he reached her side, and tugged on the leash. "Heel, Tophet, heel."

The dog froze, then sat, casting Ramsay a glance over his shoulder.

"Oh my, Tophet has never disobeyed me like that," Cassandra said, gasping to catch her breath. "I think he recognized someone among the people."

"But who would the dog know here?" Ramsay asked, though he'd seen the answer for himself. Tophet was barking at Graham.

Graham obviously felt cheated that he was not to make the trip on the river. So now he had endangered everything by showing up on the stairs. He ran the risk of Cassie recognizing him and becoming suspicious about Ramsay's true identity.

"I'm not sure whom Tophet would recognize," Cassandra replied, uncertainty in her voice. "The bushy-haired man who disappeared under the bridge there. He was glaring at me and he seemed so familiar. I can't imagine where I've seen him before, or how Tophet would know him."

"Tophet probably saw a stray cat," Ramsay said, urging her to turn back to the barge. "And the man probably just has an eye for a pretty lady."

"I suppose," Cassie granted.

"Our barge is over here." Ramsay steered her back toward the craft. He climbed aboard first. Tophet eagerly followed. Then Ramsay turned to help Cassie onto the barge. Without any reluctance now, she placed her hand in his and stepped aboard.

The moment her silk boot touched the deck, he knew she was his—for the afternoon at least. He'd overcome her reluctance. The thought filled him with a strange mixture of victory and trepidation. Though their afternoon in the zoological gardens could be declared his victory—she'd sneaked away from her family to see him—their meeting had not gone precisely as he'd expected. The pleasantness of it, and the kiss, had not been in his plans. Cassandra could not be counted on to be predictable. The thought made him wary—yet it excited him, too.

"This is wonderfully old-fashioned," she said, eyeing the pavilion erected on the deck of the barge to shade them from the heat of the sun." Shall we pretend we are Elizabethans?"

"Indeed, why not?" Ramsay asked, deciding to go along with whatever game seemed to please her. "Who are you going to be? The Virgin Queen herself?"

Cassandra cocked her head thoughtfully. She looked delightfully feminine today, wearing a flower-trimmed bonnet and a gown of the palest pink with a wide, pleated collar and a hem edged in lace and tucks. "Why not? What fun to rule a country and a court."

Ramsay knew in an instant that Cassandra St. John was a virgin. Not that her virginity was any great surprise. But her airy innocence in accepting the queen's role gave her away. According to gossips Cassandra had trod an interesting line between decorum and outrageousness. That she and Dudley might have experimented in their unconventional relationship was entirely possible, but he knew instinctively that she hadn't surrendered that final piece of herself. He was glad.

Did her father know that? Ramsay wondered. How far was Davis St. John willing to go to protect his daughter's prize?

"And who will you be?" she asked. "And why?"

"Let me think," he said, his mind rapidly discarding dashing

Elizabethans who might displease the lady. "I believe I'll be Sir Walter Raleigh."

"And why?" she insisted.

"Because he was a courtier, a poet, a scholar," Ramsay said, watching for Cassandra's reaction, "and he was a gentleman willing to make sacrifices for his queen, as well."

"And the Queen's favorite," Cassandra added, regarding him thoughtfully. "A very clever answer, Ravencliff. You are a flatterer, my lord, a worthy courtier."

"Can you blame me?" Ramsay asked, alert to the assessing gaze she leveled on him. She was young and naive, but not necessarily a fool. He understood women well enough to know that nothing annoyed an intelligent woman more than insincere flattery. "Sir Walter Raleigh lived quite an exciting and productive life. Besides being a favorite of the Queen, he was a military man who fought the Spanish. He was an explorer in the New World and a successful merchant. As a scholar he was author of *The History of the World*. A rich life."

She nodded in acknowledgment. "A full life indeed. So where is your cape and sword, Sir Walter?"

Ramsay put his hand to his side as if grasping the hilt of a rapier and flung his arm into the air as if to swirl a cape. "You're the one with the imagination."

"I do see it," she said, smiling. "I think you'd look quite handsome in feathers, ruff, and trunk hose."

"Need we be too literal?" Ramsay asked, quite unprepared to wear any costume beyond what he'd donned for the day. "What are you wearing, Your Majesty?"

"Perhaps you're right about being too literal," Cassandra agreed after a moment of thought. "I rather like the ropes of pearls and those jewel-encrusted high collars, but a farthingale is quite too much."

"I agree about the farthingale, and about the pearls." Ramsay gestured toward her bonnet. "Take it off."

"You are speaking to a queen, Sir Walter." She laughed

but obeyed him, revealing her bright red hair neatly arranged in curls.

"I see it now," he said, "the headdress of pearls that you are wearing, their smooth luster shiny against your fiery hair."

"Poetic, too. You are very good at this game, my lord," Cassandra said with a shake of her head, and settled herself among the pillows he had indicated for her. "I hope I won't be an impediment to your business transaction today."

"Not at all," Ramsay said, amused by the game she had instigated. He took her bonnet from her and tossed it aside. "In fact, I'm delighted to have you along. Your company will make an otherwise long, tedious trip much more pleasant. After all, it isn't every day a man has the pleasure of traveling with exalted royalty. Please make yourself comfortable. Forgive me, but I fear the barge of musicians and thespians have gone ahead of us."

"We shall have no entertainment, then?" Cassandra asked, with an imperiousness worthy of a queen.

"Save ourselves," Ramsay said.

"We shall rub along quite nicely, I'm sure," Cassandra said.

"So we shall," Ramsay said, praying that she was right. He'd always left the problem of entertaining to his mistresses in Scotland. Now that he was the suitor, he was at something of a disadvantage. If playing Queen amused the lady, then he'd go along with it.

As the waterman steered them out into the traffic on the Thames, Ramsay helped Cassie arrange the pillows and rugs beneath a canvas pavilion out of the sun.

Nose to the wood, Tophet investigated the farthest reaches of the barge. Then he settled down between their feet.

Cassandra watched. "It is so strange how content Tophet is in your company. Normally he sits only at my feet."

"Dogs have always liked me," Ramsay said, as casually and as truthfully as possible.

"You should take that as a compliment, my lord," Cassie said, peering down the river. "Tophet never liked Dudley. I should have made note of his doggy wisdom. How long will it take us to reach our destination?"

"It will take us about an hour to get there," Ramsay said, removing his hat and setting it aside as well. "We'll be beyond the less lovely sights of the docks soon. Then the scenery will improve. So we might as well be comfortable. Do you mind if I take off my coat?"

"You mean your cape, Sir Walter?" Cassie said with an understanding smile. "Of course not. It is a lovely warm day, is it not?"

"How about something cool to drink?" Ramsay asked, tossing his coat down beside her bonnet and turning to retrieve a pitcher from behind him. "Our waterman said he would have something to refresh us. Ah yes, lemonade."

When she turned her head to watch the passing scenery, he caught an enticing glimpse of her nape. The coppery curls lying against her pale skin made her complexion translucent. Her throat was delicate and vulnerable. He wondered what she would do if he put his lips there, nuzzled her neck, and nibbled her ear. Would she turn her face to his and invite more kisses? Or would she act the prim, virgin queen?

Ramsay's hand trembled as he poured a pewter goblet full and handed it to her. He'd purposely avoided having servants other than the necessary waterman aboard. Witnesses were one thing. Witnesses who could overhear conversations were another.

He sipped from his goblet and watched her, aware of a greedy, selfish pleasure in having her all to himself.

Queen she was. How long a virgin queen, was another matter. For soon her virtue would be given to some man. Should he be the one to take it? That part of his scheme he'd never been clear on. His intention was to do whatever it took to win Glen Gray.

Now he was developing a certain fascination for the lady. Therein lay the complication. Now that he had the St. John princess to himself, just what did he intend to do with her?

CHAPTER SEVEN

"You were right about it being a lovely day to be on the river," Cassandra said as the waterman rowed them beyond the Vauxhall stairs and on to the Battersea Field and Chelsea vicinity. Fishermen stood along the bank. The air freshened and the noises of the city faded so they could hear the trumpeting of the swans swimming along the banks and the lowing of the cattle in the riverside meadows. A cargo barge laden with red fruits and green vegetables floated passed them.

Tophet jumped up to bark. The friendly bargeman waved.

To Ramsay's surprise, Cassandra smiled a sedate response and returned the wave with a queenly, but cordial gesture. He marveled at the strange contrasts existing side by side in the lady—she could be an exuberant lass younger than her score of years, or a regal woman proper as a patrician twice her age.

The remainder of their boat ride was uneventful. The riverside presented a series of changing tableaux worthy of comment. Their conversation ranged from the inconsequential to the sublimely humorous. The gentle rocking of the boat lulled Ramsay into relaxing and he soon found himself more comfortable in Cassandra's company than he'd been in anyone's presence—other than Graham's—for years.

The landing at the Two Yews Inn was deserted when they arrived. The barge slipped easily up to the dock. As soon as the craft was tied up, Ramsay jumped onto the stones and reached back to help Cassandra off the boat just as a good courtier would. The day had turned cloudy so they decided to leave her bonnet behind, but they brought Tophet along.

"The inn courtyard is shaded and cool," Ramsay assured her as they strolled along the stone quay toward the inn. The stone house sat back from the river among a stand of beeches. He reached down for Tophet's leash. "Let's let the dog enjoy a bit of freedom too."

Liberated, Tophet loped ahead, scouting out a zigzag path well in advance of them.

"It's a charming place," Cassandra said, smiling in the direction of the inn. "So peaceful-looking after the bustle of London. So bucolic."

"My thoughts exactly," Ramsay said, pleased that she was not disappointed in the quaint setting.

"If I may ask, what is the nature of the business you've come to transact?" Cassandra asked, as they listened to the soft cooing coming from the dovecote they passed.

Ramsay smiled down at her. If he understood women as well as he thought he did, she was going to like this surprise. "You'll see soon enough. Are you hungry, Your Majesty?"

"Yes, indeed I am," Cassandra said, smiling up at him. "Is being a courtier like Sir Walter as exhausting as being Queen? I can't imagine doing this day in and day out."

"I believe you're doing very well," Ramsay said, thinking queenliness came quite naturally to her. "I, on the other hand, feel quite at a disadvantage."

"How's that, my lord?" she asked, a faint frown crossing her brow.

"I have no cloak to throw down upon the ground for my

Queen to walk on,'' he said, reminding her of the old tale about Raleigh and Queen Elizabeth.

Cassandra laughed, her pretty white teeth flashing in the summer sunlight. ''No need to trouble yourself, my lord, for there are no mudholes for me to cross. Your absent cloak is unneeded.''

''I am delivered,'' Ramsay said, looking thankfully toward the sky as if he'd been saved from a grim fate.

Cassandra laughed again. The melodic sound made him smile, not a movement that he had to force to his lips, but a natural expression he'd like to try more often. It came spontaneously. He allowed it to linger and it made him feel lighter than he remembered feeling for a long time.

As planned, his instructions regarding luncheon had gotten there before them. A table with a white cloth was laid in the shade of the old oak tree in the inn's courtyard. Though the innkeeper and his wife were there to serve them, no other guests were about to intrude. Luncheon was simple but satisfactory: cold meats, bread, cheese, butter, jam, and fresh berries with cream.

Ramsay and Cassandra sat in the shade of the old tree, nibbling on the simple food and savoring the tartness of the berries. The breeze off the river tugged at the table linen and toyed with the lace at the throat of Cassandra's gown. Ramsay watched the delicate points of lace touch the porcelain white skin of her throat, flutter against her fragile collarbone, and caress the back of her neck. How he longed to follow their path with his fingers, with his lips.

''Do you think Raleigh did this for the queen?'' Cassandra asked, taking a bite of a raspberry.

Ramsay watched her lick a drip of cream from her lips. The berry juice glistened on her mouth and reddened her tongue. His body tightened. He ached to move to her side and feed her himself, berry by berry. Maybe he could sample the flavor on her lips. With another woman, he would have done just that and taken full advantage of the flirtation. But with Cassandra, he sensed he'd moved as fast as he could without making her suspicious or fearful of him.

Instead of feeding her berries, he shoved the whole bowl of fruit and cream at her. "I feel certain Raleigh romanced the queen after a fashion. Every courtier does."

"You think he brought her along on a business trip and fed her bread and cheese?" Cassandra asked, nibbling on another berry.

"It probably didn't happen quite like that," Ramsay said, unable to take his eyes off the drop of cream at the corner of her mouth. Her tongue flicked out and it was gone.

Suddenly Cassandra extended a berry to him. Ramsay watched with fascination as a dollop of cream, pink with berry juice, trickled down the berry and dropped onto the table. He glanced across to see Cassandra lick her lips once more.

"These are delicious, don't you want one?"

"No." Ramsay swallowed the tightness in his throat. What he wanted was to kiss her, tasting the red juice of the berries and cream on her lips. But he didn't dare. His body was telling him that once begun, this kiss would have to be carried through to completion. "No, not now. Where is the innkeeper? The man I was going to see should be arriving at any time."

He shifted in his chair to call to the innkeeper who instantly appeared. Ramsay learned that the man he was to talk with had indeed arrived. None too soon, Ramsay thought, regretting that he'd been rescued from painful, eternal unrequited desire. "Tell Mr. Brown to bring his basket here."

Before long, a well-dressed farmer wearing a straw hat appeared at the courtyard gate. He strode across the flags carrying a huge lidded basket large enough for laundry. When he reached the table, he set his basket on the flagstones, doffed his hat, and greeted Ramsay with many respectful bows. Tophet had risen and was already nosing the basket, whose contents whined and rocked the woven-willow container.

"What on earth?" Cassandra exclaimed, bending over the basket. "What's in here?"

"Thank you for coming today, Mr. Brown," Ramsay said. "Please show us what you have brought."

"Very good, my lord." With a nod from Ramsay, the farmer pulled off the woven lid to reveal a basket full of shiny black noses, liquid ebony eyes, and wagging tails. Round-bellied writhing black bodies tumbled onto the courtyard flagstones.

"Puppies! But they are adorable," Cassandra cried. She jumped up from her chair and reached into the basket to scoop up an eager little hound. She seized one who had climbed atop his litter mates and was about to escape. Then she sank down onto the stone curb around the tree, without regard for her muslin skirts billowing out around her, and she gathered as many of the puppies as she could onto her lap.

"I'm looking to add several bitches to my kennel," Ramsay explained, picking up another of the pups as he grinned to himself. He'd been right. The lady liked the pups. "Mr. Brown is said to raise some of the best Nairns here in the south."

"A litter of ten fine pups, my lord," Mr. Brown said.

"But these are Tophet's breed, are they not?" Cassandra asked, holding a puppy up to her face and allowing it to lick the tip of her nose. Wrinkling her nose, she giggled. Ramsay was ready to take both of them home, the plan for Glen Gray be damned. "You have a kennel of Nairn hounds? That must be why Tophet takes to you so naturally. He senses your fondness for dogs."

"That must be it," Ramsay agreed, stroking the small head of the pup in his hand without meeting Cassandra's gaze.

"Of course, but that still doesn't explain how you knew Tophet's name without asking me," Cassandra said, rubbing the sleek pup against her cheek.

Suddenly alert, Ramsay forced himself to pick up another of the pups and stroke it as if she'd not asked a meaningful question. Perhaps she was going to draw the connection sooner than he thought. Despite her nuzzling of the pup in her hands, Ramsay could feel her gaze upon him.

"Did I know Tophet's name without asking you?" he asked,

as casually as he could manage. He remembered very well speaking the words on the doorstep of Seacombe House before he'd caught his mistake. When she'd said nothing, he'd concluded she had not noticed. "I don't recall that. Surely I heard you call to him or some such thing. Here, what do you think of this sassy little girl?"

He lifted another pup—a squirming, squealing female, he noted—and thrust it into her arms. "Are they all weaned, Mr. Brown?"

"All ten be ready for you to take them home, my lord," Brown replied, as proudly as if he'd sired the litter himself. "From the best sire and bitch in my kennel they are, and they will serve you well—hunters or fighters or companions."

"Which ones do you think I should take home to Ravencliff?" Ramsay asked Cassandra.

"But you must take them all," she said, looking up at him as if astonished that he could consider any other decision. "You can't separate them from their brothers and sisters. They would be too unhappy. You must take them all."

"Even the runt?" Ramsay asked with a laugh.

But he understood what she was saying about the pain of separation. He'd known it once in his life, too—that black moment when you know even the dearest person in your life doesn't want you. Ramsay held up the smallest of the litter, a tiny black pup with stubby legs and uneven ears. It struggled valiantly to lick his face. "Taking them all is hardly practical, Your Majesty."

"But he has spirit, my lord," Cassandra said with a laugh. "Look at his determination to greet you. I could never bear to be separated from my sister. See, I warned you I would be of little help in business. My heart is too soft to make a queen's harsh choices."

"Is a woman's heart ever too soft?" Ramsay asked, regarding the energetic runt in his hand. He'd never known a woman who truly had a truly tender heart—despite all the poetry and tales to the contrary. Not his mother. Not his former fiancée.

Not even Ellen, his younger sister, though she'd never been cruel to him. But mistresses never made pretense of possessing such a weak bodily organ. Arrangements with them were business affairs. And that was the way he preferred his women. No pretenses. No heartstrings.

What about Cassandra St. John's heart?

He glanced at her as she talked to the puppies. He knew nothing of her heart, yet here he was playing courtier to her—a spoiled heiress—and he was feeling as lusty as a boy who had just learned what his pizzle was for. He frowned at the puppy in his hand. He would not allow himself to be seduced by her trim ankles peeking out from beneath her lacy hem. Or that wealth of hair, priceless gleaming tresses that would slide between his fingers like silk. He knew nothing of what lay in Cassandra's heart. He did not care to. It was not her heart he was trying to win. Only her favor. Favor enough to frighten her father. "I'll take them all, Mr. Brown."

"All ten, my lord?" Brown asked, obviously surprised.

"Every last wriggling one of them. Make arrangements with my man to send them all north."

"Right away, my lord," Brown said, bowing several more times.

"Well done, my lord." Cassandra tossed her head back and laughed. "But now I know you for what you are—a faker."

"Faker" echoed in Ramsay's ears. Guiltily, he tensed and forced himself to turn to her as nonchalantly as he could. "How's that, Your Majesty? I don't understand."

Cassandra smiled up at him, her lap and arms full of squirming puppies—her skirt rumpled up so that her delicate white-stockinged ankles seemed to call to him—her blue eyes soft and shining. "You are a faker. Behind that stern face of yours lurks a kind heart."

Relief washed over Ramsay—along with a foolish lightheartedness. Inwardly he blanched. *What nonsense,* he told himself. *I'm too old for this. A mere girl smiles approval at me and my heart flutters.* Still, an involuntary grin spread across his face.

Just play the game, he told himself. *Play the game.* He offered her a courtly bow. "But Your Majesty, Sir Walter could do no less."

Ravencliff offered Cassie the choice of one of the pups to take home with her, but she declined, regretfully. She could not choose which to separate from its companions.

"I have Tophet," she told him as she watched Mr. Brown gather the puppies up in the basket. She'd been surprised that Ravencliff had ordered all the pups sent to his home. Nairn hounds were worth a fortune, as evidenced by Mr. Brown's beaming smile. Undoubtedly the day's sale had increased his income considerably. Ravencliff seemed to give the expenditure little thought. Then, most aristocrats, even the impoverished ones, seemed to give the expense of any of their favorite indulgences little thought.

They left soon after Mr. Brown had packed up his little dogs. Soft heavy clouds had gathered to darken the day and the breeze had become cool and moist, bearing the promise of rain. As they walked to the landing, their steps became more hurried. But Ravencliff still played the part of Raleigh to her Queen Elizabeth. Cassie couldn't help but laugh at the whole charade. Ravencliff made such a good Raleigh. In her mind, the explorer and military strategist must have seemed a man's man in a royal court full of dandies in satin bloomers, trunk hose, and codpieces.

During lunch in the courtyard Ravencliff had removed his cravat and loosened his shirt collar—with her permission of course—to reveal a sprinkling of golden hair at his throat. The sight had made her throat go dry. She tried not to stare at the wiry curls or think about how they would trail downward. She'd seen bare-chested men before, she'd reminded herself. She'd watched Connor McKensie fight several times in only his kilt. While the sight had been pleasing to her eye, it had not created the same melting heat inside her that a glimpse of Ravencliff did. She could not resist stealing repeated looks at him throughout their meal. She noted then, too, his dark eyelashes and the tigerlike intensity of his eyes.

Raindrops began to fall as they reached the barge—fat, wet drops that soaked through clothing or rolled off bare skin. One here, then one there. Not many. But they speckled the landing stones with dark circles and pockmarked the smooth surface of the river.

Tophet jumped aboard the barge without urging.

Ravencliff leaped onto the barge and turned, reaching out for Cassie. The moment she put her hand in his, thunder rumbled overhead. Out of the sky a big raindrop plopped on the back of her hand. They both saw it, a beaded circle of water between her wrist and her knuckles. For an instant it held them both transfixed. Then the sky opened up. Rain plummeted down on them. Ravencliff literally dragged her aboard the barge and into the protection of the pavilion.

The waterman shoved off, knocking them both off balance so they toppled onto the pillows and rugs.

"I hope you aren't too soaked," Ravencliff said, his hand still clutching hers.

Cassie smoothed her hair, aware of some rainwater soaked through to her scalp, but she was only a bit damp. "I knew when I saw that raindrop on my hand that it was going to be a downpour," she said with a small laugh.

Ravencliff watched her intently, his green eyes dark and searching as he raised her hand between them. Before Cassie realized what he was doing, he put his mouth to the spot where the raindrop had fallen. He sipped up the moisture on her skin. The pliant warmth of his lips against the back of her hand held her spellbound. When she did not pull her hand away, he began to move over her skin tenderly, his lips warm with relish.

Cassie sucked in a breath. His touch set her hand afire. She leaned toward him, confused and uncertain about what he wanted of her. But willing to find out. "My lord?"

He pulled her into his arms and held her for the space of a

dozen heartbeats, her face tipped upward to his. She waited. He touched her chin with one finger, then bent to capture her mouth in a kiss. That long-awaited kiss. The kiss she'd known he wanted to give her in the zoological gardens but had offered her only a sample of. Physical shock shook her as his mouth moved against hers. She trembled. Passion followed the first touch of their lips, quick and hot.

She wrapped her arms around his neck and kissed him back, hungry for the taste of his mouth, for the melting surrender and the fierce pleasure. Her hands rested on his chest and her fingertips tingled from the accelerating beat of his heart. She wanted to lie even closer to him and explore every solid inch of his body.

But then his mouth made her forget everything beyond their lips. Before she realized quite how he had accomplished it, he'd seduced her lips apart and she was receiving his tongue. And she liked the sensation.

He didn't make stabs at the seam of her lips like Dudley had done. Ravencliff's tongue enticed and seduced and entered to stroke and explore and taste thoroughly. She tasted in return—and it was delicious. The only thing abrupt and shocking was her response. She pressed herself closer to him, aligning her body with his on the pillows.

Then she submitted fully to his lips. He applied just enough pressure and a delightful degree of suction. His mastery was captivating, and too marvelous to stop. Her stomach fluttered weightlessly, and her limbs felt heavy. She was light-headed and breathless. Her breasts tingled and between her thighs in her secret places she experienced a dull, feverish ache.

Without releasing her mouth, he moved his hands from her shoulders down her back, then over her derriere. He pulled her against him though they were already pressed so close together she had not thought being closer was possible.

Then, feeling his hardness through her skirts' petticoats, Cassie went still. She'd never allowed such closeness with Dudley. Nevertheless, her bones seemed to have melted so she had no choice but to press into Ravencliff for support. Though she knew it wasn't proper, the evidence of his desire thrilled her. She laid her hands on his shirt, her fingers involuntarily curling to fists.

He released her and pulled his head back, ending the kiss.

Her eyelids were heavy. Her body ached for his lips, for his touch. When she looked up into his eyes she saw that he was as stunned—but as hungry for more—as she.

Abruptly he reached for the door flap of the barge pavilion and pulled it closed. Not that the bargeman rowing in the rain had noticed anything amiss. And from what little she could see of the river beyond the barge, there were few others on the river because of the rain. But Cassie was glad Ravencliff thought of their privacy.

In the dim light he peered into her face. "You must say if this is not to your liking. You are not obliged in any way to accept my attentions."

" 'Tis to my liking," she said, her arms still wrapped around his neck. She thought she would die if he didn't go on kissing her.

Then Ravencliff pressed her down into the pillows once more. The scent of him filled her nostrils. He smelled of leather and lemon and puppies. As he lowered his head to hers again, she reached for his lips with her own. When his tongue slid into her mouth, he made a low wanting sound and angled his body against hers, pressing into her softness. She reached up and sank her fingers into his fair hair.

By the time they broke apart for breath, they were panting. Cassie was certain her face was flushed. Her body burned with yearning and her heart pounded with excitement.

"Damnation," he murmured again, burying his face in her neck.

"What is it, my lord?" Cassie gasped, fearful this bliss would end too soon.

"You taste divine." He kissed her neck hungrily.

The heat of his lips seeped into her now. She ran her hands

up and down the corded muscles of Ravencliff's back, dropping her head back and giving him access to her throat.

At first he only caressed her shoulders and nudged aside the lace of her collar. Then he was loosening her bodice buttons and sampling the skin of her throat. His hands slipped down over her breasts, his touch light. But the sensation of his caress made her tremble. The yearning coalesced into a heavy aching in her breasts. She wanted his hands on her—and his lips. As if he knew her thoughts, he brushed aside her gown, baring her throat and shoulder and trailed feathery kisses to the edge of her shift. When he reached the lace, he continued downward. The tiny kisses trailed fire along her skin even through the fabric. She arched her back, urging him on, but he seemed to know exactly what she needed. When his lips descended on her nipple, she gasped and shivered. The sensation reached down deep inside of her. She lay weak and mindless in his arms, only knowing the rapture he brought her.

When he took his mouth away he quickly covered her throbbing nipple with his hand.

"Cassandra?" He whispered into her ear. "Princess?"

She could only whimper and roll her head from side to side on the pillows. She needed him.

He leaned above her now. She could feel his breath against her face. "Cassandra, we—"

"My lord?" called the waterman. "If you please, I need to speak to ye."

Ravencliff cursed. He freed himself of her slowly, then rose, adjusting his clothes as if he was the one half undressed and not she.

"Cover yourself, " he ordered in a rasping voice at the door of the pavilion. "This is not the place for any more of this nonsense."

Then he was gone.

His exit admitted the damp river-breeze, which drifted across Cassie's fevered skin. She shivered in the sudden chill. Her body yearned for him to return to her. But clearly he would not. Slowly she sat up and began to fasten her bodice as he'd ordered. But her hands shook so she had to work slowly. She could hear the men's voices outside the pavilion, but she could not make out what they were saying. Although they sounded concerned, it did not seem to be a serious discussion. She drew a deep breath and tried to force herself to concentrate on dressing.

From the tolling of the church bells she realized they were closer to the city than she'd realized and that it was much later than she had thought. They were going to have to hurry if she was going to get home without her anyone suspecting that she'd done something besides go off to luncheon with a friend.

When Ravencliff reappeared, he ran his fingers through his hair as though troubled.

"Is it serious, my lord?" Cassie asked, smoothing the front of her bodice.

His eyes flicked over her quickly, obviously taking in her hasty repairs. He frowned and handed her the bonnet that had been discarded earlier. "Here, tuck your hair under this. No, no problems," he said, "but I think a fortuitous interruption nonetheless."

Cassie pulled on her bonnet and eyed him cautiously. "I'm not certain I understand, my lord."

"I don't mean that I . . . we didn't . . . I appreciate what we have just shared." He shook his head and reached for his coat without looking at her. She noted several beads of perspiration on his brow. "But as it is not what is accepted by society, we have already been indiscreet. You are here without a chaperone. We must be circumspect."

"But why?" Cassie said. "I'm not ashamed. In fact, I am quite flattered that you find me—desirable, my lord. I'm not afraid of what people think."

"Well, you should be and I'm certain your father is." His head came up and he stared at her, his eyes darker and more searching than ever. "I do find you desirable, princess. But that does not excuse my lack of restraint. I'm afraid you owe the waterman a debt of gratitude for curbing my excess."

Cassie thought he was jesting. "I hardly think you intemperate, my lord."

She longed for the return of the ease that had grown between them earlier. When her eyes met his, the small laugh she was about to give caught in her throat.

He was serious, deadly serious. A chill settled over Cassie, a delicious chill. Ravencliff had wanted her, had almost taken her. A real man had held her in his arms and almost— It had been a near thing. The wonder of it was quite unlike anything she'd ever known with Dudley or any of the young bucks who had stolen kisses in the garden. With Ravencliff she'd almost become an initiated woman. But that fact seemed to displease him.

His green eyes lightened and she saw a spark of anger in their depths. It frightened her. "I am not a man to toy with, princess."

"I never thought you were, my lord," Cassie said, confused, but not ready to accept blame or to shirk responsibility. She remembered clearly the way he'd kissed the back of her hand, hungrily, greedily. Without any encouragement from her. "Nor am I a lady to trifle with."

Ravencliff's glare hardened, then softened a fraction and he ducked his head. "So I have learned. Let's remember that about each other, shall we?"

In the silence they listened to the waterman calling out to the dock hands on the stairs.

Ravencliff got to his feet and reached down to help her up. "We just have time to get you home without raising suspicions."

CHAPTER EIGHT

"It canna be," Erik Drummond muttered to himself when he saw Ramsay Forbes and the St. John girl appear at the top of the St. James stairs. Shocked by the sight of the two—together—Erik almost stepped from his dry hiding place into the drizzle to get a better look. To confirm what he was certain was an impossibility—Charlotte St. John on the arm of the Marquis of Linirk. "It canna be."

He caught himself before he stepped out into the open. To make himself known to Graham Andrews now was the last thing he needed to do. Erik had been following Graham all afternoon. What he'd learned about the McKensies' hated foe had not been particularly enlightening. Graham had scurried around the streets of London hiring carriages and paying stablekeepers and ordering food in the name of Forbes. Erik's watch had been damned dull, until now.

It had taken him and Connor a month to confirm that Linirk was in London—and not at Ravencliff. The marquis could be near invisible when he wished. When you did see him, you could be sure he wanted to be seen. Except for now. Erik knew in his Scots gut that Ramsay Forbes did not want anyone watching him now, alone with Charlotte St. John. He squired her along the street with an unmistakable air of possessiveness. With his hand on the small of her back he helped her climb into the hackney Graham had hired earlier. Then the marquis glanced around as if to see whether they'd been observed. Apparently satisfied that they had not been seen, he climbed in after her. The hackney started off at a hasty pace.

Erik had never seen Linirk with a lady. He'd declared his sister's son as his heir five years ago. Mothers of marriageable lassies had struck him from their eligible list. It was known that he kept a mistress from time to time. But he was not known to keep company with a lady—not since he nearly murdered his fiancée and ruined her lover. That had been many long years ago.

Erik watched Forbes's hired carriage disappear in the direction of Mayfair and shook his head. None of this made any sense. Connor and Charlotte were attending an all-day function at the Foundling Shelter, Erik reminded himself. " 'Tis impossible for that to be Charlotte."

Erik sucked in a shallow breath. Of course it wasn't Charlotte. The lass on Forbes's arm had to be her twin sister, Cassandra—the twin who could look you in the eye like she thought she was a man's equal, or better. He'd met few women who could do that, and never a lass. Erik recalled hearing whispers among the servants about Cassandra's fiancé crying off recently. He'd not been surprised. Who wanted to marry a lass with that kind of arrogance—heiress or not?

But now a new understanding grew, and a chill settled over Erik. Coincidence? Was Forbes that vile? Of course he was. The whole cursed clan Forbes had been that evil for centuries. Forbes—the snake. If an opportunity the man wanted didn't exist, the heartless marquis created it.

Had Ramsay Forbes linked himself up with Cassandra St. John to strike at Connor McKensie? When? How? Questions hatched like chicks in a clutch and the hatred of the clan Forbes grew inside Erik.

He glanced around to see what Graham was doing. He glimpsed Forbes's foster brother ducking into a shop doorway to get out of the rain just as he himself had done. He was making no effort to show himself to Forbes. Why had Graham remained hidden?

So the lady wouldn't see him, Erik decided. Cassandra and Charlotte knew Graham already. They'd been introduced when Graham had presented the lovebirds and Tophet at Charlotte and Connor's engagement breakfast. So why hide? Even more curious, why would Cassandra agree to be seen in the Marquis of Linirk's company when she knew that he'd engineered Connor's kidnapping? She had risked herself, along with her sister, to rescue Connor. Charlotte and Cassandra were unwaveringly loyal to one another. So why would Cassandra attach herself to Connor McKensie's foe?

Erik decided to give up following Graham Andrews for the day. He could always pick up Andrews's trail at the townhouse whenever he needed to. Right now he had news to report to Connor.

Ramsay dropped down in the chair before a glowing fire and stared into his brandy morosely. "I must tell her the truth soon."

"Why? Looked like ye had her eating out of yer hand to me," Graham said from the dark corner of the room where the scotch bottle and brandy decanter sat. He joined Ramsay at the fireside, a glass of scotch in his own hand. "What did ye do all that time at the inn and on the river?"

"I'm not certain." Ramsay sipped his brandy and allowed it to warm his throat. The day with Cassandra had left him contemplative. His plan had been to entertain and seduce her. Seduction, or romancing a woman, was a many-stepped effort. He'd never expected to take complete advantage of Cassandra on the barge. That was not the point. That had never been the point of this whole plan. The point was to intimidate her father when the right time came. When Cassandra seemed to trust him, when her reputation was on the line. That was the time to intimidate Davis St. John. And the time would come soon.

What troubled Ramsay was that he'd come close to throwing caution to the wind and completing his seduction that day. Cassandra was the most tempting morsel he'd ever seduced. No woman besides Aileen had ever made him lose his head before, and he did not like feeling those emotions again. He did not like losing control of his feelings. "We talked and flirted and played at being Queen Elizabeth and Sir Walter Raleigh. And the time slipped past."

"Ye played Queen Elizabeth and who?" Graham asked, looking amazed.

"She always has some game she wants to play." Ramsay found himself chuckling. "She had me yodeling in a tunnel like a Swiss mountaineer the first day, and today we playacted at being a courtier and a queen in a bygone time. 'Tis all a game."

"Ye are the Marquis of Linirk," Graham said with an injured frown. Ramsay knew his foster brother's clan pride was offended. "Ye are the Forbes. Ye have no need to be playacting at anythin'."

"I'll admit I wasn't quite prepared for her games," Ramsay said, vaguely aware of the smile on his lips as he recalled Cassandra drawing him into the tunnel to sing schoolroom ditties. Silly as listening to their echoes had seemed, it was a unique experience, one he would not have missed for any price. A lighthearted pleasure he would have missed if she'd not cajoled him into it. "Her fantasies are not what I expected, not the kind of games other women I've known play."

"So what happened today?" Graham asked, obviously curious now. "Besides yer playacting."

"She liked the pups," Ramsay said, remembering Cassandra sitting on the curb at the base of the tree with her lap full of squirming black dogs.

"I didna think it wise to take her to see the hounds," Graham said. "She's bound to connect ye and Tophet eventually."

"I'm not certain whether she has or not," Ramsay said, remembering how she'd asked him about Tophet's name. Recalling the strange sensation that had spun through him, the half hope, half fear, that she was going to catch him in his lie. She suspected something, or she would not have asked him about the slip. But how much did she question? "I admit she does not trust me as completely as I'd like yet."

"Ye two looked cozy enough when ye climbed up the stairs and into the hackney," Graham said.

"It was a good afternoon together," Ramsay said. The memory of the kiss was fresh enough to make him uncomfortable.

"How many of the Nairn pups did ye decide to send to Ravencliff?" Graham asked, a tone of irritation in his voice.

Ramsay knew that his foster brother was still annoyed that he'd been left behind and Cassandra taken along instead. "I decided to take all of them."

"All?" The scotch in Graham's goblet sloshed over the side. "Are ye daft? That litter is worth a fortune."

"Now the ten puppies are part of my fortune," Ramsay said, unperturbed by Graham's criticism. "Cassandra didn't want to see them separated."

"So the spoiled heiress is making decisions for ye now?"

Ramsay's anger flared, but he never allowed it to show. "You know better than that."

"Aye, I do." Graham ducked his head and studied the scotch in his glass. "So, is it time to go to her father yet?"

"No," Ramsay said without hesitation. He knew Graham was eager to be done with this scheme, but he was not going to rush a single step of it and lose all they'd managed to gain. "It's too soon to let Davis St. John know that his daughter is under the influence of the Marquis of Linirk. But if I don't tell her the truth soon, someone will recognize me. If she learns my identity from someone else, all our efforts will be for naught."

"Ye donna think she'll run straight to her father when you tell her?" Graham asked.

"I don't think so," Ramsay said, surprised by his concern and understanding of Cassandra. "As she would see it, it is one thing for her to keep her father in the dark about what she is doing. But quite another thing for me to deceive her."

"So ye are going to tell her?" Graham asked.

"I believe so." Ramsay did not voice his own guilty misgivings.

"How?" Graham asked. "When?"

"I'm not certain." The kiss on the barge had thrown Ramsay's sense of timing into turmoil. Just when nothing was moving as fast as he'd like, he suddenly felt as if he was hurtling along some unexpected path. But he did understand there was no turning back, not after Cassandra had wrapped her arms around his neck and allowed him to press close.

As it was, Cassandra was going to be hurt or angry when she learned the truth. He had no idea which, but he did not relish the scene. Hopefully he would be spared the retribution she had unleashed on Dudley. But if he did not tell her, he risked the chance that someone else would. Then all would be lost. He was certain of it. If the truth came from him, face-to-face, he had the opportunity to plead his case—or to instill fear. Whichever would hold her. Whichever emotion would allow him to manipulate her father.

Now he wanted something more than Glen Gray. He wanted Cassandra St. John to continue to playact with him.

"Whatever I do, I must tell her the truth, before it's too late," he muttered. Before she learned the truth from someone else and refused to playact with him—ever again.

The day after the kiss on the river, Cassandra went to Lackington's bookshop on an errand for Charlotte. She had nothing else planned for the morning and she was too dazed and restless

to be content at home. Ravencliff's kisses had left her too
unsettled to stay indoors at home without company.

After picking up her sister's order, Cassie decided to while
away an hour or so among the bookshelves. She liked books.
There was nothing quite as wonderful as a good novel, a warm
fire, and a dish of tea on a rainy afternoon. She just wasn't
quite as obsessed by the volumes as Charlotte was. So while
Betsy waited for her downstairs with the other servants on a
bench at the entrance, Cassie strolled along the railing of the
upstairs rotunda. She took little heed of the titles on the bookshelves or of the busy clerks and patrons at the central desk
below. She walked about in a bit of a euphoric daze. The
memory of Ravencliff's kiss was still rich, and so vivid that
at moments her lips still felt tender.

Mama was off with her Greek-study society and Papa had
gone to his office. After luncheon Charlotte, Mama, and she
would meet at Aunt Dorian's and discuss Charlotte's wedding
plans. But for the moment she had little to occupy her but the
memories of Ravencliff's touch. And if she dwelled on the
warm tingle of his fingers on her skin, a blush warmed her
cheeks. Her body came alive in ways she'd never been aware
of before: the flutter in her belly and the ache in her nether
regions. If she was not obligated to those blasted luncheon plans,
she would rush off to Regent's Park and loiter shamelessly until
two o'clock when she could see Ramsay on his daily ride again.

Over the next few days, her calendar was full of a multitude
of obligations and she would be unable to see him. But that
did not keep her from wishing for more of his company. She
wondered if Ravencliff would wait for her in the park, if he
missed her as much as she missed him. She liked to think he
did.

Cassie turned to wander back into the shadows of the stacks,
sorry that she would be unable to go to the park today.

Ravencliff stepped out of the shadows into her path.

Surprised, Cassie almost dropped the books she was carrying.
Though she'd been thinking about him, his sudden appearance

startled her. A small cry escaped her and she stepped backward, bumping her shoulder against the bookshelf. A couple of books plopped over on their sides.

"Cassandra?" He took off his hat and offered her a small bow. His fair hair gleamed in the light streaming in from the skylight above. As usual he was dressed all in black. His waistcoat on this morning appeared to be a rich, black-striped damask weave.

"My lord," Cassie began, her breathless surprise flashing into irritation. "What on earth are you doing lurking in the shadows? You gave me a start. Do you often loiter in the dark and startle a lady without warning?"

"I am sorry." He spoke softly, as if truly apologetic. "I didn't mean to frighten you, Cassandra. I just happened to be passing by the bookshop and I saw Betsy sitting on the bench by the door and I suspected that you were here."

"How opportune," Cassie said, noting how odd and vexing it was that Ravencliff always seemed to discover her when she least expected him—and always when she was alone.

"I was hoping you might do me the honor of accompanying me for a ride in the park," he said.

"'Tis early." She gazed up at him, vexed with herself and him. Despite her vexation, she was glad to see him, to note once again how very genteel he could be, in a masculine way that sent tiny shivers of pleasure through her body. Even though she'd just been yearning for him, she found annoying his presumption that she would be willing to put aside what she was doing for him. He didn't own her. He wasn't even officially a suitor or a friend.

"I must get back to the house with these books," Cassie lied. "Charlotte is expecting them. This one on the labor conditions for children in the factories is of great interest to her."

Ravencliff took her elbow and ushered her out of the shadows and into the light from above. "That's easily taken care of. We'll send Betsy home in the carriage with the valuable tomes and a message that you're with a friend."

"My lord." Cassie resisted his hold on her arm. "It's not as simple as that."

"Why not?" Ravencliff said with a perfect air of innocence. His grasp on her remained firm. "I wish to see you. We have servants to do our bidding."

"Because I find your invitation presumptuous," Cassie said, allowing him to maneuver her around the shop only because she did not wish to make a scene.

Ravencliff stared at her as if he did not understand a word she'd said.

"I'm not certain how ladies comport themselves in the north, my lord," Cassie felt compelled to explain, "but in London a gentleman just doesn't expect a lady to put aside what she is doing to satisfy his whim."

A dark look crossed Ravencliff's face, menacing and obstinate. Surprised, Cassie bit her lip. With Dudley she'd never hesitated to alert him to his faux pas. Perhaps she'd gone too far in reprimanding the baron.

"I assure you this is not a whim," Ravencliff said, frowning more severely than Cassie had ever seen him frown. A sense of gravity clung to him. "I need to speak with you today. It is of the utmost importance that we have this conversation and that we have it in private."

His intensity alarmed Cassie. "Why didn't you say so? Has something happened? Is someone ill?"

"Nothing quite as dramatic as all that, but 'tis important," Ravencliff assured her with a shake of his head. He relieved her of the books and handed them to a clerk. Soon Betsy was dispatched toward home with Charlotte's books. Ravencliff handed Cassie and Tophet into his phaeton and they were off toward Hyde Park.

At this hour of the day there was no one of note in the park.

"I hardly expected to see you this morning, my lord," she said, bracing herself against the seat as he hastily turned onto a less-traveled path. Ravencliff drove in silence, but she could see that he was brooding on something. His seriousness wiped away some of her vexation.

"After yesterday, I discovered that I have no patience for waiting to see you again," he said.

"So it was no accident that you found me at the bookshop?" she asked.

"No, it was not. I came seeking you." He turned to stare at her, his eyes dark and intent.

His admission made her heart flutter.

"I admit you have been at the fore in my thoughts too," she said, as calmly as she could. Inside, excitement bubbled and her heart pounded. Surely this meant he was as bewitched by her as she was by him. Had he brought her here to declare his feelings? Dudley had been agitated when he'd taken her into the garden and confessed his ardor, she remembered. "Here we are alone and our conversation quite private, my lord. What is it you wish to tell me?"

Ravencliff slowed the horses to a walk and his frown deepened to a scowl. Suddenly Cassie realized he wasn't about to declare anything she wanted to hear. She forced herself to take a deep breath and remain calm.

"Cassandra," he began without looking at her. "How much do you know about me?"

Cassie glanced at him. "I was just thinking about that very thing in the bookstore. I don't even know your family name or where you are staying in London. But I think I know the important things. I know that you are a stern man, a man of discipline, of traditional tastes and simple habits. I know that your favorite place in the world is Ravencliff and that you like dogs."

His scowl became forbidding. "As dull and dour as that?"

She laughed and offered him an encouraging smile. "I also know that despite that austere face and your strict ways, you are kind and generous, caring, and you even have a sense of humor."

Miraculously, his scowl softened into the touching expression of a man-boy who desperately needed to hear her words of approval. Cassie's heart fluttered again. She longed once more to smooth the way for the confession that seemed to be difficult for him to make.

But before she could say more, he faced forward, concentrating on the horses as if driving a walking team demanded his full attention. His expression hardened once again. "I believe it is vital that you know the truth about me before we go on."

"By all means, you must tell me now, my lord," Cassie urged with a nervous laugh. "My curiosity has become quite unbearable."

"The fact is, I possess several other titles."

Cassie sat still, listening intently. Several titles meant that Ravencliff's true rank was surely higher than baron. That would be no surprise to her. Everything about his demeanor, his manners, interests, education, and spending habits hinted at a man of wealth and position. "Should I be addressing you as Your Grace?"

"No, nothing quite as exalted as all that," Ravencliff muttered without looking at her. "However, I have reason to believe that my family name will be of significance to you."

"And that is?" she asked lightly. The truth could hardly be as ominous as he seemed to think it was. "Pray do not torture me any longer."

He paused as if he were having second thoughts about telling her, then he added in a low voice, "My family name is Forbes. I am Ramsay Forbes, the fourteenth Marquis of Linirk."

CHAPTER NINE

Ramsay waited for Cassandra to unleash her anger on him. But she remained silent, staring at the bridle path ahead of the phaeton. He feared she had not heard him. "I am the laird of the clan Forbes, the clan that feuds with the McKensies."

"I know who the Marquis of Linirk is," Cassandra said, her voice ominously well modulated, but her face averted. Only Tophet was willing to meet his gaze.

When Ramsay studied her expression, she appeared uncharacteristically sober. She was wearing a willow-green muslin gown and a bonnet with a shallow crown and a closed brim. The summer breeze toyed with a stray tendril of red hair at her nape. Tiny gold earbobs swung with the bounce of the phaeton. Her small, velvet-slippered feet remained still on the floorboards. Now that the phaeton barely moved along the path, her gloved hands rested in her lap as motionless as a statue's. Ramsay watched her pulse beating rapidly in her throat and waited for her reaction.

"I realize this must be a shock," Ramsay said, growing impatient with her lack of response.

Still she stared ahead, her face pale and her eyes unfocused.

Confronted with this uncharacteristic silence, Ramsay decided to answer the questions she was bound to ask. "I introduced myself with one of my lesser titles because I knew my real name might put you off. I had no way of knowing what lies McKensie has told about me. I wanted you to have the opportunity to get to know me without any preconceptions."

"You certainly managed that," Cassandra said, again in the same careful tone.

Ramsay bit his tongue. Lord, he hated this: explaining himself, tossing out excuses like some powerless tenant groveling before a landlord. He didn't have to do this. So why was he?

Ramsay glanced across at Cassandra again. Where were the hysterics he'd been prepared for? No foot-stomping or tears. Where was the explosion of anger? No thunder or fire. But he could feel an invisible curtain of icy silence threatening to come down between them. Where was her spirit?

With a start he recalled what he should have remembered earlier, the scene in the tea shop. There had been no hysterics over Dudley, either. In fact, he'd never seen hysterics from Cassandra over anything. High spirits and high jinks—even revenge, yes—but never hysterics, never tears.

He eyed her more closely, pondering the possibility that he hadn't anticipated her reaction as thoroughly as he should have. "Cassandra, say what you think."

"Never fear," she said crisply. "I shall."

That was better, Ramsay thought. Her anger was beginning to show. They passed another equipage, but the passengers were strangers. At a fork in the path, he turned the phaeton down a more secluded fork.

"So you knew who I was when you came to my rescue that day on the street?" Cassandra asked as soon as the other carriage was out of hearing.

"Yes, I did," he admitted. " 'Twas not difficult. The red-haired St. John twins are well known in Town. I did not want to frighten you more than you had been by the footpads. If I'd introduced myself as Linirk you undoubtedly would have thought of me as the greater of two evils, perhaps even as an archenemy.''

"Enemy?" she repeated softly. "So you decided to lie to me instead?"

"Be honest. How would you have treated me if I'd introduced myself as the Marquis of Linirk?"

"I certainly would never have allowed you to take me home," Cassandra said, still frozen in her stiff pose. "You had Connor kidnapped. Your henchmen told us so."

Ramsay's hands tightened on the reins and the horses tossed their heads. "That was an unfortunate, botched attempt to dissuade Kinleith from fighting in a prizefight. That's all it was."

"It was an effort to keep him from fighting so he'd forfeit any opportunity to win a championship title," Cassandra countered, her voice still surprisingly even. "It was an effort to keep him from having a chance to purchase Glen Gray. You endangered his well-being and you caused my sister great anguish."

Ramsay winced. There was no evading these accusations.

Cassandra whirled on him. This time her voice was low and loaded with emotion. "And you lied to me. Not just on one occasion, but every time we were together. By letting me continue in ignorance of your true identity. You lied to me."

"I had good reason," Ramsay maintained, suddenly feeling that he'd tied his cravat too tight.

"I will not accept that," she said, tapping a finger on the seat between them. "Stop the carriage."

"No, I'll take you home when we have settled this."

"There is nothing to settle," Cassandra said. "A lie is a lie. I will not abide dishonesty. Stop this carriage this instant. I will ride no farther with you."

Ramsay ignored her command and urged the horses into a trot.

"Listen to me." Cassandra lurched from her seat and grabbed for the reins. The phaeton rocked. "If you won't stop this carriage so I can get out, then I shall stop it."

"Here, stop that," Ramsay said, leaning away and holding the reins beyond her reach. Her quick angry reaction startled him. "Are you insane?"

"No, I'm outraged." Cassandra made another, but less strenuous, attempt to seize the reins. "I want to have nothing more to do with you ever again."

Ramsay evaded her grasp once more.

"If you don't stop this vehicle, then I shall jump out."

Ramsay cursed under his breath. She was going to wreck them or hurt herself. He pulled the horses to a halt. "And if you get out, just how do you think you will get home?"

"I shall manage quite well, thank you." Cassandra jumped from the phaeton with amazing agility for a woman who required a man's arm to walk across a drawing room. Tophet followed her. She turned on her heel and marched back down the path in the opposite direction, toward the park entrance.

What now? Ramsay quickly brought the phaeton and team around and drove slowly alongside her. If he'd paid attention at the tea shop when she'd walked out on Dudley he would have foreseen this. "Get back in, Cassandra, and I will take you home. You may rail at me all the way. I will make no excuses or protests. Call me any name that you like. I shall take you home."

"Get away from me," Cassandra snapped, marching straight ahead without even deigning to look up at him. "I never want to see you again."

"I will not have you gadding about this park or the London streets unescorted," Ramsay said, at a loss for how to make her obey without resorting to physical violence. Customarily people instantly did as he commanded. "It is unsafe. Remember what happened last time? Remember the footpads?"

"I remember and rest assured, I shan't go home unescorted," Cassandra said, without a pause in her determined stride. "Do not trouble yourself over my welfare, my lord. Ever again."

"Cassandra, stop this foolishness this instant," Ramsay demanded, feeling oddly helpless and growing angry.

"How dare you suggest my behavior is foolish," Cassandra muttered as she trudged along. "After what you've done. Foolish doesn't even begin to describe this—this—this insult, this deceit."

She halted, her skirts swirling about her ankles, and glared up at him. "Not just insult and deceit, my lord, this is betrayal. You betrayed me. I have no desire to associate with you any longer."

The word *betrayal* sent an icy barb through Ramsay's gut. He frowned and grew impatient. He knew more about the pain of betrayal than she ever would in her sheltered, indulged life. "You overdramatize, Cassandra."

"Do I?" She cast him a frosty scowl before continuing on her way. "I think not."

At that moment another carriage came along, an open landau with a handsome young couple out for an early, but private ride. When the pair saw Ramsay driving his phaeton and Cassandra striding alongside on the path, their mouths dropped open. Ramsay urged his team on and ignored the other carriage. He prayed the passengers were strangers.

"Halt, driver," the young man called out. He stood up in the landau and took off his hat in greeting. "I say, Cassandra St. John, is that you? Cyril Smedgewood here, Tony's friend. Remember me? We went boating together last spring at Henley-on-the-Thames."

Cassandra stopped and her face brightened.

Ramsay cursed silently and pulled his team to a halt.

"Why, yes, Mr. Smedgewood, I remember you," Cassandra said, moving across the path in front of Ramsay's team toward Smedgewood's equipage. "And what a delightful day on the Thames that was, too. How are you, sir?"

"Quite well, Miss St. John, thank you," Smedgewood said though he was eyeing Ramsay with suspicion. "You know my fiancée, I believe, Miss Alice Meadforth. And you, sir—Linirk, is it not? I'd not heard you were in Town, my lord."

"I just arrived," Ramsay muttered, in no mood to be polite.

He longed to order the young buck and his lady on their way so he could get back to his conversation with Cassandra.

"I see," Smedgewood said, regarding Cassandra this time with a faint questioning smile. "Might I be of some service, Miss St. John?"

"Mr. Smedgewood, but of course, this all looks quite strange and you must be wondering what is going on," Cassandra said, with a gay laugh and a bright smile set in place on her lips. Ramsay cursed silently. He'd totally and completely underestimated her.

Cassandra continued. "It's really quite simple. The bar— *marquis* and I were just undertaking to prove a wager that I could walk faster than his fine team of horses. Isn't that so, my lord?"

"Umm," Ramsay allowed reluctantly. She exchanged a quick assessing glance with him. He wasn't about to compound his sins now by disputing her word before her friends. He suspected she would take full advantage of his reluctance.

"A wager?" Smedgewood repeated, clearly mystified, but gamely ready to go along with her story.

"How unique," Miss Meadforth said as if it must be a charming game. "And pray tell, who is winning?"

"Miss St. John," Ramsay snapped in disgust. No reason to hide the truth.

"My lord is being kind." Cassandra simpered and smiled up at Smedgewood. "But what is most important is that it seems the marquis is late for a very important appointment."

"I am not—" Ramsay began, unwilling to go along with anything she said.

"At the King's palace," she interjected, raising her voice to be heard over him. "His lordship is too modest to make much of it. But he has an audience with the King."

Ramsay clamped his mouth shut again, annoyed with her audacity.

"I say, I have heard you have the King's ear whenever you want it, Linirk," Smedgewood said with awe in his voice.

Ramsay silently cursed his lofty connections. He glared at Cassandra. Denying that he had an appointment with the King would only make him look ridiculous and ensure protest that he must be on his way—which was exactly what she wanted. He'd never faced a craftier opponent.

Cassandra smiled back at him, smug defiance in the curve of her lips. Then she returned to Smedgewood. "Would you be so kind as to give me a ride to Tony's house, sir? You seem to be going in that direction. So sorry to trouble you, Miss Meadforth, but I simply cannot detain the marquis any longer."

"Not at all, Miss St. John," Miss Meadforth said, scooting over to make room for Cassandra. "Anything we can do to speed the marquis on his way to the King's palace."

"Indeed, we would not delay you, Linirk," Smedgewood agreed, opening the landau door and offering a hand to Cassandra.

Damned obliging, these English, Ramsay groused silently.

"Just so," Cassandra said, seating herself next to Miss Meadforth. "See, my lord, you need not trouble yourself over me gadding about London unescorted. We owe Smedgewood a word of thanks, do we not?"

"Indeed," Ramsay muttered between gritted teeth. There was nothing to do but end this farce. He would confront her again, in another time and another place. "So good of you to see Miss St. John safely to her cousin's house, Smedgewood."

"My pleasure," the young buck said, resuming his seat and speaking a command to his driver.

As their carriage pulled away, Cassandra offered Ramsay a small wave. "Good-bye, my lord."

Ramsay did not miss the finality of her words and it made him coolly angry. She might think this was over, but he knew better. Staying one step ahead of her was not going to be easy, especially now that she knew who he was.

He tipped his tall black hat. "Until we meet again, Miss St. John."

* * *

"Let me make certain I understand what you've just told me."
Tony Derrington spoke with calm deliberation—as if he
thought Cassie was mad. "You have been seeing the Marquis
of Linirk over the past two weeks and Uncle Davis and Aunt
Susanna don't know anything about it?"

"Yes, I'm afraid that's what it amounts to," Cassie conceded, feeling like a witless child. "I fell for everything that
Ravencliff—or Linirk—or whoever he is—told me."

After Linirk's revelation she'd been too upset to go straight
home, and the fact that Smedgewood was Tony's friend was
too fortuitous to ignore. She'd found herself on Seacombe
House's doorstep asking if Tony was at home. Without Charlotte to talk to, he'd become her confidant. Fortunately he was
in the house, and thankfully, Aunt Dorian was out. Cassandra
had no wish to confess her foolishness to her aunt. But she'd
been unable to hide her agitation from Tony.

The moment he'd finished ordering tea, she'd poured out
her entire confession without preamble.

"But, you see, I didn't know Ravencliff is Linirk until
today," Cassie repeated, her anger and humiliation no longer
governable. She paced back and forth before the French doors
of the Derrington family parlor. "I can't believe what an idiot
I have been. Poor Mama and Papa had been wondering where
Linirk was, and all the time the bloody scoundrel has been
deceiving me."

"Exactly when did all this happen?" Tony lounged back on
the settee facing the view of the garden. Because he'd not been
out of the house yet, he wore only a white shirt with his cravat
half-tied and fitted nankeen stirruped trousers pulled tight over
his black boots. "When did he save you from the footpads?"

"The day that Dudley cried off." Cassie still remembered
her first meeting with Ravencliff clearly. The sight of him
coming out of nowhere to her rescue had been miraculous.
He'd been wonderful: tall, calm, quick, and strong. His fair

good looks accented by his black garb made him look like the archangel Michael swooping down on Satan's army. Just the memory made her heart beat faster. "I was on my way home and not being very observant. Thinking about Dudley, I suppose. Suddenly there they were. The old woman. Then the man came up behind me. Then Ravencliff came out of nowhere and sent them packing."

"And he introduced himself as Ravencliff?" Tony asked, his broad, handsome brow furrowed.

"Yes, he told me today that is one of his lesser titles." Cassie glanced down at Tophet, who'd stationed himself at doors open to the garden where he could watch the birds at the birdbath. "You were his dog, weren't you, Tophet? That's why you never barked at him when you growl at nearly every other man in my life."

Tophet looked up at her and wagged his tail.

"Botheration, Tony, what else do you think Rav—Linirk has lied about?"

"Precisely my next question." Tony frowned deeply. "But if it's any consolation, Ravencliff Court is where Linirk is known to spend most of his time. It's on the northern border. So he was truthful about that."

"Small comfort," Cassie said, staring out at Aunt Dorian's garden, without seeing the beauty of a single rose or shrub. She could hardly believe what was happening to her life. First Charlotte became betrothed to a Scotsman and would soon be married and gone from the St. John townhouse. Then Dudley cried off as if he'd just discovered she had leprosy. Now this. Her hero was a villain.

"So when Ramsay Forbes decided that his other attempts to acquire Glen Gray failed, he came to London and just happened along in time to save one of Davis St. John's daughters from footpads," Tony recounted thoughtfully. "Damned good luck, don't you think?"

"What are you saying?" Cassie threw herself down in one of the chairs by the window. Her aching heart pounded in her ears. "Are you suggesting that the footpads were no coincidence?"

Tony shrugged. "We're dealing with the man who arranged for Connor to be kidnapped. What do you think?"

Cassie frowned, remembering how miraculously the hackney carriage had materialized out of nowhere. She groaned. "I think you might be right."

Tony shook his head and a lock of his dark hair fell across his brow. "Just as I suspect that it wasn't coincidence that he visited you at the Newmarket races when I went to the betting circle. But how did he know that you wouldn't tell anyone about meeting the Baron of Ravencliff?"

The bottom spiraled out of Cassie stomach and she groaned. Had Ravencliff set that up, too? She felt like an inch-tall fool and her head began to ache as much as her heart. "He said we should keep our meetings secret."

"Secret?" Tony repeated with a tone of disbelief in his voice. "You allowed him to talk you into that?"

"I know," Cassie said as another wave of shame swept over her. "I can't believe I've been such a peagoose. He said our meetings were too special to share with others. I thought so, too. I thought it wonderfully romantic and mature. I thought I was having my own special tryst while Charlotte is getting all the attention as a bride-to-be."

A knock on the door announced the arrival of the maid with their tea. As soon as she'd placed the tray on the table and left, Cassie set about pouring. The steaming fragrance of the hot brew and the familiar tea ritual eased her despair a bit.

Tony sat up and leaned forward, facing her across the tea table with his elbows on his knees. "You know, through all of this, the little adventure at the brothel where we found Connor and all, I don't think I've ever really heard what the story is behind Glen Gray."

"Charlotte told me the story that Connor told her," Cassie said, dropping a lump of sugar in each teacup. "I don't recall all the details, but it seems that the glen was part of the dowry of a Forbes girl who married into the McKensie clan. She was carried off by pirates soon after the wedding, something like in the first six months, and there were no children. The Forbes clan asked for the return of the dowry property, but the McKensie groom was so grieved he wouldn't hear of returning it. He thought she might still return or something like that. That's how it started. Later there was an arranged battle to settle the matter, but the McKensies claimed the Forbeses cheated or some such thing, so nothing was ever resolved.''

"After the battle of Culloden I suppose the land was confiscated from the McKensies," Tony finished.

"Yes, I believe that was the way of it," Cassie said. "Then somehow last year Papa unwittingly acquired it as part of his factory and land purchases. Next thing you know we have Connor McKensie on our doorstep and now Linirk too."

Tony frowned. "Cassie, how many times have you seen Linirk?"

"I only set out to meet him once that day in Regent's Park," she said, thinking how he'd given her a pink rose to apologize for Dudley's bad behavior. She still had it, pressed deep in the pages of her lady's comportment book. That day she'd thought Ravencliff—Linirk—was the most gallant man she'd ever met. "Other than that, we happened upon each other in the street."

"Are you sure you happened upon each other?" Tony peered at her over the tea tray. "Either way, how many times have you met with Linirk?"

"Coincidental and intended?" Cassie tried to sum it up in her head. "Four times, I guess."

"Tell me about each one," Tony urged, sipping his tea.

"Yes, of course," Cassie said, forgetting her teacup. "The first time after the footpads was at the races. Then I went riding to find him in Regent's Park. Then yesterday I was shopping in Henrietta Street, then today at the bookstore we . . ." Cassie allowed her words to trail off as she saw skepticism cross her cousin's face.

"Do you think the Marquis of Linirk regularly does business

in Henrietta Street?'' Tony asked with a grin. "Primarily drapery and millinery shops line the way. I can't image it, unless he is buying clothes for a lady.''

Cassie groaned once more and buried her face in her hands. She'd been so intrigued with the man she'd not thought of that herself.

"Where did you go?'' Tony said. "What did you do?''

"It was all harmless enough,'' Cassie said, not even wanting to remember the intimacies she allowed Ravencliff on the barge. She certainly was not going to describe for Tony how passionate Ravencliff's kisses were and how tender his caresses. The lying cad. "The first time we went to the zoological gardens. Today we went for a drive in the park. He took me to see some puppies at an inn upriver. It was perfectly harmless.''

"But you had no chaperone or servant with you?'' Tony asked. "No one saw you together?''

"No one we know,'' Cassie said. The sweet treasured moments on the barge in Ravencliff's arms began to take on a more sinister hue. She closed her eyes against the dark thoughts, but they came anyway. There was no denying the full implications of what Ravencliff had been up to. He had kissed her and held her in his arms because she was Cassandra St. John, not because he cared about her. He'd swept her off her feet because he thought that he could gain Glen Gray, or at least could gain influence over Papa, by seducing her.

"Cassie, you must be honest with me.'' Tony set aside his cup, his face grim, and the first sign of anger gleaming in his violet eyes. "Did Linirk force himself on you improperly? Out with it. If anything happened—if he so much as put a stray hand on you, I'll call him out.''

"No, Tony,'' Cassie protested, horrified at the thought of Tony and Ravencliff facing each other at twenty paces with pistols. "Nothing like that happened.''

Tony raised his chin and tilted a skeptical gaze at her. "Are you certain? You can tell me the truth, Cassie. Don't protect the scoundrel. He's caused enough trouble to deserve to be called out anyway."

"I swear, other than deceiving me, he did not force anything improper on me," Cassie said, gazing back at Tony with as steady a gaze as she could manage. She spoke the truth, she told herself. Ravencliff had forced none of his attention on her. She'd eagerly accepted every kiss and caress.

Apparently satisfied with her answer, Tony sat back again. "What are you going to do?"

"Well, I'm not going to see his lordship again," Cassie vowed.

"That may not be as easy as you think," Tony said. "He must be having you followed. How else would he so conveniently find you in the street or the bookshop?"

"Of course," Cassie said. "That was how he'd always managed to turn up at the most propitious moments."

The thought frightened and angered Cassie. She remembered her tea and sipped from it again, hoping the steaming brew would comfort her. It didn't.

"And he is not likely to give up until he gets what he wants," Tony added. "What are you going to tell Uncle Davis?"

"Tell Papa? I'm going to tell him nothing," Cassie said, the image of Linirk sitting in his carriage in the park still clear in her mind. "I don't see why Papa needs to know anything about this. He and Mama have enough on their mind as it is with the wedding. I will just have to be certain that I go nowhere unescorted. I made my feelings clear to Rav— I'll never remember to call him Linirk. But I told him what I thought in the park. Surely he will take his planning and plotting elsewhere. He must know now that he'll win no help from me."

"This is the man who had Connor McKensie kidnapped to keep him from fighting in a prizefight," Tony reminded her. "There is this rumor, that he ruined another man, some old family friend of the Forbeses Linirk took a dislike to. Totally wiped out the man's fortune so that he died in poverty and in exile in Italy. It would seem the marquis is a very determined man."

Cassie heard the truth in Tony's words. "Just what would you have me do? Surely he wouldn't be foolish enough to try another kidnapping."

"I don't think so either," Tony said, "but I think you should be certain that you never go out without me or your mother or sister for your escort. Someone who will serve as a witness which Linirk would not care to have at a seduction attempt."

The thought made Cassie purse her lips, then she took another sip of tea. Now, there was a new mystery. "Tony, why do you think he confessed?"

Her cousin shrugged. "Who knows? Just consider yourself lucky that he did."

"Of course I'm glad," Cassie said, considering herself a lucky fool. "I'm so grateful to know the truth. I was a fool once, but I won't be one again."

CHAPTER TEN

"Miss Cassandra, your father and mother wish to see you in the study immediately," Horton said the moment he opened the door to Cassie and Tony.

They hadn't even stepped across the threshold into the hallway. A bad sign, Cassie thought. Horton, who never smiled, looked absolutely grim. She exchanged a quick glance with her cousin, then led the way into the hall.

"Did Papa say what this is about?" Cassie asked, handing Tophet's leash and her bonnet to the butler. The dog tolerated the servant only because he fed him.

"No, miss," Horton said, avoiding her gaze. He'd been the St. Johns' butler since Papa was a boy and Cassie knew Horton always knew what was going on in the house. He made it his business to know. In the past he'd often been a subtle ally in her and her sister's escapades, but today he offered no help. His aloofness unsettled Cassie.

When she glanced at Tony again, her cousin shrugged. "Do you want me to wait for you?"

"No, it's probably something to do about the wedding," Cassie said, certain nothing could be worse than the scene in the park she had just suffered through with Linirk. "You'd be bored. Off you go to your club or your tailor. I feel quite fortified. Thank you for your advice."

Tony offered a mock bow. "My pleasure. Call on me when you need an escort."

Cassie threw her arms around him. "Never fear, I shall."

"Cassandra, please grace us with your presence without delay," came Papa's voice from the study, raised in an impatient manner Cassie had never heard before. Charlotte's wedding to Connor McKensie was wearing on his composure.

"Coming, Papa." She brushed a quick kiss of gratitude on Tony's cheek, certain that the secret of her meetings with Linirk was safe. Then she hastened toward the sound of Papa's voice.

The study seemed positively crowded when she entered. She surveyed the room as she heard Horton close the door softly behind her. Her father stood behind his desk with Mama on his right, seated in a chair, and Erik Drummond stood ill-at-ease on Papa's left. Cassie nodded a greeting to the Scotsman, wondering why Connor's kinsman was present.

"We have another guest as well," Papa said, gesturing in the direction of the fireplace.

Cassie turned to see Linirk step forward.

"You!" she blurted, even as her heart fluttered at the sight of the man who yesterday had held her in his arms and kissed her; even before she realized that Mama, Papa, and Erik were watching with great interest. "What on earth are you doing here? I thought I made myself very pl—"

"Cassandra." Linirk cut her off. His gaze caught hers and refused to release her. In his eyes there was something of a warning.

Cassie took a deep breath and struggled to hold on to her composure.

Linirk offered her a small bow, his movement graceful, powerful, and darkly handsome as always. "It seems we've been found out."

"Found out?" Cassie choked out, so astonished by his smooth words she was nearly speechless.

"I came to tell your father about us, but Drummond arrived to tell him before I could," Linirk said, his emerald-green gaze still holding Cassie's.

"I saw ye at the St. James Street stairs yesterday," Erik said with a righteous shake of his head. Hatred filled his voice. "Connor and I agreed I should come here and report the fact this morning. You have a lot of gall, Linirk, you insolent knave, deceiving this family just because ye hate the McKensies."

Mama gasped softly.

"Drummond, please, there are ladies present," Papa said, his voice edged with strain. "We appreciate your concern, but kindly allow me to handle this."

"Aye, I will," Erik said, glowering across the room at Linirk. "But be warned, sir, the marquis is slippery as an eel."

"So it is true, then, Cassie?" Papa asked. "What Erik came here to tell us?"

Cassie tore her gaze away from Linirk to look from Papa to Mama, her dear, loving parents who had been so patient with her games and escapades. She owed them better than this kind of embarrassment.

Mama leaned forward, clasping her hands in her lap. "Have you and the marquis been meeting secretly these past few weeks?"

Cassie balled her hands into fists and bit out the words she loathed to say. "Yes, it is true, Mama."

"You have raised an honorable daughter, Mrs. St. John," Linirk said, stepping toward Cassie and reaching for her hand.

Defiantly she tucked her fists deeper into the folds of her skirt and stared at him. "Why are you doing this?" she whispered to him.

"Because it is not over between us, princess," Linirk replied softly, so that only she could hear. Then, speaking more loudly, he added, "Of course, I explained to your father that I misled you at first, after I rescued you from the footpads. Your father has been very understanding.''

Cassie glanced at Papa to read his reaction.

"We understand that you must have been grateful for the marquis's assistance," Papa said.

"Yes, I was." Cassie frowned at Linirk, sending him a message of reproach. How dare he come to her parents and spill what he'd told her was a secret between them. *And did you tell them how you hired the footpads to attack me?* she wanted to demand. Apparently untroubled, Ramsay smiled back politely as if he was performing some perfectly acceptable, honorable duty.

"And he did not reveal his true name to you?" Papa continued, clearly wanting to believe that she was a pawn of the marquis as indeed she had been.

"No, he did not," Cassie said. "He did not reveal himself to me until—"

Cassie stopped, unwilling to admit that she'd allowed Linirk to lure her from the bookshop, away from her maid, and into his carriage that very morning. Mama and Papa would never approve of such behavior—especially where gentlemen were concerned. She glimpsed a knowing quirk of Linirk's brow. The cad was enjoying her dilemma.

Cassie glowered at him with as much ferocity as she could summon. "His lordship did not reveal himself to me until recently. I was shocked and disappointed by his deception."

"My behavior was unforgivable," Linirk agreed, hanging his head ever so briefly as if he were truly ashamed.

What a sham the man is, Cassie fumed.

"I'm displeased with your actions myself, my lord," Papa said, folding his arms across his chest as he stood behind his massive desk. "Have you an explanation?"

"My only defense is that at the time of the attack, Miss St. John's well-being was my primary concern." Linirk turned to Papa and spoke with the utmost reason and humility.

Cassie smoldered in silence.

"I extend my most profound apologies for any harm done," Linirk added, his fair brow furrowed in sorrow. Anyone who'd never met the man would believe his regret was genuine. "I did not want to distress Miss St. John, given the complicated relations between our families. Once the misrepresentation had been made, I confess it was far too easy to let it stand."

Cassie almost gave an unladylike snort.

"Aside from the fact that I'm deeply troubled that you did not notify me of the attack on my daughter," Papa said, his expression still grave, "you have truly offended my daughter, Linirk. You deceived her. It is for her to accept or reject your apology. Cassandra, are you satisfied with Linirk's confession?"

"Accept an apology, my eye," Erik snapped, his agitation evident in the sway of his kilt and the low key of his voice. "Yer a-tryin' to weasel yer way into the family because ye hope to gain Glen Gray. Mr. St. John, I think ye should order him from yer house and tell him to never darken yer door again."

"Thank you, Mr. Drummond," Papa said, a polite strain returning to his voice. "I understand what you are saying. Unfortunately, I feel this is Cassandra's decision."

Cassie studied Linirk, searching his eyes for a glimpse of the truth, for a glimpse of the man she'd known as Ravencliff, the solitary baron from the north with whom she'd felt safe. With whom she'd laughed and sung. With whom she'd discovered a passion in herself that no one else had awakened.

But the man who had betrayed her gazed back, wearing a polite, unreadable smile. His face, his eyes, told her nothing. Any lingering trust she had in him had vanished during their ride in the park. There wasn't a soul in the room who didn't believe that he'd made her acquaintance because he wanted Glen Gray.

Disappointed, Cassie glanced away. Whatever she felt about Linirk, she could not allow him to threaten her family's happi-

ness or security through her folly. "I am satisfied with the
marquis's apology."

Silently she prayed her acceptance would send him on his
way. This was the man who had arranged for Connor's kidnapping. Papa knew little of those details and she wasn't going to
be the one to tell him. But the sooner Linirk was out of the
house, the sooner she would feel that her family was safe.
"Your lordship may leave here with an unburdened conscience."

"I'm so relieved to hear that my apology is accepted." He
allowed her to take him by the arm. She led him from the
hearth toward the door, but his steps lagged.

In the center of the room, he stopped and put his hand over
hers, and turned to smile at Papa, the same bloody-unreadable
smile he'd offered her. No amount of gentle tugging would
budge him. His feet were firmly planted on the Oriental carpet.
"My conscience is indeed freed of its burden, of the shadow cast
by the knowledge that I had deceived you and your daughter."

"Good," Cassie said, tugging once more, less concerned
about appearances this time. "Then you may leave and trouble
yourself over it no more, my lord."

"But you see, my purpose in being here is twofold," Linirk
continued, his voice oily-smooth. "I also wish to clear the way
for Cassandra and I to put this unhappy episode behind us. I
wish to ask permission to pay suit to your daughter, St. John."

Cassie's mouth dropped open.

"Why, you foul—" Erik would have charged across the
room if Papa had not put out a hand to block him.

"Linirk." Papa braced his hands on the desktop and leaned
across the surface, his scowl deepening. The temperature in
the room dropped from cool to freezing. Cassie shivered. She
tried to pull away from Linirk, but he would not release her.

"Don't play games with me, Linirk," Papa said. "You've
made your apology and my daughter has seen fit to accept it.
My daughters are not and will never be pawns in the McKensie-

Forbes feud nor in the dealings between you and me. If you think I'm going to offer you—''

''Davis,'' Mama interrupted, rising from her chair, warning Papa of something Cassie didn't understand. ''Please don't bring up the marquis's past offers and your ambitions now.''

Papa stopped, his gaze flickering in Cassie's direction. She felt Linirk's gaze slide over her, also. Then the two men glared at each other once again, something passing silently between the two of them.

''Of course, I expect nothing,'' Linirk said, finishing Papa's sentence as smoothly as if it had been his own. ''We are both gentlemen of principle. I made you an offer for Glen Gray and you turned it down. No grudges held.''

Cassie stared open-mouthed at her father. What offer? What had Papa refused? Something was going on here she did not understand. She'd never heard Papa mention an offer from Linirk.

''Of course, no grudges,'' Papa said, appearing relieved his secret was not revealed. ''I'm glad you understand.''

''Not at all, sir,'' Linirk said, his voice full of sympathy, his hand continuing to imprison Cassie's hand on his arm.

Unseen by anyone else in the room, his thumb stroked Cassie's palm, sending shivers of awareness through her. Her face grew warm and she studied the floor, hardly seeing the intricate design woven in the rug. The seductive pressure of his thumb stirred all the reactions that their intimacies on the river had brought her. He had destroyed her trust in him, but her body's reaction to him remained strong as ever.

''Very well, then,'' Papa declared. ''You will withdraw your request, my lord.''

Oh yes, please, Cassie wanted to cry in his ear, though she knew in her heart that Linirk would not back down. He'd already laid his cards on the table exactly the way he wanted them.

''But you allowed Connor McKensie to pay suit to your daughter Charlotte,'' Linirk said, a tone of injury in his voice.

"And you would deny me? How unfair it would look to Society—even to the King—if I am refused the same privilege."

"Don't threaten me, Linirk," Papa said. "I was never pleased about Kinleith's suit. And as I recall, he came with a formal recommendation from my sister."

"I see." Linirk released Cassie's hand long enough to rub his chin in reflection. "I, too, could provide recommendations, if that would satisfy you, St. John. I would prefer not to trouble the King over this. But how about a letter from, say, the Duke and Duchess of Deander?"

This time it was Erik who snorted. The old duke and duchess ranked among the King's favorites.

"It was more than recommendations that influenced Charlotte's father and me, my lord," Mama added. "We allowed our daughter to follow her heart."

"As generous and loving parents would." Linirk bowed to Mama, then suddenly turned to Cassie. "But don't you think Cassandra should have the same choice you allowed her sister?"

Cassie stared up at him, so cold in her fear and awareness of his power and potency that she shivered once more.

"That's enough, Linirk," Papa said, standing upright, away from his desk. "I'm not playing your game. I believe you were on your way—"

"Wait, Papa." Cassie gazed up at Linirk—the golden-maned lion in gentleman's clothing who dared to walk into the sheep-fold, her family's home. She shivered again. She was not frightened of him for herself, but for Papa and Mama. For Charlotte and Connor. It was her fault that he was standing in Papa's study forcing this situation on them. If she'd been more observant, if she'd been more cautious, she never would have allowed Linirk's deception to go beyond their first meeting—or the second—because she never would have fallen for his lies.

"What will it be, Cassandra?" Linirk asked, eyeing her closely. This time Cassie glimpsed the calculation in his eyes. "Will you agree to my suit?"

Cassie took a deep breath and tested the waters. "The Little Season is about to begin."

"That's true," Mama murmured distractedly. "But it does make for an awkward situation, you must admit, my lord. You calling on Cassie with the tension between you and Kinleith."

" 'Awkward' is a polite term," Erik said. " 'Tis pure folly."

"I vow I shall be a gentleman, Mrs. St. John," Linirk said, bowing ever so slightly in Mama's direction. Then he leaned in Cassie's direction, imprisoning her hand once more. "What will it be, Cassandra?"

Cassie gazed back at him, realizing that—whether he understood it or not—he was offering her the perfect way to know exactly what he was up to, just what Papa and Mama had to be concerned about. She still remembered clearly what she'd overheard them say of Linirk when she'd last heard them talking of the wedding. *"Better to know what he's doing."*

She'd be a fool to refuse to take advantage of the opportunity, for her family's sake, for Charlotte's sake.

The wedding was only weeks away. All she had to do was allow Linirk to pay her court through the Little Season or until Charlotte and Connor were safely wed. She could do this. She could. She had the strength. She had the courage. She forced a smile to her lips and gazed back at Linirk as bravely as she could manage. For his deceit he deserved no better. "I should be honored by your suit, my lord."

An outraged bellow echoed through the study. Everyone turned toward Erik. The Scotsman's face glowed red with anger. He pounded his fist on the corner of Papa's desk, then pointed a menacing finger at Linirk. "Connor McKensie wonna be pleased with this bloody news. Nay, not at all. Watch yer step, Linirk. Watch yer bloody step."

"That's enough, Drummond," Papa snapped. "I won't have any more threats made in my house."

But Erik was already stomping toward the door.

Cassie held her breath until the Scotsman had slammed his way out of the study. Linirk squeezed her hand gently.

"Ignore him," he murmured so only she could hear. "I am very pleased, Princess."

But Cassie was too numbed by what she'd just done to smile back at him. She took no pleasure in his satisfaction. She could not ignore the Scotsman's reaction because she knew that Charlotte was going to be just as outraged. Charlotte would never understand, no matter how carefully Cassie explained it to her twin sister. If Charlotte knew the truth, she would tell Mama and Papa. If Mama and Papa knew Cassie was plotting, they would forbid her to see Ramsay. And she knew she must see him again—for Papa's sake, for Charlotte's sake. For some mysterious reason she didn't understand, she would allow the Marquis of Linirk to court her.

"I'd like to know why ye look so pleased with yerself," Graham demanded the moment Ramsay had finished recounting what had happened in Davis St. John's study. They were seated in Graham's favorite tavern, The Foxed Goose. The aging barmaid had just served their drinks and taken their order for the meal of the day. "Ye just went a-grovelin' to a glorified merchant and gave away our whole plan."

"I did not go groveling," Ramsay said, sorry he'd told his foster brother the whole story. Until Graham had started complaining, he'd been in a celebratory mood. The confrontation had been a success as far as he was concerned.. He couldn't exactly explain why he felt so elated. He just knew that he'd revealed his true identity to Cassandra St. John and she was still speaking to him. What's more, she and that stubborn father of hers had agreed to allow him to call on her. "I do not grovel for anyone. I simply headed off a nasty turn of events. It might have turned out much worse, Graham. Much worse."

A haze of tobacco smoke hung in the crowded taproom, and the patrons, an affluent lot of tradesmen and merchants, were noisily engaged in their own conversations. A game of darts was in progress on the far side of the room and a terrier sat at his master's foot near the serving counter. Amid the babel, neither Ramsay or Graham were concerned about being overheard.

"I'd like to know how it could be worse," Graham said. "We've gained nothing."

"We've lost nothing, either," Ramsay said, aware that Graham never would have the vision to understand how things had changed; the plans had to be modified. Nearly everything about their original plan had gone awry and he needed desperately to reconsider his next course. One reason for their predicament was Graham's own oversight. "We might have lost everything if I'd not gone to St. John's Mayfair home. Our old friend Erik Drummond was there when I arrived. He'd already told St. John that he'd seen Cassandra and me together. Would you happen to know anything about that?"

Graham's face went slack with shock and he banged his mug down on the table. "Nay, I didna know. You mean that Drummond, the McKensie weasel, has been prowling the streets and I didna sense it? Nay. 'Tis impossible. I'd have seen him."

"Apparently you did not," Ramsay said, unable to hide his irritation. "You should have been keeping a keener eye open for the McKensie and Drummond. He said he saw us at the St. James Street stairs."

Graham frowned. "But how? I was there. I saw no one."

"His details were too exact to be speculation," Ramsay said. "I count on you to be aware of anyone following us."

"Aye, I promise I'll not miss that scoundrel again," Graham growled, his face twisted in anger and humiliation.

"Once Drummond had told all he knew," Ramsay continued, "Cassandra came in. If I'd not told her in the park, she would have learned it from him. And how do you think she would have reacted if she learned the truth about my identity from Drummond before she heard it from me?"

"She's but a common lass," Graham said with a dismissive shrug. "She'd fuss, but she canna snub a man of your rank. She canna snub a marquis."

"She may be a common lass, but her aunt is a countess, her uncle is the Earl of Seacombe and a war hero, and her father is a very rich man," Ramsay said, once again growing irritated with Graham's narrow vision. "Nearly as rich as I am. Don't underestimate Miss Cassandra St. John. She will snub me if she chooses to. This is not Scotland, Graham, we're not in the Highlands. My rank gives me advantages, but not absolute power."

Graham frowned rebelliously, like a rebuked adolescent. "But why not just play the daughter card, then? Humiliate St. John with the fact that you've been seeing his daughter without proper chaperone and be done with it?"

"Because Cassandra could claim, and rightly so, that she did not know who I was," Ramsay explained patiently. "And because the matter at this point is my word against hers. If I pressed the matter, I would look ungentlemanly and become the villain."

"That never bothered ye before," Graham said, with a surprised lift of his bushy brows.

"What's the point if I don't get what I want? We are still a long ways from getting Glen Gray."

"So how does calling on Miss St. John make us any closer to our goal?" Graham growled, raising his mug of ale to his lips.

"Because it almost puts me back in control of the situation," Ramsay said, sensing some dark anger in his foster brother that he didn't understand. But he forged ahead with his explanation. "I underestimated the man. It's not knighthood that is his weakness. I don't know why I didn't discover this before. 'Tis his daughters. And if I'm right, Cassandra is his favorite."

"Why?" Graham exclaimed, staring into his mug. "The lass is willful, contrary, and altogether too intelligent for a woman."

"Perhaps," Ramsay admitted. "When the time comes, St. John will do whatever is necessary to protect her. He has already lost one daughter to a Scotsman. I don't think he is going to allow that to happen again."

"So how is what yer doin' now different from before?" Graham asked, his brows drawn together in perplexity.

"I will be courting Miss St. John in a more conventional fashion," Ramsay said, realizing as he spoke the disadvantage of courting Cassandra formally. All the sweet, playful secrecy of their meetings would be gone. The sense that everything that happened between them was his alone to treasure would disappear. Their secret games, once unsullied by the opinion of the outside world, were over. He could hardly play Sir Walter Raleigh to her Queen Elizabeth at a formal dinner party.

"But we have a new problem," Ramsay said, the full implication of what rights he had won coming down on him.

"And what might that be?"

"Cassandra knows the truth," Ramsay said, surprised how glad he was that he need hide nothing more from her. Yet the truth had robbed him of something important. "She no longer trusts me."

"How important is that?"

"It is vital to our plan," Ramsay said, forgetting that his port glass was empty. "How do I regain her confidence? What string do I pull? What price must I pay?"

"Glen Gray is worth any price," Graham said, slamming his mug down on the table. "Give her anything. Shower her with gifts. Take her to the best places. Glen Gray is worth any price. Any sacrifice. Donna ye forget that."

"I have not forgotten," Ramsay said, remembering the mixture of fear and anger in Cassandra's eyes when she gazed up at him in her father's study. She would be harder than ever to win over now. Ramsay's elation began to evaporate. Maybe he hadn't gained as much as he'd first thought.

CHAPTER ELEVEN

Ravencliff brushed a trail of feathery kisses down Cassie's throat. She moaned softly and trembled. The warmth of his lips melted through her skin. The sweet heat seeped into her bones, spread along the core of her limbs, then coalesced into a pool in her middle. Cassie stretched beneath the bedcovers and whispered his name. "Ravencliff." No matter what anyone said, he would always be her Ravencliff.

He made no reply, but moved down her body, kissing her through the thin fabric of her nightrail. One hand spread across her hip. The other held her hand, stroking her palm. The heat inside Cassie grew. Pleasure swelled into a deep aching thrill that thirsted for more of his caresses. She touched the fevered skin of her throat where his kisses still burned. The pressure of his thumb branded her palm. She surrendered to the pleasure, allowing it to sweep her toward some wonderful destination.

"Cassandra, have you taken leave of your senses?" demanded Charlotte's voice from far away.

Cassie struggled against the blanket of lethargy Ravencliff's kisses had layered over her. A cruel light fell across her face. She whimpered and shielded her eyes against it.

"Get up," Charlotte said, closer now. Her voice was sharp and unfamiliar. "We're going to talk about what you've done and we're going to talk about this now."

With a gasp, Cassie surfaced from her dream and squinted up at her sister looming over her bed. A lighted candle rested on the bedside table. The door connecting Cassie's bedchamber with Charlotte's stood open, lamplight streaming into Cassie darkened room. She bolted up, her dream shattered and her heart thudding in her ears.

"What time is it?" Cassie tugged at her nightgown, which was sticking to her damp body. She hadn't seen her sister since breakfast when Charlotte had asked Cassie to pick up the books at Lackington's. As her eyes grew accustomed to the light she saw Charlotte's jewelry glitter with the rapid rise and fall of her breasts. The plumes in her hair trembled. She and Connor had spent the evening at a party. Despite the lateness of the hour, she still looked fresh and glamorous, ready to be entertained as the Season's bride-to-be.

"Time for us to talk," Charlotte said, without sitting on the edge of the bed as she customarily did. "Erik told us what you agreed to, and Papa confirmed it. Linirk is going to pay you suit? How could you?"

Cassie tried to rub the sleep from her eyes. With everything that had happened that day—Linirk's betrayal, the hidden truths she and Tony had uncovered, the confrontation in Papa's study—the day had seemed interminably long. Cassie was exhausted.

Although she'd known this encounter was coming, she'd hoped it could be postponed until morning when she was rested. She wanted to have her wits about her. "Charlotte, don't take this so badly."

"Badly?" Charlotte exclaimed, throwing her hands into the air. "How am I supposed to take it?"

Charlotte had changed over the past three months since she'd first met Connor and begun to make changes in her life. Though her happiness pleased Cassie, she couldn't help but regret that they were being torn apart.

Cassie had always felt protective of her younger sister, though Cassie was only twenty minutes older. Still, Charlotte had always been the gentler of the two, the more vulnerable, less able to fend for herself. Cassie had always sheltered Charlotte, and she would go on sheltering her, no matter who came between them.

" 'Tis difficult to explain," Cassie said, knowing her sister would never quite understand or approve. Knowing that if she tried to explain how this was her way of spying on Ramsay until the wedding was over, Charlotte would carry the tale to Mama and Papa. She'd always tended to be a Goody Two-shoes. If Mama and Papa thought Cassie was plotting and did not truly welcome Linirk's suit, they would forbid her to see him.

"Please give it your best effort," Charlotte said, bracing her fists on her hips. "Tell me Linirk has threatened you with bodily harm or something else that makes sense."

"Of course Linirk has not threatened me," Cassie protested, glimpses of the sensual dream flashing through her mind. "Linirk is a gentleman. Didn't Papa tell you how the marquis was of great service to me when I was accosted on the street? I'm flattered that he is willing to be my escort through the Little Season."

"Cassie, he probably hired the footpads himself to win your trust," Charlotte said, leaning across the bed to make her point.

Cassie winced, mortified and vexed. Charlotte had seen through Linirk without even having to think about it. But Cassie could not admit that now. "We don't know any such thing for certain."

"Even so, have you forgotten that this was the man who had Connor kidnapped and held prisoner in a brothel cellar?" Charlotte paced around to the foot of the bed. "You were there, weren't you? I thought it was my twin sister who posed with me as twins fresh from the country who willingly showed their ankles to Molly.''

"I was there," Cassie muttered, remembering the escapade as if it had happened only a week ago, although three months had passed. She and Charlotte had posed as naive country girls looking for work in London as they searched for Connor. "But you must admit, Charlotte, no one was hurt. Connor fought his fight. Tony was arrested for starting a brawl, but Uncle Nicholas was able to settle the matter with the magistrate. Only Harby went to jail and Lord knows what horrible things that man had been up to. But there was never any direct link to Linirk.''

"You don't think that Linirk would have ordered murder if it had suited his purposes?" Charlotte demanded. "Are you siding with that blackguard?''

"Of course not." Cassie waved the possibility away. She didn't even want to contemplate Charlotte's accusations against Ravencliff—Linirk.

"Cassie, you met those men, great brutes with fists and clubs in Molly's house of ill repute. You think they would not have committed murder?''

"I can't say," Cassie said, though she knew only too well how deceptive Linirk could be. Manipulation and intrigue she could believe of him, but murder she could not credit.

"There you are, defending him," Charlotte said, her voice full of anger and disbelief. "He is evil. I can't believe you are doing this.''

"Charlotte, there are things you don't understand," Cassie muttered. The embarrassment of having been so foolish as to permit Linirk to win her trust filled Cassie once more. The shame of it—the guilt of liking him despite his deceit—made her determined to make up for her foolishness.

"He is using you, Cassie," Charlotte said, her voice cracking with emotion. "You are nothing more than a puppet to him. And you are going to permit such a man to squire you around as if he'd committed no crime.''

"That is not so," Cassie said, pained by Charlotte's accusation. "I'm no one's puppet and you know it."

"And Papa, he is another mystery," Charlotte said, raising her hands in a gesture of helplessness. "Papa does not like Linirk. I know he doesn't, but now he's prepared to allow you to be seen with him?"

"Because he allowed you to see Connor," Cassie snapped in return. "Why should he deny Linirk the same privilege?"

Charlotte gasped, her exasperation obvious. "How can you even speak of Connor and Linirk in the same breath?"

"Because you are letting them come between us," Cassie said, trying to remind her sister of what they were losing.

"No, *you* are allowing it." Charlotte grew still, sober, and more serious than she'd appeared since she'd come into Cassie's room. "I can forgive Papa misunderstanding what Linirk is up to. He doesn't know the marquis like we do. Papa doesn't know the details of Connor's kidnapping. But you do, Cassandra. You know exactly what Linirk is. You know he is using you as a pawn against your family and against Connor and me. *You,* I cannot forgive."

Her sister's words wounded Cassie, but she hid her pain. She dare not tell Charlotte the truth, for that would surely bring an end to her plan. "You just don't understand. Linirk has proven himself of service to me and he has been good company and I intend to see him. He gave me Tophet and has entertained me in a considerate manner. Connor and you have come to no great harm. So I see no reason to turn my back on the marquis."

Charlotte stared at Cassie as if she was suddenly gazing at a stranger instead of her twin sister.

"I can't believe you are doing this," Charlotte repeated, shaking her head with a frown of regret on her face. "I thought we had promised each other that we were going to stay close no matter what the men in our lives did."

"That was before Dudley cried off," Cassie pointed out, aware of the sour twist of her mouth.

"And that has changed everything for you?" Charlotte asked.

"Yes, in many ways," Cassie said, sorry to admit a truth that she herself had just discovered. That her life had changed, not because Dudley had cried off, but because she'd met Ravencliff.

Charlotte was silent for a long moment before she said, "We have made our separate choices so we will go our separate ways."

"Only if that is truly necessary," Cassie managed to say, despite the tightness in her throat. But the harshness in Charlotte's face remained unchanged. "If we must, we must."

"Good night, then." Charlotte took up the candle and left the room, closing the door noisily and leaving only darkness behind her.

Suddenly chilled, Cassie slid down under the covers. Her pillow seemed lumpy. She beat it into submission, then lay back, closing her eyes tight in hopes of falling asleep again. But sleep did not come. Instead hot tears spilled down her cheeks—tears of pain, humiliation, and anger. What a fool she had been to believe Linirk that day on the street! She should have known something was very strange just from the way Tophet accepted the man. Foolish. Foolish. Foolish.

Now she must pay the price of her folly. If Linirk sought to pay her suit to win his way into her family, then she would fight to keep him out—in her own way. If she must suffer, then he would suffer too. But Mama and Papa need never know. Charlotte and Connor would be safely wed and happily on their way to Kinleith Manor. Cassie would have protected them all. Then someday maybe Charlotte would see how foolish this separation was.

The dark one! The thought popped into Cassie's head with such suddenness that she gave a start. She sat up in bed. Now she knew who the gypsy had referred to in her fortune-telling. Linirk dressed in his black, of course. The dark one! And murder? What murder? Oh yes, she knew the answer to that

now, too. The only murder that was going to be committed
was his, at Cassie's hands. All she had to do was think of a
sufficiently prolonged and painful method with which to finish
him off.

Comforted by that thought, she lay down again, her thoughts
returning to Charlotte. She was going to miss her sister—the
hair brushing, the jewelry trading, the joint shopping ventures,
the shared confidences. A dry sob escaped Cassie. Isolated,
vulnerable, and as alone as she'd ever been in her life, she
curled up in a ball and waited for sleep.

The thought of accepting social invitations did not please Ramsay. He'd never cared to go out in Society. Required too much
hypocrisy by half, to his way of thinking, mouthing all those
polite phrases and bowing to people who hardly deserved such
respect. But he had a price to pay for his deception and he had
little doubt that Cassandra would exact it. So, socialize he
would. Glen Gray was worth any price. Graham's words echoed
in his head.

He'd arrived on the doorstep on Thursday fighting to keep
the smug victorious smile from his face until Cassandra had
seated him in the bloodiest uncomfortable chair in the world.
Who would have thought St. John would have allowed such a
piece of furniture in his drawing room?

Cassandra had greeted him coolly. Across from him, she sat
on the settee, her pretty head bowed over the stack of invitations
which seemed ever so much more interesting than his company.

As if she'd heard his thoughts, Cassandra glanced up at him.
Tendrils of red hair brushed against her neck just behind her
ear. Ramsay remembered the fragrance of her skin and shifted
once again on the delicate chair. He longed for the day when
they had sat side by side on a barge rug.

"Here is an invitation to tea at the Smith-Ryans' and another
for a card party with Mr. Smedgewood," Cassandra said. "Do
you remember Mr. Smedgewood and Miss Meadworth?"

"Yes," Ramsay said, taking a sip of tea from the teacup. "Quite unforgettable, that meeting."

"Hmm," was all that Cassandra said without looking up at him. She flipped through another invitation or two. "A boating party."

"Let's accept that invitation," Ramsay said, suddenly prepared to keep up his end of the battle. "You seem to enjoy activities on the water."

Cassandra flashed a look of outrage at him and he knew she understood exactly what he meant. "I do sometimes. Let's see what else is here, shall we?"

She flipped through several more. "A soirée and a musicale. Oh, look at this. I'd quite forgotten Mama and Aunt Dorian had applied for vouchers to Almack's. What a wonderful opportunity to get you out into Society. We shall go dancing at Almack's."

Ramsay frowned.

Cassandra glanced across at him, hope flickering across her face to be quickly replaced by a studied expression of innocence. "You do like to dance, don't you, my lord?"

"Of course." Ramsay was determined not to be baited by her. "It's just that I'm a bit out of practice."

"That should be no obstacle," Cassandra said. "We can practice here if you like, or at Aunt Dorian's. She will play piano accompaniment for us. We might even waltz."

Ramsay shifted uncomfortably on the infernal chair again.

"Are you comfortable, my lord?" Cassandra asked, the hint of a wicked smile mixed with her wide-eyed, guileless regard.

"No, as a matter of fact, I am not." Ramsay rose from the chair, set his teacup down on the table and strode across to the settee. Cassandra stared at him in surprise as he settled himself next to her. The cushion was considerably softer and the seat deeper. He sat back and faced her. "But this is better."

She did not shrink away, but her eyes narrowed. A glance at the door seemed to satisfy her that her mother was not about to return. "Don't think I don't know what you are up to."

Ramsay quirked a brow at her. "What am I up to?"

"All of this, the footpads, the coincidental meetings, the request to court me, it's all part of your plan to get Glen Gray," Cassandra said, her face hard and tense.

Ramsay studied her earnestness. She stared back at him, her blue eyes dark with indignation. So she had figured out the truth behind the attack in the street. So he was paying for that, too. He would have to remember to arrange things more subtly in the future.

"If you believe that is so," Ramsay began, speaking quietly so that Horton, the butler loitering in the hall, could not overhear. "If you think my proposal is nothing more than a bid for Glen Gray, why did you agree to the arrangement? You could have said no. It was plain your father would have accepted your decision."

"Because I have no intention of allowing you to work behind the scenes," Cassandra said without hesitation. "No more kidnappings."

Ramsay frowned. "I thought I explained that."

"You explained it," Cassandra said, biting off her words crisply, " but I have not forgotten the sorry affair, nor has my sister or Connor. I will not have her happiness threatened. I will not have my family's welfare endangered by a selfish man who cares nothing for others and will do anything to have his way."

Ramsay schooled his expression to hide his surprise and the unexpected pain that Cassandra's words caused him. *Blackguard. Cad. Cruel. Heartless.* He'd been called many things in his time, but he'd prided himself on being unstintingly generous with those loyal to him. Being called selfish hurt.

"So you sacrifice yourself to the villain," he said, unable to keep the bitterness from his voice. He'd intimidated her into accepting his courtship proposal. He knew that, but he'd also wanted to believe that she might have agreed to it because she found something attractive about him.

"I make no sacrifice," she replied, shuffling through the

invitations once more. "*You* proposed this arrangement. I agreed to it so I would know what you are up to. And to put Dudley to shame. *You* are the one calling yourself a villain, not I."

Ramsay opened his mouth to counter her words, but could find nothing to say.

Rapid footsteps rang out on the marble floor of the hall. They both turned their heads toward a welcomed interruption.

Susanna St. John entered the drawing room with a tremulous smile of greeting on her lips. She was a pretty woman with lustrous, amber-colored eyes and shining red hair as bright and rich as her daughters', but wrought in unfashionable curls that suited her. The warmth and acceptance in her smile never failed to put her guests at ease. "I'm so sorry I've been neglecting you, Lord Linirk. I'm afraid I was distracted by a bit of disappointing news that just arrived. But I am so glad you were able to call today. I see that tea has been served and Cassandra has brought out the invitations."

Ramsay rose and bowed. "Yes, we were just considering which ones to accept."

"We're going to dance at Almack's for certain," Cassandra said, busy once again with the elegant cards and envelopes.

"How nice," Mrs. St. John said, an uncertain smile on her face. "Of course, we'll want to be sure it's an appropriate evening."

"Of course." Ramsay knew she meant an evening when Kinleith and Charlotte St. John were not also at Almack's. Then, to appear polite, he added, "I hope your disappointing news concerned nothing of importance."

"No. Well, yes," Mrs. St. John said, settling into a chair on the other side of the settee, a comfortable-looking piece of furniture. "It has to do with my Hellenistic studies."

Cassandra frowned as she poured tea for her mother. "Mama, is this about the exhibit?"

"Unfortunately, yes," Mrs. St. John said, accepting the dish of tea from her daughter. "I'm afraid the Duke of Deander has refused to exhibit his extensive collection of Greek pottery at the Egyptian Hall. It is my pet project, Lord Linirk. The proceeds are to go for more work on the Parthenon. I had such high hopes that this last appeal would persuade him, but alas, I'm afraid even Dorian can't seem to bring the old duke around.''

"I hear he can be an obtuse man," Ramsay said, unwilling to mention that he'd had some personal experience with the man.

"Indeed," Mrs. St. John said. "But let's not dwell on this disappointment. What other invitations have you decided to accept?"

Cassandra drew several from the handful and described them to her mother. Ramsay made no objections or encouragements. He suspected any comment from him would only bring an opposite reaction from Cassandra.

"And you are in agreement, my lord?" Mrs. St. John asked when Cassandra had finished.

Ramsay inclined his head in assent. "I believe Cassandra has selected well. I shall be very pleased to be her escort. In fact, to demonstrate my pleasure, I brought a gift for your daughter."

"How nice, my lord," Mrs. St. John said, with a smile of genuine pleasure spreading across her face. Ramsay realized that Susanna St. John's reputation for graciousness and generosity was well deserved. "Isn't that nice, Cassandra?"

"Yes, indeed," Cassandra muttered, her glance at him suspicious at best.

Ramsay reached into his pocket and brought out the small box he'd discovered at a vendor's stall at Covent Garden. Though Graham had been right about the necessity of bestowing gifts, Ramsay knew better than to buy her something costly. Cassandra would dismiss such a gift as a payoff. Ramsay would not chance offending her like that. Each offering had to be meaningful.

The workmanship on the wooden box was good but plain,

yet the moment Ramsay had opened this little treasure, he'd known it was the perfect gift. He held out the small box wrapped in plain brown paper and tied up with string.

Cassandra stared at it distrustfully as if she expected it to bite her.

"It's just a small token that I thought you might enjoy," Ramsay said, beginning to wonder from the resentful mistrust in her eyes if she was going to refuse it.

Her glance flicked across his face once more before she took the box and carefully unwrapped it. When she dropped the paper and string to the floor, she held a wooden, inlaid box in her hand. She stared at it.

"Is it a music box?" Mrs. St. John asked, glancing at Ramsay.

"Yes, open it," Ramsay urged, fearful now that he'd been mistaken about the appeal of such a humble gift.

Slowly Cassandra lifted the lid. Instantly the box chimed out the schoolroom ditty that they'd sung in the tunnel at Regent's Park.

Ramsay peered into Cassandra's face, waiting for the smile of delight he'd been certain the music would bring to her lips as she remembered that moment as he did. But she only stared at the box as if it were some strange, bizarre object.

"How charming," Mrs. St. John said, smiling fondly at her daughter. "That was always one of your favorite songs as a little girl, Cassie."

"Yes, it was." Cassie snapped the box closed. The music ended abruptly. She glared at Ramsay, anger swimming in her eyes—and tears.

Ramsay cursed silently. What had he done now? She did recognize it as the song they'd sung in the tunnel. He knew she did. Why should the music box anger her? Why should it bring tears? He tried to peer into her face again, but she turned toward her mother. "See, Mama, how the lid is decorated with ivory and ebony."

" 'Tis lovely, Cassie," Mrs. St. John said. "Do have more

tea, my lord, and tell me about your home in the borderland. What is it called? Ravencliff?''

Drawing on his steely self-discipline, Ramsay obliged Cassandra's mother, describing his home in some detail, aware all the time of Cassandra's silence at his side. He did not understand why the gift had not delighted her. One music box would not heal the rift between them entirely. He knew that. But he'd hoped that it would be the beginning of reclaiming her trust. Yet it had failed.

But he would not give up. If he had to go dancing at Almack's to regain her confidence, he'd buy himself new dancing shoes. Glen Gray was worth the price.

CHAPTER TWELVE

At first Cassie stuffed the music box into the back of her dressing-table drawer and ignored it. She loathed the thing. She loathed Linirk for giving it to her. How she wished he'd given her rubies or sapphires, something inappropriate. Jewels she could have thrown back in his face. Gems she could have rejected as a bribe rather than the gift he claimed it was. She wanted no gifts from him.

But a humble music box that played a song both he and she had sung together—it bordered on charming. The man was shameless—and cunning.

She loathed him for several other reasons, too: his deception, his persistence, his high-handedness. But the music box served to sum up her feelings. How dare he give her a reminder of their good times together, of a time when she liked and trusted him; of a moment when he'd kissed her and she'd kissed him, and she thought he liked her for herself. How dare he! It had all been false.

But she exacted her retribution. She dragged Linirk to every party they were invited to and every entertainment she could think of. They'd played whist at Mr. Smedgewood's townhouse.

They'd joined the boating party in an outing to Greenwich and enjoyed a clandestine tour of the Queen's House. The King was not in residence and someone in the party knew someone who prevailed on someone. Cassie fell in love with the lofty, well-proportioned rooms and the graceful spiral stairwell. They attended musicales and soirées—always when she and Mama knew that Charlotte and Connor would not be in attendance.

Then she insisted on enjoying a performance of the opera. And to his credit, Ramsay—as he'd requested she call him— Ramsay had behaved as if he attended the theater every week.

His conduct as her escort was flawless. He was punctual. His dress was always appropriate, though black. His arm was ever ready for her hand. He smiled when he should and conversed tolerably well.

If he hated Society as was rumored, he showed little impatience or discomfort in it. Cassie was hard-pressed to think of how to harass him next.

Sometimes in the conversation she learned things about him, such as the fact that he'd been educated at St. Andrews University, just as Connor McKensie had. Like Connor, Ramsay had studied the sciences. She also discovered that as a young man Ramsay had done a grand tour of the Continent as was the custom for young gentlemen of aristocratic families. He'd been particularly fond of sunny Italy.

"Venice was my favorite city," he'd told her when she asked one evening as they danced. A wistful smile of pleasure crossed his face. "You must see Venice. You'd like it too."

"I don't know, with all those watery canals and bridges," Cassie had said—she who'd been no farther from home than Edinburgh.

"No, not the canals, they do not signify," Ramsay had said, waving away her notions. The light of pleasure brightened his eyes and his smile softened his stern forbidding features. "Venice is a city of beauty, mystery, intrigue, and make-believe. Oh, Princess, you have never seen such beautiful carnival costumes and masks. Lights on the piazza. Red flowers in windows. Tabby cats in doorways. Narrow, meandering ways that lead deep into a maze. Yes, you'd like Venice.''

After a description like that, Cassie was convinced he was right. She gazed up at him, entranced by his enthusiasm for the city on the Adriatic. His obvious affection for the northern Italian city brought other questions to mind, questions she lacked the courage to ask. What of the women in his life? Had there been a woman in Venice that brought such a smile to his lips? Why was he thirty-some years of age and without a wife? Why had he declared his nephew his heir? Questions that no one asked. Cassie sensed that if others would not pose them, she dared not submit them. And then, there was always the possibility she would not like the answers.

Throughout the two weeks of their social whirl he offered her other gifts—little things: a cheap souvenir paper fan from Greenwich that had made her laugh, despite her vow not to show pleasure in his offerings or company; and later he brought her a handkerchief embroidered with black Nairn puppies. That she had tucked into the wrist of her gown, and carried it frequently.

While nothing in his conduct could be criticized, Cassie knew from their first outing that being with Ramsay was a totally different experience from being with Dudley.

This should have been no surprise to her. The first difference she noted was the way that people treated her in Linirk's company. When Dudley had been her escort, no gentleman hesitated to ask her to dance or to converse. But with Ramsay at her side conversation was polite, and people greeted them warmly enough, but curiosity always lingered in their eyes when they moved on as soon as it was polite to do so. When the dancing began, only Tony—with a defiant gleam in his eye—had the courage to ask her to dance.

At the card party gentlemen had seemed uneasy about being her partner. She hated cards and ordinarily seldom attended card parties. She had only accepted the invitation to this one because she intended to keep Ramsay busy. With him as her partner, they'd won every game despite her bungling. He never said a cross word to her about her incorrect leads and inept bidding.

By the time the evening arrived for their appearance at Almack's, Cassie was exasperated with Ramsay's exemplary behavior. He'd done nothing she could even remotely criticize. He was attentive, polite, and at moments, he even touched her—on the hand, the small of her back, a stroke just above her elbow—with seeming affection.

Because he'd been initially reluctant about appearing at Almack's, she had no idea what to expect of him at Society's most-talked-about social club. But she had the satisfaction of knowing that however he behaved, tongues would wag. And Dudley would be sure to hear that she was being courted by the Marquis of Linirk.

Mama and Papa served as their chaperones. Upon entering the establishment, just before the doors were closed for the evening, the rooms proved warm and stuffy with the heavy scent of perfumes hovering in the air. Brocades and satins whispered as the ladies moved around the room and heirloom jewels glittered in candlelight.

Cassie and Ramsay were spoken to politely but briefly by Lady Cowper, the grand dame of the salon these days. She eyed him, taking in the fine cut of his clothes and the tartan sash across his shoulder, but made no remark about it. After mouthing some polite words about being honored to have the Marquis of Linirk at Almack's, the lady had moved on to speak with the select others who had vouchers for the evening. A few aristocrats delivered obligatory greetings and hurried on to speak to other acquaintances.

"I swear, if I didn't know better, I'd think people don't like you," Cassie said, vexed by Lady Cowper's cursory greeting.

"They don't like me," Ramsay said, escorting Cassie along behind her parents. He wore his customary black, but the suit was in a formal style and his shirt was of the finest white linen, a surprising concession to the rigors of dress required by London's famous social club. But in addition to his formal attire he wore a Scottish tartan sash draped across his chest from his shoulder to his hip and fastened with a jeweled brooch of the Marquis of Linirk's family crest.

"But they don't even know you well enough to have made a proper decision," Cassie said, amazed to find herself practically defending the man.

"Perhaps they know all they need to know," he said, gazing out over the crowded room.

"I doubt it," Cassie said, also scanning the room for familiar faces. That was why one came to Almack's, to see and be seen. Otherwise, she'd always felt the place was overrated. The food was terrible and the music only tolerable at best. But there was little doubt that word of her appearance there on the arm of the Marquis of Linirk would reach Dudley. "I know more about you than they do, and I still can't make up my mind."

Cassie glanced aside at Ramsay in time to see conflict on his face. But it vanished in an instant.

"Then I'm flattered that at least the decision has not come down against me."

"Mrs. St. John," called a rotund man from across the dance floor.

At Cassandra's side Mama turned and smiled. When she recognized the man, she muttered, "Heavens, it's the Duke of Deander. What can he want?"

"Mrs. St. John, I'm so glad that you are here this evening," the round-bellied aristocrat said, dodging his way across the middle of the crowded dance floor. Lady Cowper frowned at him, but he forged ahead undaunted, ducking the dancers.

Cassie and Mama dropped a polite curtsy to him.

"Your Grace, how good to see you here," Mama said.

The duke puffed and bowed to the ladies then to Papa and Ramsay. Proper greetings were exchanged. "Mrs. St. John, I thought I might take this opportunity to say that I've had second thoughts about agreeing to show my pottery collection at the

Egyptian Hall as you and the Hellenistic-studies group had so kindly requested.''

Mama gasped. ''But that is wonderful news, Your Grace. St. John, His Grace is considering showing his pottery for the benefit of the Parthenon.''

''Good news indeed,'' Papa said, with a nod of acknowledgment.

''But I shall be so happy to inform the other officers of the study group,'' Mama said. ''Oh, Your Grace, you don't know how wonderful this is.''

''Well, you can thank the marquis here for bringing a few facts to light that made me reconsider my hasty, early decision.''

Cassie stared up at Ramsay in surprise.

''My lord,'' Mama said, facing Ramsay. ''How kind of you.''

Ramsay took a step back and—if Cassie hadn't known it was quite impossible—he actually looked abashed. ''I merely detailed a few points about the benefits of such an exhibit for His Grace that I feared he was not aware of.''

''Well, Linirk's advice did the trick for me,'' Deander said, linking his arm through Mama's. ''Mind if I borrow your wife long enough to work out some of the details, St. John?''

Papa agreed and Mama and Deander strolled away, heads together in deep discussion. Papa excused himself to have a smoke in the garden.

Cassie turned to Linirk. ''Now, there is an example of exactly what I was talking about. I actually believe that you prefer that people not like you. It's like your excuse for wearing black. You say it eliminates decision-making. If someone dislikes you, you have no verdict to come to. Their rebuff simply enables you to rebuff them in return.''

''An interesting theory,'' Ramsay said. Her remarks offended him and he refused to meet her gaze. ''Makes me sound lazy at best.''

''No, you don't do it because you're lazy,'' Cassie said, wondering for the first time why a man of Ramsay's rank would prefer to keep people at a distance. "I'm certain of that. You have other, better reasons. I just don't know what they are."

"Would you like to dance?" Ramsay asked, with a small bow.

"I knew you'd change the subject," Cassie said, hearing the strains of a waltz begin.

"I thought we came to Almack's to dance," Ramsay said. "Do you wish to waltz or not?"

"Yes, I do," Cassie said, amused with the irritation she heard in his voice. He'd been on such good behavior over the last two weeks she'd almost given up getting a rise out of him. She smiled with satisfaction. He returned her smile. With guilty pleasure she allowed him to draw her out onto the floor and into his arms.

He'd held her several times in the last two weeks of parties and social events. His touch had always been proper, just the right amount of pressure on her waist, just the proper distance between them as they waltzed across the floor. Cassie had encouraged nothing more and he'd attempted nothing more. But this evening Ramsay's hand seemed to press more familiarly on her waist, his fingers spreading up to her ribs. He drew her a bit closer. Not enough to invite comment. But enough for Cassie to be conscious of the heat Ramsay stirred in her. She looked up into his face, tingling under his scrutiny so like that which he'd settled on her that day on the river barge.

Her heart skipped a beat. She looked away from him lest he see in her eyes the desire he awoke in her; the desire to be held close and be touched intimately. Part of her longed for him to take her into the garden, into the dark where they might exchange something more intimate than clasped hands on the dance floor. The other part of her was mortified that this man, who'd threatened her family, could make her want to melt into his arms.

Cassie and Ramsay danced together several more times. No other gentleman dared ask. By the end of the evening the gossips were whispering about them. Cassie had no regrets.

The smile of pleasure would not be wiped from her face. Despite his sins, Ramsay made her feel admired and desired and very much like a woman. Let tongues wag.

Later, in Cassie's bedchamber as Betsy helped her undress, Cassie's head was full of unruly thoughts. How generous of Ramsay to help her mother with her Greek pottery exhibition. It was no great sacrifice on his part, yet he'd gone to the trouble to speak to the Duke of Deander. And he'd asked for no reward. She was having difficulty reconciling the man who had held her in his arms with the man who would commit kidnapping. Was he truly guilty of having Connor abducted so he would have to forfeit the championship prizefight? Was he guilty of hiring henchmen to attack her in the street? Or had she and Tony been too quick to lay the blame on Ramsay?

If Ramsay was to blame for one or both crimes, a few gifts and helping Mama achieve her desired Greek pottery exhibition, hardly erased his guilt.

Cassie donned her nightrail and dropped down on the edge of her bed. But how evil was Ramsay, truly? How evil did she want him to be?

"Will there be anything more, miss?" Betsy asked, stifling a yawn.

"No, thank you," Cassie said. "I think I may read for a while, but you go to bed."

Betsy offered a sleepy curtsy and left the room.

As soon as she was alone, Cassie opened the door to her sister's room. "Charlotte?"

In the moonlight pouring through the windows, Cassie spied her sister asleep in bed. The wedding was only a week away and Charlotte's days were filled with preparations and obligations: fittings, favors, food selections, flowers. Cassie found that she was seldom consulted about any decision. Before Kinleith and Linirk came into their lives, the girls had consulted each other about everything, from how they wore their hair to the choice of lace for their undergarments. Their nightly talks had virtually ended. Cassie missed them. Cassie didn't even know where Charlotte was spending most of her time these days. If it weren't for the effort to keep the men separated, Cassie wouldn't have any idea about Charlotte's social calendar. She felt cut off from her sister in a way she thought could never happen. And it made her sad.

"Charlotte, are you asleep?" Cassie asked quietly, hoping that her sister might be awake enough to talk to her. She ventured a few steps into the room. "I want to talk to you. I want to tell you what Ramsay did for Mama."

Charlotte's form remained still, her breathing deep and even. If she wasn't asleep, she was faking effectively. Cassie lingered for a moment, wishing that Charlotte would roll over, smile sleepily at her, and begin talking. Cassie wanted to share her doubts about Ramsay, but she knew her sister would have little interest in that topic. To Charlotte he was a villain, plain and simple. Deciding it best to leave her sister undisturbed, Cassie tiptoed back to the door and pulled it shut.

"I wish we'd never met them," Cassie said aloud. "If I'd never sent you off to that prizefight where you met Connor, if I'd let Dudley take me home the day he cried off, none of this would have happened."

Thoughtfully Cassie ambled to her dressing table, opened the drawer and reached far back inside to find the music box she'd stashed there, out of sight and out of mind. She closed the drawer and set Ramsay's gift in the center of the table. After a moment's thought, she opened the box. The song she and Ramsay had sung in the Regent's Park tunnel filled the room.

Cassie whispered the lyrics, the memory of the fun and camaraderie she'd shared with the man who had rescued her from the footpads flooding over her. Try as she might she could not summon up the vision of a villain that she'd come to connect with the Marquis of Linirk.

The song slowed, then stopped. Cassie stood alone in the

quiet of the night, feeling lonelier than she'd ever felt in her life. Taking up the key which resided in the box, she wound the box for the first time and the music started up again, light and cheerful.

Cassie carried the box to the bedside table and set it down. She kicked off her slippers and crawled under the covers. With the strains of the music box reminding her of Ramsay's generosity, she settled down to the novel she was reading, her mind's eye giving the storybook hero Ramsay's face.

CHAPTER
THIRTEEN

"Well, did ye impress the elite at Almack's last night?" Graham demanded of Ramsay as they strode down St. James Street.

The sun was shining and the street was crowded with dandies and their carriages, gentlemen out to order the latest fashions for the winter. Ramsay had little interest in clothes at the moment. They already had ordered and arranged for delivery of a pair of enormous candlesticks as a wedding gift to Charlotte and Connor. Now he was scanning the shopfronts in search of a particular establishment he'd heard of for another purpose.

"It was so late when ye came in last night, I didn't hear ye," Graham added when Ramsay didn't answer. "Are ye gainin' anythin' from all these parties and dances?"

"I'm gaining ground," Ramsay said. The round of parties and entertainments were beginning to exhaust him. "But I'm not as in control as I'd like to be."

"Then last night was no success?"

"On the contrary," Ramsay said, thinking the next shop on the corner was the one he sought. "Last night was an important step in the right direction. If there was someone of importance in London who did not know that I'm courting Cassandra St. John, they know it now. The tongues were wagging before we left Almack's. I saw the chaperones' heads together and I could feel their eyes on us before the first dance was over. Last night was an important success.''

''But Kinleith's wedding is only a few days away,'' Graham said, stepping aside for a dandy and his lady, then quickening his step to catch up with Ramsay. ''Has nothing been settled about Glen Gray? Do you think St. John will give it to his daughter for a wedding gift?''

''There was a time when I feared he might,'' Ramsay said, with a shake of his head. ''But I think St. John is too shrewd to do that now with Cassandra being courted by me. He doesn't want anything to spoil the wedding. And he must show an even hand with his twin daughters.''

''Then do we have a chance at Glen Gray?'' Graham asked.

''I think we will when our plan is carried through.'' Ramsay stopped in front of the shop on the corner. ''Here we are. This is the establishment I'm seeking.''

'' 'Tis a walking-stick shop.'' Graham stopped in front of the shop and stared at the display in the window. ''There be a right good stick. And look at that knobby one in the dark wood.''

''I'm buying a gift,'' Ramsay said.

''Does the lady need a staff?'' Graham began, a twinkle sparkling in his eye. ''Ye don't need to come to a shop on St. James Street to provide her with that, now do ye?''

Ramsay shook his head. ''Mind your manners, man. I've decided you're never going to take to the horse I purchased for you, so you'd best pick out the exact walking stick you want because it seems you're going to spend the rest of your days on foot.''

Graham tossed back his head and laughed. ''Well, that's a relief. A walking stick 'tis what I've a need for. But do you think the English can make a fine-enough one?''

Ramsay leaned toward Graham and spoke in confidence. ''I

have it on good authority that there's a Scotsman in the workroom who makes the best the shop has to offer. I think you should be able to find something useful here.''

''Aye, well, so I shall,'' Graham said, sobering and striding into the shop with an air of purpose.

Ramsay followed his kinsman through the door, and accepted the chair the proprietor offered him while Graham searched through canes and walking sticks. But Ramsay did not forget their conversation about Glen Gray and Cassandra. He'd detected a shift in her attitude toward him at last. His talk with Deander had done the trick, he thought. But now that he'd regained her trust a bit, he was uncertain what came next. But he had to make his move soon.

There was indeed a Scots workman in the shop workroom. Graham insisted on meeting the man and asking his expert advice. It took more than an hour of discussion, careful examination, and trial, to determine just which walking stick would suffice. Ultimately he selected a long sturdy stick, unlike the typical short, tapered canes Englishmen favored.

Then they were back out on the street again, Graham striding along with new vigor, the sterling-silver lion's head of his new walking stick gleaming in the sunlight.

''Now, this is the way God meant men to travel,'' Graham said. ''None of that silly four-legged-creature transportation or those new steam machines. A good walking stick is the best mode of travel.''

Ramsay laughed. ''If you say so.''

''But seriously, back to the St. John lass,'' Graham continued, as if their conversation had not been interrupted by an hour of shopping. ''Ye've been seeing the girl every day for two weeks and ye are chaperoned everywhere ye go with her. The St. John lass and McKensie are still scheduled to wed next week. I donna understand where this is taking us any closer to winning Glen Gray.''

''What we want is for Davis St. John to be willing to pay any price to get me out of his daughter's life,'' Ramsay said.

On the surface, the plan still sounded good, but the reality of it was beginning to trouble him.

"And how are ye going to do that?" Graham said. "How do you make that merchant ready to damn near give you Glen Gray? It's the seduction, right?"

"No, more than just seduction is required, I believe," Ramsay said. "Danger must be implicit, though I see no reason to harm the lady, but we do need to get her out of Town to scare the man properly."

"So we kidnap her," Graham said. "Why didn't you say so. 'Tis easy enough to do."

"No, no, 'tis not that easy," Ramsay said as they walked. "This must be done with finesse and subtlety. St. John is who we want to frighten, not Cassandra."

Graham frowned. "Then what do you suggest? An overnight tryst somewhere. We can always arrange for the carriage to break down in some remote place. Then ye can—"

"I don't think she would fall for that," Ramsay said, remembering only too well the caution he still glimpsed in Cassandra's fine blue eyes. She was beginning to trust him again. He'd felt it in the way she allowed him to hold her as they danced at Almack's. And as obliging as she might be on the dance floor, she wasn't likely to blindly allow him to lead her anywhere.

"Then what do ye suggest?" Graham asked. "Time grows short."

"I don't know," Ramsay said. "I don't know."

"I thought ye had this all planned out," Graham said, his impatience surfacing again.

Ramsay knew his foster brother was right. He usually had each step of his plan plotted out with few details left to chance, but once he'd revealed himself to Cassandra and she had stepped out of his carriage in the park, he'd had to improvise. For the last two weeks improvisation had served him well, but Graham was right. Time was growing short and he was going to have to take some action. Instinct told him that the clue to what he needed to do lay with Cassandra. She would tell him—purposely or unwittingly—how to frighten her father.

The sense of urgency hovered in the shadows of Ramsay's consciousness as he dressed for the rehearsal dinner that evening. He had to make his move for Glen Gray soon. Tonight, for the first time he would be in the same room as Kinleith, he thought, as he tied his cravat with his usual fastidiousness. There was no way the St. Johns could avoid the encounter.

But Cassandra had exacted a promise from him that he would be on his best behavior. He'd agreed. And he had little doubt the same vow had been extracted from Kinleith and the Highlander had agreed, just as he had.

When he'd finished with the cravat, his manservant helped him into his black coat, a formal cutaway for the evening. Then he draped his tartan sash across his shoulder and fastened it at his hip with the crested brooch.

They would behave as civilized men, for the sake of the ladies, Ramsay thought, as he posed before the mirror to satisfy himself that his dress was suitable for the evening. But he intended to make it clear to Davis St. John that he still anticipated receiving Glen Gray or there would be a price to pay. He expected to clarify his position soon. St. John had to know that the Forbes clan would not lose this property in a wedding again.

But when Ramsay laid eyes on Cassandra in the hallway of the St. John townhouse where the rehearsal dinner was being held, he banished the urgency from his mind. She smiled at him and curtsied as she always did, no less welcoming than she'd become over the past few weeks. The welcome warmed him. This evening she looked beautiful in a gown of green and pink that exposed her shoulders in an alluring way. And her coppery hair was piled on her head, leaving her neck bare and defenseless.

But the loveliness of her appearance could not hide the truth from Ramsay. Sadness and dismay lurked in her eyes. His determination to regain Glen Gray faded. He had no idea what might have happened to dampen Cassandra's usual light spirits, but her subdued mood troubled him.

"Has something gone amiss?" he asked the moment they could talk without being overheard by the other guests. "Did everything go as it should at the church rehearsal?"

"Yes, the rehearsal was fine," Cassandra said, wistfully watching Kinleith and her sister at the other side of the drawing room. "I guess I'm just becoming sentimental. Look at them. They are so happy and I wouldn't have it any other way, but I'm going to miss my sister."

"Of course," Ramsay said, also watching the happy couple. At first he thought Cassandra's strange mood the product of jealousy. She liked to be the center of attention and her sister was receiving most of it these days. Yet her sadness seemed to run deeper than mere envy.

"I hope it does not trouble you much to be in the same room with a McKensie," Cassandra said, looking up at him with wide-eyed concern. "I don't understand much about feuds. You always seem to go stiff when I mention my sister and Connor."

"I can abide by a promise," Ramsay said. "I am a gentleman, after all."

"Yes, of course," Cassandra said, still preoccupied with observing her sister. "I love all the wedding parties, but the festivities will soon be over and Connor will take Charlotte away. Then I'll be . . . without my sister."

Ramsay almost groaned as all the pieces fell into place for him. Cassandra was feeling left out and left behind. And he was the reason. As much as he'd like to deny the truth, her relationship with him had no doubt come between Cassandra and her sister. Bloody hell, how could he have foreseen that complication? He didn't care much how St. John felt, but Cassandra . . . There must be something he could say to ease her pain. "Far too much ado is made over weddings. I don't know why there's all this fuss, unless it is just an excuse for a party."

"This afternoon at the church Connor said that a Highland wedding celebration can go on for days," Cassandra said, glancing in the direction of the happy couple. "Is that so? Do you know much about the Highlanders?"

"Aye, I lived with a Highland family for ten years, Graham's family as a matter of fact," Ramsay said. "I just don't go about in a kilt to prove my manhood."

Surprise and curiosity stole the sorrow from Cassandra's expression. She looked up into his face. "Truly? You've lived among the Highlanders?"

"Aye, my mother was of a Highland family and she convinced my father to practice the old custom of fostering his heir to another family," Ramsay said, carefully holding bitter memories at bay. It would not do for Cassandra to see his true feelings about his mother and father. His purpose was to spin a few tales to entertain her. "So that's how Graham and I became brothers, if you will."

"I didn't know that," Cassandra said, a smile of wonder coming to her moist lips. "Then Connor's ways should not seem strange to you."

"No, not particularly," Ramsay admitted. He and Kinleith understood each other well enough. "But there are other practices in the Highlands that don't include riotous wedding festivities."

"Such as?" Cassandra leaned closer, clearly intrigued by his suggestion. "Tell me."

"In the old days," Ramsay began, trying to recall the tales and folklore he'd heard told around the fire during the long winter nights, "Highlanders were sometimes known to kidnap their brides if the lassies' families showed any reluctance to accept the match."

"Kidnap her?" Cassandra raised her brows. "How amazing. But didn't that cause a feud?"

"Actually it made feuding difficult," Ramsay said, wonder-

ing how much embellishment he should add to his story. "Once
a lass became the laird's bride, her family would be fighting
family."

"I see," Cassandra murmured. "So how was it done? Did
the laird scale the castle walls?"

"It usually wasn't necessary to go to that much trouble,"
Ramsay said, captivated by the light of enchantment in Cassandra's eyes. "The laird would scoop the lass up as she was
walking to church or to market. Then he'd wrap his tartan
around her and carry her off for a wedding night."

"Without a church ceremony?" Shock sobered Cassandra's
face.

"Sometimes the laird bribed a priest to preside over a ceremony, but usually it was naught more than a handfasting,"
Ramsay explained, certain that she wasn't as shocked as she
appeared to be. "Do you know what handfasting is?"

Cassandra shook her head.

" 'Tis an old custom where a lad and lass pledge to live
together for a year and a day as man and wife," Ramsay
explained. "At the end of the year, if there were children or
the lass was with child, they were wed. If there were no wee
ones, but the pair still wished to be together, they were wed
and no one could gainsay them."

"How romantic," Cassandra said, gazing off into space, her
head clearly full of images more romantic than realistic.

"Romantic?" Ramsay frowned. "How so?"

"So beautifully simple." She tugged gently on Ramsay tartan sash. Then she added, with a disarming laugh, "I mean
wrapping a tartan around your lover and then pledging your
troth. How wonderfully practical and romantic coming from a
bunch of knobby-kneed Scotsmen. So the laird and the lass
meet. All they need is to see each other's eyes and they know
they are meant to be together. But her family dislikes them
knowing each other. Perhaps they have another laird in mind
for her. But the first handsome laird is undaunted so he comes

for her and carries her away to his castle. It's almost as romantic as Romeo and Juliet, only with a happier ending.''

"Who said the first laird was handsome?" Ramsay asked, watching her closely, amused by her fairy-tale view of what probably had been kidnapping and rape as often as not. The castle was probably little more than a crumbling thatched cottage. "He was just more persistent, I suspect. It was a very ancient custom, princess. 'Tis hardly ever practiced these days.''

The conversation turned to more mundane things when Tony approached them. Ramsay managed to get through the remainder of the evening with an obligatory wish for the couple's happiness. He brushed a polite kiss across Charlotte's cheek, but he did not shake Kinleith's hand. Nor did Kinleith offer to allow it.

But Cassandra accepted and bestowed on him the warmest kiss since their day on the Thames together—since she'd learned who he truly was. Ramsay left St. John's home with ideas and a plan forming in his head.

When he reached his own home he barged into the drawing room without taking off his hat. Just as he'd expected, he found Graham sipping scotch and waiting for him in front of a warm fire.

"Well, what is it?" Graham demanded the moment he caught sight of Ramsay's face. He rose from his chair. "Ye are grinning like the very devil himself. Did St. John surprise ye with the gift of Glen Gray?''

"No, but he is going to." Ramsay threw his hat at the sleepy manservant, then reached for the scotch decanter and poured himself a drink. He was unable to keep his delight from spreading across his face. "But I know exactly how to make him do it. I need your help and we're going to have to work fast. The timing has to be perfect. There are many things to arrange.

We have only tomorrow and a few hours on the day of the wedding.''

''To help ye is why I'm here,'' Graham said, setting aside his glass of scotch and rubbing his hands together in anticipation. ''What are we going to do?''

''First we're going to drink to you bloody Highlanders and your barbarian ways,'' Ramsay said, pouring himself a glass of scotch and joining his foster brother beside the fire. ''Then we're going to lay out exactly how to get Cassandra out of town.''

CHAPTER
FOURTEEN

The next two days—the day before and the day of Charlotte's wedding—were so full Cassie had no difficulty in putting out of her mind how much she was going to miss her sister. She helped direct the packing and the shuttling of gifts and household goods to the new townhouse. She supervised Cook and the servants in food preparation. She even dealt with the tradesmen and messengers for Mama and Charlotte. They were occupied with the last-minute details at the church and at Aunt Dorian's house, where the wedding breakfast was going to be held.

When Cassie had a spare moment, she saw to the final alterations to her own gown and the setting out of her slippers and jewelry. All the while she was glad to be useful wherever she could and she ignored the fact that the wedding was going to bring her a great loss.

Until she stood at the back of the church and awaited her musical cue to walk down the aisle ahead of Charlotte and Papa she hardly even had time to think of Ramsay. Everything was finally in place for the ceremony. The pews and the altar were draped in summer flowers and greenery. Sunlight poured through the upper windows, bathing the graceful Gothic arches of St. Margaret's, Westminster, in a cheery brightness. Cassie was glad that Charlotte had chosen St. Margaret's instead of the dark and dreary St. George's of Hanover Square. A wedding should take place in a light, joyful setting.

Once more Cassie scanned the guests who had assembled at St. Margaret's for the wedding. The small crowd was no surprise. Most of the guests would extend their good wishes and pay their respects at the wedding breakfast later. But she'd invited Ramsay to the church and he'd agreed to come, she thought. But she could not find him anywhere. Perhaps he'd had a change of heart, Cassie thought, shaking an imagined wrinkle from her pink satin-and-lace skirt. His absence wasn't important. She could depend on Tony to serve as her escort if Ramsay did not appear.

Connor and Tony took their places at the front of the church. Erik sat nearby in the first pew. True to his heritage, Connor wore a well-tailored kilt and a formal cutaway coat. Cassie found that she was becoming accustomed to the Scots costume she'd once found original and unfashionable. It looked right on Connor.

The music began and Cassie lifted her head and prepared herself to lead her sister and father down the aisle to the altar.

The ceremony proceeded without mishap. Charlotte recited her vows in a clear, determined voice, her gaze on Connor's face as she spoke. Connor said his vows with strength and tenderness, his gaze moving from their clasped hands up to her face. Their golden wedding bands gleamed in the sunlight.

Cassie wondered if she'd ever be as fortunate as her sister to declare her love, honor, and loyalty to the man she truly loved. Aunt Dorian had had that good fortune, and Mama too. Cassie stole a glance at her parents. Papa looked grim and sad all at once. Mama sniffed into her handkerchief as Papa slipped a protective arm around her. They were losing a daughter, Cassie realized. She wasn't the only one who was going to miss Charlotte. With a sniff she stifled her tears—except for the single teardrop that escaped to rain on her handful of pink roses.

The couple was blessed, and the organ blared a triumphant march. At the back of the church, just under the choirloft, Connor swung Charlotte around, made quick work of turning back her Brussels-lace veil, grasped her around the waist, and kissed her soundly, bending her over backward.

Cassie watched with envy, wondering what it would be like to be wanted by a man so passionately. To have him take you in his arms and kiss you for all the world to see. And to want him so passionately in return that you would leave your family to become the lady of the manor in the north, as Charlotte was about to do.

The kiss lengthened. Charlotte's arms went limp as her head tipped back and she dropped her white rose–and–orange blossom bouquet.

The wedding guests chuckled and applauded.

Cassie hurried forward to retrieve the bridal bouquet before it was trod upon, then she backed away. It was not her day to be the center of attention. From afar she watched her sister and her new husband with gladness. Maybe Papa and Mama had their doubts, but Cassie thought it was a good match. Connor's boisterous good humor was a perfect compliment to Charlotte's somber studiousness. They would do well together. Cassie had little doubt of it.

When Connor and Charlotte parted, Connor laughed and Charlotte smiled, blushing furiously. Well wishers laughed and chattered, ushering the couple out onto the church steps. The organ music ended with a flourish and the organist departed. The guests' noise faded as they climbed into their waiting carriages.

Cassie stood back in the shadow of the choirloft waiting for the guests to leave. When she was certain most everyone was gone, she ventured back down the aisle to look around one more time to be certain that nothing else had been left inadvertently. When she started back up the aisle, Betsy was waving to her from the front door.

"Miss Cassandra, the carriage is waiting," she called.

"I'm coming," Cassie said, hurrying up the aisle with the bridal bouquet in her hand.

Betsy disappeared out the door before she got there. Cassie turned to look around at the church one more time. Strange how a few moments in a lovely place like this could change everything about so many people's lives. She sighed and turned back toward the door. When she stepped out onto the church porch, no one was there. They'd left her behind.

"Drat," Cassie muttered. "Betsy, I thought you were waiting for me."

A large hand reached out and seized her arm. "She did, but I told her I would wait for you."

"What?" Startled, Cassie lurched away from the sudden restraint. She found herself staring up into Ramsay's face.

"I said, I'm waiting for you," he said, quietly withdrawing his hand and offering her a soft, apologetic smile. Cassie gaped at him. She'd never seen him dressed in anything but black boots, trousers, coat, waistcoat, and tall hat. But there he stood gloriously handsome in a kilt—of all things. A kilt, a white ruffled shirt, and a dark blue velvet coat. Perhaps most startling of all was the jaunty, pheasant feather–trimmed hat perched atop his fair head.

In his native costume he seemed larger and less contained than he did in a frock coat. Cassie couldn't keep a soft laugh of surprise from escaping her.

" 'Tis not meant to create laughter," Ramsay said, seeming to smile and frown all at once.

"I'm laughing with pleasure, my lord," Cassie said, fearing she'd offended him. "You look quite dashing."

"For a Highlander?" Though his expression was polite and controlled as ever, an air of excitement swirled about him— an air of danger. A thrill tingled through Cassie.

He added, "I told your coachman that I would take you to the breakfast myself. But I lied."

"You lied—how so?" Cassie asked, stepping back from Ramsay, still overwhelmed by the change in his looks. It was almost like meeting a whole new person, but someone she'd known existed all along, and he'd emerged to stand before her at last.

"I've been here waiting for you," he said, smiling more secretively now than apologetically, "but not to take you to your sister's wedding breakfast. I've been waiting to take my partner in adventure away."

"An adventure? Today?" Cassie asked, immediately intrigued—but wary. She looked around to see Graham standing near a coach on the street. Her maid stood next to the Scots retainer. It seemed that preparations already had been made. "But this is Charlotte and Connor's wedding day."

"And so you've seen them wed," Ramsay said, taking her arm and tucking it around his. The velvet of his coat felt soft and warm while his arm beneath was steely. "And what will go on for the rest of the day? Drinking and dancing. A crush of people all wanting to greet the bride and groom and wish them well. And if you aren't there, will you be missed?"

"Well, probably not, but—" Cassie began, remembering the things she should be doing for her sister as maid of honor.

"You were so fascinated by the story I told you the night of the rehearsal dinner, remember, the kidnapped Highland bride?" Ramsay said, peering into her face. "I thought, why not make a game of this? Why not an adventure? So here I am, a Highlander out to kidnap his bride."

"And I'm the bride?" Cassie laughed, but pulled away from him, still intrigued but oddly uncomfortable with his suggestion. " 'Tis a daring premise for an adventure, my lord."

"No more daring than being a highwayman," Ramsay said, smiling more like himself now. " 'Tis but a game, princess. I don't mean to frighten or vex you. I'm inviting you to come away with me and I'll show you how the puppies have grown."

"I thought you sent them to Ravencliff," Cassie said, thinking of the darling puppies she'd held on her lap not so long ago at the riverside inn.

"I did." Ramsay's gaze met hers. "Wouldn't you like to see Ravencliff? Leave all this fuss to your sister and Kinleith. It is their day. Come with me. Be my guest."

"I don't know." Cassie liked the idea of seeing Ravencliff. Ramsay had not talked of the place often, but when he had, his affection for it had been obvious. She wanted to see his family's seat for herself. "Ravencliff must be several days away and 'tis not fitting—"

"When has propriety ever troubled you?" Ramsay asked with a laugh. He gestured toward the other side of the church porch. "Ravencliff is three days' journey. I've made all the arrangements for your comfort at the best inns along the way. And bring Betsy along to serve you and be your companion."

Betsy turned an unhappy, woeful face toward her, and Cassie knew that her maid was not thrilled with the idea of a journey north.

"But Mama and Papa—" Cassie tried once more, sorely tempted to run away from festivities that would only remind her of the loss of her sister, of her own failure—her own broken betrothal. And there was another, even better, reason to go with him. There would be no possibility of an embarrassing scene between Ramsay and Connor at the wedding breakfast. If Cassie went with Ramsay now, Charlotte and Connor's wedding and honeymoon would be unmarred.

He leaned closer, apparently concerned that she was having second thoughts. "We'll send a note to your parents so they'll not worry about you. There is writing paper and ink in the carriage. I always take good care of my guests."

Cassie laughed now, almost lighthearted at the thought of saving the day for Charlotte. And how dangerous could this adventure be, with her maid accompanying her and her parents informed of where she was? " 'Tis hardly a kidnapping the way you describe it, my lord."

"Ah, but if you come with me now, from this place, it will be a kidnapping," Ramsay said, speaking softly in a conspiratorial manner. "The lovely lass swept away by a Highland laird."

Cassie caught the scent of his spicy shaving soap. His nearness made her heart flutter. So did the thought of being clutched passionately in his arms. She couldn't resist casting him a smile. He could be so charming when they were alone together—an even better partner in an adventure than Dudley had ever thought of being. "If it is not against my will, is it still a kidnapping?"

"Of course, you are carried off with nothing but the clothes on your back," Ramsay added, with an open-palmed gesture of appeal. "What lady is willingly carried away without her travel trunk?"

Cassie laughed once more. "How true, my lord."

"Never fear, princess," Ramsay said, taking her hand again and leading her down the church steps. "I have thought of everything."

"I'm sure you have," Cassie said, allowing him to lead her toward the carriage, the thought of a trip to Scotland and a great adventure at a marquis's country home dispelling the sadness that had enveloped her throughout the wedding. "So, carry me away, my lord."

Ramsay did not pause. He released her hand and swept her up in his arms. Cassie cried out in surprise, just barely managing to hang on to her two flower bouquets. He jogged down the steps. She threw her arms around his neck, lest her struggles throw him off balance.

But his arms were strong and his gait steady. Cassie laughed as he carried her down the remaining steps toward the coach. Graham threw open the coach door. Ramsay set her down on the coach step and urged her inside.

"Come on, Betsy," Cassie called as she settled herself on the coach seat, delighted with her decision. This was going to be a grand adventure. "We're going to Scotland."

"Yes, miss, if you say so," Betsy said, frowning unhappily

as she settled down on the seat across from Cassie who was reaching for the lap desk she'd found to write the note to Papa. Soon the missive was dispatched via a messenger, and the Marquis of Linirk's coach was trundling its way out of London, headed due north.

Davis stood at the desk in his brother-in-law's library and read the two notes again. With each reading he hoped to find something new or different. He prayed to find in the handwriting of his daughter and of Linirk some clue about her whereabouts not written in words. He was disappointed once again. He cursed aloud this time. After the third reading—and the troubling fact that he and Susanna had noticed Cassie missing—the messages were taking on a nauseating reality. He'd received them only minutes ago, after the last wedding guest had departed from the Earl of Seacombe's townhouse. Odd timing.

"Those were my instructions, yer lordship," the messenger had vowed when Davis had glimpsed Cassie's handwriting and demanded to know where the messenger had come from and why now. "The lord what gave them to me said to deliver them letters after the last wedding guest had departed. And that's what I done. I waited until the last carriage rolled away, I did."

Davis questioned the man further, but he clearly knew nothing beyond his instructions. So Davis had ordered him tipped and sent on his way.

Then he'd opened letters. As he read, the champagne fog he'd been in most of the day cleared immediately. His heart had popped into his mouth. He'd forced himself to sit down and get a grip on his emotions. Cassie was in the hands of Linirk—and on her way to some remote place. How was he going to tell Susanna? What was he going to do?

"This had better be important, dear brother," Dorian said as she swept into the study with Susanna following. Nicholas ambled in behind the ladies.

"Close the door, would you, old chap," Davis said to his brother-in-law. The tall, stately earl arched a questioning brow at Davis, but did as he was bid. Nicholas was not a man to stand on ceremony.

"Yes, Davis, the wedding has been a great success," Susanna said, crossing the room to her husband with the satisfied smile of a mother of the bride. "We should leave your sister and her family to their own home again. The hour is late and we're all rather weary."

Davis absently patted his wife's hand on his arm. "Did any of you see Cassie today?"

"But of course," Dorian said, glancing around at the others for their agreement. "I saw her at the church and she looked lovely, too."

"Yes, we all saw her at the church," Susanna said, frowning a bit. "But I never did see her here. Did you, Davis?"

"These notes were just delivered to me," Davis said, holding up the papers. "One is from Cassie. It seems she has gone with the Marquis of Linirk to be his guest."

"What? May I see the note?" Susanna asked, reaching for Cassie's letter. Davis gave it to her.

Nicholas frowned. "Any word from Linirk?"

Davis held up the other note. "Indeed, he assures me that our daughter and her maid are safe under his protection. He asks if I've reconsidered the disposition of Glen Gray. And if I do, I should inform his agent here in London. Cassie could be home very soon, he says."

"The blackguard," Dorian cried.

"She wrote where they are going here, but someone has blacked it out," Susanna said, clearly troubled and perplexed. "But why would Cassie go off with Linirk like that? She's always been headstrong, but never utterly foolish."

"Obviously someone tampered with Cassie's note because he doesn't want us to know where he took her," Davis said. From the look of worry on Susanna's face he decided that this was not the time to admit that he'd never told her all he knew about Cassie's past daring escapades. Unfortunately, this was not as out of their daughter's character as her mother would like to believe.

"I'm afraid I'm to blame," Dorian said, innocently coming to Davis's rescue. "You see, Cassie came to me immediately after Dudley cried off, that very day. She looked so downcast. I advised her to throw propriety out the window, buy a new bonnet, and go about enjoying herself."

"Do you think that's why she agreed to Linirk's suit?" Susanna asked, turning to her husband.

Davis shook his head. "I don't know. But Linirk had best not harm her or I'll—"

"I really didn't think the marquis would go this far." Nicholas reached for the missive Davis held. "But when it comes to the Scots and their feuds, who knows? May I see Linirk's note?"

Thankful for his brother-in-law's cool head, Davis handed the letter to Nicholas.

"You're not going to say anything to Connor, are you?" Susanna asked, clutching at Davis's arm. "They'll be leaving for the Continent tomorrow. I don't want them upset."

"No, of course not now," Davis said, unwilling to disturb their daughter and her new husband on their honeymoon. "Charlotte and Connor don't need to know anything about this for now. But I will not have my daughter threatened nor will I be intimidated by Linirk."

"But surely Lord Linirk won't harm Cassie," Susanna began, looking from one to another of them for reassurance.

"She does not sound the least frightened in this note," Dorian observed.

"Cassandra is never frightened, not even when she should be." Davis stared at his wife in exasperation. "Susanna, don't you understand? The courtship was all a sham. I feared it was from the beginning. He approached Cassie when Dudley cried off. When she was vulnerable. He won her trust. Then he arranged for the Greek pottery exhibition that you had your heart set upon—all of it in an effort to win his way into our good graces.''

Susanna's eyes widened and her mouth trembled. "How very cynical, Davis."

"Nonsense," Davis said, growing frustrated and angry. His daughter was somewhere on the road in the company of a man who was angry with him for not accepting his offer for Glen Gray. "Linirk is heartless and ruthless. There's hardly a businessman who has ever dealt with him who doesn't know so."

"I have trouble imagining that," Susanna said, seemingly determined to side with the villain.

"I think what your husband would like for us to recall is that the marquis was probably the man who had Kinleith kidnapped," Nicholas explained gently.

"Thank you," Davis muttered, gratified to have Nicholas speak on his behalf. "I was beginning to think I was the only one who remembers Linirk's reputation. The Marquis of Linirk ruins men. Why would he not ruin our daughter?"

In the silence that followed, Susanna turned to him. With a sinking heart, Davis saw tears fill his wife's eyes.

"Oh, surely not," Susanna whispered, brushing away the tears threatening to stream down her face. "Surely he would not be so cruel to our baby girl. What has Cassandra done to deserve this?"

Davis's heart sank lower. He silently berated himself for speaking so plainly before the women. Slipping an arm around Susanna's waist, he pulled her close. Over her head, Davis met Nicholas's gaze.

"Say the word," Nicholas said. "I will serve as intermediary. I can be on the marquis's agent's doorstep in a matter of minutes."

"I hate giving in to the man," Davis muttered between his teeth.

"But you can't risk Cassie's safety," Dorian said. "I'll go myself. I'd like to tell him what I think of his disreputable behavior."

"That won't be necessary, Dorian," Nicholas said, touching his wife's shoulder. "Though I'm sure you'd have the man quailing in his boots. Let me do this."

"I'm not going to give up Glen Gray to that man." In Davis's arms Susanna began to tremble. When Davis turned toward his sister, he saw fear and concern in Dorian's eyes. He hated Linirk. "I won't set the McKensie-Forbes feud back into motion."

"You needn't do that," Nicholas said with calm and reason. He pointed at Linirk's note still in his hand. "The marquis simply asked if you would be willing to reconsider your disposition of Glen Gray. All he wants at this point—as I see it—is your agreement to discuss the matter. Tell him yes, provided he returns Cassie at the earliest possible date."

"Do it, Nicholas," Davis said. "Deliver the message."

CHAPTER FIFTEEN

By the second night on the road north, Cassie began to have second thoughts. Not because of Ramsay. He was a perfect gentleman. And with him in her company and out of London, there was little possibility that the heartless marquis could interfere with Charlotte and Connor before they left on their continental honeymoon. But the trip was longer and more arduous than she'd remembered.

Arrangements had been made for them at the best inns. Good food. Clean bed linens. Even clothing awaited them each night—fine nightrails and pretty morning gowns with a fine wool Forbes tartan shawl to wear against the chill of the early morn. Ramsay's company at meals was charming—in a restrained way. But when they traveled, he rode his black horse alongside the coach. Graham, who always seemed to be frowning, sat up front with the coachman.

Cassie sensed that the Forbes clansman was not pleased with the trip, though she had no idea why. The long hours confined to the coach were exhausting, but sometimes Ramsay rode close enough to the coach window to point out some landmark or sight of interest along the way.

Mostly they kept on the move, starting before dawn each day and driving until after dark. They stopped often to change coach horses. But Ramsay pressed the coachman to keep a fast pace.

Cassie wondered what Papa and Mama had thought when they received her note. She hoped that they would not be worrying about her.

By the end of the second day the neat, grassy meadows, the fertile wheat fields, and the dark forests of the south gave way to rolling treeless hills and shaded rocky glens.

"We'll reach Ravencliff late tomorrow," Ramsay told her when he walked her and Betsy to the door of their room that night.

"I hadn't thought being kidnapped could be so exhausting," Cassie said with a laugh.

"You're not having second thoughts, are you?" he asked, peering at her with a questioning look.

"No, of course not," Cassie replied quickly, ashamed of losing heart in an adventure he'd obviously gone to a great deal of trouble to arrange.

"I know it's a long trip, but it will be over tomorrow." Ramsay brushed a chaste kiss across her cheek. "I promise it will be worth the effort."

The warmth of his lips tingled through Cassie. She prayed he was right about the journey. She clung to him and turned her mouth toward his, hoping he would give her a real kiss. To her disappointment, he released her, his gaze glancing in Betsy's direction. Her mother might as well be standing beside her, Cassie thought.

"Sleep well, princess," Ramsay said, leaving her at the door of her chamber.

And she did sleep well. The next morning they were off before light again. When she caught sight of Ramsay from time to time, she noticed that he had begun to ride ahead instead of alongside. His face was always turned north, ahead of them, eagerness in the tension of his lips and the set of his jaw. He was impatient to catch sight of his home. Cassie was, also. Primarily she wanted to climb out of the lurching coach, too, and plant her feet on solid ground once again.

At twilight they'd crested the hill and halted long enough for Ramsay to point out the slate rooftop and twelve chimneys barely visible among the trees in the glen. The house and grounds were much larger than she'd expected, but she'd not realized how much larger until another half hour had passed before they drove up the drive and halted in front of the house.

"And this is where you grew up?" Cassie asked, stepping out of the carriage in front of Ravencliff Court. She was glad of his hand to steady her as she stretched her limbs. Her body ached from the long ride. She was glad to be out of the rough rocking of the coach and eager to see what answers Ravencliff would provide to the riddle of Ramsay Forbes.

"I was born here and lived in this house until I was ten," Ramsay said, ushering her into the house. She could feel his eyes on her, wanting to know what she thought of the place, wanting her to be favorably impressed, no doubt. And she was.

"It's beautiful," she said, as she strolled into a room that must be a drawing room. A carved and ornately painted wooden panel ceiling soared overhead. A fireplace big enough to walk into stood on the facing wall, and the western light of the day flooded into the room through the diamond-pane windows, making the room bright and welcoming.

"You've only seen the entrance," Ramsay said, at her side. "And the drawing room."

"I know," Cassie said, breathless with excitement. "But I can tell I love it. The wood is beautiful, rich and well-rubbed with love. Love always shows. And the furniture looks comfortable."

She stroked the back of massive carved wooden chair near the fireplace. " 'Tis Tudor."

"I think there may be a few French pieces somewhere,"

Ramsay said, looking around the room for something he did not find. "The house is built on the foundation of a house built by a knight who returned from the Crusades. He built the chapel, too. It remains intact. We'll see that tomorrow. Then various ancestors down through the ages have added a library here, a ballroom there, and so forth."

Around them, the servants bobbed curtsies and scurried about, taking wraps and opening doors and carrying mysterious parcels Cassie knew nothing of.

"This is my butler, Briggs. He will see to anything you need, and he will see to Betsy's welfare as well."

The tall, thin man with a full head of gray hair and sharp blue eyes bowed to Cassie.

She handed her tartan shawl to Betsy who handed the garment to Briggs who passed it to one of the maids.

"But you must show me the rest of the house," Cassie said, walking down the hallway, gazing up at the decorated ceiling.

"Now? The sun is going down."

"Now," Cassie said without hesitation. "I have not traveled all this way to be confined to one room because of the darkness."

Obviously pleased, Ramsay smiled and reached for her hand. "Then I shall indeed show you the rest of the house. Graham, candles."

Ramsay's kinsman mumbled some unintelligible answer and soon appeared with a branch of burning candles.

So they, she and Ramsay, rambled throughout the house for the next hour, Cassie taking her time to absorb all the things she saw. The library boasted a fine collection of books. An elegant chandelier appointed the ballroom with an intricately inlaid wooden floor and ornate musicians' gallery. Palms and lemon trees filled the orangery. But in the dining room, Cassie found what she was most interested in—the family portraits.

The room was quite dark, with royal-blue damask wall covering and an elaborate plastered ceiling that hovered high above them. But Cassie peered at the pictures undaunted.

"The old laird up there near the ceiling was the Forbes the year the feud began with the McKensies," Ramsay said, holding the branch of candles higher and pointing out an old small dark painting of a bearded man in a feather-trimmed bonnet.

"And who was laird when the pitched battle was fought to settle the feud?" Cassie asked, her gaze feasting on the thirteen faces of the lairds of Forbes.

"That would be Ian," Ramsay said, stepping toward another wall. "He is over here."

"He looks like a lion," Cassie said, following Ramsay's gaze. "Did he truly send more men on the field than was allowed?"

Ramsay frowned. "The McKensies lie about that. The additional Forbes men were sent onto the field to aid the wounded."

"But the battle settled nothing," Cassie said, wondering where the truth of the story lay. Had the Forbeses cheated, or had they simply tried to aid their wounded as Ramsay said? One hundred and fifty years later, the truth would probably never be known.

"Are you looking for someone special?" Ramsay asked, as Cassie examined the faces that gazed back at them from the walls. "I can have the servants light the chandelier overhead."

"I'll come to look again tomorrow," Cassie said, aware that the servants were busy in the small dining room next door, laying out an informal supper for them. "Where are your mother and father? And your sister? I want to see what they look like. You have the advantage. You have met my family."

Ramsay ceased following her and said no more as she paced around the room. For a moment, she was so intent on the men and women who stared back from the canvases that she didn't notice that he was no longer at her side. When she did, she stopped and turned back to him. He was watching her coolly.

"Is something amiss?" Cassie asked. "Oh my, what did I say? I've been babbling and I fear from that look in your eye that I've said something I shouldn't have."

"No, nothing like that," Ramsay said, carrying the branch

of candles to the side of the room where she stood, but his distant expression did not improve. He gestured upward. "That's my grandfather up there. And the boy at his side is my father."

Cassie turned to examine a portrait of a stern, brown-haired man with a surprisingly somber boy at his side. The shape of the face and the strength of the jawline were reminiscent of Ramsay's face. "The Forbeses are such serious men. Where is your mother?"

"My mother died on the Continent some years ago," Ramsay said, reaching for Cassie's arm and drawing her toward the small dining room. "There is no portrait of her in the house. However, a portrait of my sister hangs in the stairway. I'll show it to you later. Now let's have some supper."

Cassie thought his indifference strange, but decided not to question it. She was too hungry. During their meal Cassie extracted a promise from him to show her the puppies soon. But the absence of the portrait of Ramsay's mother troubled her. She thought it very strange in a house where hung a likeness of every significant relative who'd lived during the last three hundred years. Why was Ramsay's mother's picture missing?

Cassie slept well into the morning in the big tester bed of the rose bedchamber. She awakened rested to the sound of song-birds outside her window and the sun intruding between the drawn draperies. Betsy offered to carry breakfast up, but Cassie was so excited about seeing more of Ravencliff and Ramsay that she refused. As soon as she was dressed in the simple gown and tartan shawl provided, she found the breakfast room where adequate fare awaited her on the sideboard. As Cassie ate, Briggs told her that Ramsay had eaten early and was in his study seeing to estate business. He would join her later.

Though disappointed, Cassie was not particularly surprised that Ramsay had duties to see to. He'd been in London for a number of weeks. No doubt there were matters that needed his attention after such a long absence. She assumed that Graham was probably in the study with him and they might be occupied for some time. So she asked if she could view the family portraits again. Clearly relieved that the London miss would be so easily entertained, the butler readily showed her to the formal dining room.

"The sets of antlers are quite impressive," Cassie remarked, glancing at the racks over the doors. "So large."

"Yes, miss," Briggs said. "If I may explain."

"Please," Cassie said, gazing up at the wide racks of hard, shiny brown antlers.

"All the Forbeses have been first-rate shots," Briggs began, pride bristling from the square set of his shoulders. "That rack you are looking at is of a royal stag. See the twelve points, six on each side."

"Yes, I see," Cassie said, counting the points. "And that one over there is even larger, fourteen."

"Yes, that stag was brought down by his lordship himself on his tenth birthday," Briggs said, with a gleam of immodesty lingering in his eye. "Fourteen points is an imperial stag. 'Tis the only one ever shot at Ravencliff."

"Quite an accomplishment," Cassie said, admiring the majestic rack. "I'm sure that was quite an occasion for celebration."

"Yes, miss, the old marquis declared a holiday and there was feasting," Briggs said, a nostalgic grin lighting his face. "The young lord was the hero of the day."

Cassie could just imagine Ramsay strutting about, pleased as a peacock with himself. Each glimpse of him in the place where he grew up conspired to erase the villainy from the man she knew. "And where would I find the portrait of his lordship's sister, Ellen?"

"In the stairwell, miss, on the wall opposite the window," Briggs said, standing politely at the door. " 'Tis a portrait of his lordship and his sister done some years ago. Would you like me to point it out for you?"

"No, thank you, Briggs, I can find it myself," Cassie said,

studying the framed faces again. "Carry on. I can amuse
myself."

The butler bowed and left her alone.

Cassie rambled around the room, her hands clasped behind
her as she peered into the faces of generation after generation
of Forbeses. The older portraits hung near the ceiling and like-
nesses of the more recent marquises and marchionesses hung
nearer eye level. She reviewed each portrait, studying the fit-
tingly sober poses of the clan lairds. The men were posed with
their favorite dogs or horses and often in their kilts—even in
times when Cassie knew wearing of the tartan had been out-
lawed. The ladies were frequently pictured with their children.
About all of these ancestors hung the aura of self-confidence
and practicality. A glint of no-nonsense. Exacting men who
made hard choices when necessary. Some of the men had the
faraway look of visionaries, of seers of destiny. Some posed
with military bearing and gruffness. Others appeared ready to
declare a celebration. She suspected Ramsay possessed all those
qualities and more.

She moved toward the stairwell, all the while marveling how
Ravencliff, even by daylight, was so different from what she
had expected. The downstairs rooms were lofty, well-lit, and
comfortable, with thick rugs on the floor and deep chairs by the
fireside. It was a home where people dwelled, not an untouched
showplace meant to impress, like so many of the London homes
or country houses.

In the stairwell she found the portrait of Ramsay and his
sister Ellen opposite the mullioned window where Briggs said
it would be. It was a large portrait of a blond boy and a girl
sitting with a basket of playful Nairn puppies. Both children
were so absorbed in the pups that neither looked out at the
viewer. A moment in time captured by a talented artist. Ellen
appeared to be much like her brother: graceful, elegant, fair,
and aristocratic. Even as a boy Ramsay displayed his trademark
refinement, quite unlike the demeanor of the other Forbeses
Cassie had seen in the dining room. Those faces were of solid,

rosy-cheeked, hardy Scottish stock. Boisterous. Bold. Energetic. All brown-haired and suitably decked out for their station in life, yet prosaic. Ramsay and Ellen's mother must have brought that dark-blond fairness into the family. Cassie suspected that their mother looked much like Ellen. She would have been a lovely woman. How strange that her portrait was not to be found in the collection.

"Have ye ferreted out what ye were looking for?"

The grating sound of Graham's voice was so near and so unexpected, it startled Cassie. She jumped, then rounded on the man. He stood on the landing just below, glaring at her as if he'd caught her snooping through the personal family closet.

"I wanted to see what Ellen looked like," Cassie snapped. All she was doing was studying family portraits and she was not going to let his unfair implication embarrass her. "And I'd appreciate it if you would not creep up on me like that."

"Perhaps if ye were no poking around alone, ye wouldna have to be fearful of others surprising ye," Graham said with a sneer.

"The marquis forbade no part of the house to me," Cassie replied, meeting his gaze levelly. She'd disliked Graham from the first day she'd met him at Charlotte's engagement breakfast, the day he'd delivered the betrothal gifts from Ramsay. He had cold, gray eyes. From the beginning of her courtship with Ramsay, it had been obvious that Graham was no fonder of her than she was of him. Yet this morning the virulence of his hostility surprised her. "I merely wanted to get to know the family better."

"Well, donna spend much time or trouble on that study," Graham said, his fists planted on his hips like a factor delivering orders to a tenant. "I'll never know why he brought ye all this way. He donna open his home to his women, ever."

Cassie stared at Graham and her heart went still. She knew that this man wanted to hurt her. She could feel it, but wasn't going to let that frighten her. "Just what do you mean by 'his women'?"

"I mean his mistresses, and donna think ye are not one of them," Graham said. "The fact he brought you here when he's not brought any of the others donna mean nothing. All ye need to know is ye'll never be any more than a mistress to him. So donna set yer sights on his lordship. Donna get any silly idears in yer head."

She took a deep breath and forced her expression to remain as bland as possible. "I'm afraid I don't understand what you are trying to say."

"I mean, banish any lovesick notions from yer head," Graham said. "His mother banished him to the Highlands when he'd just celebrated his tenth birthday. Then his fiancée, Aileen, he worshiped the ground she walked on. She eloped with another. Every woman in his life has betrayed him. He will never marry, lass."

Indeed, her head was spinning with what Graham had just told her. She'd had no idea that Ramsay had been sent away by his mother or that he'd once had a fiancée. Sadness filled her for Ramsay the boy, who must have hated being sent from Ravencliff. "I know his mother is dead. What happened to Aileen?"

"She lives on the Continent in poverty with her husband," Graham said with a frown, strangely smug with satisfaction. "But she was unworthy to become marchioness. Few young ladies, even those of good family, are qualified to take up such a title. I'm a-warnin' ye, get any pretty ideas like that out of yer head. As soon as he be satisfied, he will be finished with ye. And ye will be on yer way home to London with yer head a-spinnin'."

His tone clearly implied that Cassie ranked among the unworthy for the title. When he met her gaze, this time Cassie saw the spitefulness in his gray eyes.

Astonished by Graham's maliciousness, Cassie drew herself up and glared at him. As suspicious as she might be of Ramsay's intentions, she had few illusions about Graham's goals. He did not like her. She didn't understand why. Perhaps he was jealous of the attention that Ramsay bestowed on her. But she was not about to allow Graham to humiliate her. Nor would she permit him to believe her a fool.

"Thank you for the warning." With an imperious lift of her chin Cassie continued. "Rest assured, Mr. Andrews, that I have a better understanding of why I'm here than you may think. You see, an heiress has a fair sense of her value."

The surprise that crossed Graham's face pleased her, but she did not allow it to show.

The ring of Ramsay's footsteps on the floor below brought them both around to face him. The interruption brought a welcome air of relief.

"Good morning, my lord," Cassie called, with genuine pleasure.

Ramsay stopped at the bottom of the stairway. "There you two are."

"Aye, here we be," Graham said, his glance silently declaring the confidentiality of their conversation. Cassie ignored the look.

"Discussing family portraits, my lord," Cassie said, her heart tripping at the sight of Ramsay's stern good looks. He stood with his hand carelessly resting on the newel post and his foot on the first step. He was informally dressed in a white shirt, a long, black old-fashioned waistcoat, trousers, and boots. His cravat was meticulously fashioned, as ever. He looked rested, and more at ease than she ever recalled seeing him. Being at Ravencliff seemed to agree with him. Despite Graham's attitude and her own misgivings, she was glad she'd come.

She smiled at Ramsay. When she looked down into his green eyes, she saw pleasure at the sight of her. He hardly looked like a motherless boy or a woman-hating man as his eyes roamed over her. Unable to resist the urge, she touched her hair to be certain any stray tendrils were in place.

Graham frowned. "I was just showing Miss St. John the portrait of you and your sister."

"Yes, I see you were partial to Nairn hounds even in those days," Cassie said, seeing no reason to spoil the moment by tattling on Graham's rudeness.

"Does that surprise you?" Ramsay asked, a soft smile on his lips. "Dogs are such good companions. Unlike people. Once you've made friends with a dog, he will remain loyal. He won't betray you."

"That's true, my lord," Cassie said, glancing briefly at Graham. But Graham turned away, leaving her more perplexed than ever.

Determined to remain aloof from Graham, she took Ramsay's arm as she glanced back at the clansman one last time. When she caught his eye, she added, "Indeed, my lord, loyalty is so important. Don't you agree, Mr. Andrews?"

"Aye," Graham said, his frown deepening at the sight of Cassie on Ramsay's arm. "Loyalty is everything."

CHAPTER SIXTEEN

"If there is a ghost anywhere at Ravencliff, it is here in the chapel," Ramsay said, standing back from the sanctuary door so that Cassie could enter first. His voice was full of amusement. She knew he was patronizing her, but she didn't care. His company was a welcome change after that unsettling confrontation with Graham.

"A ghost? But you told me there was no ghost." Cassie stepped into the small dark stone house of worship and waited for her eyes to adjust to the gloom. From the outside, the little chapel was as grand and dignified as a small cathedral, complete with small graceful spires and stone-carved gargoyles and saints.

From what Cassie could make out inside, the interior was just as detailed. Delicate stone flowers graced the pillars. Along the inside walls, tombstones of long-dead Forbeses—the dates so old they'd been worn away from the passing of many feet— flagged the floor.

"Remember, you asked about a gray lady at Ravencliff?" Ramsay said, pulling the door closed and remaining so near her that his breath tickled her ear.

"And you said there was none." Cassie's belly quivered. She stepped away from him lest her knees become as soft.

"There is no gray lady walking the halls of the house," Ramsay said, his voice full of mock apology now. "I'm afraid the best I can do is a knight in the chapel."

"Who is he? An ancestor? Does anyone know?" Cassie asked, delighted with the prospect of seeing a ghost. Her eyes having adjusted to the gloom, she stepped farther into the chapel.

"The common tale is that the apparition is the ghost of Sir Calum who came home from the Holy Land in the eleven hundreds and built the chapel to give thanks for his safe return," Ramsay explained. "His home was the foundation for Ravencliff."

"What a delightful story." Cassie admired the trinity of stained-glass windows facing south over the altar. "Where is this gray knight seen?"

Ramsay paused as if he was reluctant to answer her question. "At the altar, and he's more golden in color, actually."

"A golden ghost?" Suddenly realizing what he was saying, Cassie turned to Ramsay in excitement. "You've seen him?"

"When I was a boy," Ramsay added with a shrug, as if his young age made the experience doubtful. "That was so long ago, I almost wonder if it was real or just the figment of a boy's imagination."

"Do tell me about it," Cassie urged, not just because she loved ghost stories, but because she was eager to have Ramsay share something so special with her. "What did the ghost knight look like? Did he glow?"

"It happened in broad daylight," Ramsay said, eyeing her as if he wanted to be certain that she wasn't going to laugh at him.

"Yes, do go on," she implored, smiling to herself. His uncertainty touched her. Ramsay, the villain of every plot, feared her laughter. "Please tell me. I love ghost stories too much to ever make fun of one."

Her earnestness seemed to convince him. "It was a summer day, and I must have been about eight or nine at the time. I was playing some game with Ellen and one of the steward's sons. I ran in here where I knew it would be cool and quiet and neither of them would think to look for me. At first I stood at the door much as we did today. As my eyes adjusted to the darkness I saw the form of a knight—at least it appeared to be a knight—in armor and helmet, kneeling at the altar, his head bowed in prayer."

Cassie whirled around to peer at the altar, hoping in a silly, futile way that the ghost knight might appear for her also. But the altar was bare, awash in the colored sunlight falling through the chapel windows. "Had you heard of him before?"

"I'd heard of Sir Calum," Ramsay said, with a nod. "We all knew his story. Of how he'd returned from the Holy Land to find his wife and his house still awaiting his return. None of that a small miracle in those times when Scotland was fighting for her independence from England. Sir Calum was so grateful, he built the chapel and named it after his wife's patron saint, Saint Margaret. Though the story goes that he appears during the full moon, no one had ever told me of seeing him. No one has ever been afraid of the chapel."

"But then what happened?" Cassie asked, anxious to know all the denials. "Did the ghost move from the altar?"

"No, I saw no movement," Ramsay said, smiling a bit more now. "He did not turn and point a finger at me to pronounce a curse or anything melodramatic like that."

"I didn't mean that," Cassie sputtered in exasperation. "What happened? Did he disappear? Did he turn so you could see his face? Were you frightened?"

"No, not especially," Ramsay said, an uncharacteristically faraway look in his eye as he recalled the details. "It was strange, but not overly frightening at the moment. I knew he was not real. I mean, the apparition was real, but his corporeal existence was not like ours. I could see the altar vaguely through him. The feeling in the chapel was very peaceful. Serene. I felt no threat or menace. But I knew somehow that he was praying and that I should not intrude on him.''

Cassie nodded. "Then?"

Ramsay shrugged. "The sun went behind the cloud, and his image faded with the dwindling of the light. As I watched, the altar became vacant.''

"Did you ever see him again?" she asked, turning again to watch the altar in fascination.

"One other time I thought I glimpsed him, during a Sunday-morning service with everyone from the house sitting right here with me," Ramsay said, "but his image was not as sharp as before and no one else seemed to notice him.''

"Did you ever tell anyone?" Cassie asked, thinking how strange it was that this boy would see what no one else could.

"My sister, Ellen, which was a mistake," Ramsay said, with an endearingly sheepish smile. "She mocked the idea of a ghost in the chapel. My younger sister is a very practical woman. She doesn't believe in ghosts or second sight. I'm sure she's never seen an apparition of any kind. And foolish would be the ghost who dared trouble her.''

Cassie laughed softly as she looked up into Ramsay's green eyes, pleased to see a new softness there that she'd never seen in London. "You know, my lord, until this very morning I would have voiced the same sentiments about you. Skeptical and cynical and deserving of your reputation as a cold man.''

"Aye, that is my reputation." Ramsay looked away from her, and a painful frown crossed his face so quickly Cassie almost doubted she'd seen it. He turned his back toward her and paced toward the altar. "And what do you think now that you've seen my home? Now that you've heard my ghost story?''

"Do you truly want to know?" Cassie asked, butterflies of uncertainty fluttering in her belly.

"Yes, I want to know," he said, turning to face her, his face open, even a light of curiosity in his eyes.

"I think you are a complex man who prefers to obscure his

real self behind a scurrilous reputation," Cassie said, praying that her honest opinion was the right thing to confess.

Ramsay laughed, a soft, bitter laugh that sent chills down Cassie's back. "I assure you my reputation is earned, princess."

"I did not mean to say that it was not earned, my lord," Cassie said, strolling to the opposite side of the chapel. "I merely meant to say that there is so much more to you than your reputation. If everyone knew that your mother had banished you from your family home when you were ten and that your fiancée had deserted you, they might view your actions differently."

"Who told you those things?" Ramsay demanded in a sharp voice.

"I must have overheard them somewhere," Cassie said, looking at him with her eyes wide and innocent.

"Bloody hell . . ." Ramsay turned away from her, muttering under his breath, obviously displeased. "Graham's been talking, hasn't he?"

Cassie shrugged.

"It is not his place to go about spilling family secrets to visitors to Ravencliff," Ramsay said.

"Be that as it may," Cassie said, "it must have been very difficult for you to be sent away from a place that you obviously love so much."

Ramsay paused for a long moment, clearly struggling for an answer. Finally he spoke. "It may be hard for you to understand, princess. But I lost more than a place that I love when she sent me away. Your mother is a delightful, loving woman. But I lost my mother when I was ten, not because she sent me away, but because she betrayed my father and me—with another man."

Cassie gasped. "You mean—?"

"I walked in on her and her lover," Ramsay said, his mouth pressed into a thin white line.

"How awful," Cassie said, her mind barely able to comprehend the pain and shock of such a scene.

"She extracted a promise from me that I not tell my father,"

Ramsay said, turning away slightly. "I tried to honor that vow. But I was only ten. To me, my mother's indiscretion not only shocked my sensibilities, it also cast doubts on every word of love and concern that she'd spoken—to me or to my father."

"That's perfectly understandable," Cassie said, looking up into his face, longing to make these unhappy memories easier for him to bear. "Perhaps there were things that you did not know. Perhaps she was very unhappy. Perhaps if you could have heard her side of the story, you would forgive her."

He shook his head. Though the deep frown left his face, ghosts of pain haunted his green eyes. "I learned later that the man I discovered her with was not her first lover, nor her last. How can a son forgive that?"

"So you've never gotten over your mother's betrayal?" Cassie asked, realizing how his life had been shaped by that one defining moment.

"But I have," Ramsay said, with a forced smile. "The man in me has gotten beyond it. I hardly ever think of my mother." He tapped his chest. "But the boy inside . . ."

Responding to the urge to touch him, Cassie placed her hand on his chest, over his heart. The body beneath her hand was warm and solid. She stared at her hand, taking pleasure in the powerful heartbeat beneath her fingers. "You mean the boy in here where I can feel the thudding of your heart?"

Ramsay's eyes widened in surprise, but he did not draw away. Cassie felt a shudder pass through him. Then slowly he raised his hand and put it over hers. His palm was warm and dry and his hand steady. "Yes, that boy still hates her for what she did to my father and me."

"There's no wounded heart here," she said, holding his gaze. "This organ is strong. I think it wants to heal. I believe the boy can heal too."

Ramsay's face suddenly grew stern, almost hard. He shook his head and pushed her hand away. "No, some wounds are too deep and too angry to heal properly. Perhaps 'tis better to accept that one is maimed and get on with it."

Disappointed with his unwillingness to accept her commiseration, Cassie stepped away from him.

"Come now, no pity needed here," he said with a dry laugh. "I did not suffer overly much. Graham and his family became my family, too. Make no sad faces on my account, princess. I did not bring you here to make you unhappy. Now, let's forget about things long past."

"Yes, let's," Cassie agreed, though she knew this was unfinished business. She also still longed to know about his fiancée, Aileen—and the fabled mistresses. But clearly now wasn't the time to ask more questions. She took his hand. "As I recall, my lord, you brought me here to show me the puppies you purchased on the Thames."

"Let me give you a tour of the grounds first," Ramsay said. "Then we'll find the pups."

He showed her the dovecote and the dairy. They strolled through the kitchen garden at the back of the sprawling house and through the formal French garden to the east, just barely visible from the deer park that stretched from the hills down into the valley and along the river. Ramsay described it all for her, smiling at her innocent questions. Though he seemed to endeavor to remain nonplussed by all that he showed her, Cassie could see the pride in his face and hear it in his voice. He truly loved Ravencliff and it wasn't difficult to believe that he'd much rather spend his time in this lovely place than in London.

The puppies were in the kennel between a stableful of fine riding and coaching horses and a coach-house full of vehicles of every description. Cassie continued to ask him questions just because she liked seeing that pride in his eyes and hearing its richness in his voice.

In the warmth of the day, as he explained a plan he had for improving his cattle, Ramsay unwrapped the cravat from around his throat as he talked. He opened his shirt down to his collarbone. Enough for Cassie to catch a glimpse of the pulse in his throat and the hint of golden hair that must cover his chest. Eyeing the sight, she had difficulty concentrating on his words.

Inside the kennel, Cassie dropped down into the fresh straw near the door. The scent of straw and piney sawdust filled the air. The trainer and his helpers, the sons of servants and farmers, carried the litter in, black and squirming, armful by armful. The puppies were sleek and fat, with mouthfuls of sharp teeth. Finding herself attacked by a swarm of pink-tongued, floppy-eared pups, she opened her arms to them. They leaped at her, tugging at her gown and licking her face, leaving her helpless with laughter.

To save the lace on the sleeves of her gown, she unbuttoned them and rolled them up to the elbow, then undid the restrictive hook at her throat. Absently she tried to tuck loose tendrils back into her coif, but her heavy red hair refused to oblige and she gave up.

She caught Ramsay staring at her. "Do I look too disreputable, my lord?"

His lips thinned as if something displeased him. "The puppies don't seem to think so."

"But look how they've grown," she exclaimed, mystified by his frown and determined to ignore it. She rubbed the round belly of one little female. "I know they don't remember me, but it's fun to think they do."

"I'm convinced they remember you," Ramsay said, crouching down beside her, his frown of displeasure disappearing. "If it weren't for you, I probably would have split the litter up. They owe you much."

Cassie laughed. "What are their names? How goes their training?"

The trainer, a gray-haired man named Tanner, obligingly pointed out their names and explained that they were all excellent pupils and would undoubtedly prove valuable beasts once their training was complete.

She and Ramsay played with the pups, then watched as the trainer put them through their paces. Ramsay assisted. Cassie was amazed at his patience with the young dogs. The stern man in black that she'd first met in London hardly seemed the type to sit in the straw with her and play tug-of-war with puppies. With boyish enthusiasm he led them in Follow the Leader and nearly all the pups followed Ramsay. Then Cassie called, and they romped after her, nipping at her skirts and yapping at the toy in her hand.

"And who can fetch?" Cassie challenged, tossing the ball toward the door. Nearly all bound after the prize. The pups romped, tumbled, and sprawled, sleek black balls of flailing legs and tails. It seemed perfectly natural for Ramsay and Cassie to brush hands and rub shoulders together as they played with the dogs.

When they paused for a moment to take count and see who was missing, Cassie smiled at Ramsay and sank down onto the straw again. "I'm so glad you talked me into coming here with you."

Ramsay settled down beside her, gently shaking himself free of a particularly persistent pup which would not release his sleeve. He handed it to Tanner. Then he turned back to Cassie, peering into her face for a long silent moment. Then he took her hand and kissed it, an endearing, spontaneous gesture that startled Cassie. Their eyes met over her hand while it was still pressed against his mouth. Desire burned in his green eyes. Cassie swallowed dryly.

Ramsay turned toward the trainer who'd remained to help them contain the puppies.

"Leave us," he ordered. The man tipped his hat and disappeared out the door.

"I'm glad you agreed to come, too," he murmured, his lips brushing against the sensitive skin of her knuckles once more.

Though it was her hand that he kissed, a surge of heat rushed through Cassie's belly and breasts. Did it show, that his touch affected her body? Certain that he could see how he thrilled her, a blush burned in her cheeks.

Swiftly he dropped her hand. His eyes searching hers, he seized her shoulders, drew her close, and kissed her hotly, hungrily. Cassie surrendered to the kiss Almost guiltily she slipped her arms around his neck and acknowledged to herself that this was what she'd wanted and hoped for from the moment she'd agreed to go away with him. This kiss, this intimacy that he'd introduced her to on the river barge. This piece of himself that she knew he kept hidden and protected.

He wanted her and she wanted him. No man's touch had ever made her feel so desirable—so hungry—as his did. She gave herself over to it.

They sank down on the kennel straw, him above her, pressing her down into the softness. His lean body covered hers and blocked the light. Cassie willed her body to melt into his. She arched against him until she could feel the buttons of his clothing bite into her flesh. He groaned, slipping his arms around her, his hands sliding down her back to stroke her derriere and to press her leg against his long, powerful thighs.

Something yanked at Cassie's loose hair. She gently attempted to brush away the puppy. Tiny sharp teeth nipped at her earlobe. Cassie whimpered a protest. Without releasing her mouth, Ramsay moved, fending off the eager puppy onslaught. Then a puppy's cold and wet nose nuzzled her ear. The sensation was so startling Cassie choked.

Ramsay released her immediately and pulled her up into a sitting position so they faced each other. "Are you all right?"

"Yes, I'm sorry, my lord," Cassie said with a gasp, feeling foolish and quite unwilling to stop just because of the dogs. She couldn't help but giggle.

"I should have known better than to try to compete with a litter of pups," he said, quickly moving away from her, putting more than an arm's length between them. The pups instantly invaded the gap.

Cassie yearned for the warmth of his arms around her. It seemed almost cruel to have the strength and passion of his embrace withdrawn so suddenly.

"But I much prefer your mauling to theirs," she said, laughing unabashedly as she reached for him, hoping to draw him near for another kiss.

To her surprise, he resisted, leaning away, his lips thinning as if he regretted what had just passed between them. "You shouldn't accept either mauling, if you don't wish it." His voice was cold.

Cassie froze, trying to imagine what she'd said or done to make him pull away. Was she not experienced enough? She'd only seriously practiced kissing on Dudley. He'd always seemed pleased with her efforts. And on the barge Ramsay had seemed satisfied—until the waterman had interrupted. Maybe she'd not been as successful that day as she thought. "But I don't mind. Honestly. They're but puppies and you—"

"I'm a heartless man," he said without looking at her. "Don't forget it."

"I don't forget," Cassie said, more puzzled than ever. "I just don't believe it."

"Believe it," Ramsay said and turned his back on her.

"Straighten your gown," Ramsay ordered over his shoulder, his back still toward Cassandra. He got to his feet without facing her. He feared his face would betray the fierce desire burning within him. Certainly his body would. Thankfully he'd worn his favorite long waistcoat which covered his body's treason. Now his conscience troubled him, too. His conscience was more difficult to deal with. He wanted Cassandra more than he'd ever wanted a woman. Panic wormed painfully in his gut. Not because he was afraid of her father, but because he was afraid of her—of what she could do to him. " 'Tis time to go back to the house."

"We were having such a good time." Bewilderment filled her voice and touched his heart. "I'm sorry if I said something wrong."

Ramsay felt like an oaf and a scoundrel all wrapped up in one. He glanced over his shoulder at her and caught a glimpse of the straw clinging to her red tresses and the wrinkles he'd pressed into her plain gown. She stared back at him crestfallen.

Once, he had thought her a spoiled chit, nothing more than a pawn in a deadly game he played. As long as she'd been nothing more, it had been all right to kiss her, to touch her, to seduce her. Heaven knew she was willing enough to be seduced.

But she'd given his conscience its final kick when she'd put her hand on his heart and declared it strong enough to heal. The very organ he'd denied possessing had pounded like a steam engine when the warmth of her small palm had soaked into it.

He'd never known until that moment a heart still beat inside him—a wounded heart. But she had put her hand on his chest and found it—raw and bleeding though it was. He'd looked into her eyes and discovered no pity there. Only caring.

She cared for him. The man who'd chosen to be the villain of her life. How dare he repay such generosity with seduction?

"You said nothing wrong," Ramsay muttered, wishing he could think of something to make him angry with her. Wishing for some way to blame this awkward moment on her. Some excuse to send her away so he could gather his wits. Life was so much simpler when a woman was at fault for your troubles. "Don't you need to freshen up before dinner or something?"

That was the bloody wrong thing to say. She stared down at herself in dismay, at her rumpled gown and twisted bodice.

"I'm sorry if there is something about my person that gives offense," she began, looking up at him again with a brave face that stirred tender feelings he'd only lately discovered he owned. For a moment he thought his fearless Cassandra was going to weep. Silently he cursed his hasty words. But she shed no tears. He should have known.

Ramsay sighed in exasperation, with himself and her. He could not have her thinking that his folly was her fault. He turned and reached for her hand to help her up. "Come here. Nothing about you gives offense, princess. That's not what I meant to say."

She accepted his hand and got up gracefully, the line of her mouth somber. She tugged her bodice aright and shook straw from her skirt. When she looked up at him again, doubt clouded her blue eyes.

He couldn't resist pulling her close once more to reassure her.

"You've done nothing wrong," he whispered against her mouth, longing to taste her again, to savor deeply of her once more. Familiar panic wormed in his gut again. Gently he set her away from him. "Go back to the house and dress for dinner. I'll be along later. It's all right."

She peered into his face, searching for the truth in his words. He prayed that she found it there. Apparently she did, for at last a smile touched her lips. As if she was satisfied with his answer, she turned without saying a word and left the kennel.

Ramsay remained where he was, his head lowered, listening to the crunch of her light, rapid footsteps on the gravel fade away toward the house. He closed his eyes against the knowledge that he'd lied to her once again. He'd only wanted to reassure her. But it wasn't "all right," his rediscovered heart told him. Nothing about her being at Ravencliff was "all right." And nothing about his life would be all right again.

CHAPTER
SEVENTEEN

"Damnation, why didna ye do the deed?" Graham demanded hardly an hour later when he strode into Ramsay's study in response to a summons. He'd already heard about the little tryst between Ramsay and the St. John lass in the kennel. He could hardly believe that Ramsay had failed to get beneath her skirts. This whole kidnapping and seduction was drawing out longer than Graham had expected. It played havoc with his nerves. He dropped down into a chair before Ramsay's desk. "Tanner told me all about it, the two of ye in the straw. I canna believe ye didna put yer pizzle to her and be done with it."

Ramsay frowned from behind his desk. "I shall have to warn Mr. Tanner to mind his mouth. I asked you to come here to discuss this letter from McNeal. It was waiting for me when I returned to the house."

"Ye should have bedded her in the straw like you did Lady Moreen afore she knew what happened," Graham pressed, unable to keep the impatience from his voice. He was annoyed with Ramsay and with the lass. She seemed to like Ramsay— too well. Graham had tried to put her off with the truth about Ramsay's mistresses only this morning. But from the way she'd romped in the hay with the puppies and Ramsay, according to Tanner, she'd hardly listened. "The lass could hardly call it ravishment the way she is throwing herself at ye."

"The kennel was not the time or the place to seduce a lady," Ramsay snapped, a deep frown lining his face. "I'd appreciate it if you would keep your barnyard thoughts to yourself."

"Well, ain't ye the refined gentleman now," Graham goaded, sitting farther back in his chair and contemplating the irritation on Ramsay's face. What was going on with his foster brother and the lass? Graham was beginning to think he'd underestimated her. "So what are we doing now? Treating the lady like a houseguest? Squiring her around the manor like she were the King himself? And she no more than a commoner with a rich papa."

"I'll entertain her the way I see fit." Without so much as a flicker of acknowledgment of Graham's taunt, Ramsay tapped a finger on the letter before him. "According to this missive sent by our good neighbor, McNeal, our tenant John Jenner has been rustling again."

"Blast it, I don't give a pig's ear about McNeal and Jenner," Graham said, leaning forward in his chair. Ramsay's evasiveness was making him angry. "I wanna know what's happenin' between ye and the lass. Because I keep gettin' the feelin' this whole blasted scheme is one bloody mistake. Am I wrong? She's got ye wrapped around her finger and she's running the bloody conspiracy now."

"That's not true." Ramsay glared at Graham across the desk. As Graham watched, Ramsay's fiery anger turned to ice— green and murderously cold. Instinctively Graham leaned back, beyond Ramsay's reach.

"Yer not losin' sight of our goal, are ye?" Graham continued to query. "I remember when mention of Glen Gray put a fire in yer gut and a light in your eyes, lad. I remember when there were fightin' words on yer lips at the mention of the McKensie name. Where's that fightin' spirit now?"

"I have not lost my fighting spirit, as you call it," Ramsay muttered between tight lips. "Rest assured I have not forgotten what we're after. And I'll remind *you* of some things. First, seduction was never an essential part of the plan. Surely you understood that."

"I did not," Graham said, astonished by Ramsay's revelation. "When did that part of the plan change?"

"That never changed," Ramsay said with a shake of his head. "To win over Cassandra was, and has always been, a ploy to generate fear in her father. If physical seduction is required, then so be it. But the threat of it should be enough. I might add, I've taken my mistresses when and where I wanted them, but I've never sunk to seducing a lady to get what I wanted—I fail to see why it is so bloody damned important now."

Graham gave a harsh laugh of disbelief. "So we brought the lass here instead of an inn outside of London to offer her hospitality until her father begins to see things differently?"

"I decided to bring her here because being in Scotland makes it difficult for the long arm of British law to do anything," Ramsay said. "If we'd stayed around London her father or her uncle, the earl, would have been certain to find us."

"Aye, that I understand," Graham agreed. He'd felt safer the moment they'd crossed the border, though technically the magistrate could still come after them. And their local magistrate was McNeal, their nearest neighbor. "So, have we had any message from London?"

" 'Tis too soon," Ramsay said, returning his interest to the letter on the desk. "We must be patient."

"Aye, I suppose," Graham said, his anger and doubts only partially mollified.

"Rest assured that everything is going as planned," Ramsay said. "We must have patience. We must allow St. John to pull himself together and calm his wife once they understand what has happened. Then I can tell you exactly what will be going through Davis St. John's head. He will be thinking that he could have saved his daughter from this peril. If he'd accepted

my last proposal, she would be safe. And he would be introduc-
ing himself and his lovely wife to Society as Sir Davis and
Lady Susanna.''

''Aye, so he could be.'' Graham chuckled at the thought of
the dismaying dilemma St. John now faced. ''But he didna
accept and here we are. What happens if her father willna take
her back? He's gonna think ye've had yer way with her whether
ye did or no. Don't laugh. I've seen it happen. Sometimes a
father be no more willin' to take back a ruined daughter than
a husband be.''

Now Ramsay was chuckling. ''St. John will take her back.
Never fear.''

''And ye'll return her in exchange for Glen Gray?'' Graham
said.

''Of course, why do you ask that?''

'' 'Tis impossible not to see,'' Graham said, shifting impatiently in his chair again. ''Ye want the lass. If I thought it
possible that ye could be corrupted by an English girl, I'd never
'ave agreed to this folly.''

''Remember, you're talking to the man who has no heart,''
Ramsay said, but something about his tone lacked conviction.
''It shriveled up and died long ago, my friend. Smooth your
feathers back into place.''

''Aye, so I seemed to recall.'' Graham met his gaze, remembering something he'd heard that he knew Ramsay would want
to hear. ''By the way, news reached me that Aileen's husband
lost his position at the customshouse in Amsterdam and he's
too ill to work.''

''Such a shame,'' Ramsay replied, without a single note of
sympathy in his voice. ''But her children are being provided
for by her mother, are they not?''

''Aye, the children thrive with their grandmother,'' Graham
said, reassured by his foster brother's ongoing pleasure in the
vengeance he had wreaked on his former fiancée.

''Then shall we get back to business?'' Ramsay said, looking down at the letter on his desk once more. "Let's devote ourselves to the matters we can control for now."

"Aye, back to business—so what do ye want me to do about Jenner?" Graham asked.

"Get yourself up to his place today," Ramsay ordered. "Count his cattle and any sheep you find, too. And remind him that if he has any more grand ideas about stealing the beasts, he'd best take his rustling farther from home. Aren't there some McKensies or Drummonds he can pester? Tell Jenner if he goes after our friendly local magistrate, McNeal, again, I'll have his hide."

"Aye, consider it done," Graham said, rising from his chair and grinning at his laird. These orders sounded like the Ramsay he knew. Laying down the rules hard and clear. "I'll make sure Jenner knows what's good for him. I'll leave the lass to you."

" 'Tis the most beautiful dinner dress I've ever seen," Betsy exclaimed, hovering behind Cassie who gazed at herself in the mirror. Silently Cassie had to agree.

Betsy had found the dinner gown of the amaranthus-colored fabric that they'd admired not long ago in the Henrietta Street shop window. It had been hanging in the dressing room of the rose bedchamber. In fact, everything Cassie needed had been neatly stored in the dressing room, everything from lacy silk undergarments to a beribboned nightrail of the finest linen. Stockings. Slippers. Garters and petticoats. Combs and brushes. Nothing had been overlooked.

"So well-made," Betsy added. "Look how the fabric drapes just so here."

Indeed it was exquisite, thought Cassie, the gown's color— a shade of purple with a pinkish tint—and its design, an off-the-shoulder style with a draped collar and puff sleeves. The gown suited her perfectly.

"I could not have chosen better myself," she murmured as

she turned slightly to admire the lay of the collar across her shoulder. The thoughtfulness was impressive, but the presumption of selecting her personal things troubled Cassie.

What an enigma Ramsay was. He'd been generous and thoughtful throughout this entire trip. Then suddenly in the kennel, just when he'd begun to kiss her with all the tenderness and passion she'd sampled on the barge, he turned his back on her and became a stranger again.

"How do you think his lordship knew about the fabric?" Betsy asked.

"He must have seen us lingering in front of the shop window," Cassie speculated, unsurprised by Ramsay's skillful observations—or spying. He'd proved himself to be alert and attentive more than once, even if only for his own purposes. But his rejection of her in the kennel troubled Cassie. In fact, it hurt.

After he'd told her about his mother so openly, she'd begun to feel as if they were growing close, beginning to know each other as friends at least, if not as intimates. She'd almost thought he'd been affected when she'd touched his heart and encouraged him to forgive his mother. But perhaps that had only been an act. He had also proved himself an able play actor. Now she couldn't be certain about his reaction to her in the chapel. Perhaps Graham was right about his foster brother and his dislike for women. After all, Graham knew Ramsay at least as well as she did, she reminded herself.

Her heart ached for the boy who'd found his mother in a scandalous position with another man. How he must have doubted his mother's love after that. Despite all he'd said and done she couldn't help but feel that he'd deserved better. And in time he would find it, if he could give the people around him a chance. If he would give her a chance. It might be Glen Gray that he wanted. But Cassie knew it was not what he needed.

When the dinner gong sounded, Cassie found Ramsay staring into the fire in the dining-room hearth. The flames lit his face.

He'd not heard her enter the room and she took the moment to admire him. He wore his usual black attire with a black cashmere waistcoat intricately trimmed in black silk braid. The firelight brightened his dark blond hair to gold and softened the stern repose of his face. He seemed so serious and engrossed in thought that she feared his mood had not improved since their kiss in the kennel.

"My lord, I'm certain this is quite improper," Cassie said, stepping into the room. The rustle of her gown announced her as grandly as any words.

When he turned to her, a slow smile of appreciation spread across his face. Cassie warmed under his scrutiny. Stepping toward her, he reached for her hand. "If you mean the dress, I assure you that you are mistaken. Nothing that turns out so lovely can be improper."

"But 'tis not quite the proper sort of gift." Cassie accepted his hand and curtsied. "And how did you know I wanted it?"

"Know what?" he asked, gazing into her eyes. "I saw the fabric in the window and thought it perfect for you. When I knew I'd . . . uh, that we would be journeying north, I ordered it. The dressmaker was full of questions. So I described your pretty shoulders and your lovely throat which I discovered that day of our barge trip. She drew this up. I believe she added the sleeves for fashion."

"You truly did think of everything," Cassie said, surprised and a bit embarrassed by his reference to their intimate moment on the river. Then she leaned closer to speak so that the servants would not overhear her. "But Betsy is quite outraged. 'Tis not fitting, she says, for a man to give a gown to a lady other than his wife."

Dismay slipped into Ramsay's expression. "But Miss St. John, I'm merely providing for my guest."

"And how successfully you have done that," Cassie said with a laugh, delighted that the irritation he'd displayed earlier in the kennel was gone.

"I hope you find dinner to your liking," Ramsay said, leading her toward the table. "Cook was pleased to have guests to prove her skills to."

"I'm sure I'll love it," Cassie said, unable to resist touching her mouth with her fingertips as the memory of his kiss came flooding back. She let her eyes close as the memories made her flushed and languid. The marquis was certainly full of surprises. Full of heat and passion—and denial. She opened her eyes again at the thought of how quickly he'd set her away from him and drawn an invisible barrier between them in the kennel, but now he was himself again.

With all the decorum of a London gentleman, Ramsay seated her at his right at the long, shiny dining-room table. The meal proceeded smoothly with Briggs, the butler, serving them himself. Her wineglass seemed bottomless. The food was flavorful and deliciously prepared. Ramsay's company was charming. They talked of the things he'd shown her at Ravencliff. But Cassie was careful to avoid mention of the kennel. Still, there were questions she longed to ask.

Briggs removed the last plate.

Ramsay looked to Cassie. "Shall we go to the drawing room?"

A sudden inspiration seized Cassie. Call it whimsy. Call it a test. "You know, what I'd like to do is have brandy and cigars in the dining room with the men."

Ramsay stared at her for a moment as if he'd not heard her clearly. "Cigars?"

"Yes, cigars. Surely they taste better than they smell," Cassie said, realizing as she glanced at her wineglass that she might have drunk more than usual. But she couldn't help but wonder whether he would fall back on all the old male taboos. No tobacco for the ladies. Did he have the courage to share a truly new experience with her? "I've always wondered what you men do in the dining room over brandy and cigars when we women are sent away to the drawing room. We must endure some matron's stories about her children who are the brightest and handsomest ever born while the gentlemen huddle around the table. Just what is it like to talk in the dining room over brandy and cigars?''

Ramsay continued to stare at her, his expression betraying only a hint of surprise. Then he glanced at Briggs over her head. Still his expression did not change. ''Briggs, bring us the brandy and the cigars from the study. Be sure to bring the fresh batch I brought back from London. We can't have our guest smoking stale tobacco.''

''Yes, my lord.'' Briggs left the room.

''Thank you, my lord.'' Cassie clapped her hands together. ''Now, next, who shall I be sitting at your table, sharing a cigar with you?''

''Queen Elizabeth, of course,'' he said instantly, to her surprise.

Cassie sat back in her chair. ''Do you think she smoked cigars with Sir Walter?''

''Why would she not?'' Ramsay replied, smiling an enigmatic half-smile. ''They might have been sampling some of the fine tobacco from the New World.''

''Yes, I see,'' Cassie said, liking the thought. ''Queen Elizabeth I shall be. Then I shan't have to pretend to be a man.''

''Yes,'' Ramsay said, his half-smile broadening into a grin. ''I'm relieved about that also.''

Briggs returned with a silver tray bearing the brandy decanter, two glasses, and a carved wooden box that held the cigars.

''That will be all.'' Ramsay dismissed the butler as he reached for the brandy decanter.

Cassie inched to the edge of her chair to observe Ramsay better. ''Is there an etiquette to this? Brandy first? Then cigars? I've taken part in countless tea parties. I've never been privy to this particular ritual, you understand.''

With a long-suffering expression Ramsay glanced at her as he poured the amber liquid into the snifters. ''Usually at a formal dinner party the butler pours the brandy. When all are served, he passes the box of cigars, allowing each guest to select his own.''

Ramsay set Cassie's glass of brandy before her, then picked up the cigar box, opened it and presented it to her.

"What do I look for in a good cigar?" she asked, studying the dozens of tobacco-leaf cylinders lying in the box. The rich, pungent fragrance of fresh tobacco assailed her. The cigars all looked alike to her.

"Shall I select one for you?" he asked, reaching into the box.

"No," Cassie said, before he touched a cigar. "I prefer to make my own choice. But what should I look for?"

"Of course you must make your own selection," Ramsay said, watching her closely, a smile full of soft, suggestive amusement on his lips. "You want a smoke that is rolled tight. One with a good, even, rich brown color. And though it should appear to be moist, it must be firm to the touch."

"Like this one?" Cassie asked, suddenly suspicious that he was teasing her in some way she didn't quite understand. She chose a cigar and held it up to the candlelight. "This one is firm and straight."

"Yes, straight is good," he agreed with a soft chuckle.

"Then what's next?"

He picked up a metal tool that looked like a clipper. He offered it to Cassie. "Clip off both ends. That will allow the air to flow into the cigar so it will burn properly and you can draw the flavor from it."

Cassie stared at the clipper. Then she held out the cigar to him. "Would you be so kind, my lord? I wouldn't want to get it wrong."

Patiently Ramsay took her cigar, speaking as he put the clippers to it. "Usually the gentleman does this for himself. I've seen some smokers have particular preferences as to how the cut is done. There, that should do nicely."

Cassie accepted the cigar from him. "Now, are we ready to light it?"

"Indeed." Ramsay took up a rush light from the silver holder on the tray and put it to the candle. A flame flared softly,

"When I put the rush light to your cigar, you want to draw on it gently. That will encourage the tobacco to burn evenly and burn without going out."

Cassie nodded and leaned forward, the cigar to her lips.

Ramsay paused before he put the rush flame to it, then shook his head.

"What is it, my lord?" Cassie asked.

"Your mother and father are going to have me crucified."

"I won't tell them about this," Cassie said, hoping to reassure him.

"That's of no account," he said, a strange regretful smile on his lips. "I assure you I shall deserve whatever justice your father decides to mete out to me. Hold still. Draw gently. There."

"Oh, mmmm." Cassie sucked on the tobacco, its flavor filling her mouth with a rich smoky taste, almost as aromatic as the scent of the cigar itself.

"Now don't swallow the smoke," Ramsay warned, a look of concern on his face. "Just taste it then blow it out. We don't want you to get sick."

Cassie held her breath, then puffed the smoke out into the air. "Like that? That's not so dreadful."

Ramsay grinned and sat back to light his own cigar. "Now, have a sip of brandy and see what you think."

Cassie picked up her brandy snifter and took a small sip. She knew this was a considerably stronger drink than the champagne and sherry her parents had sometimes allowed her to drink on special occasions. The brandy filled her mouth with a rich sweet flavor, then burned all the way down her throat, leaving her feeling slightly flushed. But the effect was not entirely unpleasant.

She could feel Ramsay's eyes on her as she took another puff on her cigar, then a sip from her snifter. She closed her eyes to better concentrate on the full rich flavors and aromas mixing in her mouth. When the brandy had burned its way down her throat, she turned to her host. "No wonder you gentlemen don't share this disgusting habit with the ladies. It's quite pleasant.''

Ramsay smiled indulgently and puffed on his cigar. "You mustn't tell anyone I gave away the secret. I might be drummed out of my London club.''

The smoke curled up around his blond head. He looked incredibly handsome, contentedly in control, and supremely male. A thrill of attraction coursed through Cassie and her breathing quickened. She wondered how many of his mistresses' hearts he'd broken. She wondered if he would break hers.

'' 'Tis our secret,'' she said with a giggle, then helped herself to another sip of brandy.

He went on with his instructions. "You must also remember about smoking, that a gentleman never smokes without consent in the presence of a clergyman and he must never offer a cigar to any churchman above a curate.''

"Truly?'' Cassie said, surprised by the rules. "I did not know that about curates. They just fill ladies' heads with strictures about not crossing our ankles and never shake an acquaintance's hand. Just offer a cordial pressure. And so forth. I wonder about queens. Does a gentleman offer a cigar to a queen?''

Ramsay laughed softly. "Only if she expresses interest.''

Determined to be queenly, Cassie drew herself up in her chair. Deciding that she wasn't quite tall enough, she rearranged herself, sitting down on her foot and holding her head high. "I thank you for your advice, Sir Walter,'' she said in a low, authoritative voice. Then in her own voice she added, "Does that sound queenly enough?''

"Too low,'' Ramsay said, watching her with cool, but definite interest as he swirled his brandy in its snifter.

"How about this?'' She took a quick sip of brandy, cleared her throat and tried again. "I say, Raleigh, fine cigar.''

She used a higher voice with a lofty accent like Lady Cowper's at Almack's.

Ramsay chuckled once more, a deep warm sound that rumbled in his chest, a sound Cassie was becoming quite fond of.

"Well, what do you think?" she asked, eager for his approval for several reasons. "Does that sound queenly enough?"

"Close," he said, still smiling.

Cassie cleared her throat once more and resumed the accent. "I say, Sir Walter, it's come to my attention that you and I have something in common."

The interest in his eyes deepened, despite his hooded regard of her. She could feel his gaze traveling across her face, down her throat, and almost caressingly along her shoulders. She looked down at her crystal brandy snifter and resisted the desire to shiver under his gaze. She could not be more affected if he'd actually touched her with his hands.

"I can't imagine what we might have in common, Your Majesty," he replied, drawing on his cigar.

"It seems we both have undergone the heart-wrenching disappointment of a broken engagement," Cassie said, using the Cowper accent once more. She stole a glance at Ramsay, but continued to twist the snifter on the table before her.

"Did Graham inform you of this also?" Ramsay asked at last.

"He mentioned Aileen when he talked about your mother," Cassie said, making no pretense at her silly accent again. "I thought it ironic that we should find ourselves suffering from the same unfortunate affairs of the heart."

Ramsay stubbed out his cigar in the dish Briggs had left on the silver tray for that purpose. His lips were thin and bitter as he spoke. "I can tell you that the pain fades over the years."

"I'm glad to know that," Cassie said, watching him carefully, longing to know all the details, but unwilling to mention the elopement Graham had described to her. "Graham indicated some problem about the lady's ability to fulfill the role of marchioness."

"If that's what he said. However, I fear my foster brother has represented the facts in the best light," Ramsay said without looking at her. The smile he'd bestowed on her earlier was completely gone. "I cried off. Aileen was a great disappointment to me. If it seems to you that I've been unfortunate in my relationships with women, you're quite right."

Cassie stared up at Ramsay, shocked and dismayed by the evidence of the pain he still suffered. An unfaithful mother and an unsuitable fiancée. He'd indeed been most unfortunate. "If it serves as any consolation, my lord, I happen to think Aileen foolish to have disappointed you."

"Aileen got what she wanted—and deserved." Abruptly, he got up from the table. "I believe that's enough cigar smoking. Shall we adjourn to the drawing room? Perhaps you'd honor me with some music or another song."

She rose from the table, accepted Ramsay's arm, and allowed him to lead her into the hallway. "This has been so much fun, let's not end it with something so conventional as music in the drawing room."

"You have another idea?" Ramsay asked, eyeing her suspiciously.

"Was my last one so frightful?" Cassie asked with a laugh.

"I survived," Ramsay said, seeming to have recovered his good humor after their brief discussion about Aileen. "What is it Your Majesty would like to do? What is mine is yours. Wither shall we wander? What dost thou desire?"

"Let's go to the chapel," Cassie said, pleased with the return of his good humor.

"Why the chapel?"

"To wait for the ghost of Sir Calum to appear," she said, tugging on his arm as she turned toward the door. "Doesn't the legend say he appears on the night of the full moon?"

"Cassandra, 'tis but an old legend," Ramsay said. "If there was ever a ghost, he long ago gave up saying his prayers and crossed over into eternity—or wherever ghosts go."

"Let's go find out," Cassie said. "Are you not ready for an adventure?"

Ramsay shook his head in resignation. "Briggs?"

"My lord?" The butler appeared out of nowhere.

"Bring a lantern and Miss St. John's shawl," Ramsay ordered, smiling down in Cassie's face. "It may get chilly in St. Margaret's Chapel while we wait for the ghosts."

CHAPTER EIGHTEEN

With the lantern in hand Ramsay walked Cassandra to the chapel. She chattered about one thing then another all the way from the house, through the park of rowan and spruce trees. Along the drive, the brightness of the moonlight neutralized the lantern's light. Cassie talked on, seeming to expect no reply from him. He did not mind. Her company was comfort enough.

"So you mean after you saw Sir Calum you never came to the chapel in the full moon to see if he appeared again?" Cassie asked as Ramsay let them into the chapel.

"Truly, Princess, I did not think seeing the old knight was all that remarkable," Ramsay said, nearly sorry that he'd told her about his experience. "I certainly never thought the ghost of the old Crusader would provide entertainment for my houseguest."

Shadows fled before the lantern as he set it down on a bench at the back of the chapel. The door closed behind them with a slow, agonizing creak.

"Ooooh," Cassie said with a visible shiver that made him smile. She paced toward the altar. "Are there any more tales about Sir Calum? Did he have sons?"

"Yes, and daughters. Ravencliff was handed down to the Forbes clan through the daughters," Ramsay said. "The story goes that he and his lady were hardworking, kindly, and devout."

"What a fine ancestor to claim," Cassie said as she stood in the middle of the chapel, turning slowly to examine the place. If the prospect of confronting a ghost troubled her, it did not show. She stared up at the ceiling, the line of her throat and bosom visible and tempting in the lantern light.

"What fine mellowness of the stone," she commented. "Graceful arches and the rich color of the stained-glass windows. And look at that moonlight."

Ramsay gazed at the triple windows over the altar which admitted the bright nocturnal light. He'd never noticed the sight of the moonlight pouring through the stained glass before and it was indeed beautiful.

"Put out the lantern," Cassie suggested in a whisper. "We really don't need it with this moonlight."

Ramsay did as she asked. When the lantern was extinguished, they stood in the jeweled light, hardly a detail of her person obscured from him. Cassie smiled, her face smooth and white, her lips curving in invitation. The rosy color that the brandy and cigars had brought to her cheeks faded in the soft moonlight. Even in the dinner gown with the shawl wrapped around her, she looked as at home as a Scots lass.

"Do you still have services in here?" Cassie asked, pulling her shawl closer around her shoulders.

"At Christmas and Easter we make special donations to the village church to encourage the rector to come out here," Ramsay said, reminding himself of his second thoughts about seducing her. It was best not to become too distracted by the lady's charms. "Otherwise we join the village church congregation. It's a bit of a trip into the village, but we help fill the church pews. 'Tis enough to make the rector smile. But in the old days, when Sir Calum built the chapel, there would have been a priest who lived here to perform all the rites and services for the household.''

"Ravencliff would have been its own little village, then," Cassie said, turning once more to examine the small sanctuary. She swayed slightly, but seemed to find her balance again. Ramsay suppressed the urge to slip an arm around her.

"Were those the days when the Highlanders carried off their women?" Cassie asked, grinning as she turned to Ramsay once more.

"It probably was," he said, unsurprised that she remembered the ploy he'd used to get her to come to Ravencliff.

"Well, I've been thinking about what you told me about handfasting," Cassie said, examining a corner of her tartan shawl. "Show me how it is done. Pretend I'm your kidnapped bride and I agree to handfast with you."

"Cassandra, 'tis a silly old-fashioned custom." Ramsay hesitated. His instinct told him they were treading on dangerous ground. " 'Tis done no longer. I've never seen the ceremony performed."

"But you must have some idea of how it was done," Cassandra said, looking up at him with imploring eyes. "Did the village participate?"

"I suppose, if the laird intended for the union to be binding," Ramsay said. "He could have little claim to his bride's dowry if it weren't. The groom undoubtedly would gather around his allies and relatives."

"Come, you must demonstrate this handfasting for me." Cassandra took his hand and led him through the moonlight to the altar. " 'Tis only playacting. We clasp hands, I suppose."

"Yes, but we clasp left hands," Ramsay said. " 'Tis also called a left-handed marriage."

"Oh, I see." Cassandra smiled up at him. The scoop of her gown revealed the rise and fall of her flawless breasts. The moonlight cast a seductive shadow of cleavage. Her dark pink lips gleamed moist and inviting. Her white teeth flashed in the soft moonglow. The bluish light colored her hair rich and dark as mahogany wood. Ramsay's body stirred. "Why left hands?"

"Because, I suspect," Ramsay began, "the tradition is not recognized by the Church or the state as legal."

She offered her left hand. "Here, like this?"

"Yes, that's it." Ramsay tenderly took her left hand in his left hand; cradled in his palm, it was small and warm and fragile. Her fingers pressed ever so lightly against the inside of his. She stood alone with him in a haunted chapel, hundreds of miles from her home and her family. She knew he wanted something her father possessed. She was either very foolish or very trusting. At the moment, he wanted to think she trusted him.

Something cold and stony inside of Ramsay began to crumble, one stone after another toppled. He peered down into her face and she smiled up into his. The collapse of his defenses set off warnings deep in his gut. Yet the sight of Cassandra's confidence touched his heart. He shoved the warnings away.

Slipping his right hand around her waist, he drew her closer until they stood hip-to-hip, their hands clasped against his chest much as they had been earlier when she'd discovered his heart. But this time they stood so close that the back of his left hand pressed between her soft warm breasts. He could feel her heart beating, fluttering strong, and determined as a captured bird.

She felt so perfect pressed against him. He would play the role of Highland groom to please her. He could make up the words, or read the story in her eyes. "Here, give me a corner of the shawl. That's it. And we wrap our clasped hands in the tartan."

"And are there words to say?" Cassandra asked, gazing up into his face again, her lips wet and enticing under his gaze. "You know. Vows we make to each other. You, the Highland laird, and me, the kidnapped bride?"

Ramsay nodded, though vows were the last thing he had an interest in at the moment. "I begin by promising to honor, protect, and provide for you for a year and a day. That's the true handfasting promise.''

"That's the vow?'' Cassandra asked, a hint of disappointment taking the delight out of her smile. "No declaration of love?''

"No.'' Ramsay shook his head. If there was one, he'd never heard it. And Scotland could sink into the sea before he'd vow his love to anyone ever again—even on this night.

"What does the bride promise?'' Cassandra asked, grinning up at him. "The same thing?''

"Aye, the same,'' Ramsay said, without a clue as to what the bride would pledge.

"I promise to honor, and care for you for a year and a day,'' Cassandra declared.

With her other arm she flung a corner of the tartan shawl up around his neck, pulled him down close to her. "And if I handfast with a man, *I promise* to love him at least a year and a day.''

Ramsay sucked in a soft breath, searching her face for the truth. Would she be standing here with him if they weren't playacting? He found it there in the deep blue of her eyes. She might be a skillful play actress, but she would give him what she'd vowed. He knew it. She would never be like Aileen. No secret betrayal. No lovers in the shadows. No false face in his presence. Whimsical and imaginative, spoiled and indulged as Cassandra might be, she would never cheat those she loved.

"Now what, my lord?'' she asked. "A kiss?''

He sealed their mouths in a fiery kiss. His hand pressed into the small of her back pressing her against him, the feminine curves of her body surrendering to the hard planes of his. She yielded to the thrust of his tongue as he plundered her mouth again and again.

The taste of Cassandra reawakened Ramsay's unsatisfied appetite, whetted only four hours before in the kennel. Desperately wanting her, he angled his body closer, sent his tongue deeper into her mouth, and tilted his hips, nudging the delta between her thighs. Soft whimpers of arousal escaped her.

Coming to his senses, Ramsay raised his head to look into her face.

Cassandra's eyes were closed. Her face remained tilted up toward his. She sucked in a breath of air.

"We don't dare stay here any longer," he said, releasing her from his embrace, and beginning to free their hands from the binding of the shawl.

"But why?" she said, watching his efforts with a puzzled expression. "Where are we going?'

"To the laird's bedchamber," he said, without waiting for her protest. But she made none. " 'Tis the final step of the handfast."

"Of course," she whispered, without looking at him again. A deep blush colored her cheeks, but she did not demur.

Once they were unbound, he grasped her hand and led her out of the chapel and back to the house. Neither of them said anything as they hurried across the shadowed park. The moonlight was still bright enough to show them the way. They slipped back into the house. Ramsay led them silently up the stairs and directly into the marquis's suite. The moment they were inside, he closed the double doors and bolted them.

When he turned to Cassandra, she stood in the middle of the room watching him, her face solemn. He wondered if she was frightened.

"You're not going to become fainthearted with our play-acting now, are you?" he asked softly as he walked toward her. Only moonlight lit the room, but they needed nothing more to see each other.

"No, my lord," she said, smiling at him softly, her eyes following him as he neared her. "Are you?"

"It's much too late for that," he said, coming to a stop

before her. How lovely she was. How confident. "I'll soon show you why."

He led her to the bay windows where the brightest moonlight streamed into the room.

First he tipped her face up to his and kissed the tip of her nose lightly. She closed her eyes and smiled. He was glad to see no uncertainty in her face. Then slowly, article by article, he removed her clothing. First the shawl dropped away, and he kissed her bare throat and shoulders. Then with fingers clumsier than they'd ever been, he loosened her bodice lacing, the tapes of her skirt, the ribbons of her shift. Little by little, garments drifted to the floor.

He stopped occasionally to admire, pet, to kiss parts of her that he'd only dreamed of. As badly as he wanted her he would not rush any part of this. Her body, each curve and contour, offered him a sensual feast. She was lovely all over.

As he bared her skin, he kissed the pale underside of her arms, the curve beneath her breast. She moaned, tipped her head back, closed her eyes, and raked her fingers through his hair. Her small pink nipples pearled and her breasts grew firm in his hands. Then he stroked lower, kissing each contour, her navel, her belly. He sank to his knees. He kissed her mound and stroked her legs from her thighs to her dainty ankles as he rolled off her stockings. Inhaling the woman scent of her, he drew a finger along the inside of the arch of her foot. She whimpered again.

Crying out his name, she tugged on his hair. "Hold me."

Swiftly Ramsay got to his feet and scooped her up into his arms and carried her to the bed. His manservant had turned it down earlier in the evening. Ramsay laid her on the sheets and stood back to admire his prize. The moonlight limned every contour of her, her breasts, her belly, her thighs, and the red-curl-covered mound—the promise of the deepest pleasure she had to give.

When she suddenly moved to cover herself with the damask counterpane, he realized he must be watching her too hungrily.

"No, don't hide yourself," Ramsay said, as he shrugged his way out of his clothing which had become painfully confining long ago. "I want to see it all."

She stopped, the bedcover lightly draped over her hip. With a taunting smile, she took her breast in her hand as if she was offering it to him. "Is this what you want, my lord?"

Eyeing the lovely peaked nipple, Ramsay struggled to divest himself of the last of his clothing. When he was naked, he stood at the side of the bed, allowing her to view him as he viewed her. She looked him up and down, her eyes widening as they lingered on his arousal.

"So much more vigorous than those pictured in the books," Cassandra whispered. Then she made room for him next to her.

"What book?" Ramsay asked as he stretched out beside her.

"The book Charlotte and I found," Cassandra murmured. She offered her lips to him. "Never mind."

Ramsay kissed her soundly, then lowered his head, capturing her alluring nipple with his mouth. She tasted good and the bud felt wonderful against his tongue. Each flick of his tongue across it elicited a moan from her.

Gently he guided her hand from her breast down to his erection's hardness. As her fingers closed firmly around him, he sucked in a breath though his lips never left her breast. When she didn't draw her hand away in shock, he tongued her again. She moaned. Her response thrilled him.

She stroked him uncertainly at first, then with more confidence—and desire. The more hungrily he suckled her, the more passionate her caresses, exploring his sex from the strong root, up the smooth length, and to the tip where he could not prevent the bead of moisture from forming.

Groaning in agonized ecstasy, he pulled her hand away. A man could only take so much of that torture. But he rubbed his open mouth over her other flushed breast until it, too, was stiff. Then he began to move downward, wantonly kissing her belly and her navel and the soft delta of red curls. She moved restlessly under his mouth, imploring with whimpered sounds. No matter how tormented, he was not going to rush this. He wanted to be certain that she was ready. He kissed the inside of her thighs, encouraging her to open for him. With a sigh she did. She was soft, warm, and so incredibly wet that his fingers delved easily into her. She clutched desperately at the hair of his head as he bent over her. The temptation was too great. Gently he marked the tender white flesh of the inside of her thigh with a kiss of passion.

She tossed her head on the pillow. "Ramsay, please?"

At the sound of her pleading, he could wait no longer. Clumsily he fumbled for the protection he'd put in a box on the bedside table.

"What are you doing?" she asked.

"Safeguarding you," he muttered, quickly preparing himself as he always did for a woman. He'd decided long ago there would be no by-blows to lay claim to his name. Then he rose up over Cassandra, parting her thighs and gently forcing his way into her.

A hoarse cry escaped him as her virgin body gave way, then closed around him like a silken fist. This was nothing like lying with one of his mistresses. He cared about this woman from the part of him that was buried in her, to the far reaches of his spirit. This act engaged all of him from his manhood to his heart. There was no escape from this bond. This was forever.

He fought away all the demonic fears caring for her brought him and peered into her face. Resting his weight on his elbows, he laced his fingers through her fiery hair and kissed her brows. She opened her eyes, her face sober in her passion. "What do I—?"

"Move with me, princess." Ramsay murmured. "We are dancing."

She matched his even strokes with a subtle undulation of her hips.

The closer they moved to climax, the tighter she clung to him and the deeper he penetrated. Gritting his teeth, he held back until he felt waves of sensation shimmy through her, felt her gentle contractions around his manhood, and saw the light of ecstasy explode and glimmer in her green eyes.

Only then did he release the rigid control he had imposed on himself. He buried his face in the soft fragrance of her hair and gave himself over to the encompassing pleasure that erupted within him into Cassandra.

CHAPTER
NINETEEN

"Are you all right?" He felt the nod of her head against his chest where she lay cradled next to him. His lips grazed the top of her head. "You're still so small. I know it can't be very pleasurable for you."

He was already becoming aroused again. Readjusting their bodies slightly he heard Cassandra whimper, not with pain, but protest.

"You're certain I didn't hurt you?"

"No," she whispered, her breath tickling his chest hair.

"I must have."

"Only a small bit." She cuddled closer.

Of its own accord, his body stirred. They lay so close, he knew she could feel him growing.

"My lord," she whispered, her lips still brushing against his chest. "Doesn't it ever—I mean, doesn't it go down?"

"Apparently not tonight," Ramsay said, slightly amazed by his own stamina. He gathered her closer, trying to ignore the demands of his body, but it was impossible, especially when she tilted her head back, and kissed his jaw. Her breasts pressed against him, no less aroused than his manhood.

Then he groaned her name again and covered her once more, sinking deep into the snug liquid heat of her. They danced again, a slower waltz this time. His sated need gave him more time to please her. With steady fingers he stroked away damp strands of hair that clung to her flushed face. With the rest of his body he stroked the satiny warmth inside her. Her eyes were limpid as though she was enthralled. As they neared the pinnacle of pleasure, she arched her throat, offering it to him. He caressed the fragile skin with his lips. They reached release together, moaning in a soft duet.

Ramsay rolled to her side and gathered her into his arms. She whispered his name once more, but then fell asleep. He held her until he, too, drifted off. Later, he awoke to find her awake also. The room had fallen into near darkness. The moon had set. But the passage of time seemed to have changed nothing between them.

She found his lips with her fingers. He kissed the tips, sucking them softly. Then it all began again, the need as strong, the pleasure as intense. As much as he wanted to hold himself back for her sake, for the sake of her body's inexperience, he buried himself deep inside of her again. Nothing of the experience had diminished from before. He took her once more after that, just before dawn. Both found pleasure again—their last before the cock crowed.

Cassie awoke to the sound of thunder, or of someone pounding somewhere in the house. Suddenly the weight on the mattress beside her disappeared. Realizing where she was, Cassie bolted up in bed, clutching the sheets to her chin. By the palest morning light Cassie saw the butler wearing only his trousers and shirt standing in the doorway.

"See to it, Briggs," Ramsay's voice called from across the room from where he was hastily pulling on his clothes.

"Very good, my lord," Briggs said, as if he found a lady in his master's bed every morning, then disappeared.

Ramsay sat down in a chair and began pulling on his boots. Cassie watched him, too confused and muddled with sleep to know what to say. As he worked, a lock of his dark blond hair fell across his brow. She could see that his mouth was thinned and a night's growth of beard shadowed his face, making him appear grim and angry.

When he finished with his boots, he glared at her across the tousled bed. She hardly recognized him as the same man who had made love to her only a few hours before.

"As soon as I leave this room, gather up your things and be prepared to depart for London within the hour," he said, speaking in barely more than a whisper. "I'll send Betsy to you."

"But I thought—" Cassie began, her head beginning to clear. They had so many things to say to each other now, after they had shared a lovers' dream—and a lovers' bed. She'd wanted to believe in the handfasting last night. She wanted to believe they had a year and a day to love each other.

Ramsay surged to his feet. Even with his shirt hanging loose about him and his hair awry, he looked wonderful to Cassie. But she couldn't understand why he was being so cross with her after the glorious night they'd passed together.

"I don't care what you thought," he said, his voice nearly a growl. "You are going home."

He strode out of the room and slammed the door behind him. The bedcurtains trembled with the force. Cassie sat frozen for a moment, listening to his footsteps as he went down the hall toward the stairs. The pounding on the door had ceased. Now she heard the sound of men's voices raised in excitement and urgency.

She suddenly understood whatever was happening had to do with her. Without another moment of hesitation, she climbed out of bed.

Her first exertion slowed her. She was sore where she'd never been sore before and she longed for a bath. However, the circumstances didn't permit. Moving as swiftly as she dared, she found her shift and petticoats, donned them, then grabbed her shawl as she scurried to the door. On the threshold she paused to listen for a moment. Still she could only hear voices, no clear words. Gathering the shawl and her courage about her, she hurried in barefoot silence down the hallway.

From the top of the stairs she saw the front hall below was vacant, so she dashed down the stairs, following the sound of male voices in Ramsay's study. Now she was beginning to make out words. She pressed herself into the corner near the study door and listened, holding her breath so she would not miss an utterance.

"Where in the bloody hell have you been, is what I'd like to know," Ramsay demanded of someone, apparently the man who had been pounding on the door and had been admitted by Briggs.

"I've been riding through rain and shine, light and dark for two days, my lord," the man stammered. "The roads were nigh impossible near Berwick. Flooding. I did the best I could."

"Well, let's see what Fredericks and St. John have to say," Ramsay said.

Cassie heard the crackle of paper being unfolded. She recalled Ramsay mentioning that his agent's name was Fredericks, or something like that. Why would Papa have contacted the Forbeses' agent—unless he was uncertain of where to find her and Ramsay? But she'd told them where they were going in her note.

"So now St. John is willing to talk, as soon as he sees his daughter," Ramsay bellowed aloud.

Cassie understood the implication of Ramsay's words. She closed her eyes against the thought that last night had not been as dear to him as it had been for her. She rested her forehead against the wall.

"But he makes no commitment," Ramsay continued. "Just like him. I don't know if he's a fool or just damned cunning. Why does he hang on to a piece of property that is of little use to him?"

" 'Tis the greed of the English," Graham said.

At the sound of Graham's voice, Cassie rolled her eyes heavenward. No doubt he knew, or would know, about last night, too. There was hardly any way to hide it. Her heart began to ache. She'd always known what this was about—the feud. Why had she dared to think—even hope—for anything more? Because she'd learned that a heart beat inside him? Because she'd foolishly thought she could help him discover the heart he'd lost? She was the fool.

Cassie shrank back into the corner, wondering if she'd only dreamed the wonderful things she and the man in the next room had shared in his bed. Of vows exchanged in an old chapel. Of hands bound with Forbes plaid. Of ecstasy only a man and woman can share.

"Miss St. John?"

The voices in the study went silent.

Cassie started and found herself staring up at Briggs. The butler had shrugged into a proper coat, but his cravat remained untidy. He stared back at her, his brow arched in surprise and embarrassment. Then she realized he was hardly as disheveled as she was.

"May I get you something, Miss St. John?"

Cassie never looked down at herself. It was none of his concern if she looked like a half-naked woman who'd just crawled from her master's bed. She lifted her chin and pulled the shawl around her. "Yes, as a matter of fact, Briggs, I came in search of some tea and some of those wonderful scones that Cook makes. Please put them on my breakfast tray and send it to my room."

Relief settled in the slope of Briggs's shoulders as he took her cue. His face arranged itself into the perfect stoic butler's mask. "Yes, Miss St. John. I'll send a tray to your room directly."

"Thank you," Cassie said as she marched away from the corner, past the study door. She'd heard the men's voices resume briefly, but she could make out nothing more. As soon as Briggs had disappeared from sight, she prepared to bound up the stairs to her room.

"Cassandra."

Cassie froze at the sound of Ramsay's voice. "My lord?"

"Come into my study," he said, sounding as if he were issuing a perfectly ordinary invitation.

She turned toward Ramsay, listening to the footsteps of Graham and the messenger as they left the study. She wondered what Ramsay had told them.

"I'd prefer to dress first," Cassie replied in the vain hope of escaping.

"Now," he said, his tone offering no alternatives. "Please."

Slowly Cassie crossed the hall and padded into the study. Ramsay followed her. She heard him close the door, softly this time.

She remained standing in front of the desk, staring down at the cigar box that Briggs had brought to the dining-room table the night before. Why had she not noticed what a lovely box it was? she wondered inanely.

"I imagine you heard enough to have an idea of the news the messenger brought," Ramsay said.

"A message from Papa sent through your agent," Cassie replied, studying the fringe of her shawl, wondering how much to say; how much to keep to herself. "I thought Papa knew where I was. Is he too dreadfully angry with us?"

"I believe he's primarily angry with me," Ramsay said, still standing behind her. "I had Graham alter your note. Your father knows nothing more than that you are with me of your own will."

"I see," Cassie said, astonished at how calm she was, though her knees had suddenly gone weak. She sank down onto the footstool by the cold hearth. "Why does that not surprise me? Of course last night was all a deception, too."

Speaking softly, he launched into a string of invectives she would have thought marvelously creative under other circumstances.

"I'd hoped there was more between us, my lord," Cassie went on, her pain and confusion spilling out before she could call them back. She clutched her shawl so tightly around her that her knuckles went white. But she had no desire to cry. Her head was incredibly calm and cool and her heart had stopped beating.

"Last night was playacting, Cassandra, you knew that," Ramsay said, pacing the floor behind her. "I never led you to think any different."

Cassie turned slowly, endeavoring to get a look at his face. Clearly he had no intention of facing her across the desk. "No, you did not. And I never asked you to promise me more."

He ceased his pacing and turned slightly toward her, his hands still clasped behind his back. When his gaze finally met hers, Cassie would have sworn that the harsh light in his green eyes softened.

"What I want to know is, did you get what you wanted from all this?" she asked. "Is Papa going to give you Glen Gray?"

Ramsay met her gaze honestly for the first time that morning. "He is willing to discuss the possibility now. He wouldn't even negotiate before."

"You don't understand Papa," Cassie said, secretly proud of her father's implacability in the face of a marquis's power. "He is a very unemotional businessman."

"But I do understand him," Ramsay said. "He is devoted to his daughters. An offer of knighthood might not tempt him, but a threat to his daughters catches his attention."

"Papa would never turn down an offer of knighthood," Cassie stammered.

"Indeed, he could have been Sir Davis St. John for several months now," Ramsay said. "But he clings to Glen Gray— why, I'll never know. That is why I brought you here. And you came with me willingly."

The gleam of victory in Ramsay's eyes did it. Anger blossomed inside Cassie at last. Her heart began to beat again, fast and angry. She would do anything to wipe that look of triumph from his face.

"And do you know why I came so willingly?" she asked, unwilling to allow him to think he had made a conquest. "You think it was because you were so clever? Because I was so desperate for your company? To see Ravencliff?"

"You're here because you love an adventure, princess." He smiled at her indulgently. "Admit it. I tempted and you could not resist."

"Hardly," Cassie said, scrutinizing his face to be certain that her words had the effect she wanted. "I came because I wanted to be sure Connor and Charlotte would be safe from you and your henchmen. I wanted to be certain there would be no more kidnappings of Connor or hired footpad attacks."

Her words hit their target. He blinked at her, clearly surprised.

"The moment you made the offer on the church porch, I knew my problem was solved," Cassie said, taking small satisfaction in the astonishment on his face. She cast him a bitter smile. "I knew I could protect my sister. Now, four days later, she is safe on the continent. You have what you wanted, so it is time to send me home. You are finished with me, just as Graham predicted. But I don't care. Because I got what I wanted and I'm finished with you as well."

Ramsay glared at her, astonishment in the lift of his brows. Anger thinned the line of his mouth and deep in his eyes lurked just a hint—ever so faint—of pain.

So be it, then, Cassie thought, lifting her chin defiantly. Despite her self-control, the hint of pain in his eyes touched her. She could not fathom why he should be hurt. He'd seduced her for gain. Did he expect her to thank him for it? And for heaven's sakes, why did she care? Cassie swallowed the lump in her throat. "I shall be ready to leave within the hour, just as you wish."

Struggling with her aching heart and her knees, weak from the confrontation, she marched out of the room. She might be half-naked and ruined—her heart might be breaking, this time for real—but that was no reason not to hold her head high.

When she reached the rose bedchamber, she locked herself in the dressing room and cried for half an hour, muffling her sobs in a pillow.

When Cassandra left the study, Ramsay passed his hand over his face and raked his fingers through his uncombed hair. Damnation, nothing was turning out the way he'd planned.

So she'd come to Ravencliff to protect her sister. He hated that thought. Like a fool, he'd thought he'd won her trust, that she'd come because she truly wanted to see Ravencliff, because he'd invited her. Her interest had been written in her face and in every question she asked. But she'd been afraid for her sister all along.

Distractedly he walked to the window and leaned on the sill, staring at the sun rising over the ridge. He did not like the picture of him that she must see. Nor did he like to think that he was so besotted that he'd never realized she'd seen through him all along.

And last night? Last night he'd held a woman closer to his heart than he'd ever held anyone. Last night he'd lost himself in her. He'd given where he'd only taken for so long. And the joy of it had shaken him to the core. Last night had made one thing very clear. He had to get Cassandra St. John out of his bed, out of his house, and out of his life.

He'd decided that before the messenger had pounded on the door. Nothing she'd said changed his mind.

An hour later, just as she promised, dressed for travel—and her eyes suspiciously red-rimmed—Cassandra descended the stairs. Her fiery hair was confined beneath her bonnet, her face was pale, and her lips turned down. Nevertheless she descended with all the elegance of the marchioness that Ramsay was determined to never have. Betsy scurried along behind.

Ramsay awaited her at the bottom of the stairs. Despite his

determination to get her out of his house, his own emotions warred between the fantasy of demanding the dowry for a kidnapped bride and keeping her forever—Glen Gray be damned.

But returning her was the only thing that made sense, he reminded himself. 'Twas the plan. But the small voice of the lost boy who Cassandra had discovered inside him cried, *Can we keep her?*

The grown man inside said no.

Briggs was there at the bottom of the stairs, along with Graham and a footman to load Cassandra's small amount of luggage. Everything was in order for her departure.

When she reached the bottom step, she glared at Ramsay. He knew she'd been weeping and he felt like a cad—an attribute he'd once taken pride in.

"I want a gift," she said, her voice small and petulant. "I want a souvenir of my visit to Ravencliff."

The request surprised Ramsay. He pursed his lips, silently bidding himself to be considerate of her. She deserved that. "Name it."

"Your cigar box and the brandy decanter," Cassandra said, pulling on her gloves as if she was making the most natural request in the world. "Papa will never let me use his."

Briggs's eyes grew wide. Graham began to choke.

"Is that what you want?" Ramsay stared at her in disbelief. Of all the things in the house she had used and admired: the prized breakfast china or the silver hairbrushes . . . But his heart suddenly demanded that he keep the two items she asked for. "A cigar box and a brandy decanter? Why not take the silver hand-mirror from the bedchamber? Of course, the clothes are yours. Perhaps you'd like one or two of the puppies, but the cigar—"

She shook her head to all of his suggestions. "You said I had but to name my gift."

Without another word, she headed for his study. Before he

could reach the door, she emerged, his cigar box under one arm and his brandy decanter in her other hand.

Something oddly akin to grief swept over Ramsay. A ridiculous feeling, but one he could not shake. She was taking his only keepsakes of an evening unlike any he'd ever known.

"But what do you intend to do with them?" he inquired, recognizing his own childishness. He could hear the small boy in him; he clamped his mouth shut before he demanded just what keepsake was she going to leave for him.

"I intend to smoke and drink all the way home—or until I get sick," Cassandra said, marching out the door ahead of him. Then she added over her shoulder, "Whichever one comes first."

CHAPTER TWENTY

The return trip to London hardly seemed to take as long as the journey north. The most astonishing thing about the trek was Ramsay's presence.

As the coach pulled away from Ravencliff, Cassie was surprised to see the marquis riding along beside just as he had before. Sucking in a big gulp of air in amazement, she sat back in her seat, confused, but pleased. He wasn't just sending her home like so much used goods. He was taking her home.

Perhaps the difference between the two actions was small, but it was important, Cassie thought. At least he wasn't casting her off; but then, he had negotiations over Glen Gray to transact with her father. The air hissed out of her lungs like the breath from a bellows. Perhaps his company didn't mean as much as she liked to think.

"Pour me a brandy, Betsy," Cassie ordered, her feelings as tender as her body. She longed to block from her mind the memories of the night in Ramsay's arms. But the pain of being rejected went too deep to be touched. The fact was, he was sending her home. She needed to dull the misery. "For medicinal purposes. I need something to calm my nerves."

Betsy cast Cassie a skeptical glance, but did as told.

* * *

Erik spotted the coach before anyone. He was standing outside the kitchen door, sharing a pipe with Will, a St. John footman, when he saw the black vehicle without a crest round the corner. Forbes himself was riding alongside it.

" 'Tis him," Erik said, clutching the shoulder of the footman in his excitement, hardly able to believe the sight himself. Connor and he, as well as the entire St. John household, had been in turmoil for the past week over Cassandra St. John and Linirk's disappearance. Who would have thought the marquis would just turn up with her one day ? " 'Tis the bloody marquis in the flesh, bringing her back, he is. Fetch St. John. Be quick. Tell him Linirk is back."

Then Erik bounded out to the street. Before the vehicle came to a halt, he was reaching for the coach-door latch. He wanted to see the lassie's condition for himself.

"There now, Drummond," shouted Graham from atop the coach. "What do ye think yer doin'?"

Erik ignored the bloody Forbes man. He had no great love for Cassandra St. John. She was too willful and proud by half, but she was his laird's sister-in-law now. No McKensie relation deserved to be held hostage by Linirk. Erik threw open the door. "Miss St. John? Are ye in there? Are ye all right?"

"Yes, Mr. Drummond, thank you," came her voice from the darkness. She sounded sleepy and as spoiled as ever. "Where is Papa?"

Before Erik could reply, the coach lurched under moving weight. A powerful hand came down on his shoulder. He knew exactly who his attacker was and he was prepared. Erik doubled up his fist and swung. With ugly satisfaction, he felt a nose give way under his blow. The older man grunted and staggered backward. Blood spattered across Graham's face. Erik took advantage of Graham's surprise. Fists ready, he went after the Forbes clansman.

"Cease your fighting!" St. John came racing down the front steps and threw himself between the two men.

Erik almost struck the gentleman, but curtailed his swing just in time.

St. John ducked enough to avoid the blow. "I'll have none of your feuding in front of my house, before my wife and daughters. Do you hear me, Drummond? Andrews? Put your fists down and behave like civilized men this instant."

"Do as he says, Erik," came Connor's voice from the house.

Erik backed away. But he kept his eye on Graham and his fists ready. A Forbes clansman was never to be trusted.

"Graham, do as St. John says," Linirk said, jumping from his horse.

Graham backed away, holding his nose to staunch the bleeding.

"Cassie?" Mrs. St. John came running out of the house as if there weren't enough people milling around in the street. "Cassie! Are you all right?"

Erik stepped back from the coach door as the St. John lass threw herself into her mama's arms. She looked tired, but none the worse for wear. No bruises or broken limbs that he could see. But Erik had little doubt about what Linirk had been up to with her.

Linirk had the gall to stand there looking on as if he were an innocent bystander instead of the kidnapper that everyone knew him to be. Erik fumed. He glanced in Connor's direction. How could the lad take this so calmly?

"I'm all right, Mama," the lass said. "Truly, I am. I'm sorry if you were worried. I thought you knew where I was. I sent a note."

At that moment Charlotte burst from the house, crying out her sister's name.

"Charlotte!" Cassandra cried when she saw her sister. "I thought you were on your wedding trip."

"I was," Charlotte said, running down the front steps. "But

we came back as soon as we received word that you'd gone off with Linirk. Cassie, I'm so sorry for everything.''

The girls fell into each other's arms, sobbing and weeping so that a man would think someone had died. Then Mrs. St. John joined them. The women clung to each other and sobbed. St. John put his arms around all of them.

'Tis a touching reunion scene, Erik thought, impatient with tears. He shifted awkwardly from one foot to the other. There was much fluttering of hands, embraces, and kisses. Women's fuss. Even the maid was drawn into the group.

But St. John stepped back and searched out Linirk in the crowd. The man in black met his eye and approached St. John, handing the reins of his horse to the St. John groom.

''I believe you have some explaining to do.'' St. John glared at Linirk.

Erik's insides grew cold as he looked upon the face of the McKensies' archenemy, Ramsay Forbes. He'd not been this close to the marquis in years. There was no one on earth that he hated more than the Forbes laird, unless it was Graham Andrews, his foster brother. Erik looked around to see Graham still glaring at him. He was holding a bloody handkerchief to his nose. Erik knew there'd be a score to settle later. For now, he wanted to know what was going to happen to Glen Gray.

Linirk brushed passed Erik without so much as a glance.

''Yes, sir, I think we must talk,'' Linirk said. ''I see Kinleith is here.''

''No need to do this on the street, for all to see,'' St. John said. ''Let's get the women inside. Then we'll talk in the study.''

Erik turned to Will, the footman he'd been smoking with earlier. ''Fetch the Earl of Seacombe. We'll need all our allies if Linirk is going to talk with St. John.''

Hands clasped, Cassie and Charlotte followed Papa into his study. Cassie was almost speechless with the unexpected pleasure of seeing her sister. She could hardly believe that Charlotte had abandoned her wedding trip because of her disappearance with Ramsay.

"Is it true that you've been with Linirk?" Charlotte asked as soon as they were settled on the settee. "Are you all right?"

"Ramsay invited me to be his guest at Ravencliff." Cassie gazed at her sister, deliriously happy to see her again. "You needn't have worried. He was a gentleman—for the most part."

"I want to talk to Linirk and Kinleith alone." Papa moved behind his desk. He lowered his voice and frowned at Cassie. "The discussion could be awkward. Especially for you, Cassandra."

"Yes, Cassie, you should rest," Mama said, coming to stand behind them. "Let the gentlemen say what they wish in privacy."

"No, Mama," Charlotte said, her hand squeezing Cassie's. "Our future is being discussed here. We will not be hurried out of the room while our lives are planned, will we, Cassie?"

"We certainly will not," Cassie agreed, squeezing her sister's hand in return. She liked this new Charlotte and she was so relieved to have her at her side again. Tears welled in her eyes. Charlotte smiled back, her eyes also suspiciously watery. Cassie continued. "The gentlemen may say what they wish with us present, Mama. We will not hear it secondhand."

"You see, Davis, this is what comes from educating your daughters," Aunt Dorian said, sweeping into the room in a flurry of haste and excitement. Uncle Nicholas followed her. "Will brought us word of your return, Cassie. Are you well?" Dorian gathered Cassie up in her arms.

"I'm fine, Aunt Dorian. You needn't fret."

"But I think we must," Dorian said, glaring at Ramsay. "This must be settled and your reputation restored."

"I see," Cassie said, making room for Dorian beside them on the settee.

The gentlemen bowed. Aunt Dorian and Uncle Nicholas greeted each. Cassie noted that tensions eased a bit. Though Uncle Nicholas's title was of lesser consequence than Linirk's, his age and natural ship-captain's authority did much to bring a sense of order into the room.

"Close the door, Horton," Papa said as Graham and Erik came into the room. "And we are not to be disturbed."

Graham, his nose already red and swollen, moved to Ramsay's side of the room. Erik stood behind Connor, who'd seated himself in one of the high-backed library chairs.

Papa glared in Ramsay's direction. "What do you have to say for yourself, Linirk?"

"Papa, I went to Ravencliff with him willingly," Cassie said, before Ramsay could reply. She cared little for his embarrassment, but she preferred not to look the fool before her family. "He invited me and I wanted to see his home. Charlotte was wed—"

"Let Linirk answer for himself," Aunt Dorian said, regarding Ramsay with cool disdain. "And was there a proper chaperone present, my lord?"

"No, there was no chaperone," Ramsay said, catching Cassie's eye. "I apologize for being so thoughtless as to not have arranged for one."

Everyone in the room stared at the heartless marquis in astonishment. No one had expected an apology from him, least of all Cassie. She continued to study him. His grimness remained unabated and the slope of his shoulders was tight and rigid.

"What were you thinking when you took her away?" Papa asked, his voice full of incredulity.

"He was thinking that you would offer him Glen Gray to bring her back," Connor said, shifting restlessly in his chair.

"Allow the man to speak for himself," Nicholas warned Connor.

Cassie's heart jumped into her throat, choking her. She knew what her brother-in-law said was true, but she hated to hear Ramsay's ugly intentions spoken in words. It made her feel small and worthless. Helpless and used. But she had used him, too, she reminded herself. She glanced toward Ramsay again, but he still avoided her gaze.

"Kinleith sums up the idea fairly well," Ramsay said, staring into the cold, empty hearth.

Cassie sank lower in her place on the settee.

"Then why did you bring her back so suddenly?" Nicholas asked, clearly dissatisfied with Ramsay's answer.

"I brought her back because I feared staying longer at Ravencliff was not in her best interest," Ramsay said. When no one said anything, he continued. "I rather recently discovered that Cassandra's welfare is of great importance to me."

"The hell you say." Connor slapped his knee and his laughter rang out, shattering the stunned silence in the room.

"Shut your bloody mouth, Kinleith," Ramsay said in a near growl. "Nothing about this is funny."

Cassie stared at her brother-in-law uncomprehendingly. Charlotte squeezed her hand. When Cassie turned to her sister, Charlotte was smiling, a knowing gleam in her eye.

"I'm not certain I see what is so amusing," Papa said as Mama dropped down into the nearest chair, her eyes wide and her hands clasped tightly in her lap.

Glowering, Graham shifted uneasily behind his foster brother.

Connor gasped for breath. "But it is too funny. Don't you see? Your heart has been stolen, too. Don't you see the humor in it? We never had a chance, Linirk. Neither one of us. We were doomed to lose from the beginning."

Laughter overcame the prizefighter once more. From the way he held his sides, Cassie feared he was going to fall off the chair and start rolling on the floor. She frowned, hardly as amused as her brother-in-law.

Ramsay shook his head in disgust. "My heart has nothing to do with it. 'Tis my conscience she prompted. And you, St. John, you're to blame, too. If you'd taken the offer of knighthood that I made you, none of this would have happened."

"How dare you blame Papa!" Cassie cried, jumping to her

feet. "You wanted to show me Ravencliff. You know you did."

"Don't you blame me or my daughter for your shortcomings, Linirk," Papa boomed, starting around the desk toward Ramsay.

Nicholas put himself between the two men.

Connor sobered instantly and shot from his chair. "Thank your good fortune, Linirk, that St. John is not so easily bought. Because if he had been, the McKensies would be warring on the Forbeses here and now."

"Nobody is warring on anyone here," Nicholas said, stretching out his arms to keep the two at a distance. "Sit down, everyone."

Connor sat. Papa moved back behind the desk.

But Cassie glared at Ramsay. "No one is to blame for me going to Ravencliff except Ramsay and me. He asked me and I accepted. I knew there was no chaperone other than my maid."

Ramsay met her gaze at last. What she saw there was astonishing. Sadness. Stubbornness. And even a little glimmer of— was it possible?—regret.

"Let me make something very clear right now," Papa said, from behind his desk. "I've said this in a variety of ways all along, but there seems to be some reluctance to believe me."

"Go ahead." Nicholas moved to Papa's side. "I think everyone is listening now."

"I have no intention of selling or gifting Glen Gray to the McKensies or the Forbeses," Papa said. "I will do nothing to encourage feuding or any other activity against Crown law. Is that plain enough for all of you?"

Silence reigned for an instant before the men began to talk, all at once.

"Just what do you intend to do with the property?" Graham demanded.

"Glen Gray has been sold to a newly formed company," Papa said.

"Sold?" exclaimed Erik. "What company?"

"You never said anything about selling the property to me," Connor said, staring at his father-in-law in amazement.

Papa held up his hand to quiet everyone. "A railroad will be cutting across it. I received a substantial price for the land. In an effort to settle this feud, I have split the proceeds into two trusts for the education of the McKensie and Forbes clans' children. All the two of you need to do is sign the papers agreeing that hostilities will cease between your clans."

The brilliance of Papa's gesture stunned Cassie.

"Papa, that is a wonderful thing to do," Charlotte cried.

"Ye canna do that," cried Graham in his now-nasal voice, his bushy brows coming together in anger. From his place near the hearth, he took a step into the center of the room. "The glen rightfully belongs to the Forbeses. 'Tis in your power to restore the property to its rightful owner and settle the dispute. Ye must return it to the Forbeses."

"Nay, it belongs to the McKensies," Erik shouted, his ruddy face contorted in anger.

Cassie stared at the men, suddenly struck by how deep the feelings over Glen Gray went. It wasn't just a piece of ground that Connor and Ramsay claimed, their entire families laid claim to the ground.

Papa opened his mouth, but Uncle Nicholas silenced him by putting a hand on his arm. "St. John gained the property in a legal sale. It has been out of Forbes or McKensie ownership and in British hands for almost a century. He has no obligation to do any such thing with it."

Cassie glanced in Ramsay's direction. He remained by the hearth, staring at the floor. Was he angry? Surprised? Disappointed? Three days ago she would have claimed to be able to predict his response. Anger. But now she wasn't so sure.

"Neither of you Scottish gentleman is going to get Glen Gray," Uncle Nicholas repeated. "So there is no more need for kidnapping or any other nefarious plotting. That applies to all of you. Mr. Drummond? Mr. Andrews as well. Are you listening?"

"So, Linirk, all your courting and kidnapping was for naught," Connor said with a derisive chuckle.

Cassie's face warmed with embarrassment.

"Connor?" Charlotte gasped in dismay.

"And you wed yourself to the bluestocking for nothing," Ramsay spit back.

Connor leaped out of his chair, fists raised and ready. Ramsay started toward him.

"Nicholas?" Dorian cried.

Unruffled, Nicholas stepped between the two men. "Mind your manners. I'll not have you taunting one another in the presence of the ladies."

"Then perhaps we should take this elsewhere," Ramsay said, glaring at Connor over Nicholas's shoulder.

"Aye, perhaps we should," said Connor, his voice low and tight.

"If you're hinting at a duel, I'll have this reported to the magistrate before either of you steps a foot out of this house," Nicholas said, his voice low, cold, and unshakable. Everyone in the family knew the story of his duel with the man who had framed him for treason. Cassie and Charlotte squeezed each other's hands again. They knew Uncle Nicholas could be trusted to do what he said. " 'Tis no honorable way to settle anything. I know from experience."

"Please sit down, Connor," Charlotte pleaded.

Her hand had turned cold in Cassie's. Connor did not acknowledge his wife's request, but he did return to his chair. Cassie watched Ramsay grudgingly stalk back to his place beside the hearth.

"Ye can keep the money," Erik declared, the red in his angry face becoming almost purple. "We donna need your charity."

"It is no more charity than if I returned the land to you *gratis*," Papa snapped. "I don't expect gratitude for this gesture, but I will not have it maligned."

"It is a thoughtful attempt at a settlement, St. John," Ramsay said, his face a study in reservation. "I don't mind admitting the move has taken me by surprise. I'm not certain how happy I am about it, but I laud your attempt to resolve this conflict."

"I didn't expect either of your clans to be particularly happy about it," Papa said, "but it seemed the only truly beneficial thing to be done with the property. The locals should also benefit from the railway coming in. Even a feud has to make way for change."

"Which side of the track will be ours?" Erik demanded.

"No one will have any side," Connor said, speaking slowly and patiently. "That's the point."

Graham frowned. "Ye canna end three hundred years of killing and raiding by selling off a piece of land. 'Tis more than an exchange of coins. People's lives were ruined. Families died over that glen."

"I believe St. John understands that," Ramsay said. "I think we need to understand better what this sale means."

"My solicitors are still drawing up the papers for the sale and the trust," Papa said. "I shall send copies of the documents for you to approve in a few days. I'm certain there are family advisors and representatives you must consult."

Connor rose from his chair. "I'll submit it to the others to look over."

"Documents will never end this dispute," Graham said, glaring across at Erik. "McKensies killed my great-great-grand-father."

"Forbes raiders killed and burned my family before my eyes," Erik shouted in return, shaking his fist at Graham. "No child's schooling can make that right!"

"Wait for me outside, Erik," Connor ordered.

Glowering over the abrupt dismissal, Erik slammed out of the room.

"Calm yourself, Graham," Ramsay said, taking his foster brother by the shoulder. "We will examine the papers before we decide our course."

"I'm glad the two of you are taking a reasonable view of

this," Nicholas said. "Think on it and look the documents over. We will have further discussion as necessary."

"Before we go on, I'd like to ask that the rest of this conversation be of a more private nature," Ramsay said. "For Cassandra's sake."

"I'm not leaving," Cassie said, glaring at Ramsay.

"But I think Seacombe and I shall," Aunt Dorian said, rising from the settee. "I don't believe Mr. Andrews needs to be present, either. Charlotte, you and Connor surely have trip arrangements to tend to."

Aunt Dorian soon had everyone except Mama, Papa, Ramsay, and Cassie out of the room. Horton closed the door once more.

"Surely you see the difficulty you have created where Cassie is concerned, my lord," Mama said, offering Ramsay an appealing half-smile. "If there was no proper chaperone, that makes things very awkward, very awkward indeed. Even though you had our permission to court our daughter, this kind of liberty— sweeping her off to your country home—is quite unseemly."

"I understand, Mrs. St. John," Ramsay said, gazing respectfully at Mama.

"Linirk," Papa began, his voice sharp and impatient. "What Cassie's mother is too polite to ask is, have you decided to ruin our daughter or are you going to propose marriage?"

"What?" Just when Cassie was certain that she'd been too embarrassed to ever blush again, fire burned in her cheeks. "Papa, how could you ask that?"

CHAPTER
TWENTY-ONE

Cassie shot up from her place on the settee. Improprieties had passed between her and Ramsay. She could not, would not deny them. But she would not be manipulated into marriage—especially not with a man who was pressured into wedding her for appearance' sake. "What on earth makes anyone think I would accept such a proposal of marriage even if his lordship offered it?"

Ramsay's eyes widened with surprise. And relief, no doubt. She'd just saved him from a fate he certainly had no interest in now that Glen Gray was beyond his reach. He frowned at her. "Cassandra, I don't think you understand how serious a blow to your reputation this will be, once it gets out."

"For once, the marquis and I agree on something," Papa said, stepping toward Ramsay as if joining ranks.

"I don't remember reputation being of great concern to anyone in this family before today," Cassie snapped, her embarrassment smoldering into anger. "Charlotte's namesake had an affair with a Polish exile and everyone seemed to think that was romantic. Who has not heard the romantic tales of Uncle Nicholas pursuing Aunt Dorian throughout several country house parties? I will not be maneuvered into a marriage for the mere purpose of stopping wagging tongues.''

"Cassandra, think of your sister," Mama said.

"Charlotte is safely and properly wed," Cassie said. "She of all people will understand.''

"But Cassandra—" Papa began once more.

"No, she's right," Ramsay said, his gaze holding hers, encouraging her in a way that she did not understand. "If I might be so bold as to offer something of a solution . . .''

"Speak it," Papa said, waving his hands impatiently.

"My sister, Ellen, would be quite happy, I'm sure, to oblige me by putting it out that she served as chaperone at Ravencliff," Ramsay said, speaking slowly and deliberately. "She and her son frequently visit me and a few letters to London acquaintances would dampen rumors of an unchaperoned visit.''

Cassie stared at Ramsay, astonished at his resourcefulness. Though why it should surprise her, she couldn't imagine. He was forever pulling something unexpected from his pocket— figuratively speaking, of course.

Mama and Papa turned to each other.

"That might serve very well." Papa nodded slowly. "I believe we could have Dorian support your sister's claims.''

"Yes, that would confirm the story nicely," Mama agreed. "But the fact that such a visit even occurred will fuel rumors of marriage.''

"I could continue to call, less and less frequently until such time as we see fit to quietly drop the courtship," Ramsay said, watching her father now. "If that is satisfactory to everyone.''

Papa glanced at Mama again. "I believe we could accept that. Would you agree to such an arrangement, Cassie?''

"It is a possible solution," she agreed with reluctance. A cold, complete break would have been the easiest to endure, she thought. She could return to her life and act as if loving Ramsay had never been part of her. She wouldn't even have to wonder when it happened, when it began. If the break was clean, she could just forget him. She glanced in his direction to find he was watching her with a closed expression. She added, " 'Twould only be until the end of the Little Season, which is a few weeks away now.''

"Actually I thought we had a year and a day," Ramsay said, his gaze holding hers.

"What does a year and a day have to do with your court-ship?" Papa asked, suspicion in his voice.

The sudden reminder of their vows brought a pang of pain to Cassie's heart and the sting of tears to her eyes. She turned away, in time to hide them, she hoped.

"Cassandra knows," Ramsay said, his voice low and caress-ing. Cassie stared at her hands clasped before her.

"Just a silly game," she said, relieved when Ramsay did not pursue his comment, but she could feel his gaze on her, seeking something. She did not understand what he wanted.

Then Papa frowned and asked the strangest question. "Lin-irk, is there any reason why marriage should be considered?''

Ramsay paused only briefly, glancing uncomfortably in Cass-ie's direction before replying, "No, sir, I protected your daughter.''

Cassie stared up at him and Papa in confusion, uncertain about the meaning of the question.

Papa's face fell, a mixture of relief and sorrow shaping his features. His gaze flickered in Cassie's direction, then turned away. She knew she had let him down. She suddenly hated Ramsay for putting her through this ordeal over a piece of property.

"I am not an irresponsible man, St. John. I shall marry your daughter if you wish it—and if she will have me. Or I shall have my sister make it known that she was a chaperone and we will end our courtship at a less conspicuous time in the future. Whichever you wish.''

"Marriage is out of the question." Cassie shook her head. "Write your sister, do whatever is necessary if we must cover this up.''

Papa scrutinized Cassie closely before he replied. "You have your answer."

Ramsay bowed to her wishes. "I shall dispatch the letter today."

Papa nodded. He suddenly appeared older than his years and very weary. Aware that she was the cause, Cassie sank back down on the settee. Mama slipped a reassuring arm around her. But Cassie knew she'd disappointed them all.

As she stared into her lap, the exhaustion of the trip crept over her. She didn't want to think any longer about property and clans, proprieties and improprieties, betrothals or weddings. She wanted to sink into a hot bath and wash away all her thoughts and feelings for Ramsay. She wanted to forget about Graham, Connor and Erik, Papa and Mama. All the people she'd disappointed and hurt. Perhaps life as a nun would offer her some peace, she thought. A barren cell with a simple hard bed seemed to have a lot of appeal. Maybe not the hard bed, she decided as a shadow fell over her.

"Lord Linirk wishes to speak to you alone," Mama was saying. "Do you feel up to it?"

Cassie glanced up to see Ramsay standing before her, sober and unemotional as ever.

"Do you wish me to stay?" Mama asked.

Cassie's first reaction was to say yes, but the soft hint of contrition in Ramsay's eyes made her hesitate. "I can't imagine what we have to say to each other, but I'll talk with him."

"We'll be right outside in the hallway if you need anything," Mama said. "Don't keep her long, Linirk. She needs her rest."

As soon as Mama and Papa were out of the room, Ramsay sat down beside her. He reached for her hand, but she pulled it from his grasp. She was too exhausted, too heartworn to play games with him. "Papa's sale of Glen Gray must be a great disappointment to you."

" 'Tis a surprise, I grant." Ramsay sighed, an oddly regretful sound. "We have used each other ill, princess. I used you in the hopes of obtaining Glen Gray. You used me to spite Dudley.''

''There was more to it than that,'' Cassie reminded him, lest he think her as manipulative as he. ''I was protecting my sister.''

''Aye, there is that virtuous motivation,'' he said with a dark chuckle. ''I would have never harmed your sister. McKensie maybe, but not your sister—or you.''

The door squeaked, then moved ever so slightly.

''We'll be finished in a moment,'' Cassie called out, thinking that Mama had become impatient. But as she watched a black nose appeared, then Tophet came trotting into the room, his tongue lolling happily from his mouth and his tail beating a furious wag. He put his head in her lap and licked her hand in greeting. At the moment he seemed the only family member truly happy to see her.

Then the hound greeted Ramsay, too, as if all was just as it should be.

''He reminds me of happier times,'' Ramsay said, giving the dog a pat on the head.

His words echoed Cassie's thoughts, but she would not tell him so. ''Please say what you have to say, my lord, and let's be done with this.''

''I can assure you that my sister will be more than happy to put herself forth as your chaperone while you were at Ravencliff,'' he said, putting his arm along the back of the settee and leaning closer to her as he scratched the dog behind the ears. ''You consented to your father's suggestion that we appear to be courting for the remainder of the Little Season?''

''Yes, I believe you heard me,'' Cassie said, refusing to look at him and wishing he was not so close that she could feel the warmth of his breath on her neck. She hurried on. ''I realize this will be as awkward for you as it is for me. However, you do not need to see it through for my sake. I will survive a few unkind rumors. I have before.''

''I would not have agreed to the strategy if I was not willing to do my part," Ramsay said. "I wondered if it might make the courtship easier for us both if we pretended it was all new."

A silly little hope fluttered in Cassie's belly, but she forced it away. "Why should we do that, my lord? I'm not even certain that I'm capable of playacting anymore."

"You do have Dudley to consider," Ramsay said quietly. She could feel his eyes assessing her. Drat! He understood just how important it was to her to present a proud face to the world.

"And for myself," he continued, "I don't care to be considered the rejected suitor one more time."

"So you are offering this as a way for both of us to save face," Cassie said, remembering the story of Aileen, Ramsay's former fiancée, that Graham had told her. The merit of the suggestion was immediately clear to her—as well as the awkwardness of it.

"I see we understand one another," he said.

"Too well, I fear," Cassie said.

Ramsay rose from the settee and ambled toward Papa's desk. "So, how do you think we should proceed?"

"We shall continue to be seen together," Cassie said, wondering what on earth he was doing. He seemed to be looking for something. When he didn't find it, he turned toward the hearth. "Until the end of the Little Season, just as we'd planned before."

Ramsay turned toward her as if he was about to ask something.

"Don't you dare tell Papa about the handfasting," Cassie said. "He will read more into it than he should."

"As you please," he said, continuing to survey the mantel, his hands nonchalantly stuck deep in his pockets. "We could go for rides in the park again. Always a good place to be seen."

"As long as the weather is fair," Cassie said, now more puzzled than ever about what he was looking for in the room and exactly what he was proposing between them. "And we will be properly accompanied by grooms, of course."

"Of course, and I could be of service to your mother with her exhibition," he offered. "I like your mother. You are very fortunate, Cassandra, to have such a lady to watch over you."

"And Papa?"

"Ah, well, your father and I may be another story," he said, his face brightening at last. "Here's what I was looking for."

He opened Papa's cigar box. "A fine selection. May I choose one for you, or do you wish to select your own?"

"I prefer to make my own choices," Cassie asserted.

"Of course," he said, offering her the box. "How could I forget? Make your choice."

Despite her weariness, a smile slowly spread across her face. This was the man she'd known at Ravencliff and she knew in that moment that she loved him. The man who knew and understood her games. The realization struck her so deeply that she feared she was going to weep. If he saw her, she'd have to explain her tears away as playacting and he'd think that very strange.

Cassie swallowed the lump in her throat and took a cigar from the box. Ramsay returned the box to its place on the mantel and proceeded to find the clipper, then the rush lights. As the smoke curled up around their heads, they discussed the possibility of accepting an invitation to another card party at Smedgewood's or of obtaining vouchers to Almack's. Walks in the park with Tophet. All the appearances that would reassure Society that their courtship continued unmarred by scandal.

Ramsay leaned against the hearth, one hand hooked in his waistcoat pocket as he held his cigar with the other. He seemed to enjoy their plotting. Cassie's heartache eased as they talked. Her exhaustion evaporated. She quite forgot where they were and what they were doing until Mama stepped into the room and nearly fainted at the sight of her daughter smoking a cigar with the Marquis of Linirk.

* * *

One morning a fortnight later, Graham watched Ramsay sitting at his desk, reading through the Glen Gray documents that the St. John footman had delivered earlier that morning.

Even with two weeks to think about it, Graham could not bring himself to accept this whimpering end to the feud. Glen Gray sold off like a mere piece of land—not a cause to fight for, not a holy quest to pursue, just signed away for a few pounds in a bank. It was unacceptable. He paced the study floor, his head down and his hands clasped behind his back. "Ye canna erase three centuries of wrong in a few sheets of paper," he railed. " 'Tis an abomination to even think it. Men have fought and died for that land. Ye disgrace their memory to relinquish the clan's claim just like that."

"So you've been saying," Ramsay said without looking up from the papers. "Don't you think Kinleith is going through this very thing with the McKensies?"

"I donna care what Kinleith does," Graham said. "My great-great-grandfather—God rest his soul—is a-spinnin' in his grave."

"I doubt that peace is a disgrace to a good soldier." Ramsay glowered up at him. "I don't appreciate what you're saying, about me or Cassandra. Besides, there are other things to consider."

"The money? We can give our children a fine education without St. John's charity."

"I agree, but this is not charity," Ramsay asserted, finally looking up from the document. "The funds for the trust are the proceeds of the sale. Be practical. Even if Glen Gray belonged to the Forbeses, I'd have to consider selling to the railroad company, especially for this price. It would take a couple of centuries of grazing livestock to bring in the profit this transaction will reap."

"You'd give up the feud for money?" Graham demanded. "Have ye no principle?"

"What good did principle do your great-great-grandfather?" Ramsay challenged, his voice taking on the hard edge that

Graham knew too well. There were times when Ramsay could be persuaded and times when he was immovable.

Furious, Graham slammed his fists down on the desk, leaned over, and peered into Ramsay's face. Ramsay had been seeing the St. John lass nearly every day for the last two weeks. He left for every assignation with a smile of anticipation on his face and returned with the glow of pleasure in his eyes. Ramsay's growing attachment to the lass could only mean ill for the feud. All of Graham's anger and frustration boiled up at once. "I know what ye want. 'Tis not money. 'Tis the lass. You'd give up the feud for her. You'd turn your back on my great-great-grandfather's honor and that of all the other loyal Forbeses who have laid down their lives to win back Glen Gray.

"My father and I knelt at my great-grandfather's bedside as he lay dying from a McKensie blade stuck in his back during a raid. It was a long, slow, painful death. I remember the sight of red blood on the sheets, the smell of putrid flesh, and the sound of our women weeping. We clasped hands and vowed to him that we'd see this feud won. Now look at you. You'd disgrace me and my father and my great-grandfather—all of them—just to lie between that English lassie's legs again.

"Ye will no even deny it, will ye?" Graham taunted.

"Why should I?" Ramsay looked down at the documents again. "Is it such a terrible thing for me to find pleasure in a woman's company? Is it such a dreadful prospect to give up ground that we haven't possessed for three hundred years in exchange for profit that will benefit clan children? Perhaps it is time for us to reexamine what we're doing, Graham."

"Bloody damnation, have ye turned as daft as a churchman?" Graham straightened and planted his fists on his hips. "Canna ye no see it? Yer dancing to her tune, no the other way round. Handfasted with her in the chapel and took her to bed. When ye loaded her into the carriage and brought her home, I thought ye still had yer head on straight. I thought ye'd twist her father's arm and get want we wanted from him.

But what do ye do? Ye damn near apologize to her papa—a commoner—for beddin' a ripe lass who should have been married off for her own good when she was fifteen."

Ramsay slowly rose from his chair to his full height, spread his hands on the desk and leaned over until he was eye level with Graham. "You go too far, Graham."

"Do I? What makes ye think this woman is any better than the others?" Graham quizzed, truly fearful his kinsman could be hurt by a woman's betrayal again. "Ye court her now for appearance' sake, but what makes you think this one won't turn on you just like your mother and Aileen?"

"She is different," Ramsay said without a pause. "Entirely different. You'll see. Whether we accept this agreement for Glen Gray or not, I intend to continue to court her as long as she's agreeable. Get that into your thick head."

"Ye intend to wed her?" Graham asked. He'd longed to hear Ramsay deny it.

"I would have offered that day in her father's study if she hadn't cut me off," Ramsay said, turning away. "Look the documents over, if you like. I think you'll find them more than fair. St. John doesn't have to do this for us. Keep that in mind. We could kiss this fortune good-bye and not regain Glen Gray, either."

Graham frowned at the documents. "Where are ye goin'?"

"I'm to escort Cassandra and her mother to the Egyptian Hall to look in on the preparations for the exhibition of Greek pottery. Do you wish to come?"

"Bloody hell, not me." Graham snorted, realizing he might as well have been ranting at a stone wall. Nothing he'd said had changed Ramsay's mind.

Ramsay rang the bell for Oliver, his manservant, and strolled out of the room with a jaunty confidence in his step. Graham's discontent deepened. The St. John lass had entirely too much influence on his foster brother. There must be something he could do about it.

"Don't wait to dine with me, Graham. I think I might be invited to sup with the St. Johns."

"How does it feel to sit across the table from Connor McKensie?" Graham goaded.

"I don't know," Ramsay said, accepting his hat and cloak from Oliver. "Charlotte and Connor are off on their wedding trip, finally. I pretty much have Mrs. St. John and Cassandra to myself except, of course, when St. John comes home. He's not a bad sort. Looking to the future for twin daughters must have its trials and tribulations. We'll talk about the documents later."

When the door closed on Ramsay, Graham went back into the library and briefly looked at the papers on the desktop. The documents that would bring to an end a three-hundred-year-old cause to live and fight lay before him. The same document lay before the McKensie. Harmless sheets of paper that would mean his ancestors had died in vain. How could he stop the feud from coming to an ignoble end?

The lass was the key. What would make her reject Ramsay? What was her Achilles' heel? If the St. John lass turned on Ramsay, if he was rejected one more time, he'd be much less interested in signing St. John's documents. The realization brought an evil smile to Graham's lips and gave him hope.

Willing to try any ploy, Graham hastily seated himself at the desk and shoved the Glen Gray documents aside. He pulled paper from the desk, opened the inkpot, and seized the quill. Pen raised over the paper, he hesitated a moment to think about what he was going to write, or more accurately, how he was going to write it. Should he sign his name to it? Or send it unsigned? Which way would make his tale more believable to the St. John lass? The timing? Timing was always important. When would be the best time to send this message? Now, Graham decided. It should be waiting for her when her day with Ramsay was over.

* * *

From the curb of Piccadilly, Ramsay looked up at the plaster Egyptian gods, their human bodies topped with sinister animal heads. Each sat between the soaring red columns of the exhibition hall. Behind them, stiff hieroglyphics covered the walls. The Egyptian Hall deserved its name.

"I can see it now," he said softly into Cassandra's ear as they waited for the morning watchman to unlock the entrance for them. They'd come early to meet Mrs. St. John there and help her with the unpacking arrangements for the Greek pottery exhibit. "You want to be Cleopatra."

"Of course." Cassandra rewarded him with a lovely smile.

"And who am I?" Ramsay prompted. "Mark Antony, Julius Caesar, or Alexander the Great?"

"Alexander, of course," she replied without pause, then she grinned at him. "Conqueror of the world."

"Indeed," Ramsay said, smiling. He was getting to like this game. "Your mother doesn't appear to have arrived yet."

"Yes, miss, that reminds me. I have a message for you." The watchman handed Cassandra a note from her mother which explained that Mrs. St. John had been unavoidably detained at the printer's, but would be joining them in half an hour or so. She apologized for keeping them waiting.

"Is this an inconvenience?" Cassandra asked, slipping the note into her reticule.

"Not at all," Ramsay replied, secretly delighted to have Cassandra's company all to himself for a change. The St. Johns had been serious about their insistence upon proper chaperoning. As cooperative as he'd endeavored to be, the constant company was wearing. How he longed to have Cassandra to himself again—just as it had been at Ravencliff.

"The pottery arrived the day before yesterday and some of the museum people began unpacking it," Cassandra said, as the watchman stood back from the unlocked the door so they could enter. "Back this way."

Inside, the place was deserted. Ramsay followed Cassandra at a slight distance, the better to admire the sway of her raspberry-pink skirts and the graceful curve of her spine as she walked. Their footsteps echoed against the lofty walls of the museum, which supposedly could hold up to fifteen thousand people. But they were alone as far as he could see, except for the guard at the door. More alone than they'd been in two weeks.

"Have you ever been here to see an exhibit?" Cassandra asked as she led the way through a series of large rooms cluttered with antiquities, foreign curiosities, and classic art reproductions.

"No, I have not," Ramsay said, stopping to get a better look at a saddle that Napoleon had allegedly owned, according to the display card. "Interesting place."

"I always enjoy my visits," Cassandra said. "But I love Mrs. Salmon's Waxworks in Fleet Street better. Charlotte thinks it absolutely too common for words, but I think it is so dramatic to see the figures posed together at some important turning point in their lives. Here we are. Yes, this is the room where the pottery will be displayed."

She stopped in the doorway. Ramsay came up behind her and peered over her head at a high-ceilinged room lighted by daylight falling from the ceiling skylight. Nearly every inch of floor space was covered with crates of varying sizes. "There is a lot of work to be done."

"Indeed there is," Cassandra said, navigating a narrow path between the crates. "I believe they started over here. Mama was very pleased with what the Duke of Deander sent. He seemed to spare none of his best pieces. Your request must have made a great impression on him. That made Mama very happy. Thank you so much for helping her with this."

"My pleasure," Ramsay said, thinking he wouldn't mind if she demonstrated her gratitude in a more obvious way. Like a kiss. It had been two weeks since they'd returned from Scotland. He'd called on her every day, in keeping with their agreement to carry out the courtship through the Little Season. She'd only deigned to brush her lips across his cheek when they'd parted the day before. Light and brief as the touch had been, Ramsay thought he could still feel her lips there on his cheek.

Being in her company so often, and yet prohibited from touching her in any intimate way, was pure hell. Perhaps it would have been different if he'd never known the delights she offered, but he did know. Being in her company and forced to behave as a gentleman was pure, heavenly hell.

"Look at that piece." Cassandra picked up a graceful urn and admired it. "To think it has survived all these centuries. Many of these depict interesting scenes. What are these people doing?"

Ramsay glanced over her shoulder. Stunned, he recognized an explicit portrayal of an act even he'd only heard of. He snatched the urn out of Cassandra's hand. "Has your mother seen this?"

"She was here yesterday when they were unpacking," Cassandra said, her eyes widening at his reaction. "Why, what is it? Something scandalous? Do tell."

"It is a lady entertaining a pair of gentlemen at the same time," Ramsay said, unwilling to lie to her, but even less willing to explain more. She still knew too little to be introduced to all the sexual mysteries. He stuffed the clay thing into a box. "I doubt the duke realized he was sending this piece along."

Before he could stop her, Cassandra reached around him for the urn. "I'd like to get a closer look, if you don't mind."

"Princess," Ramsay protested, then clamped his mouth shut. What was there to say?

"How on earth?" She studied the depiction for a long moment, then she turned the urn sideways, her eyes narrowing as if she were trying to imagine something more than what she saw there. Then a blush blossomed in her cheeks. "Yes, I see what you mean. I wouldn't have thought this possible. Isn't that uncomfortable? Have you ever done this?''

"Cassandra," Ramsay began, about to say that her question was impertinent, but the guileless curiosity in her eyes stopped him. "No, I have not. I don't share. I think you should know that what is illustrated there is not a common practice."

"Oh," she said, turning back to the urn. Her blush faded and she pursed her mouth as she assessed it once more. "They appear to be having a good time. Isn't it interesting how different cultures view men and women and their coming together? Charlotte discovered an illustrated Japanese volume in Papa's library. We found it quite enlightening. But it pictured nothing like this. I don't think Papa knew that book was there. He inherited many of those books from his aunt Charlotte."

Ramsay stood speechless as Cassandra nonchalantly placed the urn back in the crate, strolled on, and disappeared behind another packing box. With a start he realized that he was overlooking something here. Was it possible she was as frustrated with all the chaperoning as he was? Heartened, he followed Cassandra behind the large packing box.

CHAPTER
TWENTY-TWO

Cassie knew the minute Ramsay delicately explained the illustration on the urn that it had been a mistake to come into the museum before Mama arrived. When she'd read Mama's message, they should have climbed back into the carriage and gone straight home where Horton would hover over them and no word of their conversation would be private.

Mama and Papa had been most emphatic from the beginning that the remainder of her courtship with Linirk be absolutely proper. After hinting at the family's embarrassment, should the courtship be anything less, Papa recited a list of horrors Linirk had perpetrated, in addition to his plot to kidnap Connor. The career of a rich medical doctor—rumored to have been his mother's lover—had been ruined by mysterious rumors of grave-robbing. Linirk refused his mother her dowager portion unless she lived in exile. He'd also driven his former fiancée and her husband into poverty and exile. A suitor for his sister whom Linirk disliked had found himself convicted of theft and shipped off to a prison colony in Australia.

"The fact is, Cassie, the Marquis of Linirk, for all his

refinement and influence, is a ruthless man," Papa had summed up.

"But, don't you see, each of those people endangered him or his family," Cassie protested, unable to keep from defending Ramsay. The list had been dismaying, but not surprising. Ramsay protected what was his, harshly perhaps, but lashing out was his defense. She understood that about him. No one seemed to perceive in him the tenderness and compassion that she knew he kept so well hidden.

Still, in the dark of the night when she lay awake thinking of him, doubts about him encroached. Ramsay fought hard and unfairly if he felt threatened. But did she truly understand him as well as she thought?

The fact was, she shouldn't have suggested that they enter the museum before Mama had arrived. But here they were. She'd make the best of it, which meant she'd be careful about calling his attention to any more odd Greek art.

When Ramsay found her behind the crate, Cassie was desperately trying to put the urn images of the two men and the woman out of her mind. She had taken off her bonnet and had found an interesting piece of carved marble. With great care she lifted the marble from the box—a horse's head.

"It is lovely, isn't it?" she said, holding up the piece for him to see. "How the Greeks could make a hard, cold material such as marble take on life and movement is miraculous."

To her surprise Ramsay put his hat down beside her bonnet and from behind slipped his arms around her. One hand spread across her narrow rib cage and his other took the marble from her and replaced it in the box.

"Let's not trouble ourselves over your mother's Greek antiquities," he murmured against her ear. Then he found a vulnerable spot on the back of her neck beneath her ear and kissed her there.

A shiver of pleasure coursed through her. So many days spent near him, yet beyond his familiar touch had left her sensitive to every brush of his hand, every stirring of his breath, every hooded glance. Endeavoring to resist the urge to melt against him, she turned. "What are you doing, my lord?"

"Taking the moment to dwell on nothing but us, my queen of the Nile," he whispered, taking her by the waist and lifting her up to sit on an unopened box. The height was exactly right to bring her face-to-face with him. Almost as perfect as being in bed. A hot blush flooded into Cassie's cheeks again.

"But here, my lord?" Tentatively she put her hands on his shoulders and offered him a shy smile. It had been torment to keep her distance from him over the last two weeks. Even if only for appearance' sake, he'd been an attentive and ardent suitor. His very nearness day in and day out had served as a constant reminder of the pleasure they'd shared at Ravencliff. The brief touch of his hand on the small of her back. The brush of his shoulder against hers. The whisper of her skirts against his boots. And try as she might to ignore her body's cravings, Cassie longed to have him hold her again like he had that night in his bed.

"Why not here?" His mouth sought hers, taking her hungrily. They clung together, their tongues exploring and teasing. As if Ramsay knew how heavy her breasts suddenly were, he molded them in his hands. Through her gown, his fingers teased her already sensitive nipples. A thrilling need reached down inside Cassie. He glided his hands down her back, cupped her bottom, and pulled her toward him. "Open, princess. Put your legs around me."

Embarrassed, but curious and needy, Cassie did as he suggested. His hands slipped under her skirt, his warm palms caressed her bare thighs above her stockings. He kissed her again, deep and demanding.

She combed her fingers through his hair and feasted on his lips in return, her head swam with the sensation of his fingers skillfully exploring her cleft through the silk of her undergarments.

"You've been as tortured as I have, haven't you?" he murmured against her mouth.

"Is it so obvious?" she sighed as he relentlessly stroked her with his thumbs.

"Yes, even through the silk of your shift," he murmured, kissing her nose and her eyelids. "You're hot and wet, princess."

The roughness of his trousers against the inside of her thighs was seductive and wonderful. The caress of his thumbs melted every bone in her body until she pressed her forehead against his shoulder. She was incapable of protesting when he pulled at the tapes of her drawers, tugging and ripping the silk gently until his fingers found and parted her soft swollen lips. A spectacular thrill soared through her, like that she'd known that night in his bed at Ravencliff.

She murmured his name—a plea, a protest—all wrapped in one word. "What if Mother finds—"

"There's not a soul here, princess, and you're so far along now, this won't take long," he promised, unbuttoning his trousers. "I would prefer to take more time. But this will do. This will do nicely."

His entry was deliberate, torturously slow, inch by inch, until he had completely sheathed himself in her. Cassie tightened her legs around his hips, glorying in the satisfaction of holding him inside. With her arms still encircling his neck, she flung her head back, closed her eyes, and began to move with him urgently—the dance once learned, never forgotten.

He gave a low moan of gratification and followed her lead. His hands found her breasts and with his thumbs he teased the swollen buds. His touch brought her to a quick explosive climax. It had hardly peaked when another came. Cassie cried out, her body inundated with waves of astonishing pleasure. She clung to him, only vaguely aware of Ramsay's hand gently pressed against her mouth.

As she panted for air, his climax burst long and hot inside her.

When it was over, they held each other, Cassie's head tucked against his shoulder. His chin rested on her head. Neither seemed strong enough to stand alone.

She longed to tell him while they were still joined how much she loved him, despite everything. How she knew that the man who dwelled in his heart—and he did have a heart—was not an evil, villainous man, but someone who needed to protect himself. A laird who wanted to do his best for his clan. A man who could love again, if he would open his heart to her. But if she uttered those words, would he welcome them? Would he believe her? Or what if he did not feel the same toward her? A confession of love would make her look pathetic.

He kissed her temple, then withdrew from her slowly, gently. Reluctantly she released him. She was still so lethargic from their lovemaking that she allowed him to restore her clothing as best as possible. When he'd finished buttoning his trousers, he tried to take her into his arms again. But feeling oddly deserted and adrift, she pushed him away and gingerly lowered herself to the floor.

"There's no need for seduction now, you know," she declared, surprised to find herself so unsteady. She fended off his helping hand and grasped the edge of the box to regain her balance. Cassie studied him, her heart pitter-pattering in her breast. "This is hardly necessary for the pretense of a courtship. And Papa is going to settle the sale of Glen Gray and the Forbeses will receive the proceeds no matter what happens, my lord. I don't want you to get the wrong idea. We just seem to have this—"

She made a helpless gesture.

"Passion for each other?" he filled in for her.

"Passion." She nodded. Perhaps that explained what she felt with him. "Passion and love aren't the same thing, are they?"

"Not necessarily," Ramsay said, turning away from her slightly.

"Does this happen to other people?"

"I can't speak for other people, princess," Ramsay said, his voice reassuringly soft and warm. "I don't normally make love in a museum in midmorning to the queen of the Nile atop a packing crate."

"Whew, me either," Cassie said, thinking for the first time that her playacting games had truly gone too far. "We shouldn't have come in here without Mama." She pulled away and reached for her bonnet.

"Actually, I thought it was quite a good idea," Ramsay said, smiling complacently.

"You must promise me something, my lord," Cassie begged, feeling ashamed of her passionate folly.

"Of course. Anything, Princess."

"Cassandra? Linirk? Are you in here?" Mama's voice floated to them through the cavernous halls of the museum.

Disconcerted, Cassie turned on Ramsay. "Promise me you won't embarrass Mama. Not over this or over anything else."

A flash of annoyance lit his eyes. "What do you mean?"

"Just promise me," Cassie persisted, a thrill of panic stirring in her belly. She could not have Mama think anything had happened. She would not have her embarrassed just when she was finally getting the pottery exhibit that she wanted. "And don't think what just happened means anything. It was just a moment of passion."

Ramsay frowned. For a moment Cassie thought he was going to refuse her.

"I promise," he said at last. "I would never do anything to upset your mother."

Cassie sighed with relief. She trusted him to keep his promise, but his expression of disapproval mystified her. "Thank you."

"There you are," Mama said, waving to them from the doorway.

"Come in, Mrs. St. John," Ramsay called, waving a beckoning hand. "We've been looking at the treasures while you settled things with the printer."

"Yes, Mama," Cassie welcomed. "We were just admiring this marble horse's head."

"Good, I'm glad I wasn't missed," Mama said, smiling as she wove her way between the boxes toward them.

Ramsay leaned close to Cassie's ear and spoke in a taunting voice. "I agreed not to embarrass your mother, but I did not agree that our passionate interlude meant nothing."

The remainder of the day passed pleasantly enough in Ramsay's company. He behaved toward her and Mama as if nothing unusual had taken place between them in the museum. But as much as Cassie tried to put his lovemaking from her mind, her sated body soon recovered enough to be sensitive to his every touch and glance. Her concentration on the things Mama told her disappeared. She was reduced to following Mama around and taking down her dictated notes.

Ramsay shed his coat and took up the tools to open the crates as Mama directed. Cassie felt so different after Ramsay's lovemaking; how could Mama not see that they'd been up to something disgraceful before she arrived?

But Mama was immersed in her project and seemed to notice little beyond the necessary details of preparing the exhibit for opening. Even if Cassie's body had let her forget Ramsay's caresses, he would not. When Mama wasn't looking, he'd cast Cassie the most desirous of looks. At first she was horrified. Then it became funny. The Marquis of Linirk once more proved his sense of humor—and his ability to flirt outrageously. She had to suppress her giggles and force herself to concentrate on Mama's instructions.

Later Ramsay accepted Mama's invitation to dinner. Cassie had to endure more looks across the dining-room table. However, Ramsay tempered his lecherous glances in the presence of Papa, who was not as preoccupied as Mama.

By the end of a warm and immensely pleasant evening Cassie was having second thoughts about declaring herself to Linirk. Of course, a lady should wait for the gentleman to announce his feelings, but this was different. Linirk was hardly an ordinary gentleman and what reason was there for her to follow the dictates of Society?

She was pleased when Mama and Papa made their farewells and left her alone with Ramsay in the hallway to say good night.

"Am I to have you to myself again, at last?" he whispered as Mama and Papa disappeared up the stairs.

"So it would seem," Cassie replied, also in a whisper, hardly able to believe the good fortune to be left alone twice in the same day—not that she intended let happen what had happened that morning. But when Ramsay reached for her, she went into his arms. He kissed her. Not like he had that morning, but tenderly, long and slow with yearning and sweet desire. Cassie melded her mouth with his—returning the desire. Surrendering to the weakness she understood so much better now, she slipped her arms around his waist and pressed herself against him. Their mouths continued to sample and taste.

She could hold back no longer. When he released her, she rested her brow against his jaw and gasped for breath. "I have a confession to make."

"What could you possibly have to confess, princess?" Ramsay asked, his lips moving against her temple.

"You already have my heart."

He paused. She pulled away and looked up to read his face. His expression was sober and closed. She was afraid to even guess what he must be thinking.

"No, don't say anything," Cassie hurried on, touching his mouth with her fingertips. "I know you are wary of we women. Such selfish, spiteful creatures we must seem to you. The last thing you want to hear from me is that I love you. But you deserve to know that a woman who will never betray you, loves you. I don't expect you to declare likewise. That is not why I tell you this."

"Perhaps you should demand something from me, princess," Ramsay murmured against her fingertips. "I have a confession too. I did not protect you today."

Cassie didn't exactly understand what he meant. She took her fingers from his mouth. The arrogant half-smile on his lips hinted that he wasn't particularly regretful about that fact. "You don't sound concerned."

"I'm not." His smile softened into an expression oddly tinged with gratitude. "I will say no more now. But I shall see you tomorrow at tea with the Countess of Seacombe."

He bowed over her hand, his lips brushed warmly against her knuckles. Then he wrapped his black cloak around him and disappeared out the door and into the October fog.

Cassie hurried to the window to watch him stride away into the darkness. Had her declaration frightened him? she wondered. No woman in his life had been particularly good to him. Naturally he was reluctant to accept a woman's affections. But he hadn't appeared frightened by her heartfelt words. In fact, she couldn't tell how he'd felt. He'd revealed nothing.

Cassie gave a little huff. He didn't have to take her so literally. He could have at least hinted at what his true feelings were.

She turned from the window and caught a glimpse of herself in the hallway mirror. A stray tendril of hair had slipped from her coif. Her nose was shiny even in the candlelight. The starch was gone from her fitted bodice. She hardly looked her best.

He could have laughed at her, she reminded herself. That would have been wonderful. Maybe she'd been right earlier in the day. Declaring her love had been a weak and silly thing for a girl to do. But 'twas done, and she wasn't going to regret giving Ramsay her heart.

Cassie found the letter on her dressing table when she went up to bed. It had lain there awaiting her since midday, according to Betsy. A messenger boy delivered it, the maid said. He claimed he'd been paid by a groom wearing no particular livery.

After telling Ramsay her true feelings, Cassie was still so euphoric that she was hardly inclined to read correspondence. The day had been full of wonderful surprises. She considered leaving the letter until the morning; but her natural curiosity got the better of her.

Picking up the missive, she examined the handwriting, but she did not recognize it. It was not Ramsay's hand. She would have known his bold scrawl instantly. Nor was it Charlotte's or Tony's. The letters were large and painfully formed by someone who did not spend a great deal of time writing correspondence. She was sure of it.

She ordered a bath and while she was waiting for it to be prepared, Cassie ripped open the letter. It was longer than she expected and bore no signature. Curious, but unalarmed, Cassie settled down on her dressing-table stool to read.

> *15 October 1828*
> *Dear Miss Cassandra St. John,*
>   *You may wish to know that your former betrothed, Dudley Moncreff, Viscount of Monksleigh, resides in Paris at present. He pines for you. His lordship finds himself living there because he was forced out of London by the Marquis of Linirk. Also Linirk bribed his lordship to cry off on your betrothal so the marquis could make himself known to you and incur your indebtedness to him. To make certain Monksleigh did as he agreed, Linirk sat on Bunter's balcony and watched as his lordship cried off. He saw you drop the betrothal ring in his lordship's teacup. All of this is a plot to acquire the Scotland property your father owns. Beware of the heartless Marquis of Linirk.*
>   *From One Who Believes You Should Know the Truth*

Cassie stared at the letter in disbelief, a sinking feeling of betrayal gnawing in her belly. The truth of the missive could hardly be questioned. Whoever had written it had been there at the tea shop. How else could he or she know that she'd dropped her betrothal ring into Dudley's cup? And the author knew other details—things Cassie had never contemplated and never connected. Ramsay had paid Dudley to cry off? Was that possible?

She reread the letter, her eyes narrowing as she tried to make sense of it. The plot described was just the kind of scheming Ramsay was capable of—especially when he wanted something for the clan.

He'd admitted to hiring the footpads, but she'd never connected the attack with Dudley's crying off. Why should she? Footpads were for hire, men and women who earned their way by selling their services. Why would she even speculate that her fiancé's affections had a price?

Even with this letter in hand it was almost impossible for her to believe such a thing was possible. Linirk had paid Dudley to break off their engagement. She'd taken Dudley under her wing when he'd first come to Town and made him over into a fashionable, sought-after gentleman of the *ton*. His gratitude had been boundless. He'd knelt before her with his hands pressed against his heart when he'd proposed marriage. Once she'd accepted, he'd followed her around like an adoring puppy. Was it possible his love was corruptible?

Still stunned, she let the missive drop to the dressing table.

Yet how like Ramsay to attempt to buy off a lover. Heartless indeed. Cassie gave an angry, unladylike huff. How had he managed it? He could be very persuasive. He could also be intimidating. Yet Dudley had worshiped her. He'd said so, often. What true lover would be so easily parted from his beloved? How difficult had it been, she wondered with a sinking heart, for Ramsay to persuade her fiancé to leave her? What had he threatened? What had he offered? How crass had the transaction been?

She gazed into space, but in her mind's eye she saw Ramsay hand Dudley a wad of pound notes and bid him to end their engagement. Dudley nodded agreement. Then, to add insult to injury, Ramsay sat down at a cloth-covered table and watched her humiliation. According to the letter, from the balcony of the tea shop he'd played voyeur to her disgrace.

Cassie groaned aloud. And it only got worse. In the aftermath, when she'd been vulnerable, he'd paid to have her attacked and come to her rescue as if he were a hero. The blackguard. She frowned and shook her head no. She didn't have all the answers to her questions, but she knew the missive contained the truth. Damn Ramsay. Damn Dudley. Damn all men.

In her outrage she pounded her fist on the dressing table. Combs and brushes rattled against the marble.

When Betsy announced that her bath was prepared, Cassie slumped into the tub, steam rising around her. The pleasure in the day was gone and she found little satisfaction in the comfort of a hot bath. As much as she wanted to discount the letter as a lie, it answered too many questions to be dismissed. Now she knew why Dudley had cried off then lit out for the Continent so quickly. Ramsay Forbes. How could she have been so stupid as to vow her love to that villain?

Heavens, she'd allowed the man to seduce her right there in the museum, her sitting atop a box with her legs spread like a common ladybird. Yet her body warmed with the memory of his touch. She remembered how he'd admitted he'd not protected her and given her that half-smile of satisfaction.

Cassie's eyes snapped wide open. If that meant what she thought— What if she'd conceived a baby? Surely not. She'd only been unprotected that one time.

Cassie closed her eyes against the humiliation of the realization, yet despite her shame she couldn't help but wonder what Ramsay's baby would look like. Same fair hair and emerald-green eyes? The same generous nature hidden behind a facade of harshness?

Still distracted when she completed her bath, Cassie climbed out of the tub, allowed Betsy to help her dry her hair, and dress her for bed.

"Betsy, did you not tell me that the footman, Will, has a cousin who works in the stables of the Marquis of Linirk?" Cassie asked.

"Yes, Miss Cassie," Betsy said, picking up the used towels Cassie left on the floor in her wake.

"Tomorrow I would like Will to find the whereabouts of the marquis in the morning," Cassie said.

"Should be simple enough to do, Miss Cassie," Betsy said.

"Good," Cassie said. "The marquis and I have a few things to discuss."

When the maid was gone, Cassie crawled into bed, blew out the candle and sank down beneath the covers, berating herself for being so impulsive.

She didn't really love him, did she? What she felt couldn't possibly be true love. It was passion. He'd misled her from the beginning. The man she'd fallen in love with didn't really exist. He would find out soon that he could bribe and manipulate Dudley, but he couldn't exploit her—not with money, and certainly not with passion.

CHAPTER
TWENTY-THREE

"If your lordship would like to try another color besides black, how about something in gray?" the St. James Street tailor said, producing a bolt of fine, smoky-gray cloth.

Ramsay touched the fabric. As smooth as the texture was, it was nothing like the silky feel of Cassandra's thighs. With a shake of his head, he endeavored to clear his mind. "No, I think I'd like to see something in a livelier color."

"How about this?" the tailor queried, pulling out a striped cloth of dove gray with a subtle garnet thread running through it. "This just arrived in a shipment yesterday. Striking, rich, but not too brilliant. I can tell you not a gentleman in London has a waistcoat like it."

"Yes, that will do nicely," Ramsay said, thinking of Cassandra's penchant for pinks and deep reds. He was tired of black. It seemed appropriate somehow that he should wear something lighter, especially when he was in her company. "And some white shirts. No more black ones. Of your best linen, please. You have my measurements."

"Of course, my lord," the tailor said, signaling his assistant to bring in the linen samples. "And what else might we help you with today?"

The tinkle of the doorbell made them both turn to see a lady step into the shop. Ramsay blinked in mild astonishment. Not just any lady, but Cassandra, standing at the entrance. And she was alone.

The tailor frowned. "May I help you, miss?"

"I believe the lady has come in search of me." Ramsay recovered from his surprise and attempted to rescue Cassandra from the tailor's disapproval. "That is all I wish to order today. Send the things around to my London direction as soon as they're finished. Good day, sir."

Ramsay turned back to Cassandra, noting for the first time that she was positively glowering at him and her back was as stiff as an iron poker. "Cassandra, to what do I owe this pleasure? I thought we were going to see each other at Lady Dorian's for tea this afternoon."

"We have to talk, Linirk, now," she said, her voice low and husky. When he reached for her arm, she pulled away. "Alone. I will accept no lies or half-truths from you."

"As you please," Ramsay said, mystified by her words. He opened the door for her. "How did you find me?"

"The same way you always find me," she snapped cryptically.

Ramsay did not like the sound of that reply. He gestured to his curricle waiting at the curb. "I think a ride in the park is called for."

"No, I want to walk," Cassandra said, marching off down St. James Street toward Green Park.

"Take the curricle home," Ramsay muttered to the groom as he brushed past the man. He hastened to follow Cassandra, who was striding with such determined haste that Ramsay had to lengthen his stride to catch up with her.

"What is this all about, princess?" he asked when he reached her side.

"Don't 'princess' me." Her silence was as fulminating as

the glance she gave him. There was little doubt that she was upset about something of great importance to her.

"Very well, Cassandra," he said. "What is this all about?"

Without a word—or hesitation in her brisk step—Cassandra drew a letter out of her reticule and held it up for him to see. "Can you explain this to me?"

The minute Ramsay spotted Graham's writing, he groaned inwardly. He accepted the note from her without comment. What the devil was his foster brother up to now? Graham had made it plain he did not approve of Cassandra, but surely he was not foolish enough to interfere.

Ramsay quickly unfolded the paper and read it. The contents left him less shocked than annoyed. It seemed Graham was foolish indeed.

"Do you know who wrote it?" Cassandra asked, as they walked. She peered at him with narrowed eyes, ready to spot a falsehood if he uttered one.

He'd best be truthful. "It is Graham's handwriting."

"And what he says, is it true?"

"Which part?" Ramsay parried.

Cassandra snatched the note out of his hand. "Is Dudley in Paris?"

"I've heard he is," Ramsay said.

"Did you send him there?" she demanded.

"Paris was his choice."

"Don't make this any more difficult for me than it is," Cassandra appealed, pausing long enough to look up at him. The soft confusion in her eyes unnerved Ramsay. Silently he vowed to make Graham pay for this rashness. Cassandra turned and strode on. "You forced Dudley to cry off?"

He heard a quaver of pain in her voice and felt like a cur. But he was not about to let Dudley Moncreff come between them now. "Cassandra, there is a great deal you did not know about your former fiancé."

"There seems to be a great deal I don't know about you," she declared as her stride slowed a bit. "So you are telling me yes. Somehow you forced him to break off our betrothal and humiliate me and my family."

Ramsay turned toward her and tried to take her arm. She drew back. He pretended not to notice, but the gesture of withdrawal pained him.

"Cassandra, I made Dudley an offer of money," Ramsay began, speaking slowly and patiently, gauging every word. "He had a great many debts. Gambling debts."

"Doesn't every gentleman have gambling debts?" Cassandra said, clearly unfazed by the information.

"Not like the ones Dudley had," Ramsay said, suddenly impatient with her naive acceptance of the young buck's foibles. "Monksleigh has impoverished his title. He's been irresponsible and foolish and a near embarrassment to his family. They were desperate to save the situation. Marrying you was one way to do that. You are an heiress. You must have suspected as much. I'm certain your father did. All I had to do was offer Dudley the means to buy his way out of debt—without marriage."

"How very generous of you," Cassie said, stepping off the curb and heading for the gate of Green Park.

Ramsay hastened to follow her without getting hit by a speeding hackney. "If it's any consolation, he was not particularly pleased about crying off. I think he would have gone through with the wedding."

"Thank you for that," Cassandra said, passing the flower vendors and the Punch and Judy puppet show that had been set up at the gate.

The day was bright and pleasant. A crowd of children and their nurses as well as some adults were gathered around the stage. Their laughter rang out over the noise of the street traffic.

"You are better off without him, princess," Ramsay said, suddenly realizing how exhausting the pace was that she'd set for them. Annoyed with being put on the defensive, he grabbed her arm and turned her toward him. "I don't understand why you are putting on this great display of indignation. You never loved Dudley anyway.''

Cassandra gasped. Her eyes grew round and she stared up at him, her tempting lips parted in astonishment. ''What did you say?''

''I said, you never loved him.'' Ramsay spoke the words firmly this time, finally glad to have the truth out in the open. ''You should be glad that I got rid of him for you.''

She closed her eyes and shook her head as if to clear it. ''Never loved him? How do you know that?''

Ramsay hesitated. ''If you'd loved him, you would have been crushed by the broken engagement. You would have been heartbroken. Instead you were out gadding about to the races and dancing parties with your cousin.''

Cassandra's eyes narrowed. ''What do you know about what I was feeling?''

Too late Ramsay saw the unfortunate direction this was going to take. ''Now, Cassandra . . .''

''Dudley was my choice,'' she declared, pulling her arm from his grasp. ''How dare you presume I didn't love him! And you make it sound as if you sent him away for my benefit. You, who plotted to use me to get Glen Gray.''

Screeches came from the puppet stage and the children's laughter rang out again.

''Cassandra, in the beginning—''

''No, I'm not finished yet,'' Cassandra said, her voice even, clear—and oh, so cold. ''You listen to me. You're like the man behind those puppets over there. You think you can manipulate everyone into doing what you want. I suppose you could come up with some story to make Connor think his kidnapping was for *his* benefit, too. Well, you can't control everything, Lord Linirk. You can't use people like that. At least, you can't make me do your bidding. I feel what I feel. Not the emotions *you think* I should feel.''

''Cassandra,'' he pleaded softly, refusing to understand what she'd said to him. ''That comparison to the puppeteer is unfair.''

"No." Cassandra shook her head. "Oversimplified perhaps. But not unfair."

"I saved you from a disastrous marriage. As the Viscountess of Monksleigh you'd be out of money for silk undergarments before your first wedding anniversary."

Cassandra drew herself up straight. "And you know how important my frippery is to me, don't you? This must all be very amusing. 'Tis a wonder I did not hear you laughing the day Dudley left me."

"Let's walk and talk this through," Ramsay said, reaching for her arm again, desperate to make her see things his way.

"No, I'm not going anywhere with you." Cassandra pulled away from him once more, her lips pressed together in a thin, resolute line. She stepped back and surveyed him from head to toe. "And to think I confessed my love to you."

She marched on, then stopped, suddenly turning on him. "I take it back, every syllable. I must have been mad when I uttered those words." Her lip quivered. "And I wish someone would turn your own game on you. I wish someone would make you understand how it feels to lose control of your life. To suffer the insult and the disrespect of knowing your every move was orchestrated by someone behind the scenes, taking your choices away from you."

"Cassandra, you're shocked and surprised by Graham's letter," Ramsay argued, hoping to gain some time and reconsideration. "When you've had time to think about it, you'll feel differently."

"I don't believe so." Cassandra turned and strode back toward the park gate. She cast her parting words over her shoulder. "You have interfered with my life for the last time, Linirk. I do not wish to see you again. I shall see myself home."

The idea didn't actually begin to take shape in Erik Drummond's head until long after he'd watched Graham and Mr.

Fredericks, the marquis's business agent, walk into the solicitor's offices in Gray's Inn.

With Connor and Charlotte away on their continental wedding trip at last, Erik had been left to his own devices in the Mayfair townhouse. Connor had presented him with a list of things he wanted taken care of, but most of the items were small things, tasks merely intended to keep him occupied and away from Linirk and the Forbes clan.

Erik snorted in disgust as he stared up at Gray's Inn. He couldn't forget how Connor had looked upon St. John's offer of money for Glen Gray like some kind of windfall. A solution to a problem. Centuries of fighting seemed to have been forgotten like so much water under a bridge. The men killed in battle. The families left homeless ignored. The high-handedness of the Forbeses unavenged.

Perhaps Connor was too young. He'd never known the loss of someone close to him in a Forbes raid like he had, Erik reminded himself. He'd never described the details, the blood and the gore, the pain and the anger of having your family destroyed by Forbes clansmen. He'd wanted to spare his young laird that horror. Perhaps that had been his mistake. A laird needed to remember it all, to have heard the stories and made them the shared ancient memory that every generation of the clan must have, a memory sharp and long, a memory that totted up every attack, slight, injury, and offense. A laird must have such a collective memory. Book-learning was of little use to clan children. They needed to know their heritage.

Connor seemed only to think of solutions, of making his bride happy, of moving forward.

" 'Tis the nineteenth century," Connor had reminded him with a slap on the back. "The steam engine is here. Railroads are coming. Bridges will span firths where only ferries sail now. 'Tis a new age."

But why should any of that change the outcome of a feud? Erik brooded.

As soon as Connor and his bride had departed, Erik had

taken up stalking the Forbeses again. A little voice inside him said that if he watched long enough and learned enough about the marquis and Graham Andrews, he could find the solution to the Glen Gray problem.

So Erik had taken to the streets, watching the marquis's house, following the laird when he was with the other St. John twin, and sometimes following Graham. And today, when the marquis's foster brother had left the townhouse with that fancy walking stick in one hand and a leather portfolio in the other, Erik knew Andrews was the man to follow.

Graham had gone to Fredericks's office, then the two had gone off to Gray's Inn, where many solicitors kept offices. He knew they must be discussing the Glen Gray papers.

"Who would have thought three centuries of tradition and family would come down to signatures on legal papers?" Erik muttered to himself as he waited outside the solicitors' offices. "There has to be a way to stop this. There must be a way."

After two hours in the solicitors' offices, Graham and Fredericks left and retired to a nearby tavern. Erik dare not follow them for fear of being recognized. But he knew what they were doing. The business manager would order ale and the Scotsman would order whisky, fine, Scots-aged malt whisky, Graham's favorite. They would eat a substantial lunch and down several more drinks.

Erik was waiting for them when they emerged from the tavern. They walked to Fredericks's offices. Within minutes Graham was on his way back to the marquis's townhouse, the same leather portfolio tucked under his arm. Graham appeared rather grim, and Erik couldn't help but wonder if the Forbes man thought as little of St. John's offer as he did. When Graham had disappeared into the townhouse, Erik lingered a moment longer, wondering if it would be worth his trouble to wait until evening to see what else developed.

As he was trying to make the decision, a St. John footman came striding down the street with his arms full of bags and boxes.

Erik stepped back behind a lamppost in order to watch the townhouse as the footman knocked on the door. When the door opened, Erik strained his ears to hear what was said.

"Miss Cassandra St. John wishes to return these gifts to the Marquis of Linirk," the footman said, speaking formally. He shoved the items into the manservant's arms. "One cigar box, a handkerchief, a brandy decanter, a tartan shawl, and a paper fan. Please be so kind as to convey these items to the marquis."

With that, the footman turned on his heel, marched down the front steps, and headed back toward Mayfair. *Damn cheeky, these London servants, especially the liveried footman,* Erik thought. He'd had his fill of them, himself.

The manservant juggling the parcels stared after the footman, shrugged, and kicked the door shut.

But before the door closed, the late-afternoon sunlight glinted off the brandy decanter. Suddenly Erik had seen what he needed to see. He had no idea why the footman had returned the items, but he knew all he needed to know.

He knew how to foil the Glen Gray agreement. His idea was perfect. It would entangle everyone who deserved to suffer. Turning on his heel, he bolted down the street. Wasn't it a stroke of good fortune that he'd made a drinking buddy of that chemist on the east side? Funny how fate always provided the means when the time came. But he must make haste. Timing was everything.

"Grahaaam?" Even in the kitchen he heard his name roared, long and drawn out, shouted from another part of the house. The voice was Ramsay's. Graham pursed his lips and swallowed the last of the cheese Cook had favored him with. So, the St. John lass had gone straight to Ramsay with the note. That had to be the reason for all the noise. Ramsay never roared. Ramsay was usually most lethal when he was calm and quiet. Graham was not overly concerned about this confrontation. He'd known when he wrote the note that it would happen sooner or later.

He thanked Cook with a wink and strolled up the stairs to meet his angry laird.

"You just couldn't stay out of it, could you?" Ramsay demanded the minute Graham appeared in the study doorway. He held up a missive that Graham assumed was the letter he'd dispatched to the St. John house. "You just had to tell her exactly what you knew to hurt her."

"She took the truth hard, did she?" Graham asked, unable to keep the amusement from his voice or the smile from his face. "She's a pampered little chit, and to find out her fiancé had cried off for money was a good comeuppance for her."

"Hell and damnation," Ramsay muttered, the lines of his handsome face dark and harsh. "Why? Why did you do this?"

"Why not? What's the loss?" Graham asked with a shrug. "St. John has decided what he's going to do with Glen Gray. The lassie's fate is no longer connected with the property."

"Perhaps I wanted to continue seeing the lady," Ramsay said, puzzlement in his voice. "I don't understand your anger. You made it clear at Ravencliff that you didn't like the time I was spending with her. Why?"

"Because, what's the use in getting yerself involved with an English lass if she donna bring Glen Gray to the clan?"

Ramsay groaned, a curious sound somewhere between disappointment and anger. He raked his hand through his hair. "I think I'm living the curse you placed on me, princess."

"What's that?" Graham asked. A superstitious man, he hated mention of curses. "What about a curse?"

Ramsay shook his head and turned away. "Nothing, just something Cassandra said about controlling a person's life— before we parted."

"Yer no gonna be holdin' a grudge about losin' the lass, are ye now?" Graham asked, planting his hands on his hips. "She would've just turned against ye like the other women have."

Ramsay whirled around and stared at his foster brother, astonishment on his face. "Is that why you did this? Because you don't trust Cassandra? Or is it because you just don't want me to find a wife?''

"I donna want to see ye hurt again," Graham said, belatedly troubled by Ramsay's questions. The lad was taking this harder than he'd expected. "Ye donna need a wife. Ye figured that out a long time ago. Me marriage hasn't brought me any happiness. Nor did having a wife make yer father happy. Let yer sister provide the heir. Keep a mistress for the times when a man has to have a woman. That's all ye need."

"I'll decide if I need a wife or not," Ramsay said, shaking his head.

"Cassandra St. John?" Graham shouted. "She's pretty enough to bed, but ye donna have to marry her. If ye want a wife, we'll find you a fine Scots lass."

"You've gone insane," Ramsay said, turning away. "Or you've lost all your perspective. Has life become nothing more to you than acquiring Glen Gray and defying the McKensies?"

"When was life any less?" Graham demanded. "Believe me, the English chit was going to lead ye around by yer nose. I did ye a favor by writing her that letter."

Ramsay groaned, hung his head, and paced around the desk. "Leave me."

"Why?" None of Graham's arguments seemed to have convinced Ramsay of the truth. "What are you going to do? Nothing foolish, I hope."

"I mean it, Graham," Ramsay declared. "Pack your bags, because you're going north tomorrow."

The thought of going home sounded good to Graham, but he didn't like the way Ramsay suggested it. "Ye are no coming with me?"

"No, I'm staying right here and try to repair the damage you've done." Ramsay looked at Graham across the desk.

"That English bit of muslin has blinded ye that badly?" Graham taunted.

"She has," Ramsay said without looking away. "I'm going

to tell you this once, and once only. Don't you ever interfere in any of my relationships again. Do you hear me?''

"Aye, I hear ye," Graham said, uncertain as to whether he'd been victorious or not.

"Go and close the door," Ramsay said.

Graham turned slowly and left the study. Once the door was closed, he stood in the hallway trying to think of how he might have argued his point differently, more persuasively. If Ramsay was going to pursue her, then Graham's ploy had been near useless. In fact it had only served to drive a wedge between him and Ramsay. Now that was a pretty pass.

As he stood there berating himself for arguing so clumsily, he heard the front door close. Then Oliver's footsteps headed in his direction.

"There you are, Mr. Andrews," the manservant said, appearing around the corner. He was carrying a box with a note tucked into the side of it. "You saved me a trip upstairs to your chamber. This was just delivered for you."

"From who?" Graham asked, intrigued by the gift.

"A young messenger boy brought it," Oliver said. "He said a lady paid him to deliver it."

"Thank ye, Oliver," Graham said, taking the box. "I'll be in the back parlor if ye need me again."

Graham carried the box into the parlor. A fire burned in the hearth and a lamp had been lit against the October darkness outside. Graham opened the note first, too curious about the feminine handwriting to bother with the box.

> *My dear Mr. Andrews,*
>   *Please accept and enjoy this gift as a token of my thanks for your service to the marquis and myself.*
>   *With gratitude,*
>   *Cassandra St. John*

Graham laughed out loud. So the lady did appreciate knowing the truth. He thought for a moment about returning to the study to share the note with his foster brother, but decided against it. Now wasn't the time to taunt Ramsay with the lady's token of appreciation.

Still chuckling to himself, Graham dropped the note on the parlor table and opened the box to find a bottle of scotch. His favorite aged malt whisky.

"How'd the lass know?" he wondered as he pulled the bottle out to admire its rich color in the firelight. Ramsay must have said something. Maybe Graham had underestimated the chit. She couldn't be all bad if she'd think to show her gratitude with premium scotch. Graham went to the small parlor sideboard to find a glass. The wax seal broke with an easy twist. He pulled out the cork and poured himself three fingers of the fine stuff. Once more he held it up to admire it briefly.

"To a sensible lass," Graham said, toasting thin air and grinning to himself. "And good riddance."

He downed an entire glassful of liquor. It burned satisfyingly all the way down his throat to his gullet. But he smacked his lips, detecting a strange bitter afterflavor. He peered at the label on the bottle. It boasted the best contents to be had anywhere in the world.

Another glassful would take care of the aftertaste. So he poured himself another glass and drained it almost as quickly as he did the first. It tasted the same, not quite as satisfying as he'd expected. A sudden tightness began to grow in his chest.

Graham paced around the room, waiting for the discomfort to ease. But it grew all the way down into his belly. A strange shudder tore through him. The chill of an October day, he told himself. Another glass would cure that. He poured himself a third glass and downed it, eager to feel the buzz hum through his system and dull the tensions of the day. He stared into the fire, savoring the flavor, a good one—though there was that strange aftertaste.

But the third drink didn't cure the discomfort as he'd expected. Pain needled through him, especially down into his legs. His gait became stiff. He held up his glass to examine the dram remaining in the bottom. What was in that stuff? Whisky had never troubled him like this before.

The pain lanced up his neck. In anguish he slapped an open palm against his brow. Then the pain shafted down his back, into his legs once more. He tried to call out, but he'd been robbed of his voice. Then the excruciating pain seared through him, knocking him off his feet. His body shuddered once more. The back of his head hit the floor hard and his back arched from the cramps in his muscles.

The last lucid thought Graham had in a world turned to agony was that the lass wasn't as grateful as she had claimed.

CHAPTER
TWENTY-FOUR

Disheartened by his foster brother's betrayal, Ramsay sank into the leather chair by the fire and stared into the flames. The orange tongues of heat did little to repel the October chill in the room. Everything he'd attempted to accomplish suddenly seemed to be collapsing about his ears. Glen Gray would never belong to the clan again. His own blood kin had betrayed him with the letter to Cassandra. The traitor was no woman this time. But Graham, of all people. And because of it, the woman who'd captured his heart had withdrawn her declaration of love.

Ramsay released a long, low breath and leaned his head on the back of the chair. The truth be known, maybe he merited no better fate than this. Perhaps Cassie was right, the puppet master deserved to lose his power, to know the sting of injured pride and the ache of a rejected love. His heart—that fickle, unreliable organ that he claimed had shriveled to nothing—throbbed painfully inside him. It was not a good feeling and he feared it would never stop.

Still, the justice of it offered no comfort.

He'd just begun to come to terms with the disappointment of losing the glen, then Graham stirred up trouble with Cassandra. He and his foster brother had been at odds before, but Graham had never been so vengeful—never so malicious. What good did it do to hurt Cassandra? She was the one good thing that had come into his life out of this entire doomed feud.

Ramsay frowned. He understood that giving up the feud was difficult for his kinsman. Graham was older and more ingrained in the old ways, the old traditions. He could not accept that warring with another clan was not necessarily going to be to their benefit in this new age of steam engines, factories, and land enclosures. The era when clans could afford to waste men and resources on feuds was coming to an end, as had the days of Crusades and armored knights. New solutions to the old problems would dictate survival in this new age. The changes were frightening, but they were thrilling, too.

Graham would have to learn to accept them. For what he'd done, he deserved to be sent north. Let him brood alone at Ravencliff for a while. Since they'd arrived in Town last June, he'd done little but complain about life in London.

As well as he understood Graham's feelings, Ramsay would not tolerate more interference from him—considering the delicate situation existing between the Forbeses and St. Johns. Cassandra's father had offered them a respectable settlement to the feud. It would be folly to destroy the opportunity.

Ramsay's gaze fell on the stack of rejected gifts that Oliver had set on the study desk.

The sight of the tartan shawl Cassandra had returned sent an unexpected shaft of pain through him. He'd bound their hands—their lives—together with that piece of plaid. Maybe it had only been a game, but for a while—for one glorious night—he'd believed they were joined. The cigar box, the brandy decanter, the fan, and the handkerchief stood on the table, mute witnesses to his failure. Each represented a special memory. But the shawl seemed most significant.

His gaze lingered on the gifts, something niggling at his consciousness about them. Something was missing. The music box was not there. He sat forward in his chair and reexamined the items. No music box. A glimmer of hope shone in Ramsay's despair. Its absence couldn't possibly be an oversight.

Only last night Cassandra had confessed her love for him. Today—after receiving Graham's note—she'd returned everything. She'd even taken back her avowal of love. But she'd kept the music box. The gift that represented their first meeting—their first kiss. He was desperate to believe the music box symbolized something important she could not part with.

Muttering a curse, he slouched back in the chair, resting his chin on his steepled fingers. "I should have told you, princess. I should have admitted how much I love you. You deserved to know then. I'm a coward."

And if she'd known how much he cared, he wondered, if he'd said those words of love, would she have been so vulnerable to Graham's treachery?

Ramsay sucked in a deep breath of guilt and resignation. He could not blame Graham entirely for this calamity. He was guilty of not speaking when he should have—of not revealing the truth of his feelings to Cassandra.

Oliver burst into the study without knocking. "My lord, you must come quickly. I think something is wrong with Mr. Andrews."

Ramsay started, shaken out of his thoughts. He'd asked not to be disturbed. "I suspect Mr. Andrews is in a sour mood after the discussion we just had. Don't be put off by his drinking."

"No, my lord," the servant said. Ramsay noted the man's eyes were wild and his face was as white as if he'd just seen a ghost. "Mr. Andrews is on the floor in the back parlor. Something isn't right. Please come see for yourself, my lord."

Ramsay frowned. Graham usually managed to get himself to bed before he passed out from drinking. "Very well. I'm coming."

In the parlor, Ramsay found Graham rigid on the floor. A recently opened bottle of scotch sat on the table and a glass was overturned. When he bent over Graham, he found his foster brother's complexion blotched red and purple. Graham's face was a stiff mask of pain. His eyes were open and fixed. His blue lips were still wet with the scotch. Ramsay could smell it.

"Summon a physician," Ramsay ordered immediately, though he knew that Graham was dead. "Move, man."

Oliver dashed out of the parlor.

"Oh, Graham," Ramsay muttered, kneeling down by the lifeless body of the man who was more like his brother than any blood kin. His mind numb, Ramsay lifted Graham into his arms and attempted to make him comfortable, though Graham's skin was already cool to the touch.

"Relax, man, or you'll cramp your legs," Ramsay advised, vaguely aware that what he was doing made little sense. But someone had to tend to his foster brother. Graham could be such a great lout of a fool sometimes.

Ramsay was still sitting on the floor with Graham in his arms when the physician arrived. Only when the doctor, a man named Blake, prodded him, did he stand back. He watched with deadened feelings as Oliver and the footman lifted Graham's body up onto the parlor sofa. Then from a million miles away, he observed the doctor hold Graham's wrist, peer into his fixed eyes, and put an ear to Graham's chest. Then Dr. Blake looked up at Ramsay and shook his head. The little white-haired man's mouth moved, forming words that conveyed what he already knew. Graham was gone.

Ramsay stared down at his hands and his feet, astonished to see that he was in one piece. He hurt—like a hole had been ripped open in him.

"Why? How?" Ramsay queried.

"My lord, it appears to be poison," Dr. Blake said. Ramsay stared at the man, hardly comprehending what he meant.

The doctor picked up the glass and sniffed it. "I smell the bitter odor of poison in his drink. This surely is a case of foul play. Did the man have an enemy in the house? I advise you to summon the magistrate."

Oliver pointed at the bottle of scotch. "It was just delivered and here is the note what came with it."

"Let me see," Ramsay said, snatching the note out of Oliver's hand. If there was a chance of finding who did this, he would do it. Whoever had hurt Graham would regret the deed. He read the message. He did not recognize the handwriting, but he read Cassandra's name signed at the bottom.

A wave of astonishment sent him reeling. "How can this be?"

He remembered clearly Cassandra's outrage with the letter that Graham had sent her. But her anger had been aimed at him, not Graham. She'd sent back his gifts. She'd heaped wishes of unhappiness or worse upon him. She'd never said anything about making Graham pay for his deed. This didn't make sense.

"I think some questions must be asked of this lady," Dr. Blake said.

Stunned, Ramsay turned away. The betrayal of the deed was profound. The nearest and dearest person in his life was gone—and the murderer would pay. But Cassandra . . . ? Ramsay raised his head as the steps of what must be done next formed in his head. "Bring me my cloak, Oliver. Then do what the doctor says. Send for the magistrate."

Ramsay looked lost. His face was white and his eyes glazed with grief. The shock of seeing him in such anguish twisted Cassie's heart—the pain almost as overwhelming as being accused of Graham's murder.

The hour was late. She'd been summoned from her bedtime preparations by Horton who'd seemed distressed about Lord Linirk's request to see her. As she donned her wrapper, she thought the call strange, too. She'd just returned his gifts and had not expected to hear from him again so soon. She'd almost instructed Horton that the hour was too late, but then decided to see Ramsay for one last confrontation.

But when she saw him in the drawing room, wrapped in black and looming near the window like some dark malevolent caller from the underworld, she was shocked. The grief emanating from him was impossible to miss.

He made no move to approach her. His voice was low and raspy. He glared at her, his green eyes hard and cold. Then he accused her of murder. "You'll be glad to know Graham is dead, murdered."

She stared at him speechless, his pain hers. "What? Murdered? How?" she stammered. "Oh, Ramsay, you must be—"

"Have you nothing to say for yourself?" Ramsay demanded, shoving a piece of notepaper at her. "Look at the note from his murderer. His poisoner!"

Cassie glimpsed her name at the bottom of the message. A flash of understanding physically shook her.

"You don't think I—" Cassie stammered, struggling to concentrate on the letter long enough to make sense of it. The pain on Ramsay's face made her want to take him in her arms to comfort him. She reached out to touch his hand, but he recoiled. His grief was too new, too raw to accept consolation—especially from her. Sucking in a shallow breath Cassie tried to reassure him. "I didn't write this. Nor is it St. John stationery. Why would I hurt Graham?"

"Because of the part he has played in this sorry scheme," Ramsay said, wagging his head like a wounded creature, his voice low and guttural. "Because of the note he sent you about my misdeeds."

"I admit I never liked Graham," Cassie said, her mind grappling with the shock of being accused of murder. "He won no favor from me when he sent that letter about Dudley, but I would never—Poison, you say?"

" 'Tis a woman's weapon," Ramsay said, as if that sealed his case.

"Not this woman's," Cassie declared. That he was so quick to convict her hurt.

"You think I forget the unhappiness you wished on me just

this morning?'' Ramsay went on. ''You returned my gifts. You vowed to never see me again.''

''But I didn't hurt Graham,'' Cassie protested, her heart aching for Ramsay as she began to realize how diabolical Graham's murderer was. ''If I decided to take vengeance, I would make you suffer. You know that. You know me well enough to understand that.''

''Lord Linirk?'' Papa's voice came from the doorway. Cassie glanced at her father in his shirtsleeves. He walked into the room. '' 'Tis a late hour to be calling on my daughter.''

''You can take your settlement of Glen Gray and burn it,'' Ramsay stormed. ''Graham would have never agreed to it. I won't either, now.''

''I don't understand,'' Papa said, confusion in his voice. ''What's this about?''

''Lord Linirk has come to tell us that Graham is dead,'' Cassie said, without turning to her father, but thankful for his presence. Her hands had grown cold. She finally connected with Ramsay's gaze and she held it. She prayed he could read her innocence in her eyes. ''I stand accused of murder.''

''What?'' Papa said, his voice light with disbelief. ''That's preposterous.''

The door knocker sounded. Horton answered. Voices echoed in the hallway. Men filled the drawing room. A magistrate named Culpepper. A doctor named Blake. Later, Papa's solicitor, Mr. Newton, arrived. Cassie surrendered to the confusion.

Then Mama came and held her hand, her support warm and silent. Tophet sat at her feet.

Cassie cared nothing about the evening's events from that point. She remembered little about the discussions. Papa took over answering questions for her. He knew nothing about Graham's letter or of her disagreement with Ramsay earlier in the day. She had told no one of it. Shame and embarrassment had prevented her. Her fiancé had not only cried off; he'd been bought off. Hardly the kind of revelation a girl wanted to share with her parents.

So it all came out under the magistrate's questioning. Tersely Ramsay answered most of the questions. Little response was required of her. Later she only remembered holding Ramsay's gaze as he spoke. His cold eyes were full of accusation, but she did not shrink from it. All she could do was meet his gaze and will him to know her innocent.

The note was examined and discussed. Drafts of her own writing were brought from her writing desk and samples of her paper were fingered and deemed totally different from that of the note. Nothing matched—not the paper or her handwriting from any of the samples. Other issues were brought up, such as Cassie's whereabouts during the day.

Magistrate Culpepper set a bottle of scotch on the table. "Dr. Blake tells me the poison is in this drink. Do you know anything about this bottle of scotch?"

Papa's face paled. "I'm not a scotch drinker myself, but I understand it is a popular drink. As a matter of fact, I purchased a quantity of this very whisky as a wedding gift to my new son-in-law."

"Where is it now?" the magistrate asked, a light of interest gleaming in his eye.

"As far as I know, at his townhouse," Papa said. "I ordered a dozen bottles and had them delivered directly to the Earl of Kinleith's home. They are probably quite untouched. My daughter and he are on their wedding trip in Italy. This liquor is available for purchase from a number of places in Town."

Cassie's mind cleared enough to think, *What a curious coincidence.*

"Then there remains the question of the source of the poison," Dr. Blake said. "If this is strychnine as I suspect from the odor, well, it is not dispensed just willy-nilly."

"Miss St. John certainly does not have access to such a substance," asserted Mr. Newton, Papa's solicitor. "Clearly this evidence is designed by some other party to lay the blame at Miss St. John's door when it is quite impossible that she would commit such a crime."

And so the discussion went on and on. A brief search of the house was even made by Magistrate Culpepper's assistant to locate any strychnine poison. Nothing was found. In the end, they seemed to agree with Mr. Newton. But when Cassie looked across the room, Ramsay's gaze was on her again. Obviously he did not agree. The light of accusation burned in his eyes.

Cassie was beginning to understand just how clever and vicious the true murderer was. He had attacked, wounding Ramsay where he was most vulnerable—his foster brother. In addition, the murderer had endangered the agreement between the Forbeses and the McKensies. As the shock of the initial murder accusation cleared from her head, she was as determined to know who the murderer was as anyone in the room.

By the time the landing clock chimed midnight, the magistrate had decided against pressing charges. The evidence was too unsubstantial. Ramsay prowled the room, clearly unhappy with the outcome of the discussion, but willing to allow that the evidence was thin.

The other gentlemen began to make their farewells with promises to follow up on the morrow with additional questions.

"I would have a word alone with Lord Linirk, if I might," Cassie said before Ramsay left the room.

"I don't think that wise," Papa began.

But Ramsay turned, the glint of curiosity in the grim darkness of his gaze. "I will speak with Miss St. John."

"We'll be right outside the door, my dear," Mama said, taking Papa by the arm and leading him from the parlor. They left the door standing open.

"What can you possibly have to say to me?" Ramsay asked.

"I was hurt and angry when I spoke to you today about what Graham's letter revealed," Cassie said. "Learning the truth broke my heart—"

Ramsay's head came up sharply and his eyes narrowed as he studied her face.

Cassie hurried on. "But that is not the issue here. I want you to know that I would never cause you this pain. I know what Graham meant to you. I'm certainly not above a gesture or two of revenge. But no matter what you may think of me, I love—care too much about you to bring you that kind of grief for any reason.''

"A touching declaration, Miss St. John," Ramsay said, his voice full of sarcasm.

His derision grated on Cassie. She could sympathize with his pain, but his willingness to think the worst of her was beginning to do more than hurt. She lifted her chin indignantly and glared at him. ''Think what you please, but when the truth comes out—and it shall, for I shall see that it does—you will learn that you have done me a great injustice.''

Ramsay shook his head, and when he looked at her across the room, the harsh lines of skepticism and mockery had left his face. The dazed look in his eyes was gone. But the lost look she had first seen on his face when she'd entered the parlor had returned.

"Perhaps I have done you an injustice," he said. "But that is of little consequence to me now. For I have lost my dearest kinsman and my best friend. Nothing you do can bring him back.''

Ramsay dropped his gaze to the dog sitting at Cassie's feet.

"Tophet," he commanded. "Heel."

To Cassie's surprise, Tophet jumped up and trotted in Ramsay's direction. At the door the dog bestowed one quick glance at her over his shoulder, then head down, deserted her—following Ramsay out of the house.

Everything was happening faster than Erik had expected. When the magistrate, the doctor, and the St. John solicitor stepped into the October night, he turned his back to the street and slipped into the shadows. He could not afford to be seen or recognized. The strychnine weighed heavily in his coat pocket. He'd failed to plant it in the townhouse as he'd planned. By the time he'd gotten to the St. John house, Linirk had already set the place in turmoil.

Will, the footman, had turned Erik away at the door. He didn't dare take time to share a smoke or a drink, he'd told Erik. There was serious trouble being discussed in the parlor. The staff would be on call all night, probably. The master of the house was upset. Will hoped Erik would understand. And Erik said he did, of course.

But the failure to get the strychnine into the St. John house was the only thing that had gone wrong with the plan, Erik thought, in the first flush of his success. Graham Andrews was dead. Linirk was in high dudgeon. Cassandra St. John was under suspicion of murder, even without discovery of the poison in the house. Her father's solicitor might be able to keep her from being arrested for now. But there would be another way to make her look guilty. All he had to do was watch and wait. Mind his own manners so no one suspected him. But the opportunity would come.

As soon as the men had vanished from sight, Erik came out into the open again to watch the house. All the lights burned. Every window was bright. Shadows passed the windows from time to time. He could image the voices raised, the tears of the women. Was Cassandra St. John weeping? No, not that one. But she'd soon have reason to.

CHAPTER
TWENTY-FIVE

Clear and simple as it was to everyone—except Ramsay—
that Cassandra was blameless, verifying her innocence proved
more complicated than she would have ever guessed.

A day and a half later she stared disconsolately into the crate
of whisky bottles in Connor and Charlotte's small barren wine
cellar. Not a single bottle of scotch was missing. "Well, we
know that neither Connor, nor Papa, nor Erik used whisky from
this case to murder Graham."

"What did you expect to find?" Tony asked, peering into the
crate from the opposite side. The morning after the magistrate's
visit, Cassie had sent a message to her cousin pleading for help.
He'd come to her rescue. For appearance' sake and for her
safety, Papa had insisted Cassie remain confined to the house
until the murder was solved. But how could she solve it cooped
up in her room? Cassie had reasoned. After sneaking out of
the back door of the townhouse, she and Tony were soon off
on their own investigation.

"You didn't expect unraveling this mystery to be easy, did
you, Cousin?"

"We've learned nothing from all the shops we visited,"

Cassie complained, her feet aching from the day and a half's worth of walking they'd done. They'd begun with the only evidence they had, the brand of scotch used to slip the poison to Graham. From shop to shop they went, asking questions about recent purchases. She was exhausted from lack of sleep and she missed having Tophet at her feet. Just that morning she'd begun her monthly flow, confirmation she'd not conceived Ramsay's child because of their passionate liaison in the museum. She should have been relieved. But she was oddly disappointed.

Their search for the shop that had sold the whisky to the murderer had come to nothing. This particular whisky was favored by many: men and women, highborn and poor. She had no idea where else to look. "Not one of the shopkeepers could throw any light on who might have bought the whisky, and now this. We're getting nowhere."

"Surely they would have remembered a man in a kilt," Tony said.

Cassie and Tony had already been through a list of suspects and each had been discussed at length as they gone from shop to shop. They agreed that Connor would never do something so underhanded. He was an open fighter and battled with his hands. Besides, he was out of Town with Charlotte on their wedding trip.

Papa wouldn't murder anyone over a piece of land. Why would he endanger the settlement of the feud that he'd worked so hard to reconcile? The few servants in the Forbes townhouse seemed to like Graham and were nearly as grieved over his death as their master, according to what Tony could learn. That only left one suspect besides herself—Erik.

They'd come to Charlotte and Connor's townhouse as soon as they'd been certain Erik was out. The last thing needed was for the Scotsman to know that they suspected him. The servants who knew Cassie well had been glad to let them in on the imaginary errand Cassie had spun for them.

"If a bottle was gone from this crate, we'd know for certain that Erik is involved," Cassie said, disappointed to be looking down on a full case. "But it has to be Erik. I'll never forget how he walked out on Connor after the fight. And remember how he and Graham came to blows when Ramsay and I returned from Scotland? There was no love between them. And neither one wanted Connor or Ramsay to sign the papers that will bring the feud to an end."

"I remember, but even if Erik is the murderer," Tony said, "I wouldn't expect him to do something so stupid as to use his own laird's whisky to put the poison in."

Cassie shook her head. "To this day nobody knows where Erik went after the fight or who he stayed with. He must have other friends somewhere on the east side."

"You're right. He's a definite suspect, but how do we prove it?" Tony said, shoving the crate back into the corner.

"I wish Charlotte were here." Cassie said, disheartened. "Her head is always so full of miscellaneous details from her reading and research. She would know what other evidence we should look for."

"The poison," Tony said, as if he'd made a sudden discovery. "Strychnine has a distinctly unpleasant smell, or so I'm told. But don't expect Erik to have stashed it in his room. He's not stupid."

"No, he's not," Cassie said, encouraged by the idea of looking for the poison. "But let's go search his things anyway."

Erik's room was at the back of the townhouse on the third floor. Because Cassie had spent hours helping Charlotte put the newlyweds' home in order before the wedding, the servants never questioned her right to go anywhere in the house she desired.

Tony talked as they inspected the tidy room. They each moved things carefully so as not to leave Erik's belongings out of place and betray their search.

"Remember the gypsy fortune-teller at the races?" Tony asked, bending down to look under the bed. "What did she foretell? Something about beware of the dark one? And a murder?''

"Yes, I remember her, though I'd quite put her out of my mind," Cassie exclaimed, suddenly recalling that day at the Newmarket races when Jasmine had refused to take payment for telling a dark future. And now her predictions had come true. "I thought she was being dramatic. I did finally deduce that 'beware the dark one' referred to Ramsay because he wears black—But I would have never thought I'd be involved in a murder, much less accused of one."

The despair of it almost made Cassie forget why she was in Erik's room. She stood idle, staring off into space, wondering how it could all have come to this, and how a gypsy fortune-teller could have read this fate in her palm.

"I thought it all a lark then," Tony said, scrutinizing the neat top of the writing table by the window. "I only engaged the gypsy's services to raise your spirits."

Cassie gave an ironic laugh. "We should have asked about your future, too, Cousin. Maybe Jasmine could have told us something amusing about which of the ladies and their mamas who trail after you will win your proposal of marriage."

Tony straightened and turned to her with a mock frown on his lips. They both knew he was considered one of the most eligible bachelors in Society, despite his young age, and he adored being pursued by the ladies. "That's not amusing, Cassie. I don't intend to marry for many years yet. Years and years."

"You enjoy the chase too well," Cassie taunted, chuckling to herself and taking pleasure in teasing Tony. Momentarily she forgot the grim task at hand. "We should name them something, those hopeful ladies and their mamas—the Sea-combe Amethyst League would do nicely. They are so determined to see that legendary betrothal ring from the Crusades slipped onto their respective daughters' hands."

"I don't think Mother is ready to give up that particular

heirloom just yet," Tony said, turning away. "And that's fine with me."

He left the desk to search some garments hanging from a peg on the wall.

The crispness of Tony's words convinced Cassie that he was not about to rise to her bait and reveal which lady—among the throng—might have captured his heart.

"By Jove, look at this, Cassie." Tony had bent over to examine a pair of boots standing in the corner. He reached into one and held his discovery up for Cassie to see. At the sight of a half-full whisky bottle, she forgot the gypsy fortune-teller and her cousin's future, and hurried across the room to take a better look.

"It's the same brand of drink that had the poison in it," Cassie exclaimed as she examined the label.

"So Erik does know where to get the stuff," Tony said. "We simply didn't find the right shop when we were searching."

"Apparently not," Cassie agreed, staring at the bottle, feeling as though they were so close to solving Graham's murder, yet so far away. "This only supports our suspicions."

"Finding the poison in his possession is the kind of proof that we need," Tony said.

"True," Cassie conceded, looking around the room once more, certain they'd missed nothing obvious. "But wouldn't the murderer get rid of the strychnine he hadn't used as soon as the murder was committed?"

"Probably," Tony said, slipping the bottle back into the boot. "But what would be the logical way to do that?"

"Bury it?"

Tony's blue eyes grew wide as he turned to stare at Cassie. "Or plant it on the person you wanted accused of the murder. Whoever has done this is clearly trying to make it look as if you committed the murder."

"You mean he would try to plant it on me?"

"Or in your house," Tony said. "So far the murderer's attempt to place the blame at your door has failed. He must know this. He didn't go to all the trouble to write the note and sign your name just to walk away, without knowing who is arrested for Graham's death.''

"I'll grant you that," Cassie said.

"He must be looking for a way to seal your fate," Tony said, frowning at the thought.

"But how on earth would he manage to plant the poison on me or in the house?" Cassie asked, fascinated by the thought. "Unless we helped him. You know. Unless we set a trap."

"Precisely," Tony said, thoughtfully. "We may need to bait a trap. Are you willing?"

"Yes, I will do anything," Cassie said. Ramsay's lost look still haunted her, day and night. She'd thought of him often, going through the trial of arranging for Graham's remains to be taken back to Scotland. She'd learned that much through Will's cousin. Her heart continued to ache for him. She longed to comfort him, but she knew he would never allow it. She could not bring Graham back, but she could at least help Ramsay know who killed his foster brother. "For Papa's sake, at least. I'll do absolutely anything. Do you have an idea?"

"Your mother's Grecian pottery exhibit opens tomorrow night, doesn't it?" Tony asked. "We're going. Everybody who is anybody is going. And what about Erik?"

"No, he was invited, but he declined because he said he would feel out of place without Connor there," Cassie said.

"Perfect," Tony said. "I'm willing to bet that's when he'll make his move."

So they began to lay their plans for the next day. She didn't like what Tony suggested at first, but she had no better plan to offer.

Magistrate Culpepper's account of the murder investigation angered Ramsay. The burning feeling was the only emotion that had penetrated his grief in the two days since he'd found Graham dead on the parlor floor. He summoned all his will-power not to shout at Culpepper who'd been courteous enough to present a report at Ramsay's request.

"You mean you have nothing new to tell me—no more evidence, no more suspects?" Ramsay demanded as he paced his study. If the officials had something new to offer, he would have listened. He was not an unreasonable man. He was willing to consider plausible answers, but Culpepper had presented none. In view of that fact, Ramsay dismissed the man, deciding the magistrate was a fool making the investigation more difficult than it needed to be.

Culpepper had evidence. They all knew who the murderer was. The problem was, as Ramsay saw it, no one wanted to accuse a rich man's pretty young daughter of the crime. That was the sum of it, pure and simple. Justice would probably never be served in Graham's death—not under English law, anyway. Ramsay might have to take things into his own hands. Down deep inside, something rebelled against the thought that Cassandra was Graham's true murderer. But the evidence was so strong. Ramsay turned away from that thought. Time for planning revenge later. Now he had to get Graham back to Ravencliff where he could be laid to rest beside his family with all the pomp and respect that he deserved.

Ramsay had spent the last two days making the arrangements for the coffin, the London visitation and the hearse for the journey to Scotland. Oliver was put to work. Mirrors and portraits were draped. The clocks were stopped. Extra candles were ordered so there would be constant light next to the coffin. A mourning wreath was hung on the front door, mourning clothes ordered, extra servants hired and food prepared for visitors. There would be many callers and notes of condolence to be acknowledged. Susanna St. John had sent a touching note of sympathy that Ramsay had appreciated. He knew that the St. Johns would have the good taste not to appear.

But anyone acquainted with or doing business with the Forbeses would be sure to call or write before Graham was carried north to his resting place. And Ramsay would be expected to respond to them.

Before the visitors came, before the commencement of visitation, Ramsay entered the drawing room where Graham lay in his coffin, his hands crossed over his heart. The draperies were drawn. Candles burned pitifully weak against the darkness. The sickly sweet scent of lilies filled the air.

Ramsay crossed the room quickly and looked down at his foster brother. Graham looked peaceful, if unnaturally pale, now. The undertaker had managed to remove that stricken mask of anguish that had frozen in Graham's last expression. His mouth was untwisted and his forehead smoothed. Even his wild, bushy brows had been tamed. The serenity in his foster brother's face eased Ramsay's grief some. Now he could think of Graham sleeping instead of suffering.

"I will find your murderer, Graham," Ramsay vowed. "Rest assured, I will do that for you. For your family. For our clan. But justice is not always swift. Be patient, brother. Be patient."

Only the muffled clatter of horse-drawn traffic in the street could be heard in the room. Ramsay had even ordered the street strewn with straw to quiet the noise.

"I brought you something you might need," he continued, gazing at the silver-headed walking stick Graham had picked out not so long ago. Carefully he lifted Graham's hand and laid the stick in the coffin, the silver lion's head tucked in the crook of his foster brother's arm. "I don't know where you are or where you'll be going, but I'm sure you'll walk there. You'll need a good walking stick. Godspeed, Graham."

Only a moment more of silence hung in the room before the door knocker rapped loudly. Ramsay heard Oliver cross the hall to open the door. Visitation began.

Soon the house was filled with callers in black, all murmuring their condolences in soft mournful voices. Ramsay performed his duty coolly, observing himself calmly from a distance. Bowing. Shaking hands. Accepting condolences from people whose names he repeated after the newly hired secretary whispered them into his ear. He said all the proper words, surprised to find that he could do this. For Graham, he could hold his grief at bay. But he truly wanted to go somewhere and shut himself away to ache alone in the dark.

Then one name was repeated into his ear that brought him out of his grieving stupor.

"Mr. Erik Drummond, my lord," the officious but efficient secretary murmured as Ramsay saw Erik turn away from the coffin and amble toward him. He would have been less surprised to see Cassandra. "Mr. Drummond said he is calling on behalf of Connor, Earl of Kinleith," the secretary added.

Erik stopped before Ramsay. His curly dark hair was brushed into wild disarray and his dark eyes glowed unnaturally bright. He bowed before Ramsay could read more in his gaze. "My lord, I regret that we meet once again under such grievous circumstances."

Ramsay bowed formally in return, then inclined his head in acknowledgment of Erik's sentiments. He decided to say as little as possible. Let Drummond have his say and be off.

"In light of the near settlement of the feud, I come representing the McKensie," Drummond said. "We knew you and Mr. Andrews were close. I offer our condolences on your loss."

"Kind of you," Ramsay managed to say, struck by Erik's immediate introduction of the settlement of the feud.

"Of course, I suppose in light of the events—" Drummond began, casting Ramsay a sidelong glance, "that you have not been able to attend to such matters as documents and signatures."

"I have no interest in attending to the issue at all," Ramsay said, growing irritated. He owed this McKensie retainer no explanation of anything he did or did not do.

"Understandably," Drummond murmured. "Has any more evidence come to light about who committed such a heinous crime? Ye must be eager to catch the murderer."

"Nay, nothing," Ramsay said, covertly watching the man more closely now. Despite the solemnity of Drummond's errand, Ramsay thought he caught the glimmer of pleasure in the McKensie man's eye. His dislike for the man grew. Could not Drummond come to a funeral and keep the gloating out of his face? Did he think he'd won the feud because he lived and Graham was dead?

"Has the magistrate no suspect to arrest for the crime?" Drummond asked. "There are rumors that Cassandra St. John—"

"The evidence is not solid enough for an arrest," Ramsay said, even more annoyed by the mention of Cassandra.

Surprise briefly crossed Drummond's face. "I see. What happens next?"

"I will accompany Graham home to Ravencliff," Ramsay said, glancing across at the coffin. Why was Drummond so interested? "His funeral will be held there and he will be buried alongside his mother and father and the brothers and sisters who have gone before him. I've already sent orders north for the preparation."

"No, I mean what happens next with the murder?" Drummond persisted. "Are you content to allow the mystery of Graham's murder to go unsolved and unavenged?"

"Never," Ramsay said calmly, turning to study the man. Just what was Drummond up to? "Surely you never thought I would."

"No, my lord," Drummond said, a slight smile on his lips and suspicious satisfaction glowing in his dark eyes. "I never thought you would. So the magistrate continues his investigation?"

"Aye, I understand that he continues to make inquiries regarding the crime," Ramsay said.

"More evidence is bound to come to light," Drummond insisted. "I'm sure of it. Something is certain to come to light very soon."

"I pray you are right," Ramsay said, finding the McKensie man's certainty a curious thing.

Other mourners approached Ramsay. Drummond made his

farewells, but Ramsay could not dismiss the curious conversation from his mind. As Drummond left the room, Ramsay told the secretary to have the man followed. There was no harm in having the McKensie clansman tailed. In fact, it might prove enlightening.

When the last caller left the house and the lamplighters were on their appointed rounds, bringing light to the dark October streets, word came. Drummond had been followed to the St. John townhouse where he now lurked in the shadows in the mews behind the house.

Ramsay dismissed the messenger and sat quietly at his desk in the study mulling over the information. Tophet leaned against his leg. Ramsay absently scratched the pooch behind the ears.

So Drummond was watching the St. Johns' house. Susanna's Greek pottery exhibition opened tonight in the Egyptian Hall with a gala celebration. Of course the St. John family would attend. So why did Drummond watch the house? Because he suspected Cassandra of the murder? That made no sense. Did he even care who committed Graham's murder? Not likely. But he could still lead the way to something important.

Swiftly Ramsay rose from behind his desk and rang for his cloak. With an eager wag of his tail, Tophet followed him out the door. Drummond might know something that the magistrate didn't. Ramsay was ready to wager money on that.

CHAPTER TWENTY-SIX

"We must force a confession from Erik," Tony said as he and Cassie plotted their strategy in the carriage on the way back to the house. They'd already dropped Mama and Papa at the Egyptian Hall. Then, on the pretext of giving a friend a ride, they were racing back in the hopes of trapping Erik as he planted the poison in the St. John house. "But we'll need a witness to whatever he says. Will Horton do?"

"I think so," Cassie muttered. "I just hope this works."

"Erik declined his invitation to the exhibit," Tony said. "And the servants at Connor and Charlotte's house said he's not at home sitting by the fire tonight. So where is he and what is he up to?"

Cassie nodded. "But what if we missed him? What if he has already been there, to the house, I mean, and left the poison or whatever he intends to do?"

"It hasn't been that long since we left," Tony said, with an assurance that Cassie prayed was justified. Tony knocked on the carriage roof. "Drop us here, Smith. Go back to the Egyptian Hall and wait for Mr. and Mrs. St. John. We're going to walk from here."

The carriage drew to an abrupt halt. Tony flung open the door and jumped out before the groom could get the door. He turned to help Cassie down.

The coach soon disappeared and Cassie and Tony stood looking toward the corner where they could turn into the mews. The streets were nigh empty and the pavement cold and wet. The hour for Society to set off for the evening's entertainment had passed. "Ready for this adventure, Cousin?"

"Yes," Cassie said, breathlessly. She hung back, her hand gripping her cousin's arm. She was more apprehensive than she'd ever been in her life. "So much depends on what we find out tonight."

"I know. Let's go."

They did not approach the front of the house, because they did not want to alert the entire household of their presence. That had never been their plan. They wanted to go unnoticed as long as possible. For one reason, Papa had said that he thought Magistrate Culpepper was having the house watched. For another, they could not be certain where Erik was or how he planned to get into the house. But their best guess was that he'd go in through the kitchen where his friend, Will the footman, was often near the door when off duty.

They moved through the mews as quietly as they could and paused in the shadows of the carriage house just outside the kitchen door. As they waited in the darkness, they saw another figure duck back into the shadows farther down the mews.

"Culpepper's man?" Tony asked in a whisper.

"I don't know," Cassie said, finding something strangely familiar about the lurking form though she could not see his face. "He should have followed us to the Egyptian Hall."

Then recognition struck. She gasped. "That's Ramsay."

"The hell you say?" Tony blurted. "What is he doing here? I thought he was taking Graham back to Ravencliff for burial."

"Tomorrow," Cassie said. Through Will's cousin she'd managed to learn everything she could about Ramsay and how he was faring.

"Then why is he here?"

"Let's ask him," Cassie said, stepping out of the shadows to follow the figure wrapped in a black cloak. A huge black dog followed him. But man and dog had already disappeared into the darkness on the other side of the kitchen garden.

"Wait." Tony grabbed her arm and pulled her back into the shadows as another figure—one wearing a kilt—materialized out of the dark.

Cassie and Tony lurched back into the cover of the deep shadows, watching the figure's every move.

Erik did not skulk or try to cover the sound of his footsteps on the pavement. Once, he stopped to look back over his shoulder as if he thought someone was following him. As soon as he seemed satisfied that no one was behind him, he boldly marched on. When he reached the kitchen door he raised his fist and rapped on it sharply.

Fortune was on his side, Erik concluded when Will opened the kitchen door of the St. John townhouse. This time his plan was going to work.

"Evening, ol' chap," Erik greeted in his heartiest voice. "Got time to smoke a cigar with me this evenin'?"

"That I do," Will said, clapping a hand on Erik's shoulder and opening the door wider for him to come in. "We thought you would be going to the exhibition with the quality tonight."

"I would have if me lord had been here," Erik said, secretly relieved he had an excuse not to go to the stuffy affair.

"We was just sitting down to a special dinner in honor of Mrs. St. John's accomplishment," Will said. "She told Horton we was all to celebrate, too, and she gave us tickets so we could see the exhibit next week when we have our days off."

"Now, weren't that nice of her?" Erik said. He liked Mrs. St. John. She was a real lady. Too bad those daughters of hers had turned out to be such chits.

"Join us," Will invited as he shut the door behind Erik.

Nearly the entire staff was gathered in the servants' dining hall just off the kitchen. "Mrs. St. John said to make you at home, especially with Miss—I mean, Lady Charlotte and Lord Connor gone. We can't get used to the new titles."

"No, don't let me interrupt yer meal," Erik protested, as he shrugged out of his short cloak. The kitchen was light and warm, and smelled of fresh bread and well-cooked beef. He was tempted to accept the invitation, but the weight of the packet of strychnine tucked inside his shirt reminded him of his mission. "Speaking of his lordship, a letter arrived from Connor today with some instructions about the household, and in it was a note from Lady Charlotte for Miss Cassandra. Thought I'd bring it by to deliver meself, then share a smoke with ye."

"Here, Betsy can take the letter," Will said, gesturing to the maid.

"No, no, donna trouble yerself, lass," Erik said, glancing at Betsy, who made to get up from the dining table. "Donna trouble yerself, Betsy. I know where Miss Cassandra's writing desk is. I'll just take it right up there and be back in a wink. Then we'll have that smoke, Will."

"Right," Will agreed.

Erik headed for the stairs, congratulating himself on his great story and his fine acting skills. He would damn near have the house to himself. All he needed was just the right place to plant the strychnine.

"If you see Horton up there," Will called, "would you remind him dinner is on the table?"

Erik halted midway up the stairs. "Aye, I'll do that." Silently he thanked Will for the unintended warning. Horton might not be so easy to fool about his intentions.

In the hallway on the first floor, Erik paused long enough to listen for a clue as to the whereabouts of the butler. The hall was lit by a lamp burning in the parlor at the back of the house. He heard nothing. Too anxious to waste more time, he went up to the next floor where he knew he would find Cassandra's writing desk in a corner of the morning room, next to the small closet that Charlotte had used as a study. On the second floor, a single candle burned in the hallway. Erik seized it and continued into the morning room.

At Cassandra's desk, he set the candle down and studied the clutter, trying to decide where best to hide the poison. He dare not place it in too obvious a location, but it had to be easy enough to find for the magistrate's man upon a second search which would be launched after an anonymous note arrived at Culpepper's office. Erik smiled evilly to himself. He would write that note as soon as he finished here.

Where to hide the poison? Slipping his hand inside his shirt, he pulled out the packet of strychnine. Should he plant it at the back of the top drawer with her nibs, or tucked back in a cubbyful of stationery?

The floor creaked. Erik glanced up, prepared with his story for the butler about delivering a letter to Miss Cassandra from Lady Charlotte. Horton should fall for that. But in the doorway he saw Cassandra. Surprised, Erik froze. Behind her stood Anthony Derrington.

"Will said you had a letter for me," the St. John lass said, her voice cool and knowing.

Erik swallowed with difficulty. The packet of poison burned in his hand and he jammed it back inside his shirt. "I just realized I forgot to bring it with me."

"Did you?" Derrington stepped around Cassandra and into the room. "What did you just stuff back inside your shirt?"

"I donna know what ye mean," Erik said, silently cursing the fate that hindered him from accomplishing his goal. He was so close to making Cassandra St. John a murderer. And he still had a chance, if he could talk his way out of this. Then he'd leave the packet of pink poison powder somewhere incriminating. Holding out his empty hands for the lad and lass to see, he added, "See, I have nothing."

* * *

"Hand it over," Cassie demanded, without taking her eyes off Erik as she followed Tony into the morning room. She was becoming impatient and angry with this charade. This man had embarrassed her father and made Ramsay lose all faith in her. This man was a murderer. "We know you have the poison that killed Graham."

"And you came here to plant it in a way that lays the blame at Cassandra's door," Tony added without relinquishing his place between Erik and Cassie.

Erik actually had the audacity to appear shocked. "What are ye saying?"

"We know you murdered Graham and tried to blame it on me," Cassie said. "I've already sent for the magistrate. He will be here any minute. Don't dishonor the McKensie name any more. Give up and confess."

At the mention of the McKensie name Erik's face transformed. The change stunned Cassie. His features twisted into an ugly mask of hatred. "How dare ye speak to me of dishonoring the McKensie name? What know ye of honor or dishonor? Ye and yer sister, ye St. Johns who have never known suffering. Ye have never known the sorrow of defeat. Ye have never watched yer family die at the hands of Forbeses like mine did."

It took all of Cassie's courage not to back away from the Scotsman. Tony didn't move either.

"Ye want to see the poison?" Erik asked, his voice a rasping growl. "Here it is!"

With his left hand he drew the square packet out of his shirt and held it up for Cassie and Tony to see. Tony reached for it. Erik hit him in the jaw with a hard right. The powerful blow from Connor's sparring partner sent Tony staggering backward. Erik grabbed Cassie's wrist and dragged her toward the door.

Caught off balance, Cassie stumbled after him. Her wrist was locked as securely in his grip as if she were chained to him. On the threshold, with her free hand she grabbed at the door frame to stop the flight, but she could not get a firm hold.

"Tony, are you all right?" she cried as Erik pulled her from the room. "Tony?"

Tony made no reply. Terrified that Tony might be dead, Cassie's blood ran cold. She clutched at the banister, but Erik was already dragging her down the steps. She struggled to stay on her feet. She feared if she fell, he would just drag her body, bouncing down each riser. She would become senseless and be useless to anyone.

At the foot of the stairs three figures confronted her and Erik. Tophet crouched and snarled. Behind him were Horton and a figure shrouded in a cloak and a soft, black, low-crowned hat. *What is Ramsay doing here?* she wondered as Erik swung her around in front of him, painfully twisting her arm behind her back. Out of nowhere a dirk glinted at her throat. Cassie sucked in a deep breath. Her neck had never seemed so vulnerable, so bare.

"Call off the dog," Erik demanded.

"Stay, Tophet."

Cassie recognized Ramsay's voice.

At the sight of the knife blade shining in the candlelight, Horton's eyes grew wide, and without protest he backed away toward the front door. Ramsay neither advanced nor retreated.

"You, Horton, get me a hackney coach," Erik ordered.

"Do as he says, please, Horton," Cassie said, giving orders to the servant as much out of habit as out of fear.

"No, Horton." Ramsay swept off his hat and cast the corner of his cloak back over his shoulder. "No hackney."

"What are you doing here, Linirk?" Erik demanded. Still holding Cassie's arm twisted behind her, he paused, his back to the wall. Cassie stood like a shield between him and Ramsay. Ramsay seemed almost casual in his demeanor.

"I thought your call at Graham's visitation very unusual," Ramsay said, his voice smooth and calm. "So I had you followed. You see, I'm as eager to have the crime solved as you seem to be. But I'm not willing to be duped about who murdered Graham. Cassandra St. John may be many things, but I don't believe she's a murderer. I will have the truth.''

That is a relief to know now, Cassie thought wryly.

''He has the poison, Ramsay,'' she said, breathing shallowly. The knife edge was so close to her throat, she was certain she could feel the coldness of the metal breathing on her skin. But she wanted Ramsay to find the evidence, no matter what happened. ''Inside his shirt, I think.''

''She lies,'' Erik said. ''I have the poison. I found it on her desk, and unwisely picked it up.''

''And you grabbed the lady to restrain her for the magistrate,'' Ramsay finished for him. ''A good try, Drummond, but that story doesn't work. What were you doing at her desk this evening? Why didn't the magistrate find the poison the first night he was here and searched? Let her go.''

''No, send the butler for a hired carriage,'' Erik said. The blade flashed in the light again.

Cassie closed her eyes against the frightening sight of the knife.

Tophet snarled.

''No, not until you tell the truth,'' Ramsay insisted. ''You killed Graham, then?''

''I'm not taking the blame for murdering Graham.'' Erik tightened his hold on Cassie. She could hardly breathe. ''Graham Andrews deserved what he got. Ye deserved it, too, Forbes. To see yer kinsman dead in yer own house. 'Tis justice. He and his father killed my family as sure as ye stand there. He killed my father and brother and stole our livestock. My mother never recovered from her baby's death of starvation. Every last one of my kin died because of Andrews and the feud. My only blood relation was Connor's family. I swore to meself I'd make the Forbeses pay.''

Ramsay stepped closer. ''Then make me pay. Let Cassandra go and settle this with me.''

''Oh, no, it's not going to be that easy for ye.'' Erik twisted

Cassie's arm more. She bit her lip to keep from crying out. She would not give him the satisfaction. "St. John wants to end the feud, but I couldna allow that. Donna move again, Linirk, unless ye want to explain to the lassie's papa how her throat got cut."

"I've heard enough. Get him a hired carriage, like he says, Horton," Ramsay ordered, his voice calm and his expression undecipherable.

"Very good, my lord." Cassie heard the butler dash out the door.

"Cassandra, breathe," Ramsay said softly. "This is no time for you to faint."

"I will not faint," Cassie said, opening her eyes to find Ramsay's green-eyed gaze fastened on her. "I did not murder Graham. Do you believe me now?"

He nodded.

"Isna that touching?" Erik said with an evil laugh. "But ye thought she was guilty when ye saw the note, didna ye, Forbes? Ye believed she murdered yer kinsman and ye were ready to throw her over for certain. Maybe to even do murder yerself."

"Shut up, Drummond," Ramsay snapped.

She heard the hackney coach rattle up outside.

"Let's go," Erik said, nudging Cassie toward the door. They moved together, stepping sideways, an awkward, deadly gait. Erik's viselike grip never relented. His gaze swept from the door, then back toward Ramsay. "Horton, stand back. Linirk, ye stay right there in front of us. Donna make a move, or Miss Cassandra will suffer."

Ramsay did as Erik said, his gaze fixed on the blade at Cassie's throat.

Outside on the doorstep, Erik began to pull her along with him down the steps toward the waiting carriage. They were still moving sideways so Erik could see where he was going while watching Ramsay. Ramsay and Tophet followed, almost within arm's reach.

"I told ye to stay in the house," Erik bellowed as he forced

Cassie down the stone stairway. "Donna get too close, Forbes. I'll slit her pretty little throat."

Ramsay paused on the threshold.

At last Cassie saw her chance. She quickened her steps so that she was rushing Erik down the steps instead of the other way around. As she charged down sideways, she could feel his grip on her loosen. Abruptly she lurched away from him. Turning her shoulder toward the knife blade, she threw herself toward the opposite side of the steps. A pain shot through her twisted arm. Her heel caught in the hem of her dress. Fabric ripped, but she got her foot back under her. Madly she scrambled to put as much distance between herself and Erik as she could.

She heard Tophet snarl.

All Cassie could see was the paving stones rushing toward her. She threw her arms out to catch herself. At the same time she heard the knife clatter to the pavement. She knew that Tophet and Ramsay had seized the McKensie clansman. Then the sickening crack of bone and a ripping of fabric and flesh echoed across the steps. Erik screamed.

Strong arms caught Cassie.

"I've got you," Tony murmured as he set her on her feet. "It's all right."

Cassie pushed away from her cousin and turned to see where Erik was.

Ramsay had caught Erik by his right arm and yanked it back at an unnatural angle. Tophet's jaws were locked on Erik's calf. Erik tried to shake the dog. Then he swung around to strike at Ramsay. Ramsay ducked and grimaced as he twisted Erik's arm more and more until the McKensie clansman's face turned chalk white. Still Ramsay twisted Erik's arm. Graham's murderer never begged for mercy, even as he fell to his knees. Ramsay called off Tophet. Grudgingly the dog obeyed.

"If I could reach that knife you'd die here and now." Ramsay bent over the man and spoke in a low voice that Cassie could barely hear. "I'd slit open your gullet and let you watch your intestines ooze out on the flags. For murdering Graham. For your fiendish lies. For threatening Cassandra and endangering her. I'm willing to go to the gallows for the pleasure of gutting you. Do you hear me?''

Erik gave another grunt of pain. "I'd do the same to ye if I had the chance.''

"Then we understand one another,'' Ramsay hissed between his teeth.

The hatred between the two men hung in the air. Chills trickled down Cassie's spine.

Shouts rang out in the street and running footsteps could be heard.

"Culpepper's men,'' Tony said. "None too soon, I might add.''

In relief Cassie sagged against Tony. "How did you get down here?''

"I went down the servants' stairs and around the house,'' Tony explained, rubbing his chin. "I wasn't about to let that blackguard get away. Not after what he'd done to you. Not after he slugged me. I sent Will for the magistrate.''

In the doorway stood Betsy and Cook, the other footman. Just then Culpepper himself drove up and Erik was taken into custody.

Soon Cassie, Tony, Culpepper, and Ramsay were gathered before a fire in the parlor and Betsy was fussing over Cassie. Horton was issuing orders to the other servants.

"The poison is in a packet on him,'' Tony was saying to Culpepper. "He admitted everything. The murder and the planting of the evidence.''

"He confessed the murder to me,'' Ramsay put in. He stood on the far side of the room as if refusing to become one with the group of survivors who huddled before the comforting fire. Cassie was amazed at his calmness. "I'm satisfied that he committed the crime and tried to frame Miss St. John for it.''

Cassie wondered what was going through his mind. Did

this new knowledge make him feel any differently about her? Ramsay took things hard. Was the rift that Erik had created impossible to heal?

"We found the poison on him," Culpepper said, making notes in a small book he carried. "We also found some stationery paper in his room that matched the note that had arrived with the poisoned bottle."

"I never thought of looking for that." Feeling like a simpleton, Cassie glanced in Tony's direction.

"Me either," Tony admitted.

"There's definitely enough evidence to bring charges," Culpepper continued.

Relieved to hear that news, Cassie sagged against Tony. The suspicion of murder was lifted from her shoulders.

CHAPTER
TWENTY-SEVEN

"Are you all right, Miss St. John?" Culpepper asked when he saw Cassie lean against Tony. " I've sent for your parents."

"Oh, I didn't want to disturb Mama and Papa," Cassie said, dismayed at the thought of Mama's triumphant evening being spoiled.

"I think they would want to be disturbed," Tony said.

"I quite agree," Culpepper said, snapping his notebook closed with authority. "They should be here directly. Right, then, I'm going to get our Mr. Drummond down to the gaol and settle him into new quarters."

As Culpepper took his leave, Mama and Papa dashed into the house, hurling questions at Cassie and Tony. Mama rushed to Cassie's side.

"What's going on?" Papa demanded the moment he saw Ramsay. "What are you doing here?"

"Papa, it's all right. Ramsay is here because—" Cassie stopped. She turned to Ramsay, realizing that she didn't know why he was there. He bowed courteously to Mama.

"I'm here, St. John, because Erik Drummond came to pay

his respects to Graham earlier today," Ramsay explained quietly. "As a representative for Lord Kinleith, of course."

"How curious," Papa said.

Ramsay inclined his head. "I thought so, too, so I had him followed."

Then he explained briefly how when he learned that Erik had gone to the St. John townhouse, he thought that even more curious. He'd decided to find out what was going on for himself.

"Truthfully, I couldn't imagine why he'd come here until we confronted each other in the hallway and Cassandra began to speak of the poison," Ramsay said. "When I saw him hold a knife at Cassandra's throat, I began to understand. You'll have to ask Cassandra and Tony why they were here."

Papa turned on Cassie and her cousin.

"Well?" he said.

Tony began to explain their plan. Cassie let him. She could hardly take her eyes off Ramsay who seemed distracted, but unwilling to leave.

"You actually thought he'd come back here?" Papa said, turning from Tony to Cassie. "Why did you not tell me?"

"Papa we just couldn't be certain," Cassie said. "We did not want to concern you and Mama with all that was going on. We could have been wrong."

"That's not a satisfactory answer," Papa said sternly.

"Your father is right, Cassandra," Ramsay said, interrupting at last. Cassie winced at the anger in his eyes. "You should have told him what you were doing. You should have confided your suspicions in him rather than take things into your own hands, endangering yourself."

"Thank you for that." Papa regarded Ramsay with a look of grudging gratitude.

"Well, it has all worked out," Cassie said, trying to brush over her offense as quickly as possible. "Erik confessed. Lord Linirk knows the truth."

"But I think Connor is going to be shocked," Mama said. "We'd best get the news off to him so he can do what he can for his kinsman. He must deal with this as he sees fit on behalf of his family. I'm certain he's going to feel badly, Lord Linirk. I don't believe he had any idea what Erik was up to."

"I suspect as much myself," Ramsay agreed. "I want you to know, St. John, that in light of what has happened, when all has been done for Graham that I can do for him and his family, I will reconsider my position on the Glen Gray settlement. I was in shock and I spoke in haste when I refused to sign the document before."

"I understand," Papa said. "I hope you will seriously reconsider. I believe we can count on Connor to be reasonable."

"I would also like to take this opportunity to apologize to you and to your wife for being so quick to believe the worst." Ramsay spoke with great earnestness and humility, but the words clearly did not come to his lips easily. "It was a grave error on my part and I hope that you will see fit to forgive me."

"Your apology is appreciated, my lord," Papa said, glancing in Cassie and Mama's direction.

"I assure you we are very sorry for your loss," Mama said. "We understand that it was a great shock."

"Everything proclaimed my guilt," Cassie said, stroking Tophet's head. The dog had placed himself at her feet the moment they'd all gathered in the parlor. Although Cassie was touched by Ramsay's apology to her family, she was unwilling to allow him to win forgiveness too easily. "But I wish you'd had more faith in me."

Ramsay studied her for a fraction of a moment. Cassie waited, longing to hear him apologize to her. He'd gone along with accusing her of the most heinous of crimes against mankind and against him—the murder of his kinsman. Her, a woman who'd vowed her love to him. He owed her an apology. She would hear it before she forgave him.

Abruptly he turned to Papa again. "I shall do everything in my power to cooperate with Magistrate Culpepper in the case. My agent, Fredericks, will take care of things in my absence. But I can't delay Graham's funeral cortege north."

"Of course, we understand," Mama said.

"Then I shall take my leave," Ramsay said, accepting his hat from Horton. "Come, Tophet."

To Cassie's dismay, the Nairn hound glanced at her, then jumped up to do his master's bidding. With Tophet at his heels, Ramsay Forbes walked out of the St. John townhouse without making any farewell to Cassie, without asking for forgiveness.

The St. Johns heard nothing from Lord Linirk over the next six weeks.

Connor and Charlotte rushed home from Rome as soon as they received word of Erik's confession. They were in shock. Charlotte was, anyway. Connor was surprised, but not astonished. He'd known Erik's grudge against the Forbeses ran deep. He knew that Erik's family had suffered at Forbes hands, but he'd not realized it was deep enough to murder an innocent man with poison and lay the blame on another.

Charlotte ached for her husband, she confided in Cassie. Connor felt betrayed, though he did not tell anyone that but his wife. Cassie understood exactly how her brother-in-law felt. They'd all suffered from Erik's plotting.

Dispirited, Cassie found herself standing at the window, mesmerized by the fall rains glistening on the London streets or the fog drifting in the colorless, leafless garden. She saw Charlotte almost daily. There was tea at Aunt Dorian's once or twice a week. Soon the Christmas parties would begin. Though Cassie attended social events and smiled, she had not the spirit for enjoying herself. No one asked awkward questions about Ramsay. It was well known in Town that he was in mourning and that he'd returned to Scotland for the funeral of his kinsman.

Ramsay was always on her mind and she thought of Tophet often, too. At first she was angry with Ramsay for taking the Nairn hound with him. Tophet had been his gift to her, and what kind of honorable man took back his gift? But now she was glad that the dog was with him. She had her family.

She had Mama and Papa, Charlotte, Aunt Dorian, and Tony. Without Graham for a companion, Ramsay only had Tophet. And she knew Tophet's company could be soothing.

Had she and Ramsay gained nothing from their association? she wondered, as she gazed out the window, contemplating their time together. She had no answer. One highlight stood out, one victory amid the death and mourning. Ramsay had signed the Glen Gray agreement before he left London. Connor had followed suit. The feud was at an end. The rest of their relationship had been for appearances, she reminded herself. Why should she expect anything more from Ramsay?

Papa was elated. Both men expressed the feeling that Graham Andrews's murder was proof that it was time for the old feud to come to an end and for the clans to look forward to the modern world. Cassie was happy for Papa and for the McKensies and the Forbeses. Indeed a new era lay ahead. But what did the future hold for her?

One morning when the fog seemed unusually close and thick, an invitation awaited Cassie at the breakfast table. The handwriting made her heart flutter and her fingers trembled as she broke the seal.

Princess,
   Do you still make your own choices?
   Be at the entrance to the tunnel at Regent's Park Zoological Garden today at noon.

							R

After living through the longest morning of her life, Cassie was at the appointed place at the appointed time; a little early, in fact. Betsy waited for her on a nearby park bench. Cassie paced, painfully aware that in the cold, foul weather the park was nearly deserted. But how romantic that Ramsay would choose this place to meet. What would he say to her? she wondered, pacing back across the mouth of the tunnel once more. What would she say to him? She was afraid to hope for more beyond that he'd chosen this place to say good-bye to her.

She frowned to herself. No reason to get sentimental about the man. She must not forget he'd tried to control her from the first day they'd met. He'd arranged everything. Then he'd not even asked for forgiveness when he'd been so quick to think her a murderer.

The sound of footsteps reached her through the fog. Cassie stopped and turned toward them, her breath catching in her throat.

Out of the fog appeared a figure in a frock coat, not quite as tall as she remembered Ramsay. She stopped and peered through the mist, longing to see Ramsay's solemn face. As she watched the man walking jauntily toward her, she realized with a sinking heart that it wasn't Ramsay at all.

"Cassie?" Dudley cried, his footsteps quickening when he recognized her.

"Dudley," Cassie said, unable to keep the disappointment from her voice as his features became plain. "What are you doing here?"

"Cassie, how good it is to see you," Dudley said, sweeping her up into his arms before she had an opportunity to resist him. He kissed her soundly.

Sputtering, Cassie pushed him away. "Dudley, what a surprise."

The viscount stepped back and appraised her from head to toe. "By Jove, you look wonderful. A restoring sight for a lonely man. You look so good I can almost forgive you for leaving me in that tea shop with the entire bill to pay."

"Well, I'm not certain that you look good enough for me to forgive you for crying off," Cassie said, her indignation flooding back. She silently cursed Ramsay. This was his doing. It had to be. She looked out at the fog surrounding them. In fact, she was certain he was somewhere nearby, hoping to watch the results of his handiwork. "I heard you were in Paris."

"Until last week," Dudley said, his face alight with admiration for her. "My life has been hell without you, Cassie."

"Truly?" Cassie asked, unimpressed and still looking to catch a sight of Ramsay. "How is it that you've returned now?"

"I had time to reconsider my reasons for crying off," Dudley said, his smile fading a bit. "I know it's a dashed lot to ask for your understanding, Cassie. But when I thought of the wedding, I got cold feet. It happens to chaps, you know."

Cassie wasn't going to accept that. "I heard you cried off because you were offered money, Dudley. Is that true? Not very flattering to me, especially after I'd brought you into Society. Were you given money to break our engagement?"

Dudley frowned. Clearly he was not prepared for her to be so blunt. "Cassie, there were reasons that I can't share with you."

"Gambling debts?"

"Well, yes," Dudley admitted, looking away. "You can't imagine how difficult it was."

"But you vowed you loved me," Cassie said, confused every time she thought of his avowals. "Then you throw me over because you have gambling debts to pay? I could have helped you with them."

"But the temptation to pay them off and be free was too great," Dudley whined. "And I knew if you caught a breath of that wild rumor about the servant girl with child, that there would be hell to pay."

"What servant girl?" Cassie asked, blinking in disbelief at the man who'd been her fiancé once, so long ago.

"I was a fool," Dudley hurried on. "I admit it. I didn't know what I was doing, what I was throwing away. Now I've had time to reconsider."

"Now you've been asked to come back to me and apologize," Cassie said, determined to have the truth. "I'm supposed to forgive you for a servant girl, too?"

"Very well, I'll admit that I was encouraged to return to London," Dudley said, "but I wanted to. I missed you. A man can't spend his entire life at the card table. Oh, Cassie, how I missed our adventures."

Cassie numbly stared back at Dudley. He seemed like a child wheedling for her approval. Suddenly she knew the truth. Dudley's avowals of love and her own had meant nothing. They'd been empty. He did not love her and she did not love him. They'd been infatuated with each other, perhaps—or with their escapades together—but never truly in love. They'd not even known true passion. For she knew what passion was now, and Dudley had never inspired anything like it in her.

Half annoyed and half grateful, Cassie stepped away from Dudley and looked around once more. Ramsay was here. She knew it. She could feel his presence. The puppet master would never miss a meeting like this.

"Cassie, will you forgive me?" Dudley pleaded.

At last Cassie spotted a tall dark figure leaning against the balustrade of the walkway over the tunnel. As the mist drifted, she could make out a huge dog sitting at his feet. She turned on Dudley. "So what was your exact agreement with Lord Linirk?"

The last bit of hope in Dudley's face fell away. "He told me if I knew what was good for me, I'd grovel."

Cassie almost laughed.

"I was to give you every reason for why we should become engaged again," Dudley continued. "But I truly came because I've been so dashed lonely without you, Cassie."

"And what do you get for convincing me to agree to an engagement again?" Cassie asked, shaking her head. Ramsay simply could not resist meddling, could he?

"A large interest in a railroad company he is forming," Dudley admitted, reaching for Cassie's arm to turn her to face him once more. "And I'd be getting the most fascinating wife in all of London. Cassie, I know what a muddle—"

"It's over, Dudley," Cassie said with a shake of her head. She pulled away from his grasp. "I don't think we were ever intended to be wed. Anyway, it will not happen now. I appreciate that you came to me, but I think it best to leave well enough alone. I'm sorry if that upsets your agreement with Lord Linirk, but I've made my choice."

Dudley bowed his head in defeat and left Cassie with quiet words of farewell. She wasted no time in finding her way up to the walk across the top of the tunnel where she'd seen Ramsay. The fog had cleared away some. When she reached the top of the steps she could see him still standing where she'd seen him earlier, leaning against the balustrade. She knew he was waiting for her.

He did not move when she reached his side. But from his profile, he looked good. The ravages of his grief seemed to be at least partially healed. Tophet came to her, tail wagging.

Cassie stroked the dog's head.

He was the first to speak. "I did not hear you singing in the tunnel."

"I do not feel like singing today," Cassie said.

"Seeing Dudley did not please you?" Ramsay asked without looking at her. " 'Tis only fair I return him to you. As you so succinctly pointed out, it was not for me to decide whether you loved him or not."

"Well, drat it, you were right," Cassie said, still miffed with Dudley for deserting her for money and returning for money. "I don't love him. And what is this about Dudley and a servant girl?"

"You don't want to know." Ramsay turned to her at last. She thought she read relief in his eyes—relief that she'd turned away Dudley? "So your choice is made?" he asked.

Cassie stared at him, understanding in a heartbeat how wrong she'd been about what he'd just done. It might appear he was meddling. But that was not what his gesture of summoning Dudley back had been about. Bringing Dudley back to her was Ramsay's form of apology. It was his plea for forgiveness.

Cassie's stomach lurched. Of course, she'd wanted to hear him say the words. It had not been pleasant to think that the man you loved was so willing to think of you as a murderer. But how deeply felt must be his desire for forgiveness, to risk offering her former fiancé to her. How much louder his actions spoke than the sound of the words.

Talking to Dudley had revealed to her just what she'd needed to know. She did not love Dudley and never had. "No, I don't want him. How can a lady trust a gentleman who cavalierly gave her up for money?"

"A fair assessment, I think," he said.

"Then, will you concede that I'm capable of making my own decisions?" Cassie baited.

"Yes, I believe you are." Ramsay turned away from her once more, surveying the zoo below him as if there were no fog obscuring the view. "And I admit I've been unfair to you."

"I'm glad to hear you admit that," Cassie said. "Well, my lord, I have not told you of all the choices I've made."

Cassie hesitated, took a deep breath, and drew herself up to her full height. She was about to embark on the riskiest thing she'd ever done. Society would gasp over this escapade if the truth was ever known, but she'd never given a fig about Society's opinion. Why start now? What was more scary was that she might put Ramsay off. He was the one who'd sworn to never marry. But she had to know if he felt as she did.

"You've been gone a long time and hardly a day went by that I didn't think about us," Cassie said. "I know that you've made choices in your life. But I made some that might conflict with yours."

"How so?" Ramsay asked without looking at her.

"If the choice were available to me, if you hadn't already chosen to remain unwed, I'd choose you as a lover, and a husband. Of course, you are not looking for a marchioness. So it is a moot point."

Ramsay turned toward her slowly. Cassie held her breath as the silence between them stretched out forever. His face revealed no emotion. But his green eyes regarded her with an unsettling keenness. "That almost sounds like a proposal of marriage."

"Drat, I know that," Cassie muttered, feeling herself shrink in humiliation. She prayed frantically that he would be gentle in his refusal. "I'm afraid I'm about to find out that there is one thing worse than having your engagement broken. It's having your marriage proposal refused by the man you love."

"Is that truly how you feel about me, Cassandra?" Ramsay asked, almost afraid to believe that she'd spoken the words he'd just heard. "Do you love me—me with all my faults?"

He watched her swallow with difficulty.

"I'm hardly perfect myself," she said, peering into his face, her blue eyes earnest and wide. "I'm much too vain and inclined to be too outspoken and—"

"Cassandra, suffice it to say you're more perfect than I deserve," Ramsay said, to stop the recital of all the flaws he knew so well and loved so dearly. The very flaws that had brought light into his life. He smiled down at her.

"Don't torment me," Cassie pleaded. "Will you have me or not?"

Ramsay wondered at the strange look that flashed across her face.

"There is no reason why you have to marry me," she said hurriedly. "I mean, after the museum and all."

"That does not signify." Ramsay shook his head. He did not care about whether she was with child or not, but he knew it was important to her to not be trapped into marriage by a baby. "I intended marriage after our night together at Ravencliff. But I understand that it is important to you. This marriage must be of your choosing, unfettered by obligations beyond those of your heart. If you choose to have me to husband, I shall be honored to have you to wife."

"Yes, oh, yes," Cassie cried. She threw her arms around his neck, pressed herself against him, and kissed him firmly on the lips.

Ramsay slipped his arms around her waist and surrendered to the healing powers of love.

EPILOGUE

"Are you proud of yourself, St. John?" Susanna asked the moment they had a chance to themselves amid the hubbub of the wedding breakfast. Dorian had once again opened her home for her nieces. The cream of Society was present and newspapers had already hinted that Ramsay and Cassie's wedding was the Society event of the year.

How much of that was to be attributed to the feud and the murder, Davis did not know, but he suspected it all had something to do with the notoriety the affair was receiving.

"You've managed to marry one daughter off to an earl and the other to a marquis," Susanna added as she sipped her champagne. She made a lovely mother-of-the-bride with her red hair twisted into a smooth coil atop her head, and dressed in pale blue satin and pearls. "Does having a countess and a marchioness in the family satisfy your ambition?"

"I had little to do with either marriage and you know it," Davis replied, tolerably amused by his wife's gentle needling. But he was satisfied with the choices his daughters had made. Now he could relax his vigilance. His daughters each had a husband to watch over them. While they were not men he would have selected, he thought the earl and the marquis acceptable protectors for his daughters.

"But you do not answer my questions," Susanna persisted.

"I'm much more satisfied now that both lairds have signed off on the Glen Gray agreement," Davis said, aware of Susanna listening to his every word. "I had my doubts about them, but each in their own way has demonstrated good faith, and the girls certainly seem to be in love."

"Yes, they've done as we told them in the first place," Susanna said, a dreamy, faraway look in her eye as she watched Ramsay slip an arm around Cassie and draw her to his side. "Our girls married for love. They followed their hearts and that is not always the easiest road to take."

"No, it is not," Davis agreed. He'd certainly experienced a few bumps along that road himself, as a lover, a father, and a husband. Lonely Sir Benton, of the Pugilist Society, Susanna's attraction to Sir Myron of the Hellenistic Society, and the whole murder scandal they'd suffered through, had made it abundantly clear to Davis that there were more important things in his life than having a title. Though he wished that he'd received his knighthood, he found it not as compelling a need as he'd once thought it was. He had his wife, his girls, and his sister with him. How empty a title would be without them. "I've quite given up on a title. What would be the purpose in it?"

Susanna, the woman in his life whom he longed to share a title with, touched his arm and gazed up into Davis's eyes. "I'm so glad to hear that."

A flurry of movement in the crowd caught Davis's eye. He saw his sister sailing through a sea of wedding guests toward him. Dorian was dressed in the height of fashion in a lavender gown, her fair hair groomed high on her head and her throat garnished with pearls and diamonds. The Countess of Seacombe, elegant and chic as always. The earl, Nicholas, followed her, a half-smile of pleasure on his face. What were they up to?

"This just arrived for you," Dorian said, thrusting a large

envelope at him. "From the King. He regrets that he could not visit Ramsay and Cassie's wedding breakfast, but he wanted you to have this, or so his messenger said."

Davis stared down at the royal stationery and hesitated.

"Go on, open it," Dorian urged.

Davis glanced at Susanna. Her eyes were wide and solemn. She knew as little of this as he did. "Probably a note of good wishes for the happy couple."

"Open it," Cassie said. She and Ramsay and Charlotte and Connor had joined the circle.

Davis broke the seal and opened up the letter, reading hastily, barely understanding what was written there.

Susanna who was reading over his shoulder gasped. "Your knighthood. You're going to receive it. You're going to be knighted, Davis."

"Let me see." Dorian snatched the letter out of Davis's hand. " 'Knighted for services to the crown' and so forth and so forth 'and for the mediation of differences between the Scots clans of McKensie and Forbes.' You've done it, Davis. Oh, I mean, Sir Davis. Soon Sir Davis and Lady Susanna."

Dorian laughed in her delight and hugged Davis, then Susanna who looked quite stunned. Then Davis's arms were full of Charlotte and Cassie both giggling in their pleasure. Connor and Ramsay stood nearby smiling conspiratorially.

Davis suddenly became suspicious. "Do I owe this to you two? And you, Nicholas?"

Connor shook his head. "You owe it to no one, your lord-ship."

Nicholas agreed. "You quite earned this honor, Sir Davis."

Ramsay bowed to Susanna. "It pleases me much to greet my mother-in-law as Lady Susanna."

Susanna blushed. "I'm not certain I'm prepared for being addressed so."

"You'll soon become accustomed to it," said Dorian with a laugh.

His sister had adjusted to being received as a countess with amazing swiftness, Davis recalled.

"Just think, Susanna," Dorian added, "your Greek-study group will become more popular than ever."

"I'm not certain we need that," Davis said, still smarting from the memory of Sir Myron.

"Aunt Dorian, you must make an announcement to all the guests," Cassie said.

"Cassandra, this is your day with your new husband," Davis found himself saying.

"Please, I wish it and Ramsay does, too," Cassie insisted. "It is a fitting honor to share with our guests today."

Dorian agreed and Davis found himself addressed as Sir Davis just when he'd been certain he'd had everything he truly wanted.

Ramsay refused to consummate their marriage until they reached Ravencliff.

"I don't want to start making love to you knowing we're going to have to rise in the morning and spend the day traveling," he'd said when they were making their wedding plans. He'd spoken as if the decision was already made. Then he'd leaned close to her and added, "When we lie together again, princess, it won't be like in the museum."

The mention of the museum made Cassie's body grow warm. Heat burned in her cheeks. She longed for the sharp sweet pleasure he'd brought her that day. But she also dreamed of the long, slow gratification he'd given her at Ravencliff—over and over again.

"We might try the museum's form of the dance, if we wish," he added, studying her face with cool satisfaction written across his features, "but we will have all night and all day to do what we want. No one will intrude, unless we ask them to. After all, we may need to call for sustenance for time to time."

Too embarrassed by her own fantasies to say more, Cassie

had agreed, avoiding meeting Ramsay's eyes. What argument could a bride-to-be raise against that promise? Hour upon hour of passion. Every time she thought of the prospect, of Ramsay making love to her all day and night, a thrill curled through her belly. And she'd always thought the fun in the prospect of a wedding trip had been the new clothes. How young and silly she'd been only a few months ago.

What she hadn't anticipated was that a celebration awaited them when they arrived at Ravencliff. Ramsay took the swarm of relatives and friends in his stride. Cassie could do nothing but stand at his side and endeavor to remember all the names and faces. Undoubtedly she would meet them again later and be expected to remember exactly who they were.

It was late—or was it early in the hours of the morning?—when Ramsay finally shut the door of the master's rooms. He thrust the bolt home and turned to look at her.

A small fire burned in the hearth and candles glowed at the bedside. The scent of fresh roses on the table by the windows filled the room.

They stared at each other a moment. Cassie held her breath, wondering why he didn't kiss her. Then he reached for the top button of the long row down the front of her traveling dress. At last the waiting was over. Without hesitation she began to unfasten the buttons at the bottom of the bodice.

When their hands met and the buttons were all unfastened, he peeled the garment from her shoulders. He bent to kiss her shoulder, then stepped back, his gaze caressing her breasts barely covered by her shift and corset.

Cassie attacked his cravat, then the buttons of his shirt. When they had been cast aside, her fingertips roved over him in an orgy of discovery. She kissed his solid chest. He tilted his head back and closed his eyes as if reveling in her touch. Cassie marveled at the solidness of him and the springiness of his chest hair. How little of him she'd explored during their first night together. But he soon became impatient with her exploration and brushed her hands away. He reached for the hooks of the demi-corset she wore. When he'd finished with it, the undergarment fell open and dropped to the floor.

At the sight of her breasts visible through her sheer silk shift, Ramsay drew in a sharp breath. Cassie felt her breasts grow heavy and sensitive under his scrutiny. Hastily she reached for the tapes of her skirt. When it dropped to the floor, he took her hand and helped her step out of it. Then he led her to the plush rug lying before the fireplace.

Pressing her shoulders, he guided her down on to the rug. As she lay on her back, he unfastened her petticoat and pushed it down her legs. He wasn't quite so restrained when it came to untying the ribbons of her shift and stripping of her drawers.

Once her clothing was removed, he slid his hand between her thighs. She groaned in anticipation. His fingers probed her gently. He only had to stroke her a few times before her blood began to sing in her veins and the pleasure began to rise in her belly.

"Ramsay," she pleaded.

That was all he seemed to want to hear from her. He unfastened his trousers and was out of them in a flash. Cassie boldly assessed him—thrilled by the magnificence of his arousal—but only for a moment. He covered her, bracing himself above her and mating their bodies. His eyes locked with hers, he penetrated her deeply, filling her, possessing her, snatching away her breath, and stealing control of her consciousness. His dark blond hair hung over his brow, disheveled and wild. His green eyes glowed, with the firelight adding to his masculine appeal.

She wanted to concentrate on how handsome he was, but he withdrew and sank into her again. Then he dipped his head, circling her pearled nipple with his tongue. Concentration fled. Involuntarily her eyes closed. Her thighs gripped his hips. He moved again, quicker now, stroking her inside, deeper and deeper.

She sighed his name and clutched at the muscles of his back, but he did not relent until his thrust sent a tide of exquisite pleasure flooding over her, through her, eddies of sensation swirling deep inside her, then reaching out to tingle in her toes and fingers.

The tingles had barely begun to fade when she felt Ramsay shudder with his own climax. She held him close, reveling in her feminine power to give him such pleasure.

When they lay side by side, her head tucked beneath his chin, she listened in sleepy pleasure to the strong regular sound of his heart.

"It's there, your heart," she said, gazing up at him. "I can feel it beating. You are a fake, my lord, claiming you have no heart."

"But it took you to discover it." Ramsay opened his eyes and looked at her, drawing his thumb across her mouth. "And for that discovery, it is yours, as long as it beats, as long as there is breath in my body. My heart is yours."

"And mine is yours," she whispered. "You have two hearts now."

With that vow he kissed her. Cassie's mouth opened to him and her sated body came awake. And the lovemaking began again.

ABOUT THE AUTHOR

Linda Madl lives with her family in Manhattan, KS. She is the author of eight historical romances and a number of historical short stories. Linda loves to hear from her readers and you may write to her c/o Zebra Books. Please included a self-addressed stamped envelope if you wish a response.